UNTIL DARKNESS DISAPPEARS

Until Darkness Disappears

by

Will Cook

The Golden West Large Print Books
Long Preston, North Yorkshire,
BD23 4ND, England.

British Library Cataloguing in Publication Data.

Cook, Will
    Until darkness disappears.

    A catalogue record of this book is
    available from the British Library

    ISBN   978-1-84262-930-7 pbk

Published in Large Print 2014 by arrangement with
Golden West Literary Agency

The Golden West Large Print is an imprint of Library Magna Books Ltd.

Printed and bound in Great Britain by
T.J. (International) Ltd., Cornwall, PL28 8RW

*Resting here until day breaks and shadows fall
and darkness disappears.*

from the gravestone of Quanah Parker

PART ONE

1880

Chapter One

For two days Lieutenant Beeman and his detail remained in the field. They called on a rancher named Gunderson who had beef for sale, made the arrangements, and went on to another place owned by a man named Stivers. The news of Skinner's defeat seemed to have traveled fast, and by the second day Beeman was being welcomed as a Messiah. By the time he turned back toward the reservation he felt certain that the Skinner trouble was pretty much over.

They were well south of headquarters, and Beeman decided to stretch the ride out so that they arrived quite late. He expected the offices to be dark, but as they rode across the parade ground, he found the place bustling with activity. Two squads of Indian police were being formed, and rifles were being issued. He swung down, told Huckmyer to dismiss the detail, and went on into Lovering's office.

The agent was dressed as though he had been summoned from bed. The top of his nightshirt was stuffed into his pants, and he kept tugging at his suspenders as he dashed about giving orders. Then he saw Beeman

11

coming down the hall, and Lovering's face was a sunburst of relief.

He took hold of Beeman by both arms. 'Thank God, you've come back.'

'What's going on here, Mister Lovering?'

'All hell's broken loose,' Lovering said. He propelled Beeman into his office and closed the door. A woman sat in a chair, her head down, hair falling forward to hide her face. Two Indian policemen were guarding her, and Lovering waved them out.

He kicked the door shut and went back to his desk for a cigar that he lighted swiftly and drew on with furious puffs. Beeman looked at the woman and asked: 'Is she a prisoner?'

'Of course, she is! What the hell do you think?' He curbed his temper and drew on his cigar. 'Skinner is dead. I expect his cowboys to ride onto the reservation any minute.'

'Let's try and get this straight,' Beeman said, forcing himself not to hurry it. He thought of what Major Jim Gary would do. Be calm. Take one thing at a time. Be cool-headed. Get the facts straight.

He walked over and lifted the woman's head so he could look at her face. After studying her a moment, he said: 'She's not Indian. Mister Lovering, call your police-men in here and have them fill your tub so she can take a bath. Send a man to the com-missary stores for some kind of a clean dress. Get a ribbon for her hair. Women like

12

something pretty.'

Lovering's jaw dropped. 'Have you lost your mind? With Skinner's men on the way…?'

'You're wasting time,' Beeman said calmly, and polished his glasses.

With a sigh of resignation, Lovering flung open the door and gave the orders. Then he went over and sat on the edge of his desk. Pails of water were brought in and carried to his room at the back. The woman was taken there, and the door was closed. Another policeman came with a light blue dress and a ribbon. Lovering took them to the back room, rapped at the door, and thrust them through the crack that appeared when the door was opened slightly.

When he came back, Beeman said: 'Now, suppose you tell me what you know of this?'

'Skinner came back on the reservation,' Lovering said. 'He was alone. It isn't all clear to me, but he got into a quarrel with her man and killed him. Then she took a piece of firewood and beat Skinner's brains out. Hell of a ruckus! Finally the police came and brought her here. Skinner and her man are both over at the doctor's house covered with a blanket.'

'And just how do you figure the word got back to Skinner's men?'

Lovering flung his hands wide. 'How in hell do I know? I've never understood this

13

damned word-of-mouth telegraph they have out her, but news travels fast. That I do know.'

'All right, we won't worry about that for the time being,' Beeman said.

'Won't worry? You may not worry, but I'm sure...'

'Mister Lovering, try to be calm,' Beeman said, surprised that this suggestion had a soothing effect upon himself. He went to the door of the room at the back and tapped. 'Please don't dawdle in there,' he suggested.

He came back and found Lovering, standing there and gnawing on his cigar. 'Damn it, anyway!' Beeman remarked. 'There's always trouble when a white woman lives with an Indian. God-damned cowboys, always raising hell. They see a woman, and they've got to use their peckers.'

He turned his head when the door to his room opened, and the woman stepped out. The blue dress was a decent fit, and she had the ribbon tied around her hair that fell damply to her shoulders. Her moccasins padded softly as she stepped across the room.

Almost gallantly Beeman said: 'Would you please sit down?' He scratched his beard stubble and smiled. 'You must pardon my appearance, but I've been two days in the field and just returned. May I have your name, please?' He took out a small notebook and stub of a pencil.

'I'm called Fawn Eye,' the woman said.

Beeman toed a chair around and sat down facing her. 'It's obvious to me that you're not Indian. I'd like your Christian name.'

She looked at him steadily. She was in her early twenties, and her hair was a tawny brown, naturally wavy, that immediately denied her having any Indian blood. Her eyes were blue. Beeman thought she had a good face – a troubled, worn face, but good. The finger of sorrow had written lines in it, but like all truths they created no ugliness.

'Emily Brail. What are you going to do to me now?'

'Why, first, I think we ought to learn what happened.' The front door opened, interrupting Beeman. He looked up as Ben Stagg stepped inside. The old man took in the situation at a glance and moved to a chair and sat down.

Lovering said: 'Where's Bert Danniel, Stagg?'

'Couldn't find him,' the old man said. 'Word was that he lit out to Skinner's place right after the trouble.' He saw Beeman frown and added: 'Danniel's the sub-agent. This whole thing happened in his bailiwick, 'most half a day's ride from here.'

'I see,' Beeman said, and turned his attention to the woman. 'You were going to tell me what happened.'

'Was I?' She fell silent for a moment, then shrugged. 'What does it matter now? Everything's lost.'

'I'm afraid that, in spite of that, we're going to have to get to the truth of it,' Beeman said. Just then the sergeant of Indian police came in.

'We ready to go now,' he said, speaking to Lovering.

'Where is he going?' Beeman asked.

'Why to meet Skinner's men!' Lovering snapped. 'What did you think?'

For a moment Beeman stood up with his eyes closed, as though he were engaged in mortal struggle with his temper. Then he said: 'In the name of heaven, Lovering, must we resort to shooting? Will you please return your police to barracks and have them rack their arms? My God, man, confront those cowboys with rifles, and you'll have a bloody war on your hands. Is that what you want? Do you want to include in your report that you lost complete control of the situation?' He slapped his forehead. 'Mister Lovering, if you please, go back to bed if you can't do anything else.' He looked at the Indian sergeant. 'Leave. Dismiss your men.'

Lovering said: 'Go on, Sergeant. It's his responsibility, thank God.'

After the sergeant left, Beeman turned again to the woman. 'You were going to tell me what happened,' he said once more.

16

'Skinner came to our camp.'

'He'd been there before?'

She nodded, and Beeman, without thinking, plunged on. 'Your man was away?'

'He was there.'

'Well, certainly the man wouldn't...?' He stopped, and his face colored as he groped for words. 'Surely the man...?'

'Fifty cents is a lot of money to an Indian,' Emily Brail said.

Beeman waved his hand helplessly and went on. 'Was there a quarrel between Skinner and your man?'

She nodded. 'I didn't want Skinner to come back. The last time, when the Army officer hit him and ran him off, he looked at me afterward, and I decided I didn't want to see Skinner again or any of the cowboys.'

'Any of the cowboys?' Beeman said. 'Good Lord, Lovering, what are you running here?'

Ben Stagg slid his easy voice into it. 'Don't talk so green, Lootenant. This has been goin' on for a long time. She didn't start it, and she won't be the end of it. As long as there's bucks in need of tobacco, there'll be women on the blankets with the cowboys.' He held up his hand when Beeman opened his mouth to speak. 'Boy, she never had any choice. He bought her or stole her in the first place. She's his property under Indian law to do with as he wants. She'd mind him, or he'd beat her half to death. Likely he's

17

done it a few times already.' He whittled off a chew of tobacco and popped it into his mouth. 'Stick with the killin'.'

'That does seem like sound advice,' Beeman admitted. 'Who started the trouble?' he asked the woman.

'Pierced Hand ordered Skinner away from the camp,' Emily Brail said. 'He struck Pierced Hand, knocked him down. Then Skinner jumped on him with his knife in his hand. I grabbed a piece of wood and hit Skinner, but it was too late. Pierced Hand was dead.'

'That's about how we put it together,' Stagg said. 'I got there soon after. She was singin' the death song. Two policemen with me brought her here after we looked for Danniel and couldn't find him.'

'He's finished with the government,' Lovering said. 'The man's picked his side, and he'll have to make the best of it.' He looked at Emily Brail. 'What are you going to do with her, Mister Beeman?'

'Send her back to Camp Verde. What else can I do?'

Ben Stagg said: 'Her kids, too?'

It was a thought that had not occurred to Beeman. 'Do you have children?'

Emil Brail nodded. 'Two.'

'Two that lived,' Stagg said softly. 'Notice her hands, Lootenant. She's got three fingers missin'. Each one means a death in the fam-

18

ily. My guess is it'd be her kids. Now she'll go and cut off another finger for her husband. The women do that, you know ... cut off their own fingers. You ride around the reservation and you'll see old women with no fingers on either hand. They can't work or hardly care for themselves, and nobody wants 'em. They grub for scraps like a dog, and they sit wrapped in the dreams of the past and wait to die, hopin' someone will bury 'em.'

'She'll take the children with her,' Beeman said. 'Stagg, take two Indian policemen along with you. I'll have a report to send along to Major Gary.' He held up his hand. 'Now, before you tell me the reason why I shouldn't do this, let me remind you that this girl has endured enough, and it's time for her to live quietly on the post, until she can think this out for herself. I'm sure Major Gary would agree with me.'

'He would all right,' Stagg said. He got up. 'You want me to start in the mornin'?'

'Yes. Lovering, I think we can keep Miss Brail in this building tonight. The normal guard will suffice.' He stretched and rubbed the tight muscles in the small of his back. 'I think I'll take a bath, shave, and get something to eat.'

Emily Brail said: 'How can I go to Camp Verde and live with white people?'

Beeman gave it some thought, then he

19

said: 'Well, I suppose it would be fair of me to ask how you could once have lived with the Indians.'

'I had no choice.'

'And I really think you have none now,' Beeman said. 'You may want to postpone the date of making the choice, but it will eventually have to be made. I have only tried to help you.'

'Yes, I know. Thank you for letting me take a bath. And it's a very pretty dress.'

Beeman went to his quarters and shaved while water was heating. He took a bath, dressed in clean clothes from the skin out, and went to the mess hall where the cooks labored over a late meal. The troopers were just finishing, and Beeman went in and sat down next to Huckmyer. The sergeant started to get up, but Beeman put out his hand and pressed him back.

'A word, Sergeant. Quite likely the cowboys will show up. Agent Lovering thinks so. I think we're going to have to give it to them again.'

'You want me to station the men around the parade ground?'

'No, I think we'll have to be more cagey than that.' Beeman thought a moment. 'The cowboys are a bold lot. They'll come right on into the headquarters building and try to run over Lovering. Very well, we'll let them come in. When they go inside, I want their horses quietly led away. I'll be inside with Lovering. We'll try to keep them busy for a few minutes. Then Geer can quietly bring the detail in through the front and seal off their retreat. No side arms, Sergeant. Just a chunk of lead in a leather glove.'

'Leave all the details to me, sir.'

'Fine,' Beeman said. 'The men won't mind this extra duty after making an all-day march of it, will they?'

Huckmyer grinned. 'Sir, I guess they'd jump out of their graves if you yelled attention.'

'It's … good to have that confidence,' Beeman said, deeply touched.

'Well, sir, I'll tell you how it is with officers. Any enlisted man can get along without 'em, but since we got 'em and always will have 'em, we kind of like to think we've got the right to decide who's the good ones and who's the bad ones. And it's strictly up to the officer as to which he'll be.' He seemed to hesitate. 'Mind if I just talk out, sir?'

'You go right ahead.'

'Well, none of us thought you'd come to a tiddly shit, sir, meanin' no disrespect. Fact of it was, you'd kind of dogged it until Major Gary took command, and, when you took over the company, we figured we was in for it. But every man's happy to be dead wrong, and you ask 'em, and they'll tell you.' He got up and clapped on his forager cap. 'I've said

21

too much.'

'You're a good man, Huckmyer,' Beeman said, 'and I've yet to see the time when what you had to say wasn't worth listening to.'

This pleased the sergeant. He grinned, made a wry face, then hurriedly left the mess hall. The cook came out with Beeman's plate, and he began eating.

Lovering came in, his manner highly excited. 'For God's sake, you're sitting here, feeding your face, and the cowboys are...'

'Mister Lovering, getting excited isn't going to change anything.' He took the man by the arm and urged him to sit down. 'Let's look at it this way. The cowboys are going to be all lathered up and excited, aren't they? So why should we be? Wouldn't it be better if we were calm and logical?'

'Friend, you can't be calm and logical with cowboys.'

'We're going to try,' Beeman said, and went on eating. He was pleased that he could keep command of the situation when others went to pot emotionally. He felt that Gary would be this way – calm, deliberate, and, if not sure of himself, at least giving the impression to others that he was.

Lovering went back to his office, and Beeman stopped at his own quarters to get his gloves and to put up his side arms. He dropped two pieces of lead into his palm, then joined Lovering. The man had a double-barreled shotgun on his desk, and Beeman broke it open, took out the shells, and racked the gun.

'We don't want any shooting, Mister Lovering.'

'I want to see you convince the cowboys of that,' he said, and gnawed on his cigar.

Ben Stagg, escorting Emily Brail to Camp Verde, took the train as far as the tanks where he sent the Indian policemen back. Accompanied by the woman, he caught the morning mail wagon to the post, and on the way he met an ambulance with Lieutenant Flanders and Sergeant Wynn leading a ten-man escort. They stopped to have a little conversation, and, after they had gone on, Flanders knew who Emily was and how Beeman was making out. Ben Stagg knew that the ambulance and escort were going to the tanks to meet Senator Jason Ivers and his wife.

Gary was in his office when Stagg hauled onto the post. He had Emily Brail wait in the outer office and went in to give Gary the dispatches Beeman had written. Gary waved him into a chair and thumbed through the reports, a thick sheaf. 'Mister Beeman is not averse to penmanship,' Gary said, putting the reports aside for the moment. 'How is he getting along?'

'Tolerable well,' Stagg said. He told Gary about Skinner's death, and that he'd brought

Emily Brail back. 'The cowboys came to the agency around midnight. Beeman and Lovering was waitin' in the office... Lovering under the desk.' He paused to chuckle. 'While the cowboys stormed inside and raised hell, Huckmyer and the detail made off with their horses. Finally the cowboys got through threatenin' Beeman, and, after promisin' to ride south and tear the damned sub-agency up by the roots, they came out, and there warn't no horses.' He choked back a laugh. 'No horses, just Huckmyer and the detail. A couple of guns got pulled, and some more threats were made, but Beeman convinced them that they didn't really want to get hung for shootin' unarmed troopers. The upshot was that they got to fightin'. Turned out bad again for the cowboys.'

'Again? Was there another...?'

'All there in the report, Major. Anyway, as I was sayin', Beeman has twenty-six cowboys locked in the stockade, charged with disturbin' the peace, trespassin' on government property, threatenin' a public officer, displayin' firearms in a rude and threatenin' manner, usin' profanity, and failure to disburse on lawful order. He's got 'em bound over to federal court in Fort Reno.'

'My Mister Beeman did all this?' Gary asked.

Stagg grinned. 'He's a piss-cutter, ain't he? I'd say he was a better man than he ever knew. Plays it light-footed, Jim. A real fire-breather when he gets his back up. If he ain't careful, he'll make a big reputation for himself.'

'I'll be damned.'

'Figured you would be. Seems like you'll just have to write him up in a couple of dispatches. Nothin' else you can do.' He got up. 'Can I bring the woman in now?'

'Yes,' Gary said. 'And thank you, Ben. There's nothing like an eyewitness account.'

Stagg went out, and then Emily Brail came in. Stagg closed the door behind her, and Gary came around his desk and handed her into a chair. 'I'm glad to see you,' he said. 'You brought your children? I ask, because I'll want to see that you have suitable quarters.'

She looked at him questioningly. 'Quarters? I thought I was going to be locked up.' She folded her hands in her lap and studied them. 'I thought the lieutenant was sending me here to jail, and I didn't say anything to him because he'd let me take a bath and I...' She simply let it trail off and sat silently, staring down.

Jim Gary lit a cigar, went behind his desk, and sat down. He studied her and said: 'How old were you when you were taken?'

'Thirteen, I think.'

'And how old are you now?'

'Twenty-four. I think that's right.'

25

Gary turned to the filing cabinet, searched through it a moment, then opened a folder. 'You were visiting an aunt near Victoria in the summer of 'Seventy-Seven when your horse came back without you. There was a search that lasted several weeks, then the Texas Rangers came across sign of a Comanche raiding party returning north from Mexico. It was supposed that you had been taken prisoner. Is that correct?'

'Yes. My horse threw me. I was afoot when the Comanches found me.'

'Would you like to tell me about your captivity?'

She raised her eyes. 'You know about it. What's there to tell? I gave birth to my first child the next fall. He died when he was ten days old. Two squaws held me while a third cut off a finger and slashed my arms.'

'Did you ever try to escape?'

'Yes, but after the first time I never tried again. How do you know all those things you have on the paper?'

'People see things and remember them and tell me during questioning. We have a boy here, Tom Smalling, who first said he had seen someone your age, someone answering your description. So we started a file, adding to it when we could. Then we got the boy Teddy. He knew you and told me other things. Finding people is a difficult task, Emily.'

'And after you find them?'

'We try to build back the life you've lost.' He closed the folder. 'We'll have to check and find out if any of your people are alive. We'll have to talk some more, and you'll have to tell me all about your family.'

'I don't want to do that,' she said.

'No one will force you. You can live here, work if you like, go to classes if you want to. You can even leave if you want to. There are no locks on the gate, and the guards will not stop you.'

She studied him carefully. 'Why was I brought here?'

'To give you time to think,' Gary said. 'Here there is no one to blame you for anything, or to make you do what you don't want to do. Here you can live in surroundings you once knew. You can't just go back eleven years and pick up. We don't claim you can. But maybe you can find a way onward, to get past those lost years.'

'What about my children? One is four, the other a little over two.'

'They're your children,' Gary said gently. 'No matter what, we can't change some things, or deny them. You love them ... what more is there? I have children, and I love them. It's the same.'

'I want to believe you. I wanted to believe you when you came to my fire that night. You have a good face.'

'I think in time you may believe me,' Gary said. 'You may believe in others, too. We have a difficult task here, Emily. Any of the boys can tell you that we try to make them understand that all the people in the world are not good. There are some who will always call them redskins, and there isn't really anything anybody can do about it. But they learn to live with themselves, live with the past, and plan a better future.'

'When do I have to leave here?'

'When you want to. Stay a week, a month, a year ... it doesn't matter. The important thing is to leave when you know you're ready, when you know you can face anyone and anything.'

'Will it ever come to that?'

He shook his head. 'Who can know? We all grow stronger, or weaker. Either way, we learn to get along with it. Now I will call one of the sergeants and have you shown quarters.' He wrote out a piece of paper. 'Give this to the sergeant, and what you want will be brought from the quartermaster. We don't live very fancy, Emily but we have plenty to eat, and clothes, and I know you'll want a pretty dress.'

'Mister Beeman gave me this one.'

'That's because Mister Beeman is a fine man,' Gary said. 'He has a wife and a child. They'll want to meet you.'

'Do they live here?'

'Of course.'

She got up, brushed at her hair with her hand, and then she smiled. 'Will they know what I've been?'

'They'll know that you've suffered a lot,' Gary said. 'Other than that, what is there to know?'

Chapter Two

Llano Vale supposed that no other man alive could do what he was doing now, reaching back into the recesses of his memory, past the present generation to a time when all Texans made war against the Indians, and each male child became a fighter when he could lift a rifle, fire it, and reload it. They were the years of no palaver – when a man saw an Indian, he fired, not bothering to ask intent. And the Indian, a victim of custom and superstition, drew no distinct line separating friend and enemy. The white man was the enemy.

Yet Vale understood that nothing was all bad, and there never had been a time when everyone hated the Indians. The country could be aflame, united in mass determin-ation to wipe out the Indians, and there would always be those who could not bring themselves to kill when it came time to kill.

29

The War Between the States had proved this to him. Union soldiers caught behind the lines had been sheltered now and then by Southern people, and he supposed that it had worked the same the other way around.

His memory took him into the Río Pecos country because he remembered people there. He spent two days asking around, but no one remembered these people except to say that there had been trouble, and they had moved on. The clerk at the courthouse thought they had gone north, near Pope's Wells in New Mexico Territory. Llano Vale took the first available train.

He pulled in at night, unloaded his horse, stabled him, and took a room at the only hotel. When he had breakfast the next morning, he attracted considerable attention because he was so big and his mane of white hair so long, and he wore weapons and said very little. It reminded them of the old times when dangerous men rode into town with their violence and rode out again after their angers had been spent.

Llano Vale dropped a name here and there around the town and then spent his time on the hotel porch, watching everyone while they watched him. During the course of the day, Vale supposed that there was not one man, woman, or child who did not find some excuse to pass along Pope's Wells' main street and look him over. He understood that he was more than a man who just had come to their town. To them he was the past reaching out, an old hatred revived, vengeance arrived, the day of reckoning for someone. He caused them to look at each other and wonder about the hidden part of everyone's past, and they wondered who would finally go to the hotel porch and end the waiting.

The man's name was George Schneider. He was fifty-three, a man who lived alone with his daughter, and he drove into town in a farm wagon and stopped in front of the hotel. He looked at Llano Vale a moment, then said: 'It's been nearly sixteen years, Llano.'

'All of that,' Vale said. 'Sit a spell.'

Across the street all movement stopped on the sidewalk. Schneider said: 'You always did draw a crowd, Llano.'

'They stopped to see the trouble, George.'

'Is that what you brought me?'

Vale shrugged his massive shoulders. 'I could round up a lot of people who'd say that's all I ever brought anyone.'

'I'd be among those,' Schneider said. He took out a pipe, filled it, and lit it. 'We'd some strong words the last time we saw each other, Llano. Are we going to take it up again?'

'I didn't come here for that,' Vale said. 'And I wouldn't lift a hand or a weapon against you, George.'

'You know, I have reason enough to kill

you, and there isn't a jury in New Mexico who'd hang me for it.'

'That's about right.' He looked at Schneider, remembering him as he had been – younger, strong, a handsome man who had had bad luck with his women. 'Are you going to kill me, George?'

'No,' Schneider said, shaking his head. 'What good would it do? Besides, a man has time during the years to think a thing out. She was ready to leave with you. You didn't drag her away from me.' He looked at his work-hardened hands. 'Then, too, I had the little girl to think of.'

'You ran,' Vale said. 'They all called you a coward back there.'

'I don't care what they called me,' Schneider said flatly. 'I just couldn't take a chance on getting killed and leaving that little girl alone.' He studied Llano Vale. 'You'd have killed me. I wasn't any good with a gun, or my fists, or anything else. I suppose that's why Ilsa left me.' He sighed, and rekindled his pipe. 'What do you want, Llano?'

'Did you ever find out whose little girl she was, George?'

'I never tried. She was all I had.'

'She wasn't Indian,' Vale said softly. 'I think I can prove it.'

Schneider's manner became cautious. 'What are you trying to say, Llano?'

'That you picked her up on the prairie,

32

thinking she was Indian. You raised her, convinced that she was part-Indian anyway. Now I'm sure she ain't. They got a boy at Camp Verde who lost a sister. She'd be near the girl's age. The boy ain't sure where, but it's worth trying to put together, George. If she's got a brother, she ought to know about it.'

'You want to take her away from me?'

'I want to make things right,' Vale said. 'Don't you think I should, George?'

'Llano, my wife thought you was some kind of a god. She'd have gone with you that night if the horse hadn't thrown her and killed her. She left a note for me, and, because I couldn't read English then, I took it to town and had the storekeeper read it to me. I don't know whether it was her going that day or my letting everyone know about it that made me want to kill you, but you're not going to take anything more away from me.' He got up from the porch, stepped up to the wagon, and hoisted himself onto the seat. 'I'm going home. Come to my place and I'll shoot you on sight.'

'I'm working for the Army, George. I've got to talk to the girl.'

'I've warned you.'

Llano Vale said: 'George, did you ever know me not to do what I had to do?'

'Thought it would be like that,' Schneider said, and reached under the seat.

Vale had no warning until he saw the gleam

33

of the shotgun barrel, then he launched himself sideways out of the chair as Schneider
fired.

The charge hit him high, somewhere in
the shoulder, and smashed him around and
into the wall of the hotel. Schneider lashed
at his team, wheeled them, and raced out of
town as people poured across the street.
Someone yelled to fetch the doctor.

Vale was conscious when they carried him
down the street to the doctor's office, but he
hardly realized he was seeing the doctor as
he made his examination. Then someone
clapped an ether cone over his nose and told
him to breathe. A humming noise began in
his head and increased for a moment, then
blackness descended.

Schneider's team was lathered when he
pulled into his yard. He flung himself down,
after wrapping the reins around the brake
handle, and dashed toward the house. The
girl came out, drying her hands on her apron.
She seemed surprised to find him in such a
rush.

'What's wrong, Papa?'

'We have to leave. Now! Right away!'

She frowned, puckering her dark brows.
'Why, Papa?'

'I killed a man in town. The sheriff will be
after me as soon as he can get here from
Carlsbad.'

She swayed against the door, her face growing white, but she didn't burst into tears or lose control. 'You think running away...?'

'Yes, yes,' he interrupted. 'There is no other way! You pack what you can. I'll write a note. The neighbors will take the stock.' He turned her and pushed her inside. 'We have no time to lose. No more than an hour. Hurry!'

He gathered a few valuables and a metal box containing his money. He packed two canvas traveling bags with clothes. He took all these things out to the wagon. Then he went inside the house that he had built with his own hands, and sat at his desk and wrote a note to his friend Oskar Hummer who lived four miles down the creek.

Lieber Freund Oskar:

Ich würde Ihnen sehr dankbar sein... *I would appreciate it very much if you would take all my livestock and poultry as a gift from one old friend to another. By now you know what I have done, and, from what I have told you in confidence, you know why I must take Frieda and leave the country. It is possible that I will not get far, but I must go. I am too old now to give up my happy years, yet I always thought this would someday happen. I will tell Frieda everything and let her make up her own mind as to what she wants to do. But I know that her parents are*

dead. It is a feeling I've had for a long time.
Auf Wiedersehen
George

He left the note on the dining-room table and went outside to make sure the livestock had water and that there was corn pulled down from the crib to feed the hogs. Frieda came out of the house with some bedding and a canvas valise, and then they got into the wagon and drove away, taking the south road that would steer them clear of the town and anyone coming after them.

Schneider drove south along the river because he could not help himself. He was a farmer who could not live in dry, arid places or bear to travel through them. Along the river the grass was good, and the trees grew thick. He kept on going until it was nearly dark, and then he stopped to make his camp.

He had not spoken much to Frieda since they'd started. He had tried, but the words weren't ready to come out. Only after the fire had been built and the food was cooking and he had his pipe lit, did he feel he could speak.

'I'm not a good man,' he said.

She was startled. 'Papa, that's not so!'

'What do you know ... so young?' He shook his head. 'I'm not a good man, Frieda. I've lived a selfish life. My Ilsa was a child, so much younger than I, but I could never

36

understand that she wanted more of life than working hard on the farm and making a home. I could never understand why she had to have a pretty dress when she already had one to work in and one for Sunday.'

Frieda watched him, her expression grave and worried. She was a pretty girl with a small, round face and gentle eyes. 'You've never talked about her, Papa. I never heard you speak of her. Not once.' She stirred the meat and gravy and spoke without looking at him. 'It hurts me to say it, papa, but I don't remember her at all.'

He was silent for so long that she looked at him to see what was the matter. Firelight played over the lined planes of his face, and his eyes filled with tears, but they did not fall. 'You don't remember, Frieda, because you never knew her.'

Her mouth opened and closed a couple of times, then she said: 'My own mother…?'

He shook his head slowly, and she said nothing more but waited for him. 'She wasn't your mother,' he said softly. 'And I'm not your father. It was almost sixteen years ago when I found you, crying, abandoned on the prairie. You were a thin thing in a torn dress, maybe two years old. That was a hard year in Texas for everyone, Frieda. The Kiowas and the renegade Comanches were raiding everywhere. The war was on, and what was left of the settlers and ranchers rode in bunches, hunting them down. We'd been riding three days. Llano Vale, the man I killed today, was leading us. The party split, and, shortly after that, I found you. Everyone thought you were an Indian. You had dark hair, and it was 'long evening time, and your face was so dirty. One man tried to kill you, and I knocked him off his horse, picked you up, and rode back to my place. I'd had enough of it, and I didn't care what they thought.' He made a motion toward the fire. 'Don't burn the meat, Frieda. I wanted you for my Ilsa. I thought it would make her less unhappy to have a little girl. When I got home, she was gone. There was a note saying that she would meet Llano Vale in Pecos. But she never got to town. Her horse fell, or she fell. She was dead when searchers found her.' He paused to light the pipe. 'Everyone expected me to kill Llano Vale. I suppose most men would have tried, but he was a dangerous man with a repu- tation for killing, and I packed up and left, taking you with me.'

'Papa, who were my parents?'

'I honestly don't know, Frieda.'

'Did you ever try to find them?'

'No. But I never heard of anyone asking, either.' He looked at the knees of his overalls. 'I've done wrong all my life, Frieda. This time I must do right. It won't make up for anything, but they will catch me and hang me, and I must do the right thing while I can. Llano Vale told me that there is a boy at Camp Verde, in Texas, who lost a sister. She would be about your age, and he says that his sister was lost at the place where I found you, or near there. I've been a selfish man, Frieda, with you and with Ilsa. I'm going back, but I want you to take the team and wagon and go on to Camp Verde. Speak to the officer there. Tell him everything. Perhaps some good can come of this.'

'I can't leave you, Papa.'

'It isn't really leaving me,' Schneider said. 'I've stolen from you, Frieda. That's wrong... Stay on the eastside of the Pecos. Follow the roads. You'll be all right.' He got the tin box out of the wagon and gave her all the money. 'Hide it on you. Don't get friendly with strangers. There are shells for the shotgun in a box under the seat.'

'Papa, I love you.'

'I know, Frieda. And because I love you, I can do this now.' He sighed and got out the tin plates, and they each took one and began eating.

'I want you to go tonight, Frieda. Drive until you are tired and sleep in the wagon. Don't sleep on the ground because of the snakes. If it rains, be sure to...'

She put down her plate and hugged him, holding him close. 'I'll be all right, Papa. But why must I go tonight?'

'They're after me by now with a posse,' he

39

said. 'I'll stay here by the fire. They'll find me.' He patted her head. 'No one could have loved you more than I have, Frieda. Try to believe that.'

'I do. And I'll come back as soon as I can.'

After the meal she started to dawdle. She wanted to clean the dishes, to hang back, but he would have none of it. He made her go, because every minute she remained, his resolve weakened. After she pulled out with the wagon, he listened to the sound of it fading, and long afterward he sat by the fire with his pipe and his many regrets and kept feeding wood to it so the posse would have something to guide them.

He had no intention of sleeping, but he fell asleep. When he woke, he found Buck Standish and four other men standing on the other side of the fire. Standish threw some wood on the coals and, when it caught and threw out light, the badge pinned to his coat glistened.

'If you want to hang me,' George Schneider said, 'there are plenty of trees.'

'Now, we don't do things like that,' Buck Standish said. 'I wired the sheriff. He'll be down on the next train. We're going to take you back, George.'

'I know, and I'm ready to go.'

One of the men with Standish said: 'Where's Frieda, George?'

'I sent her on. To Camp Verde.'

'With the wagon?' Standish asked. He turned to a man standing behind him. 'Skinny, take your horse and catch up with her. See that she gets on a train. Bring the wagon and team back.'

'Hell, that may take two days!'

'You wanted to be deputized so damned bad, now do your job!' Standish looked at Schneider. 'It isn't safe for her to be alone like that. She'll be a lot safer on the train.'

'There was no time,' Schneider said, and got up, easing the stiffness in his joints. 'Do I walk?'

'You can ride double with Tony there,' Standish said, and they put out the fire and mounted up.

The deputy sheriff made a slow but steady ride of it, and they reached town shortly after dawn and rode down the main street to the jail. George Schneider slid off the horse and walked on inside without being told. The cellblocks were in the rear of the stone building, and he went down a short corridor, stepped inside, and closed the door. A moment later Buck Standish came and stood with a ring of keys in his hand. He slid one into the lock and turned it.

'Sure sorry things turned out this way for you, George.'

'It doesn't matter.'

'I'll have to keep you here a while,' Standish said. 'I just never knew you to do a vio-

41

lence on a body before. Took us all by surprise, although we figured that Llano Vale had come to do you in. I guess everybody in town knew what he was and what he come for.'

'It wasn't like that at all,' Schneider said quietly. 'Can I sleep now?'

'Sure,' Standish said, and went back to the front office. One of his deputies was still there, and Standish sagged into the swivel chair utterly tired out. 'It's sure hard to figure a man,' he said. 'Now you take some people, they go through life without raising their voice, then something sets 'em off, and the first thing you know you have a shooting fight on your hands and have to make an arrest. You want to mind the office a while? I'm going over to the doc's.'

He left the room and went down the street, passing off questions that came his way. He supposed that everyone knew Schneider was locked up in the jail. The doctor was in, and Standish said: 'How's Vale?'

'Awake, if you want to talk to him.'

'Is he going to make it?'

'Well, I picked nineteen pieces of shot out of him. Damned lucky Schneider was using small-sized buck. Double-O would have made a dead man out of Vale.' He nodded toward a closed door. 'Don't stay long and don't get him excited.'

'Just some questions for the sheriff when

42

he gets here,' Standish said, and went in. Vale was in bed, bandaged heavily around the chest, and from the dullness of his eyes Standish guessed that the doctor had him loaded with pain-killer.

'We brought Schneider back,' Standish said, pulling up a chair. 'No trouble. Now I'd like to hear your side of it.'

'What does George say?'

'Well, he ain't said, not yet anyway. All I've been going on is what people in the street think they saw, but I've got four or five stories from that many people. Did you come here to get Schneider?'

'What makes you think that?'

'You've done it before,' Standish said. 'Thirty years ago you sold your gun to the highest bidder. You was a trouble-shooter for the transcontinental railroad, and you shot up the opposition in a couple of range wars. All told, I'd say you've killed ten or eleven men. So it ain't unreasonable to think that you came here to kill Schneider.'

'That's kind of unfair, pinning an old reputation on a man.'

'We all know Schneider, and, putting two and two together, I figure it's like I said. You come to town, looking for him, then take up a roost on the hotel porch. George shows up, and you talk. Then suddenly there's shooting. None of us has ever known George to so much as lose his temper. Now would you tell

43

me the straight of it?'

'What are you going to do with George?'

'Well, it depends,' Standish said. 'We don't like assault with intent in this territory. If that's what it is, I'd say that George is about to do five or ten years at hard labor.'

Llano Vale thought about this a moment, his wrinkled face puckered in thought. Then he laughed, hurt himself, and quit it quickly.

Standish said: 'You think that's funny, Vale? None of us does. We like George.'

'I was just thinking that a thing can reach out a long way, Deputy. You see, George's wife once had a real shine on me. She was a pretty thing, fair, blue eyes, like most German girls. Hell, I was a free roller in those days, and, when she smiled at me, I just smiled back. Say, do you smoke? How about a cigar?'

'I don't think the doc would like it. Go on, tell me the rest of it.'

'Well,' Vale said, 'a woman is just a woman to me. Always has been. You may not believe it, but I got a couple of pretty nice-looking widows fighting over me right now.' He sensed Standish's irritation and got the train back on the track. 'George's wife was looking for some fun her husband didn't know about, so I bounced her on the bed and in the haystack and every damned place else I could. Like I say, it was fun to me, but she took it serious as hell.'

44

'Vale, you're no damned good!'

'Never said I was, so why should you be so disappointed? Anyway, she left George a note, saying she was running off with me. But she took a fall off her horse and killed herself. George swore he'd kill me if he ever laid eyes on me again.' He studied Standish carefully. 'Well, I'm an old man now, and I kept re-membering what George said, and the more I remembered it, the more I got to disliking it. So I just decided to come here and give George his chance. You know, sort of taking up the loose ends. Hell, I'm seventy-one! How long do you think I got left?'

'What happened at the hotel? Exactly?'

Vale made a wry face. 'George and I had our words. He knew why I'd come. But he didn't want to take it up. And I wouldn't forget it. Anyway, when he started to get into the wagon, I decided to make him move. As he turned to sit down and pick up the reins, I went for my pistol. But I was sitting, and the hammer caught in my coattail. Besides, I'm a lot slower than I used to be. Hate to admit it, but that damned farmer beat me to the shot. I remember thinking as I went down that I'd bought my last chips and never even got my six-shooter pulled clear of the leather. Ain't that hell?'

'You drew on George first?'

'Why, hell, you don't think a peaceful man like George would just gun down a man, do you?'

'I kind of thought it was that way,' Standish said. He got up and put on his hat. 'I'll wire the sheriff and let George out of jail. And, mister, as soon as you can ride, shag out of New Mexico. You show up here again, and there's going to be a warrant out for you. We don't need an old trouble-making bastard who never did a good thing in his life.'

He strode to the door, opening it, and went out, closing it not too gently behind him. Then Llano Vale smiled and closed his eyes, and, when the doctor looked in a moment later, he pretended that he was asleep.

Chapter Three

It was by the merest coincidence that the two new officers arrived on the same day. Captain Dan Conrad came from Fort Smith, and Captain Ellis Spawn came overland from the Presidio at San Francisco. Gary was in his office when Conrad arrived. He had the man shown in. They shook hands, and Conrad took a seat. He was tall and slender, and his left sleeve was pinned up from the elbow.

They had never met before, but the Army was not so large that they didn't know each other by reputation. Gary explained the function of his command to Conrad, and he listened intently and nodded now and then.

'In spite of what I've said,' Gary went on, 'this is pretty much a field command. It's my hope to enlarge by two companies in order to accelerate our activity. There will be times when you will find the duty brisk and a good deal of it in the field under anything but the best conditions.'

'Major, for years now I've given up hope of … well, serving in a fully functional capacity. I intend to give you no cause to complain.'

Gary saw that an orderly squared Conrad away with quarters and gave him a tour of the post. After that, his paperwork occupied him until noon. Then he went to his quarters, had lunch with his wife, and returned to the office around one.

In mid-afternoon, Captain Spawn arrived. He was a rather short, round man wearing glasses, and had a scholarly manner. Again the orderly took care of quarters and tour.

One of the men on guard duty came to Gary's office with the report that the ambulance and escort had been sighted. He shrugged into his uniform coat, settled his kepi properly, and went out a few minutes later when he heard the sentry passing the detail through the gate. He stood on his porch as they wheeled in, and he could make out the man, stocky, strongly built, with a square face and a well-trimmed dark mustache. He wore a yellow linen duster as did the woman with him. She had a scarf around her head to protect her against the dust.

When the ambulance stopped, the sergeant had already stepped down and was offering the man a hand. The senator took off his hat and whipped it against the side of the wagon to rid it of dust. Then the woman got down, bending her head forward to watch her step. When she made the ground, her legs were a bit unsteady. She laughed and put her hand on her husband's shoulder. Then she reached up, took off the scarf, and looked at Gary.

'Jim,' she exclaimed, 'I can't say that you've changed so much!'

For a moment he simply stared in awkward surprise. 'Janice Tremain!'

'Janice Ivers now, Jim.'

'Of course,' he said, hurrying forward. 'My apologies, Senator.'

'I certainly don't mind at all,' Ivers said with an incredible bass voice. 'If it hadn't been for you, Major, I wouldn't have a wife or two lovely children.' He stripped off his glove and offered his hand. 'May I, sir? I've wanted to for a number of years.'

Gary shook hands with him and studied him. He had dark eyes, very commanding; his beard stubble gave his cheeks a blue hue. He was blunt in manner, and he would make enemies. Also he would make friends.

The sergeant was standing by, and Gary said: 'Dismiss the detail, Sergeant.' He took Senator Ivers by the arm. 'If you'll come with me to my quarters, my wife is expecting you.' Then he laughed. 'In my surprise I'm afraid I've forgotten my manners, Senator.'

'If someone would tend to our luggage…,' Ivers began.

'The sergeant is already taking care of it,' Gary said, moving along with them. 'General Caswell has told me a good deal about you, Senator, and frankly I never did understand why you chose to champion my cause when we're doing work that few know about and even less care about.'

As Gary opened the gate, Jane came out, took one look at Janice Ivers, and then ran and threw her arms around her. They went into the house together, babbling as women do simultaneously, yet each understanding the other perfectly.

'I believe,' Ivers said pleasantly, 'that the next order of womanly business is bathing, talking, and what not. I'll settle for a drink and a cigar in your study, Major.'

'Your suggestion preceded mine by just about that much,' Gary said, holding thumb and forefinger an inch apart. He poured the senator a drink and gave him one of his better cigars and a light. 'I can't tell you, Senator…'

'I wish you'd call me Jason,' Ivers interrupted.

'Thank you, I will. As I was saying, I can't begin to tell you how much I appreciate your support in Washington.' He raised his drink in salute. 'I'm not a politician, sir, but I believed that once this whole affair had been placed in military hands, both houses would have quickly forgotten about it, feeling that they'd not only solved the problem but could wash their hands of it.'

Jason Ivers smiled. 'I think you have a fair grasp of politics, Jim. Of course, I admit that my interest in this is more personal than someone else's might be, yet I can't really believe it is entirely that. Let us say it's that my knowledge of the whole thing is more complete, because of what my wife has told me. Jim, I've been convinced for some time that we're only doing half a job. Oh, I know the budget hasn't been anything to crow about, and you need more men, but these things can be corrected.' He smiled through his cigar smoke. 'Politics is committee, and committee is seniority. It's as simple as that. Seniority controls votes, and this is my third term. I'm chairman of the Indian Affairs Committee and co-chairman of the military budget. That doesn't sound very important to the folks back home, but let me explain it. Assume that you are an elected official from … say, Missouri. There are military posts in

Missouri. Now I want something, so I talk to you about it to enlist your support. You may be pushing a project of your own and need my support, so we agree to be mutual in this. Or else you have no project and won't come around. I might suggest that I was also thinking of closing one of the posts in your district. That would hurt. You see the light and support me, and I don't close anything down.' He laughed quietly. 'Everyone wants something, Jim, so it's give and take all the way. But that's how the job is done.'

'Are you dissatisfied with the results we're getting, Jason?'

'Did I imply that? Good Lord, I didn't mean to. Bad habit of mine, half explaining a thing. When I said we were only doing half a job, I meant that we weren't doing much of anything for the Indians. The damned Mexican government had that bounty on Comanche scalps for many years, and unscrupulous Americans killed them for the bounty. They never have had a fair shake of it, at all. Even now, our job is to return prisoners to parents and relatives. What about the Indians? Any improvement in their station? Their schools?'

Ivers shook his head. 'No, not much, Jim.'

'I have an officer now on the reservation, straightening out some inequities,' Gary said. 'If the Indians get just what they're entitled to, it will be a big improvement.' He

51

paused to shy his cigar ash into the fireplace. 'You probably noticed the civilian camp. I have four families living there now. They've come to get to know the four returned prisoners who are ready to leave. We've taught them to read and write, taught them manners, and in many other areas broken them away from their Comanche or Kiowa training. If the whole thing is congenial, the families will leave with their recovered kin. If not...' He shrugged. 'We'll just have to take it from there. We are not, Jason, going to repeat the tragedy of some years back.'

'I concur,' Ivers said. Then he went on: 'Janice had a difficult time. Her uncle, you know, had a stroke six weeks after they returned East.'

'No, I didn't know.'

'He was actually through with politics,' Ivers said. 'He left her some money. Not wealth, but a house and enough to get her along on if she lived modestly. I met her when I attended the funeral. I saw her again four months later when I came to inquire about some of her uncle's papers. Jim, I was very attracted to her, and I knew all the rumours, all the gossip. She was a used woman to hear them tell it, but to me she was something refreshing, honest, and straightforward. I loved her.' He looked steadily at Jim Gary. 'You were very gallant to her, Jim.'

'Because I understood,' he said simply.

'Those who lived here, they understood. Her uncle didn't. But I knew that somewhere there would be a man big enough to understand. She tried to stay alive, Jason. And under the circumstances she found herself in, that was no simple thing to do.'

They heard the women on the stairs, put down their cigars, and got up when they came into the room. Janice Ivers had changed her dress and fixed her hair. She came to her husband, kissed him, then turned to Jim Gary and kissed him, too.

'Do you know what that was for?' she asked.

He shook his head.

'For not forgetting me.'

'How could I do that?' he asked. 'For a time there we were a pretty important part of each other's lives.'

'Jim, do you ever see anything of Guthrie McCabe?'

'I saw him four years ago,' Gary said. 'He put in a two-year term in the state senate then went into the Texas Rangers. He's a captain in command of F Company at Fort Concho. With your permission, I'd like to wire him that you're here.'

'I'd like to see him, yes,' Janice said. She looked at her husband and smiled. 'When you meet him, Jason, don't play cards with him, or try to out-argue him, or race horses. He can charm a bird out of a tree. He can take your life's savings and get you to thank him for it.'

'Sounds like a fascinating man,' Ivers said.

Gary glanced at his watch. 'The officers and their ladies would never forgive me if I didn't introduce you properly, Senator. I believe we can dine at eight and have an informal gathering in the officers' mess at nine, if that's convenient to you.'

'That sounds fine.'

'Then if you'll excuse me, I'll take care of the details,' Gary said.

It irritated Lieutenant Beeman to think that Danniel could desert his post at the sub-agency and just take off scotfree. It irritated Beeman so much that he had a horse saddled, filled his saddlebags, and rode off to find Danniel.

He knew the general direction of Frank Skinner's ranch, and he rode there, arriving in the late afternoon. Beeman was surprised to find that Skinner had a wife and three small children. The way the man carried on he had just naturally taken him for a single man with a strong rutting instinct.

There was no one else on the place except a Navajo horse wrangler and a Mexican cook. Mrs Skinner came to the door with a rifle in her hands and kept it pointed toward the ground while Beeman dismounted.

'I'm sorry to intrude,' Beeman said, remov-

54

ing his hat, 'but I'm looking for Danniel.'

'He ain't here,' she said, raising a hand to push hair back from her forehead.

'But he *was* here?'

'Yeah, he was.'

'Do you know where he went?'

She made a face. 'Try Rush Springs. There's a whore over there he always had a hankering for.'

Her language and her casualness shocked him. He turned as though to leave, then said: 'I'm sorry about Mister Skinner.'

'Why?'

He had to grope for an answer, 'Well … a husband and a father…'

'We was never married properly,' she said. She glanced down at the children clinging to her dress. 'And only one's his that I'm sure of.'

'My goodness,' Lieutenant Beeman said softly, and mounted his horse. Before he rode out he said: 'You've had an unfortunate life, ma'am.'

'I ain't complainin'.' She looked at him and smiled. Her thin face was pleasantly proportioned, but it was not pretty. 'You get hard up, come on back. I've entertained soldiers before.'

'Indeed!' Beeman declared, and he got out of the yard as fast as he could.

From his study of maps he knew the general direction in which Rush Springs lay and he rode across the Skinner Ranch until he found a road that he followed. Presently a sign told him that he was going in the right direction.

Darkness began to fall, but finally, ahead in a valley, he saw lights, and half an hour later he rode the length of a narrow street and tied up in front of a restaurant. A dozen men crowded the counter, and Beeman took one of the tables, gave his order, and listened to the talk around him.

The town was cattle. He could tell by the men he saw in the restaurant and out on the street. After eating, he went outside, took a turn up and down, and then headed for the back streets.

The place he looked for was not difficult to find. The house was dark, but a string of horses was tied up in front. Beeman took hold of himself, filled himself with resolve, and bravely marched to the door and knocked. A panel opened suddenly, and a woman's face appeared. She was fifty or more, flabby in the jowl, and her voice was like a file scraped against a piece of tin.

'Well, well, a soldier boy!' She opened the door. 'Come on in, handsome.' She grabbed him by the arm and pulled him into the hallway. The place was thick with perfume, and a fat Chinese figurine on a side table spewed incense out of his nostrils. A Negro woman went up and down the stairs, carrying water and towels. A lot of laughter was coming from the parlor.

'I'm looking for Danniel,' Beeman said, resisting the woman's tugging.

'Come on in and look over the girls,' she insisted, dragging him through heavily beaded draperies to the parlor. Three men sat there drinking, and four girls, two of them completely naked, sat on the arms of chairs or on laps. Beeman was almost too embarrassed to speak, but he asked: 'Is Danniel here?'

One of the men wiped foam from his mustache and pointed upstairs. 'Why don't you announce him, Edna? Danniel ought to be finished by now.'

The woman said: 'Now you know that Danniel…'

She stopped, for Beeman had slipped out of the room and was already going up the stairs. She rushed after him, yelling: 'Hey, don't go up there!'

Beeman paid no attention to her. He stopped the Negro woman at the head of the stairs. 'Which room is Danniel in?' She rolled her eyes and pointed. Beeman was at the door, butting his shoulder hard against it before she could tell him not to. The flimsy catch gave, and he barged into the room, catching Danniel in a man's most intimate and awkward position.

Cursing, Danniel flung himself off the woman, and Beeman, out of natural concern

57

for modesty, tried not to look too closely at her, although he saw that she was young and pretty. Then he made a jump toward Danniel, because the man was trying to jerk a pistol out of a holster hung on the bedstead.

Beeman was too far away to hit him with his fist, but the target was there, so he planted the toe of his boot in Danniel's crotch. The man, clutching himself, went to the floor, and threw up.

The girl got off the bed and looked at him. 'You've ruined him for the night,' she said. 'And he wasn't even finished.'

The madam and two cowboys had surged into the room. She looked at Danniel and swore because the man had soiled her rug. 'All right!' she snapped. 'I've had enough. You want him, soldier, then you get him out of here!'

'Thank you,' Beeman said. 'It was my intention to take him.'

One of the cowboys asked: 'What you want him for?'

'A witness,' Beeman said, and he picked up Danniel's clothes and flung them at the man. He said nothing to him, but Danniel knew enough to start dressing.

Bo Thomas belched and wiped the last of his gravy off his plate with a piece of bread. He looked at his son and said: 'Army grub ain't changed, but, as long as it's free, I guess a man can take it. You like it here?'

'Yes, I guess I do,' Huck said. He tried not to be ill at ease, but his father's questions bothered him. His mother just sat there like a dog that had been kicked too hard too many times.

'How come you ain't called me Pa?' Bo Thomas asked.

'Well, I guess it's because it's been so long. I just haven't got used to it.'

'It ain't my fault you got took by Injuns,' Thomas said. 'Won't do you no good to blame me, either.'

'Why, I wasn't doing that.' The boy seemed surprised that his father would think of it.

'You was a mean little critter,' Thomas said. 'Always gettin' into everything.' He looked at his wife. 'And if you hadn't spent all your time gabbin' over the clothesline with the other wives, you'd have noticed he'd got out the water gate.' He rubbed his cheeks with the flat of his hand. 'I guess you went Injun all the way, huh?'

'I tried to stay alive and keep from getting beaten,' Huck admitted. 'That's about all I could do.' He looked at his mother, and added: 'I remember you. That's the truth.' He felt compelled to say something kind, to ease the strain in her face, to make her smile, or to remember a time when she had smiled.

'That's nice, Huck,' she said, but didn't change expression at all.

He started to get up to take his plate to the sink, but Bo Thomas said: 'That's woman's work. Sit down. You want to smoke?'

Huck shook his head.

'I guess you fought the Army just like the other bucks.' He laughed. 'What was your Injun name?'

'I don't use it any more,' Huck said.

'Well, you can tell me. I'm your pa, ain't I?'

'There's no use talking about it,' Huck said. 'It's all in the past now.'

Bo Thomas reached quickly across the table and fisted the front of Huck's shirt. 'When I ask you somethin', I want an answer.'

There was no fear in the boy, but Bo Thomas didn't understand that. Huck had killed his first man at fourteen, raided deeply into Mexico a month after his fifteenth birthday, and took a Mexican girl to wife when he was sixteen. He could not remember all the times he had faced a man with a knife in hand, and now he looked at this man sitting across from him, violence smoldering in his eyes. He wondered what made him this way.

'Are you going to hit me?' he asked.

His mother came to the table, an iron skillet in her hand. 'Let the boy go, Beauregard. Let him go, or I'll dent your stupid Irish head with this pan.'

Slowly, reluctantly, Bo Thomas released his

grip, and then he laughed and made a waving motion with his hand. 'By golly, there's no need to get all het up. I got a temper, and I never denied it.' He studied the boy carefully. 'I just don't understand you. How can you look at me like I didn't exist? I gave you life, boy. You're my own.'

'You quit pumpin' the boy,' his wife said and went back to her dishwashing. 'You'll be all right once you get out of this damned place,' she said to Huck. 'You'll get to thinkin' white again when you live in a town where there's trees and nice houses. You can work in the saloon with your pa. It ain't the best, but it's a livin', and someday it'll be yours.' She tried a smile. It was a feeble thing. 'You got to remember that you've been an Injun, and you can't just expect as much as others get.'

'Your ma's right,' Bo Thomas said. He rubbed his hand across his cheek again. 'Tell me somethin'. Those letters I got … you write 'em?'

'Yes,' Huck said.

'Where'd you learn that?'

'Here. I've been going to school over two years now.'

Bo Thomas swore and slapped his hand on the table. 'Don't that beat all hell, though? I've been a hard-workin', God-fearin' man all my life, and he's lived like an Injun, killin' and stealin', and now he can read and write, and I can't.' He sounded thoroughly angry.

'I've got to get back,' Huck said, getting up quickly.

'You in a rush or somethin'?' Bo asked.

'I've just got to get back,' Huck said, and went out.

Major Gary had to admit that the party was a success even on such short notice. The punch was just right, especially after the contract surgeon added the right amount of whisky. Senator Ivers was the constant center of attention. Brevet Major Halliday was unloading his personal grievances. Halliday's wife, tightly corseted, tittered and tried to hog all the dances with the senator. She was naturally a pushy woman, and, when it came to her own selfish purposes, she was not above elbowing someone else aside.

Captain Conrad was taking the night air on the east porch, and Gary found him there. Conrad deftly rolled a cigarette with one hand and thumbed a match alight. When Gary offered him one of his cigars, Conrad shook his head and said: 'I do everything the hard way, Major. You might say that it's an attempt to prove that I can still do everything another man can do, but it's a lie, and even now I admit it.' He tapped Gary on the arm, directing his attention farther down the porch. 'Is that sergeant looking for you?'

'Over here, Wynn,' Gary said, and the sergeant changed course. 'What is it, Sergeant?'

'This is an odd time to come to you, sir,' Wynn said, 'but Huck Thomas asked me to do it.'

'To do what?'

'To get you to approve his enlistment, sir.'

'Young Thomas wants to enlist?'

'Yes, sir, six years.'

Gary pursued his lips and fingered his mustache. 'Have you asked him why?'

'Well, sir, he wants to stay with the Army for a while. He's made up his mind that he's not going back with his folks.'

'How unusual,' Gary said. 'His natural parents, too.' He sighed. 'Well, if he's made up his mind, I won't stand in his way. Do you have his papers, Sergeant?'

'Right here, sir.' He handed them to Gary and also produced a small ink pot and a pen, standing aside so that Gary had enough light to affix his signature. Then he took everything back and said: 'Shall I tell his folks, Major? The old man is liable to raise hell. He thinks everyone's trying to pull a fast one on him.'

'I'll tell him myself in the morning,' Gary said. 'You can assign Thomas yourself, Sergeant. I imagine he wants line duty.'

'Yes, sir,' Wynn said, saluting.

He left them, and then Dan Conrad said: 'That's an odd turn, isn't it?'

'Yes,' Gary admitted. 'But a man has his own life to lead.'

Chapter Four

Bo Thomas did not accept his son's decision to join the Army with good grace. The orderly working in Gary's outer office heard Thomas ranting and swearing, then there was a heavy, meaty sound, and Thomas stumbled out, a hand pressed against his mouth.

Gary looked at the orderly and said – 'Mister Thomas has a toothache.' – and closed the door. The orderly went back to his paperwork.

Tom Smalling appeared at headquarters, asked to see Gary, and was admitted. Smalling and his mother were ready to leave, and now Tom didn't know how to say good bye. The words wouldn't come to him, and he just flung his arms around Gary, hugging him briefly, and ran out. This affected Gary so that his eyes blurred a little as he looked out the window.

Shortly before noon, Teddy came to headquarters with Gary's horse. Gary and the senator were going riding because Ivers wanted to see some more of the country.

Gary came out as Teddy was tying up. The boy wore his hair short now. He had given up his bright cotton shirt and was no longer going barefoot. Dr Rynder, who was teaching in Beeman's absence, had said that Teddy was a good pupil, filled now with a desire to learn.

'Catch a horse up,' Gary said, 'and come with us, Teddy.'

The boy smiled, ran across the parade ground toward the stable. Jim Gary wondered for a moment why he had said it. He supposed it was because he liked the boy, and he thought no more about it.

Since they were to be away from the post for three days, Gary had Sergeant Wynn rig a pack horse with tent, ground cloth, and cooking gear. When Ivers arrived at headquarters, he wore duck trousers and coat and carried an enormous sporting rifle. Gary thought this a little out of place. Rather than offend Ivers, he said nothing and took along his own .50-110 Winchester.

Gary went to his quarters to say good bye to his wife and daughters. As he walked back, he saw Emily Brail hanging up clothes. Her two children played in the back yard, making mud pies where water from her washtub had splashed on the ground.

Stopping, Jim Gary said: 'There is nothing that looks so domestic as a woman hanging up her washing. Is everything all right, Emily?'

'It's a nice place to live,' she said. 'One of

the other children wanted…' She turned and looked at her own children. 'Are they permitted to play with the others?'

'Of course,' Gary said, and went on.

Teddy and Jason Ivers were talking when Gary came up, and Ivers said: 'Teddy claims there are some deer in Uvalde Cañon.'

'It's a day and a half ride,' Gary said, 'and no real promise of deer.'

'By George, I'm game for it,' Ivers said, smiling. 'Do you mind?'

'A little hunting might do us all some good,' Gary admitted. He saw that Teddy was unarmed. 'There's a Forty-Five-Seventy repeater and a box of shells in my office closet, Teddy. Fetch it along for yourself.'

The boy dashed inside, and Gary mounted up. Ivers, not accustomed to a Western saddle, had a moment of difficulty, but he swore under his breath and hoisted himself aboard.

Teddy came back with the rifle and sprang to the horse's back in one effortless leap, and Ivers said: 'God I'd give a hundred dollars to be able to do that!'

'We're both twenty years too late,' Gary said, and they rode out of the post.

They moved southwest, riding steadily, and in the late afternoon they crossed a creek that cut between grassy swales in this rolling, hummocked land. There were trees for wood and shelter, and they made camp there.

Teddy insisted on tending the fire and doing the cooking. He made pan biscuits and a stew with a thick brown gravy, and opened canned peaches for something sweet.

Ivers ate like a man who couldn't recall his last meal, then he settled back with his cigarette. 'What was this country like twenty years ago?' he asked.

'We wouldn't be sitting here with a fire burning,' Gary said. 'Not unless we were greenhorns and were fixing to be killed by Indians. If a man rode through this country well-armed and alert, he wasn't bothered. But if he let down his guard just once, he never got a chance to do it again.'

'It is difficult for an Eastern man to visualize a day-to-day danger,' Ivers said. 'In my lifetime I've faced genuine danger three or four times, and I like to think that I met it squarely. But to be on guard constantly...' He shook his head.

'It becomes a way of life,' Gary said. 'People accept what they must, Jason. A determined farmer will plant his crop in the middle of hell if he's a mind to.'

They rolled into their blankets and let the fire die. Before dawn they were up, and Teddy was fixing breakfast. Before the sun was fully over the horizon, they were mounted and moving on. All that day they rode into broken land. The prairie with its grass and rolling hills was behind them, and they entered a sparse, dry, rocky country, full of draws and short cañons and ominous buttresses.

Teddy rode ahead, his attention swinging from the ground immediately ahead to the ridges and back. Finally he said: 'Deer here, Gary.' He pointed to the game trails that led westward into the higher rocks. 'There's a spring up there.'

'Is that where we'll camp?' Ivers asked.

Teddy shook his head and pointed somewhat south. 'No, game up there. We'll camp and stake out the spring before nightfall. When it turns dark, the deer will come to the spring to drink and browse.' He pointed to his right where the trail climbed high. 'We'll wait there.'

They made camp almost a mile from the spring. Gary set up the tents, and Teddy gathered wood for the fire but did not light it. They took their rifles and, with Teddy leading the way, climbed and worked their way across the broken land to the game trail. There was a gentle breeze blowing across the trail toward them, and they hunkered down in the rocks to wait. Ivers started to light a cigarette but thought of what he was doing and put it away. He grinned foolishly, and banged himself on the head with the heel of his hand, as though he were jarring his brains into action.

The sun passed out of sight, and the sky remained a rich blue even while gray shadows built among the rocks. Then the blue faded, and the gray deepened. Teddy flicked a small stone with his finger and drew their attention.

The does came up the trail first. It was the way of deer to let the females go first. They watched them come on, a step at a time, heads turning, ears flicking, nostrils plucking at the air for scent of danger. They passed on up the trail to the high spring.

Finally a buck appeared, a great rocking chair of antlers on his head. Another, smaller than the first, came up the trail, and Ivers raised his finger and pointed to the first one, wetting his thumb and rubbing it on the front sight of his rifle to indicate which would be his shot.

Jim Gary nodded, and Ivers cocked his rifle, holding the trigger down so as to make no noise. The buck raised his head to scent the air, and Ivers's shot hit him in the neck, spun him, and dropped him. The boom of the express rifle bounded from hill to hill. The other deer leaped, turned, and raced off down the trail.

Slowly Ivers got up and climbed over the rocks to approach the fallen deer. Teddy turned and worked his way back to their camp to get the pack horse, a canvas, and some rope.

Gary joined Jason Ivers and said: 'You've

got yourself a trophy there, Senator.' He smiled and lit a cigar.

It was fully dark by the time they packed the deer back to their camp. Gary went to the spring for water while Ivers and Teddy skinned the animal out and packed the meat. Teddy, thinking of the Comanche way, was all for roasting some of the shoulder, but Gary and Ivers, long steeped in the lore that meat had to cool and cure before eating, settled for pancakes, bacon, and coffee for the evening meal, content to wait until breakfast for their venison steak.

They had a pleasant meal, and Ivers's appetite seemed boundless, but finally he could hold no more. He sighed and sat back. 'It must be the fresh air. I swear, Jim, I'd gain thirty pounds in no time in this country.'

'You'd keep it worked off,' Gary said. 'As soon as we get that trophy back to the post, I'll get Corporal Rylander to work on it for you. He's an excellent taxidermist... Lord knows where he learned it. The soldiers can come up with the damnedest talents at times.' He paused to light a cigar. 'I suppose it's because I don't stop to consider that these men had lives and professions before they joined the Army. Sometimes it seems that I was born in it, and I have a tough time remembering what it was like out of it.'

'Do you have a family, Jim?'

'Yes, two sisters, both happily married now with families of their own. Once in a while I take leave and visit them.'

'He used to send them part of his pay every month,' a voice said from the deep shadows away from the fire.

Teddy came to his feet like a released spring, and Gary wasn't far behind him. Ivers, startled, jumped right across the fire. Then the man stood up, and the firelight caught the pearl handles on his pistols. The man stepped forward, laughing softly.

'Was I hostile, you'd have been my meat,' he said. He came into the light, smiling and extending his hand to Gary. The light shone on the polished badge pinned to his vest.

'Guthrie McCabe!' Gary said. 'What in hell are you doing out here?'

'Following you,' McCabe said.

'Senator, I'd like you to meet Guthrie McCabe, who was highly instrumental in the rescue of your wife. McCabe, Senator Jason Ivers.' Then he turned and took Teddy by the arm and drew him over, keeping his arm around the boy's shoulder. 'This is Teddy,' he said. 'Now tell me how in hell you came across our trail?'

'Came down on the train,' McCabe said. 'There was some other folks aboard headin' for Camp Verde. Met a one-armed captain at Morgan Tanks. He said you'd gone this direction for a few days, so I decided to trail

71

you. Just keepin' my hand in.'

'Have some coffee?' Ivers offered, and McCabe took a cup. He was a tall man, and he wore boots with spike heels that made him even taller. His hat was wide-brimmed and had a tall crown, creased down the front, Texas-style. Across the front of his shirt dangled a heavy watch chain and a fob of gold, an immense nugget.

'If you'll pardon me for saying so,' Ivers said, 'you're exactly as I pictured a Texas Ranger to be.'

'How's that, Senator?'

'Well, just like you are. I'd have been terrible disappointed if you'd been short and wore glasses and had a bald head.'

'By golly, we've got 'em like that,' McCabe said. 'I recall your wife well, Senator. A good woman. Lot of character there.' He appraised Ivers frankly. 'I'm happy to see she got a good man. You look like you could hold your own. Can't stand a man I've got to carry along. It's tough enough to take care of myself.'

'Thank you for the compliment,' Ivers said, 'but there is something about this land that makes me feel like a little boy. And a mighty inexperienced one at that.'

They sat down around the fire, and Teddy went to get McCabe's horse and bedroll. He came back a few minutes later, put the horse on the picket with the others, and squatted by the fire.

McCabe was talking. 'So it seems that Llano Vale went all the way to New Mexico Territory after this fella. There was a shooting ... don't know the right of it ... but there was a girl on the train who said Vale was dead and that her pappy did it.' He shrugged and helped himself to more coffee. 'Likely you've picked up another stray, Jim. But you always was a do-gooder.' Then he laughed and turned to Jason Ivers. 'Tell me about Washington politics, Senator. I've always had a strong desire to be President.'

The commissioner at Fort Reno wired Washington for instructions. He had a problem that he wanted solved, but there seemed to be no solution at all because Lieutenant Carl Beeman wouldn't budge an inch. Beeman insisted on bringing charges against Bert Danniel and the civilian cowboys who had been in Frank Skinner's employ, and there was no argument that would sway Beeman. He felt that damage had been done and that the only way to stop it was to get convictions and clear up the reservation politics.

Exhausting his arguments against Beeman, the commissioner then wrote a lengthy letter to Major Jim Gary, asking that Beeman be recalled and placed on other duties, so that these charges could be gracefully dismissed before the federal government got on its high horse about it. As the commissioner put it, no great good could come of a trial. True, the guilty would probably all go to jail, but the whole Indian Affairs system would be disturbed and come under attack, which would work a hardship on the Indians and on the citizens who built their economy around the Indian agency. Which was a nice way of saying that people were just not going to stand still and lose all that easy money.

It was Gary's policy to decide things for himself, but he invited Jason Ivers to read the letter. The thing had been in Gary's stack of mail when he returned from the hunting trip.

Ivers studied the letter carefully, then laid it on Gary's desk. 'Are you asking for an opinion, Jim?'

'Yes.'

'We'll have to talk politics, then,' Ivers said, lighting one of his endless cigarettes. 'I don't think there's a politician in Washington who is personally getting rich in office. However, there are a lot of them who augment their salary by taking advantage of legislation, or of a situation. First, you must understand, Jim, that a man has to be able to afford to go into politics. It is not the thing for a poor man. Let me put this on a personal basis, if I may. My family made their money in the barrel-making business, or at least Grandfather did. My father expanded considerably, first to making furniture, and then he added another

plant that made pots and pans and silver-
ware. During the war, the barrel factory
worked ten hours a day straight through, filling government orders. The furniture factory
made rifle stocks for the government, and the
canteens turned out by the other plant ran
into the hundreds of thousands. My family,
Jim, got rich off the war.'

'That doesn't sound political,' Gary said.

'It does, because Father had … as they say
… friends in high places.' Ivers smiled. 'We
made money, and the workers made money,
and everybody profited by it. I don't think
you'll find anyone back there who thinks it
was bad. My first venture into politics was
running for county supervisor, and I spent
six hundred dollars of my own money to run
and lose. But I came awful close to winning,
Jim, and that shook a lot of people. Then
when I ran for assemblyman, I only had to
spend five hundred dollars. The party paid
for the rest. I won that, served with some distinction in the state, then entered the
national senatorial race. But because I ran as
an independent, I paid for that myself, nearly
twenty-five hundred dollars. So you see, it
takes money to be successful in politics.'

He paused to take a final puff on his cigarette and crushed it out in Gary's ashtray.
'Once I got in, it became a matter of bal-
ancing out two things. What I could do for
the good of the people nationally, and what I

could do for the folks back home who elected me. One must always think of the next election, Jim. You have to be *in office* to do any good. That might mean supporting something that you know is not quite right. I'm sure the territorial representative from Oklahoma is losing sleep over the fact that a lot of attention is going to be drawn toward his province. Jim, every territory wants to become a state even though there isn't a particular move toward that goal. Within the framework of politics, the territorial governor is trying to make his territory worth admission to the Union. I would venture to say that he is doing the best that he can with what he has, and Lieutenant Beeman, in his righteous crusade, is going to kick the bottom out of the apple cart.'

'I see,' Gary said. 'You are suggesting, then, that I respond favorably to this appeal?'

'I'm suggesting that you consider it strongly,' Jason Ivers said. 'It took me some time, Jim, to understand that I was not capable of righting every wrong I came upon. Redress is the province of God.'

'That's certainly a safe attitude,' Jim Gary admitted. 'Thank you for your views. It will help me decide.'

Jason Ivers left Gary then. For a time Gary sat at his desk, idly tapping his pencil against the top. There was no doubt in Gary's mind that Ivers was right. Profits from Indian deals were substantial, and certainly a good deal of the economy was based on this profit. Gary could not quarrel with profit. He found nothing wrong with this motive, yet he drew a distinction between fair and reasonable profit and out-and-out swindle.

He could visualize the political discomfort a trial might induce, but he could also visualize a continuance of the things that had precipitated the trial. In his mind, there was one thing outstanding about corruption. It always got worse when left unchecked.

Only last did he consider Lieutenant Beeman. A betrayal of faith now would certainly affect Beeman's attitude toward his chosen career. Although Gary understood that the man would know disillusionment, there was no reason now, other than pure political consideration, to nullify his considerable effort.

Gary drew paper and pen across the desk and wrote two messages, the first to the United States commissioner at Fort Reno.

Right Honorable Elwood K. Butler
Federal Bldg.
Fort Reno, Oklahoma Territory

Dear Sir:
Your message at hand, and contents duly noted. It is to my regret that this situation causes you concern and embarrassment, and I cannot believe that it existed with your knowledge.

77

However, since a continuance of the situation can only bring discredit upon you, and since Lieutenant Beeman has conducted himself within the framework of his orders, I see no alternative but to proceed with the charges as outlined in the arraignment.

James Gary
Major, U.S. cavalry

The other was to Lieutenant Beeman in Fort Reno.

Lieutenant Carl Beeman:
My compliments on your duties well done. Storm clouds brewing. Suggest you don poncho for foul weather. If you need assistance, wire immediately.

Gary

He called in the orderly and sent for the signal sergeant who promised to have the messages on the wires in ten minutes. Then Gary lit a cigar and contemplated what he had done.

Lieutenant Flanders interrupted his thinking. He knocked, then stepped inside. 'Sorry to disturb you, Major, but the young girl who came on the post day before yesterday wants to see you. She was here yesterday and...'

'Of course,' Gary said. 'Do you have any particulars on her?'

'Her name is Frieda Schneider, Major.

Other than that she hasn't said much.'

'Show her in,' Gary said, and laid his cigar aside. Flanders went out and in a moment or two opened the door again and ushered in Frieda Schneider. She seemed nervous and looked around quickly before taking the chair Gary offered.

'I hope you're comfortable, Frieda. Is there anything we can do for you?'

'I ... I wish you could find out what happened to my father.' She pressed her hand against her cheek. 'He's not my real father. After he killed that man, he told me that he had been with some other men who had chased Indians, and they found me on the prairie. He took me home with him because they were going to hurt me.'

Gary made some notes as she talked. 'Did he say how long again this was?'

'About sixteen years.'

Gary asked her other questions, made more notes, and finally got out a file from the cabinet and began to check one thing against another. Then he called in the lieutenant.

'Mister Flanders, send a wire to the sheriff at Pope's Wells, New Mexico Territory, and find out what happened to George Schneider. And find Teddy and tell him to come to my office.'

'Yes, sir.' He saluted, and went out closing the door.

'Now, I think we'll soon learn the best or

worst of it,' Gary said. 'But I want you to think back. Think hard and see if you can remember anything from your childhood.'

'Sometimes I've had dreams,' she said. 'Papa says they're just wishes.'

'Tell me about them,' Gary urged.

'It's not easy to remember dreams,' she said. 'They never seemed very real to me.' She spent a moment in deep thought. 'I've dreamed about another girl. She was older and rolled me on a bear rug and laughed.' Then she shook her head. 'It's hard to remember dreams.'

'Yes, of course,' Gary said. 'Did you ever dream about Indians, Frieda?'

She nodded. 'I used to wake up crying. Papa would say that it was something I ate. But I'd always dream the same thing. There was a boy, and they whipped him, and he cried and fought them until they tied him and dragged him behind a horse. Then I'd wake up.'

Gary heard steps on the porch, and Teddy dashed past his window. A moment later he knocked and stepped inside. 'Did you want me, Jim?' he asked. Then he saw the girl sitting there. He looked at her and turned his glance to Gary. Then he did a strange thing. He slowly turned his head back and looked intently at her. He walked around her, moving behind her, all the time looking at her intently. He came around to the other side

80

and stood by Jim Gary's desk and studied her face. She looked at him without embarrassment or reserve, and then Teddy knelt in front of her and gently touched her hand.

'Anna, don't you remember me? It's Ted. Don't you remember, Anna?' He glanced at Gary, and quickly turned back. 'Anna, you fell off the pony, and I tried to go back after you and they were all drunk, and they whipped me and dragged me behind a pony. Don't you remember it, Anna? I'm your brother, Ted.' He was crying now, the tears running unchecked down his cheeks. 'There was Bess, too. She was killed right away when they hit the cabin. Can you remember any of it? You were so little, Anna. So tiny. I tried to wrap you in the bear rug and hide you, but it was no good. They found you.'

He got up and put out a hand and steadied himself against Jim Gary's desk. He closed his eyes and pressed his other hand against his forehead, as though the flood of returned memory threatened to drown him.

Then he shook his head, opened his eyes, and looked at Jim Gary. 'My name is Ted Carpenter... I remember it now ... all of it. I was five years old when the Indians hit us.'

'You had a dog,' Anna Carpenter said softly. 'He bit someone, and I never saw him again. I remember crying about that.'

'That was Speck,' Teddy said softly. 'An Indian put a lance through him.' He took a

81

handkerchief from his pocket and blew his nose. He looked at Jim Gary. 'She's all I could remember, Jim. You know how I talked about her. Why was it all I could remember?'

'Love,' Gary said, 'is a bond of limitless strength.' He came around the desk and put his arms around Teddy. 'Why don't you two go for a walk? And both of you come to my quarters for supper tonight. All right?'

They nodded and went out together. After Gary closed the door, he leaned against it and shut his eyes. He felt that he had, indeed, been privileged. Surely no man could serve better, or better serve than this.

Chapter Five

Lieutenant Carl Beeman and Ben Stagg were having their supper in the Drover's Hotel when Burt Sims, the U.S. marshal, came to their table and sat down. Sims was an angular, dry-mannered man who favored brown suits and a soft-brimmed hat. He sighed before he spoke. He always did this, as though it pained him to have to say what his duties forced him to say.

'Commissioner Butler wants to see you, Lootenant. At his home.'

Beeman arched an eyebrow. 'A social

affair, Marshal?'

'Couldn't say. Likely not.' He sighed, and got up. 'I'm glad I ain't stubborn.'

'Yes,' Beeman said. 'It must be a blessing.' He watched Sims leave and finished his apple pie and coffee.

Ben Stagg leaned back in his chair, idly picking his teeth. He watched Beeman carefully. 'Daniel in the lion's den,' he said softly. 'Boy, watch yourself.'

'Yes, indeed,' Beeman said. He took a final drink of coffee, and got up. 'Are you going back to the reservation tonight?'

'Been puttin' it off,' Stagg said. 'But I guess I'd better keep an eye on Lovering. He ain't to be trusted, you know. Was he to get it in his head that this affair would be dropped, he'd turn on you. The man's only interested in keepin' his own pillow fluffed up.'

Beeman smiled, laid two fifty-cent pieces on the table, and left the dining room. He paused briefly on the street for a look up and down. There was not much traffic because the hour was early but by nine o'clock the saloons would liven up, and a man would have difficulty finding a place to tie his horse.

The commissioner lived in a large gray house three blocks off the main street. As Beeman approached, he saw two buggies parked in front. He went up the path and knocked. A Negro servant let him in.

Elwood K. Butler was holding forth in his

library. He was a robust man in his early fifties, an excellent speaker, and a man with some political promise.

'Ah, Lieutenant Beeman, so good of you to come,' Butler said. 'A drink, sir? Moses, pour the lieutenant a drink.' His fingers plucked at Beeman's sleeve, turning him to face the other two men.

'Gentlemen, may I introduce Lieutenant Beeman?' He indicated a small, sallow-complexioned man with gold-rimmed glasses and a crown of thin hair. 'Beeman, this is Mister Clive Maybank, assistant to the Secretary of Indian Affairs.' They shook hands. 'And General Tremain Caswell. I believe you've already met the general.'

'Yes,' Beeman said, 'but I expect the general doesn't remember me.'

Caswell offered his hand, and it surprised Beeman, for it was not a thing a general officer did when meeting a lieutenant. 'I recall you distinctly,' Caswell said. 'Give my regards to your wife, Mister Beeman.'

'Thank you, sir.' The servant handed him his drink.

Butler smiled, and proposed a toast. 'To friendly relations,' he said, and tossed off his drink.

'I think we can get right down to the heart of the matter,' Butler said. 'You've done an excellent job of packing our jail, Mister Beeman. It's a pity we can't channel your energy into the arrest and incarceration of our genuinely lawless elements.' He laughed, and the others smiled faintly. 'But as it is, the situation has become so alarming that Mister Maybank felt it his duty to come here and take a first-hand look. General Caswell, when apprised of the fact that the military had taken over control of the reservation, took the first train. You can see how serious this all has become, Mister Beeman.'

'Sir, I'm well aware of the seriousness. I was aware of it when I discovered that Indian women were being turned into prostitutes for fifty cents, and that the Indians were being short-changed on their beef ration, and that certain individuals were pocketing a profit by irregular dealings.'

Maybank laughed unpleasantly. 'Really, Mister Beeman, this is a schoolboy attitude. The American Indian has always been a poor horse trader. The island of Manhattan was bought for...'

'Are you quoting a precedent, sir?' Beeman stared bluntly at Maybank. 'Are you telling me, sir, that because the Indians were once cheated that this is a standard by which all dealings are measured?'

'I am saying,' Maybank declared, 'that you are pulling this thing 'way out of proportion. All right, we will admit that the agency personnel engaged in mild deceptions. We will admit that they were remiss in some areas where morality is concerned. But this doesn't warrant charges filed, men locked up and tried.'

'What do you suggest it warrants, sir?'

Butler leaped in to seize the advantage. 'Compromise, gentlemen, is the only solution here. Mister Beeman acted in good faith, as any man devoted to his duty would have done, and he is to be commended. Unfortunately Mister Beeman, without a grasp of the whole situation, let his zeal carry him into perilous waters. I feel that this whole thing can be settled without harsh or idealistic argument. Mister Beeman, dropping the charges would effect the release of the prisoners. The cowboys will likely depart or go back to their homes. Mister Danniel will be reprimanded, and a letter placed in his file. We'll find some other agency for him.' He clapped his hands together. 'So you see, we have a solution within our grasp, haven't we?'

Beeman looked at him for a long moment, then turned to General Caswell. 'Sir, you haven't spoken. I would like your views.'

'It seems to me,' Caswell said, rolling his cigar from one corner of his mouth to the other, 'that you're in a position to make a lot of unpleasant trouble for Mister Maybank and the Bureau of Indian Affairs. A trial will attract reporters, and people read newspapers, and it just may be that the uproar will cause other agencies to come under close and relentless scrutiny. In this world there are many people who only need a cause. You may be providing them that cause, Mister Beeman. You are about to hit a hornet's nest with a stick.'

'Are you criticizing my position, or applauding it, sir?'

'I must applaud it,' Caswell said, 'although that may be premature. Let me point out some facts, Mister Beeman. To carry this through will almost surely result in convictions for those accused. The evidence against them is overwhelming. You will win that battle, Mister Beeman. But what of the battles tomorrow and the next year, and ten years hence? To win on this field is to make bitter enemies who will never forgive you, and they will be powerful enemies. I can assure you of that. But you will have your champions, also men of power. Weigh one against the other, Mister Beeman. Measure them against your career. You are possibly ready, pending Major Gary's recommendation, for a promotion. Can you visualize what it might be like to grow gray in the service and not advance further? It is possible. Can you visualize one dismal command after another, one obscure post after another? This is possible, Mister Beeman. What makes a man a hero or a villain is often a fine line.'

'You have made no definite recommendation, sir.'

'And I won't,' Tremain Caswell said seriously. 'Mister Beeman, in your conduct so far you have earned my respect. You've conducted yourself in the highest traditions of honor and duty. As a general officer I cannot fault you in any way. But the decision is yours. Others have faced decisions like this and survived.'

Beeman rolled his empty shot glass between his hands and studied the play of lamplight on it. Then he said: 'Gentlemen, I'm not a smart man. I didn't graduate high in my class. My duties in the service have been routine. In fact, a sergeant could generally have performed them as capably as I.' He raised his head and looked at Maybank and Butler. 'Gentlemen, from my own observations, I would say that the Indian receives neither social nor legal justice. And from your own expressed views it seems to me that this situation is not likely to improve greatly. General Caswell has pointed out the risks I run in pursuing this, but I'll tell you this. Pursue it I will, to the damned hilt!'

A flood of angry colour came into Clive Maybank's face. He took the cigar from his mouth and snapped: 'Beeman, I wouldn't give a plugged nickel for your career!'

'I'd give less for your honor, sir,' Beeman said.

Maybank moved as though he were going to strike Beeman, but Butler quickly seized his arm and held him back. 'Mister Beeman, it is not too late to retreat.'

'There is no retreat from right,' Beeman said. 'I maybe capable of doing damned little in this world, Commissioner, but what I do will not weigh on my conscience.'

'You self-righteous fool!' Maybank barked. He went for his hat and clapped it on his head. He was in the hallway and gave Beeman a final glare and slammed out.

General Tremain Caswell put down his whisky glass and took Beeman by the arm. 'If you can stand my company, Mister Beeman, I'd be honored to buy you a drink at the hotel bar.' He clapped Beeman on the back and bowed to Butler, and they went out together.

Senator Ivers and his wife were regular dinner guests of the Gary family, and, to round it out, Dr McCaslin and Dr Rynder were often invited because they knew the value of good conversation, and they stimulated Ivers's fine mind.

McCaslin was holding forth on one of his theories; he had many of them, on a wide range of topics. 'You say it's amazing, Senator, and I say it is quite natural. Young Carpenter had not seen his sister for sixteen years, and yet he recognized her immediately. What seems odd, too, is really self-explanatory. We base recollection on memory alone. Say we haven't seen old Willis for sixteen years. Our memory of him is as he was sixteen years ago. That's all we base recognition on.' He waved his hands expansively. 'Now Ted Carpenter based recognition on emotion, the blood in his veins, and the seared remembrance of the last time he saw her. She was constantly on his mind. He talked about her a great deal. You'll recall, Jim, that he liked to watch your own children. It kept bringing things back to him. Everything lay below the surface, waiting to come up. His name ... everything.'

'This is all very interesting,' Ivers said, 'but I've heard of cases where brothers associated with each other for years and didn't know...'

'True, true,' McCaslin said, 'but we're dealing with brother and sister, the protector and protected. There's a big difference there, Senator. There's a great deal about the mind we may never know, but it seems to me that, although Ted was five at the time, he began his life from that moment on. He always said that he was about sixteen years old, and now we know he's twenty-one. Everything began for him *after* that terrible experience.'

'I'm inclined to agree with Doctor McCaslin,' Gary said. 'I've seen some strange things out here. Mothers who hadn't seen their children from infancy would immediately recognize them.'

'I wonder why the Indians abandoned the

90

little girl,' Janice Ivers said. 'That's odd, isn't it?'

'Well, there could be many reasons for it,' Gary said. 'Indians believe very strongly in medicine, and perhaps the little girl was a bad omen ... bad medicine. Or she could have cried too much. Indian children are not allowed to cry, you know.' He shrugged. 'It's hard to say exactly, although the fact that she was abandoned does not surprise me. I never gave it a questioning thought.'

Jason Ivers knocked ash off his cigarette and said: 'You know, Jim, I've been rather looking forward to meeting your Lieutenant Beeman. When is he arriving on the post?'

'Mister Beeman is occupied at Fort Reno,' Gary said, his manner casual.

Ivers's brow flicked up briefly. 'I understood that you were going to recall him, Jim.'

'The matter was discussed, yes, but I decided against it. Mister Beeman sent me a wire yesterday. The trial began this morning. Since the government prosecutors have exhibited some reluctance, Mister Beeman, as friend of the court, is conducting the prosecution for the people.'

'Why the conceited ass!' Ivers blurted.

The women were chatting softly. They stopped now, and Janice Ivers said: 'Jason, what a thing to say!'

He bit his lip and collected his temper, then leaned an elbow on the table and presented

91

to Gary a more reasonable manner. 'Jim, it was my understanding that we discussed this and reached an agreement. Not in so many words, granted, but a tacit agreement, nevertheless.'

'Jason, I'm sorry there's a misunderstanding, but in my mind it was a discussion and nothing more. The ultimate decision was military, and mine.'

Ivers frowned. 'Jim, it embarrasses me to have to spell this out for you but if I must...' He glanced at his wife and Jane Gary. 'As you know, Jim, I'm chairman of the Indian Affairs committee, and this mess your heroic, dedicated Mister Beeman is stirring up is going to come right back and perch in my lap. A mighty uncomfortable situation, I can assure you.' He crushed out his cigarette. 'I've been your champion, Jim, when you didn't have a soul who gave a damn one way or another. Now I've asked you for a favor, something easily in your power to grant, and you've turned me down. I find that difficult to understand, Jim, and I'll be frank to say it.'

'I didn't know your support had strings, Jason.'

'Well, it has!' Ivers said sharply. 'In God's name, man, try to understand how the world turns. It's you scrub me, and I'll scrub you. Pure and simple.'

'Not pure, Jason, and certainly not simple,' Gary said. 'Jason, wouldn't you like to know that your Indian Affairs Bureau was as clean as a whistle?'

'Hell, yes, but I don't want to be the one who's smeared in the clean-up.' He sighed, and shook his head. 'Jim, pull Lieutenant Beeman out of Fort Reno. They'll declare a mis-trial, and it'll be done with.'

'And if I don't?' Gary asked.

'I'll find it hard to champion a cause that doesn't have my interests at heart.'

'Jason!'

Ivers waved a hand at his wife, warning her to be quiet. He was steadily watching Jim Gary. 'I want an answer, Jim. An answer now.'

Jim Gary sat there, his head tipped forward, his lips beneath his full mustache pursed thoughtfully. Then his eyes came up to Jason's, and he said: 'Beeman stays.'

Ivers threw down his napkin and got up from the table. 'I'm sorry you've taken that track, Jim. I like you, but I've got to protect myself and my friends who support me.' He nodded to each of them. 'Now, if you'll excuse me?'

He turned and left the room, and an uncomfortable silence settled. McCaslin and Rynder hastily said good night and left. Janice Ivers fought back her tears, and said: 'Jim, I've never seen him like this. Never! I just don't understand it.'

'I suggest that you don't interfere,' Gary advised. 'There's no need in upsetting your

93

marriage by entering into this, Janice. Besides he'd tell you that it was none of your business.' He sighed, and lit a fresh cigar. 'I can't blame the man for wanting to defend himself. I can't say that he's wrong in making deals that aren't good enough to see the light of day. Jason didn't make up the rules by which he must play, and he's no less an honorable man for playing by them. The Army has its own brand of politics, Janice. Everything has its rules, good or bad. Don't blame him, that's what I'm asking.'

'How can I help it?' she said quietly. 'We're civilized, Jim, because we have the courage to fly in the face of Providence. Can you forget how it was when you brought me back?' She looked at Jane. 'You remember. It took courage for you to stand up to them, Jim. It was an unpopular thing for you to do. But you did it, and you were a big man because of it. I don't want to be married to a little man, Jim.'

'Janice, give this some time. Will you do that?' He reached out and patted her hand, then got up to answer a knock at his front door.

Lieutenant Flanders was there. 'Sorry to interrupt your evening, sir, but General Caswell is on the post. He is waiting in your office.'

'For God's sake!' Gary said, and went back to excuse himself. He went along the walk to his office where Caswell was slumped in a chair, his uniform soiled with dust. He had helped himself to a whisky and one of Gary's cigars.

'I had no idea you were coming, General,' Gary said.

'Frankly I had no idea myself,' Caswell said. 'You might say that I got lonesome, and a train ride looked good to me.' He straightened in his chair and poured another drink. 'I trust Beeman wired you that the trial has commenced.' Gary nodded, and Caswell smiled. 'Damn it, I *like* that boy. Oh, they squeezed him, Maybank and Butler. They put the screws on him and bore down, and he told them to kiss his ass. By God, there's a soldier, and, if they lean on him, I'll make him my aide-de-camp and promote him to captain.'

'General, you don't know how proud this makes me to hear you say that about Mister Beeman.' He went behind his desk and turned up the lamp a little. 'Will he get convictions?'

'I don't see how he can miss,' Caswell said. 'Milo Lovering will testify to protect himself. The cowboys will probably get a suspended sentence, but I think Bert Danniel will go to jail. That really doesn't matter. The newspaper people are there, and they've already started to carve the pieces.' He took several folded papers from his hip pocket and tossed them on Gary's desk. 'Cries of outrage and fraud.' He laughed without humor. 'What does Senator Ivers think of it?'

'I've disappointed the senator.'

'Hmm,' Caswell said, arching his brows. 'A blessing to one man is a curse to another. As chairman of the Indian Affairs committee, the senator's position is rather sensitive. Here you were, doing just dandy, recovering those poor lost people. Then you found a little something wrong at the agency, stepped in there, and *POW!*' He smacked his hands together. 'The senator, I'm sure, is disappointed. Knowing you, Jim, I'm sure you did not co-operate in a manner he thought best.'

'No, sir, I did not.'

Steps came across the porch, and Jason Ivers walked in without knocking. He nodded to Jim Gary, then said: 'General, I overheard two soldiers talking. That's how I knew you were here.' His glance went again to Gary. 'If I'm intruding, forgive me, but under the circumstances...'

'Pull up a chair, Jason,' Gary suggested. 'Care for a drink?' He took a clean glass from his desk drawer and poured for Ivers. 'I was just telling the general how I'd disappointed you.'

'Oh, Jim, I wish we wouldn't butt heads over this. I know you feel that there's a principle involved here, and I understand your reluctance to go against it, but this work you're doing here is more important than pressing this agency issue.'

'What the senator is trying to say,' Caswell said, 'is that, if you carry on with this, he's going to withdraw his support and cut you off without a dime.'

Ivers colored. 'Damn it, General, that's pretty blunt.'

'I call it honest. But he's right, Jim.'

'Did you come here to smooth this over, General?' Gary asked.

'Yes. I think I can do it. Jim, I want Lovering to withdraw his testimony. If he does, the case will be thrown out. But...' – he looked directly at Ivers – 'Lovering is to be transferred back to Washington, and Danniel is to be kicked out of the Indian Service. I want honest men to replace them. Agreed, Senator?'

'I would find that agreeable,' Ivers admitted. 'Jim?'

'There'll be no prejudice against Beeman?'

'None,' Caswell said. 'As a matter of fact, I'll personally write him up for promotion. Jim, he'll have done his job, won't he? He's cleaned up the mess, hasn't he? Does it really matter how it's been done?'

Gary thought about it for a moment, then shook his head. 'No, it doesn't. All right, gentlemen. We agree. Lovering and Danniel are out.' He raised his finger and pointed it at Ivers. 'Honest men, sir. That has to be clear.'

'God, Jim, I want honest men but sometimes I have to take what I can get.' He laughed uncomfortably and took out a handkerchief and wiped his face. 'You drive a mighty tough bargain.'

'If I didn't, Senator, you wouldn't be married now to your wife.'

'A point I'm not likely to overlook,' Ivers said. 'Jim, it might be to everyone's advantage if Mister Beeman and his detail remained at the reservation, in charge, until appropriate people can be sent out. May I use your telegraph facilities?'

'Of course, Senator.'

Jason Ivers hurried out, eager to get that telegram off to Clive Maybank. After the door closed, General Caswell said: 'Didn't hurt too much, did it, Jim?'

'No, sir, but it was a bargain I could never have made. He would have felt that I was pinching him.'

'That's why I came down. We've got to get along, Jim. This isn't a lesson for you, but it's something you should remember.' He sighed and got up, stretching to unknot the kinks in his back. 'Well, I'm going to turn in. McCabe and I are going fishing in the morning.'

'I suppose he claims he knows where they're biting.'

Caswell smiled. 'McCabe knows everything. Don't you know that?'

'He knows where there's a couple of Indian

kids, too, but he's been keeping his mouth shut about it,' Gary said. 'I know definitely that there's a family down in Uvalde County who raised an Arapaho girl. I've written McCabe to send a man down there for her, but he keeps ignoring my letters. You know, General, returning an Indian child is our job, too.'

'Maybe the subject will come up.'

'Be your usual persuasive self, sir.'

Caswell said: 'What the hell does that mean, Major Gary?'

'Oh, nothing, sir. It's just that you have charm and poise, sir ... the ability to meet people on their own terms. I noticed that right off, sir.'

'Are you comparing me to a snake oil salesman, Jim?' Then he laughed heartily. 'Listen, I was stealing horses when McCabe was messing his didies.' He winked, and went on out.

Gary waited a moment, then blew out the lamps, and followed. The guard was marching his measured post, and, as he passed in front, Gary said: 'Good night, Reilly.'

The guard was surprised, but he said: 'Good night, sir. All's quiet, sir.'

'Yes, and we want to keep it that way.' He walked on, past a row of dark quarters. There was a lamp on in Lieutenant Flanders's parlor, but Beeman's quarters were dark, and Gary was surprised to find Julia Beeman standing by her door.

He stopped, and she came to the walk. 'Major, forgive me, but I have to ask. I've heard rumors and talk and... Is Carl all right? Is he in trouble?'

Gary felt suddenly ashamed for, from her tone, he knew how much she had worried, and he had forgotten her, forgotten what it was for an Army wife to wait and wonder. 'Missus Beeman, I want you to know that I am proud of Carl. General Caswell is very impressed. He'll be coming home soon, and, unless I'm sadly mistaken, he'll be advanced over others on the promotion list. General Caswell is that delighted with his work.'

'You're not just saying ... no, I can see that you're not. Thank you. It's what Carl always wanted, to have someone proud of him.' Then she suddenly reached up and kissed his cheek and dashed for her door.

He waited until she went in. Then he walked on, whistling softly.

Chapter Six

Senator Ivers wanted to make a tour of the reservation. Although Jim Gary didn't want to interrupt his schedule, he knew that this was an opportunity to mend fences with

Ivers and, at the same time, give Captain Dan Conrad a tour of the reservation.

Gary wanted to bring Lieutenant Beeman back, and he wanted Conrad to take active command of a company in the field. So he gave Conrad his orders, and the company, with equipment and horses, boarded the next northbound train at Morgan Tanks.

There was some delay at Morgan Tanks because of a trestle washout to the south. Gary, Conrad, and the senator put up at the small inn. It had once served as a stage stop, but, with the coming of the railroad, it had been enlarged. There were three wings now, sprawling log and adobe with a plank floor, and a lively saloon occupied one corner. There was a small store across the way where travelers stopped to replenish supplies. A blacksmith had a place farther down. The railroad tracks ran through this nubbin of a town.

One long table and benches served for the dining room, and the meal was whatever Panhandle Wiggins chose to cook. That was generally stew, a culinary medium for disguising leftovers. The two officers and the senator ate one meal there and thereafter walked out to where the company was camped and took Army fare.

All during the first day of their stay Jim Gary noticed a man who seemed abnormally curious. Wherever Gary went, he could feel

101

the man's eyes on him, and, when he had had enough of it, he went over to him.

'What is it with you, friend? You've been watching me ever since I got here.'

'No offense intended, Major,' the man said, hitching up his overalls and quickly whipping off his hat. 'Been wondering how to talk to you.' He pawed the floor with one foot. 'My name's George Schneider, from New Mexico way, and…'

'In the name of God, man, I thought you'd been hung! Or were in jail, at the least. Anna Carpenter … or Frieda Schneider … was asking about you. I sent a wire and…' He took Schneider by the arm. 'How long have you been here?'

'Four days now.'

'Then may I suggest that you ride to the post with the mail orderly when he arrives? Man, you've left that girl in the air. You've got to straighten that out, understand? You just can't raise a girl like that and then get yourself in trouble and… How come they let you out of jail?'

'Llano Vale didn't die,' Schneider said. 'And Vale swears he tried to pull his gun on me first. That ain't so, and I tried to tell 'em that, but they just laughed at me.' He raised his hand as though to touch Gary but thought better of it. 'She's all right, ain't she? My little… What'd you say her name was? Anna … Anna Carpenter. She's with her brother now?'

Gary nodded.

'Then I've lost her,' Schneider said dismally.

'Oh, for God's sake, man, buck up!' Gary said roughly. 'Now you get to the post, understand? You do it, or I'll have a squad and the sheriff after you.'

It was nonsense. Gary wouldn't have wasted the time, but he suspected that George Schneider responded well to authority and a little threat.

Schneider stiffened a little and nodded his head. 'I'll do that, sir. Yes, sir, I surely will.'

Gary's manner softened. 'She'll be glad to see you, Schneider. You can't wash away those years, man. You'll see.'

'I've been afraid,' Schneider said. 'Most of my life, I guess.'

He turned away, and Gary went back to where Ivers and Captain Conrad waited. The captain wouldn't ask any questions, but Ivers had nothing against it. 'What was his complaint?'

'He wanted to know the way to the post.'

Ivers frowned. 'Anyone here could have told him that.'

Dan Conrad's blunt face showed nothing, but he was embarrassed, and it showed in his eyes. He said: 'I don't think, Senator, that he asked anyone here.'

Jason Ivers looked at him quickly, on the

103

verge of taking this further, but Conrad was half turned away, busy making a one-handed cigarette, clearly out of it.

Their train arrived in the early evening, and they boarded it. Conrad left them to see that the troopers and horses got aboard, then he came back to their coach and sat across from them. The train was a combination of flat-cars, boxcars, and cattle cars, with two coaches hooked ahead of the caboose. After the engine had taken a drink of water, they lurched out of the station with a rattle of couplings and swayed up the roadbed, slowly picking up speed on the long, shallow grade.

All that night and the next day they remained on the train. Jim Gary would never bring himself to like this means of travel. The idleness bothered him, and the noise, and the worn-in aroma of railway coaches bothered him, and the people he was forced into contact with on trains bothered him. He hoped that he was not a stuffed shirt. He liked to think that he was not, but his rather solitary life had instilled in him a distrust of people he did not know, and he disliked being pressed together with them. He would be glad when they got there.

The train pulled into Port Reno six hours late, which put the time at about one in the morning. There was not much stirring at this hour. Conrad went forward to supervise the unloading of the horses. Gary and Jason Ivers walked around the cinder platform, trying to stomp some use into their stiff legs.

Conrad came back and said: 'Major, the men have dozed and catnapped. With your permission we could push on and reach the reservation headquarters by eight o'clock.'

Ivers seemed shocked. 'Hell, Jim, I've been thinking of a bath and a bed at the hotel.'

'There are excellent accommodations at the reservation, Jason.' He nodded to Dan Conrad. 'Form the company, Captain. Have our horses saddled.' Conrad went away to attend to this, and Gary busied himself with lighting a cigar.

Ivers was put out. 'This isn't a campaign, you know. What the hell's the hurry?'

He got no answer, and he understood that Gary wasn't going to debate it with him. He jammed his hands deeply in his coat pockets and walked a little way down the platform to be alone.

There was a deep chill in the air, and they could see their breath clearly. The horses were full of pep and were giving the troopers a time of it, just holding them still. From the town side of the tracks two men came out of the darkness and into the light of the dépôt, and the badges pinned to their Mackinaws immediately identified them. They carried sawed-off shotguns and came up to Conrad first, but he pointed to Jim

Gary, and they walked over to him.

One was tall, one short. The short one said: 'I'm Hutchins, deputy marshal. This is Will Speer, the same. You're Major Gary?' He stripped off his glove and offered his hand. 'Good to see you.' He glanced at the troopers. 'Is that all you brung? Well, what the hell, two of us have been holdin' the lid on this damned town for three days now. But I'll tell you, Major, you'd better keep them damned Indians on the reservation where they belong. They start runnin' wild, and they'll get shot sure as hell.'

Some of this talk fell on Ivers farther down the platform, and he came back, the question in his eyes and in the way he looked from Gary to the marshals and back again.

'I'm not sure I know what you're talking about,' Gary said. 'We've been two days and two nights out of Camp Verde, and...'

'Then you didn't get my wire,' Hutchins said. He brushed his mustache with a finger. 'Some senator wired the commissioner from Camp Verde. An hour later Milo Lovering walked out of the hotel, and somebody cut him down from that high roof over the feed store. Speer and I was farther up the street, and, by the time we got there, Lovering was dead. I guess he died instantly, 'cause he was shot through the head.' He looked curiously at Ivers. 'Are you the guy who sent the wire to the commissioner?'

'Never mind that now,' Gary said sharply. 'What about the man who killed him?'

'He got away,' Speer said, his manner casual.

'And you didn't go after him?' Gary's tone was biting.

'Well, hell, the commissioner was yellin' at us, demandin' protection, so what could we do? A U.S. commissioner gives us orders, remember?' He rubbed his face with a gloved hand. 'But he was seen and described ... a big man, long hair, carryin' himself a little stiffly on the port side. He rode out to the south onto the reservation. That was the last we seen of him.'

'We got a name to hang on him,' Hutchins said. 'Llano Vale. He was seen around town the afternoon before the shootin'. Came in on the southbound and put up at the Drover's. The town marshal wanted to run him out of town, but with the jail full and all...' – he shrugged – 'he just never got around to it.'

'Excuse me a moment,' Gary said, and took Jason Ivers firmly by the arm and drew him down the platform until they were out of earshot of the marshals. 'Now I'm going to ask you what you said in that wire to the commissioner, Jason, and, if you even hinted that the number one witness should be shut up, I'm going to see that you never run again for public office, not even for dog-catcher.'

'For Christ's sake, Jim, I wouldn't...'

'I'm not interested in your denials, Jason. Just the truth.'

Ivers's face grew stern. 'Jim, I told him to persuade Lovering not to testify, to drop the case, and then leave the disposition of the principals to me. That is absolutely all, and in those words as near as I can recall.' He looked straight at Gary. 'And I don't like your insinuations at all.'

'That's too damned bad,' Gary said, and he went back to where the two marshals waited. 'Where is the commissioner?'

'At this hour? In bed. Where else?'

'He can wait,' Gary said, and turned to Conrad. 'Let's mount up and get on to reservation headquarters. We've got a man to hunt down.' He started to turn away, then spun back. 'Speer, you tell the commissioner to be here when I come back, or I'll come after him. Llano Vale always got paid well for his work, and I damned sure want to ask some questions about this.'

'All right,' Speer said.

After they were mounted and had turned out of town, Jason Ivers had nothing to say to Gary. He was angry, and his manner turned sulky, and, even during the rest stops, he clung to a stubborn, hurt silence.

It was dawn of a frosty morning when they came to the reservation buildings and dismounted. Lieutenant Beeman rushed out but caught himself and saluted quickly.

Gary said: 'Mister Beeman, I expected to find you in the field, searching out Llano Vale.'

'Ben Stagg has been gone part of yesterday and last night,' Beeman said. 'Please come in. It's damned nippy outside, and there's a fire and coffee.' He held the door open for them. Conrad dismissed the company and came in a moment later.

Beeman was pouring coffee. 'After the shooting I came directly to the reservation to take command. There's considerable unrest, sir. The Indians are inclined to be nervous, anyway, and they feel that there is a plan afoot to move them or something. It's hard to make them understand, sir.'

'Yes, I realise your problem,' Gary said.

'Sergeant Geer and the men are about the reservation, sir, trying to do what they can to quiet them.' He rubbed a hand across his eyes as though he were not getting enough sleep. 'Frankly, sir, I didn't know where to turn after Lovering was killed. When Ben Stagg told me he'd go after Vale, I let him, because I knew I couldn't track down that old mountain cat myself.' He shook his head slowly. 'I firmly believe that Vale was paid to kill Lovering. He came to town earlier in the day ... that much I've established. He also stayed at the Drover's, and...'

'Yes, I talked to the marshal,' Gary said. He

turned to Captain Conrad. 'I'm sorry, Dan. This is Lieutenant Carl Beeman, who's been doing Trojan service here. Dan Conrad.'

Beeman came to a heel-snapping attention, saluted, then smiled and shook Conrad's hand. 'I'm glad to see you, sir. I trust you've brought a squad. We're very short here, and...'

'I have a company,' Conrad interrupted. 'We'll relieve you any time, Mister Beeman.'

'Thank God for that! When the Indians get restless, there's no telling what they'll do. Yesterday there must have been three hundred gathered in the agency yard. Just standing there, watching, waiting.'

Gary nodded and said: 'Carl, I can't understand your not informing me of these events when they happened.'

Beeman looked as though he had been struck. 'Why, Sergeant Geer took my wire to the telegrapher before Lovering could be moved off the street!'

'I never received it,' Gary said, and set his lips. After a moment's silence he said: 'Precisely what was the time, Mister Beeman?'

'At two sixteen by my watch, sir. The day before yesterday.'

'I can't understand why the signal sergeant would fail to deliver a wire,' Gary said. 'I'm sure no one need tell him what a serious matter that would be. And certainly a message of such gravity...' He shook his head. 'No, I think it is impossible that he could fail to deliver the message. So I will assume that the signal sergeant discharged his duties properly, as he has for eighteen years.' He ticked off the point on his finger. 'Therefore, he must have given the message to someone.' He made this point two. 'And knowing the importance of the message, he would not have given it to anyone except perhaps Lieutenant Flanders.' Point three.

'But, surely, Mister Flanders...,' Beeman began.

'Yes, of course, he would have waked me out of a sound sleep. He has for much less reason.' He stopped a moment. 'Point four is that the sergeant would only have released the message to a person he believed more responsible than Mister Flanders. Who on the post'd that be, Mister Beeman?' He looked at Beeman, at Dan Conrad, and then turned to Jason Ivers and studied him intently.

For a moment Ivers stood there, then he made a turn toward the door, and stopped. Slowly the breath went out of him, and he turned back, his manner resigned. 'I really believed I could get away with it, Jim.' He spread his hands in an appeal for understanding. 'What could I do? I talked to you, and you gave me nothing, Jim. It seemed as though all I had done for you didn't matter at all. My house was being shaken badly, Jim. Lovering and this young lieutenant could rattle the windows in it, could break something.' He shrugged, and put his hands in the pockets of his overcoat. 'I sent Clive Maybank a wire twenty minutes after I left the table.'

'You told him to have Lovering killed?'

Ivers shook his head. 'No, I told him the situation was grave, and that he would have to take care of matters his own way.' He moved his eyes to the coffee pot. 'I'd like another cup of that. It's turned chilly in here.' Conrad got one for him, then Ivers went on. 'After talking to you and General Caswell, I sent Maybank another wire. I told him the situation was unchanged. It was too risky to do anything else, Jim. Can't you see that? I thought Maybank would get Lovering out of town, maybe out of the territory. Not a shooting.'

'You picked up Mister Beeman's wire?' Gary asked.

Ivers nodded. 'It was the damnedest bit of luck. I went to the signal office to wire Maybank. I hadn't heard from him, and I was a bit concerned. The sergeant was taking down the wire, and I offered to deliver it.' He smiled faintly. 'He hesitated... I give him credit for that, but I persuaded him.'

He reached into an inner coat pocket and produced the wire. It was wrinkled but clearly legible. Conrad took it and handed it to Gary, who gave it to Beeman to identify.

'That's my own wire, sir, word for word, as I gave it to Sergeant Geer.'

Jim Gary seemed to slump a little. 'Senator, I suggest that you resign for reasons of health. Please don't delay this. I'm not a patient man.'

'Yes... I...' He went over to the window and looked out on the bleak parade ground. Conrad and Beeman stirred slightly and acted as though they didn't quite know what to do. It was always that way when the mighty fell. Even in their disgrace one felt that they were entitled to a certain respect.

Gary broke the tension when he said: 'Carl, do you have anything to eat?'

'I'll tell the cook to fix...'

'I'll take care of that,' Conrad said, and went out.

Gary said: 'You might as well sit down, Jason. Everything has come to an end. And I don't feel sorry for you. You knew what you were doing, and what it could cost.' He waited, but Ivers would not look around, and Gary turned to Carl Beeman. 'General Caswell talked to me about you, Carl. He is endorsing my recommendation for your promotion. One of these days your wife will be sewing railroad tracks on your shoulder boxes.'

Conrad came back. 'Bacon and eggs in about ten minutes. The company is being fed now, sir.'

'Good,' Gary said. 'Now Mister Beeman, if you can find a bottle of whisky and some glasses, we'll all have an eye-opener.'

The peace that had descended over Texas did not lull Guthrie McCabe into a sense of relaxation. So, when he came across the tracks of two men afoot, he studied them carefully, and, without drawing Caswell's attention to them, he altered their course and followed them. McCabe could read sign as well as any man, and from the irregularity of the tracks he surmised that both men were nearly tuckered out.

Finally Caswell said: 'It's my opinion that one man is big, near two hundred pounds.'

McCabe showed his surprise, and Caswell laughed.

'I've fought Indians, too, Guthrie, and my eyes are as good as yours.' He pointed toward the river. 'Suppose we try to cut this sign farther on.'

McCabe nodded, and they turned their horses, riding faster now. It bothered him, those moccasin tracks. At first he had thought it was some Kiowa buck that had jumped the reservation, but now he didn't think so – not this far south.

They had gone perhaps a mile, staying to the ridges, because the land was rolling and they had to keep to the high ground to see, when Caswell reined in and exclaimed:

'That was a shot!'

McCabe was going to argue, but then he heard it. It was the boom of a heavy caliber rifle somewhere to the west. Together they crossed the ridge and a short valley below and climbed to the crown of a low hill where they could look down on the river. Cottonwoods choked the banks, and there was a sandbar spit in the middle of the crossing, just a patch of land and brush with a fallen log and a few trees. And a rifleman.

Tremain Caswell uncased his field glasses and had his look. He could make out the man on the sand spit clearly, then he swung the glasses to the near bank. Another man was down there, behind a skimpy rise of earth.

He handed the glasses to McCabe, saying: 'Unless I'm mistaken, that man on the bar is Llano Vale. Ben Stagg's the one on the near bank.'

While McCabe watched, there was an exchange of shots. He handed back the glasses and said – 'Let's go mix in this.' – and spurred on down the flank to the rise.

Following him, Caswell thought this was mighty foolish, for they were exposing themselves to Vale's rifle fire should he choose to open up on them. But Vale held off, and McCabe stopped on the riverbank, close enough for both of them to hear him speak. 'Hold up there! This is Cap'n Mc-

Cabe, Texas Rangers! What in thunder's goin' on here? Speak up now!'

Without exposing himself in the slightest, Ben Stagg answered: 'It ain't none of your affair, McCabe! I've chased him all the way from Fort Reno. He killed a man there. And I'll bring him back, or bury him by myself!'

McCabe wheeled his horse suddenly and said – 'Stay here, General.' – and splashed across to the sand spit. He did not dismount but sat his horse, looking at Llano Vale, who rolled half on his back so he could see McCabe squarely. 'Got yourself shot up some, ain't you?' McCabe said. 'What's this all about, Llano? You kill somebody?'

'Got paid for it, too,' Vale said. He was a worn man, gone as far as he could go with a bullet through the calf of his leg and another in the side.

McCabe said: 'Looks like you ain't goin' to spend it, Llano.'

'I don't care. I've had my fun. Ain't cryin' because it's goin' to end here. This is between me and Ben. Always hoped it'd come to that. Never did like him none. Be damned if I trust a man who's good-natured.' He wiped his gray face with his hand. 'Go on, get out of here. This ain't none of your affair, McCabe.' He tried to laugh. 'Man, I give him a run though. Killed the horse right out from under him. Damned near outran him afoot, too.' He waved his hand. 'Go on back, Mc-

Cabe. This is a quarrel that began before you was born. Git now. Let a couple of old he-bears settle it.'

'I'm going to talk to Stagg, get him to put up his gun,' McCabe said, and started back.

'Don't you do that! Don't do that, you hear!'

McCabe paid no attention and splashed across the river. He stepped out of the saddle, dropped the reins, then walked over to where Ben Stagg was stretched out.

'He hit bad?' Stagg asked. 'He's been carryin' one bullet in him all last night. We had a brush before sundown.' He rolled over on his side and patted his pockets. 'You ain't got a chaw on you, have you?'

McCabe dipped into his hip pocket and handed Stagg some cut plug. 'I want you to put up your gun, Ben. He's a done-in man, and he knows it.'

Stagg worked his jaws on the tobacco and spat. 'I chased him south clear from the reservation. He managed to catch a freight south of Wichita Falls. There we was, him on one car and me on another, and neither darin' to poke a head up.' He laughed. 'At Abilene he jumped off, stole a horse, and lit out south. I borrowed a horse from the town marshal and lit after him. He waylaid me on the San Saba, but I got in a good shot. We've footed it from the Guadalupe to here.'

From the sand pit, Vale yelled: 'Stagg, I'm

117

comin' now!' He lurched into view, stumbled, and fell. He found his feet and splashed into the water, where he fell again. He got up, and Ben Stagg rose up into view. Llano Vale stopped, knee-deep in the water. He slowly raised his rifle, but it was just too heavy for him. The muzzle was down when he pulled the trigger, and he fell forward on it.

Caswell rode forward, got a rope on Llano Vale, and dragged him to the bank. When he rolled the old man over, they all could tell that he was dead. Guthrie McCabe got down and went through his pockets, found twenty dollars and some change.

Ben Stagg studied the dead man, his expression sad. 'Twenty dollars,' he said. 'I guess that's all they paid him. There was a time thirty years ago when he got five hundred.'

He turned and walked over to the small rise of ground he had hidden behind and sat down. He hunched forward, his elbows on his knees, his body bent over, and his head way down, as though he scrutinized the ground between his feet.

Softly Tremain Caswell said: 'I thought they were enemies.'

McCabe looked at him for a long moment. 'General, how could they be when there was only two of 'em left? They just didn't know how to make up, that's all.'

118

Chapter Seven

Before the week was out, Gary met with the sub-chiefs at the agency building. Understanding well the Indian love for pomp and ceremony, he declared an extra beef issue – which was sure to bring them – and had a barbecue that ran well into the night. There was singing and dancing, and seventy gallons of ginger beer, brewed especially for the occasion, were consumed by the Indians.

Then they were ready to talk. Captain Conrad was introduced as being in charge, and, because he had only one arm, Jim Gary thought it might be a good idea if he wrestled one of the stronger braves. He had a deep understanding of their respect for strength, and Conrad, knowing a good deal about Indians, was agreeable to the match. Besides, it would provide entertainment.

A stalwart buck stepped forward and took off his store-bought cotton shirt and flexed his muscles. When he tried to grapple with Conrad, he found himself upset and suddenly was looking at Conrad from a sitting position on the ground. He got up, and they scuffled a bit, and Conrad threw him again. This seemed to satisfy everyone, and the

119

festivities began in earnest.

Senator Jason Ivers did not join in. For five hours he remained inside the agency building with his cigar and bottle and dark thoughts. Finally, after several hours of festivity, Jim Gary came in. Ivers was sitting in the dark, and, when Gary started to light the lamp, Ivers said: 'Don't, Jim. Please don't.'

'All right,' Gary said, and lit a cigar with the match he held. Then he sat down behind Lovering's desk. 'I don't like to see you like this, Jason. You've got to pull yourself together.'

'Really?' Ivers laughed. 'I've been thinking about my resigning. No one will believe it. I haven't had a sick day in twelve years. Besides, that excuse never fooled anyone.'

'No, I don't suppose it ever did,' Gary said, 'but in most cases it's better than the truth, isn't it?'

'Someday you may be in this kind of trouble and...'

'I hope not,' Gary interrupted.

Ivers remained silent for a time, 'Jim, the thing is done, isn't it? What's to be gained by my resignation? Think of the future, man. I could do you a lot of good as a senator.'

Gary's voice was hard. 'For God's sake, Jason, don't beg! Do you hear? Get off your god-damned knees!' Then he calmed himself. 'Do you think I enjoy this? Or even want it?' He blew out his breath. 'What's the use of talking about it? I suggest you leave for Fort Reno in the morning. I'll have Mister Beeman go with you. Don't delay, Jason. I'd send a wire right away.'

'How much time are you going to give me?'

'Twenty-four hours,' Gary said flatly. 'That's enough. More than you gave me or Lovering.'

'I didn't kill that man.'

'There is moral guilt,' Gary said. 'Try to understand it.'

'God, man, I do,' Ivers said. 'I just don't know how to tell Janice.'

Captain Conrad interrupted them. 'Excuse me, Major, but Sergeant Geer has just ridden in with McCabe and General Caswell. They've got Ben Stagg and Llano Vale.'

Gary put a match to the lamp and went around lighting the wall lamps, then Geer tramped onto the porch and held the door open while General Caswell came in. The others followed, but Llano Vale's body was left outside.

'You're a far piece from where I left you,' Gary said, speaking to Caswell who was backing up to the stove to toast himself. He had a beard stubble, as did McCabe. Ben Stagg went for the coffee pot.

'We took the train north,' Caswell said. 'It started here, and Ben wanted to bring him back here.'

Gary looked at Stagg. 'Want to tell me about it, Ben?'

'Nope. He got clean to the Guadalupe. He died there. It wasn't good, because it was for nothin'. All those years gone for nothin'.' He drank his coffee black and scalding. 'Twenty dollars, that's what he got. It wasn't him I hated, but the ones who give him the twenty dollars.' He turned around and showed them his back, not wanting to talk any more.

Caswell saw Jason Ivers sitting there, and he said: 'Senator, what do you think of the reservation?' He waited a polite interval for Ivers to speak, and, when he did not, Caswell asked: 'Is something the matter, man?'

'I ... I'm just very tired,' Ivers answered, and abruptly left the room.

Caswell stared after him. 'Now, what the devil's eating him?'

'Sir,' Gary said, 'I'd like to have a talk with you.'

'It can wait. I want some hot food and ten hours' sleep before I really talk to anyone.' Caswell's manner was gruff. 'Sergeant, tell the mess cook to rustle something up for us.' He moved over and put his hand on Ben Stagg's shoulder. 'It's all bad business, Ben, this using men ... bad business.'

He went out, and Guthrie McCabe eased away from the fire. 'You still smoke those good cigars, Jim? Between Ben and me, we've used up all my cut plug and...'

'You don't have to make excuses. Ben, you want one?'

Stagg shook his head, then he turned around and looked at Jim Gary. 'I don't like it none that old Llano could be used and just ... just thrown away.'

'A few heads are going to come off, Ben.'

'That a promise?'

'Yes,' Gary said. 'As good as I can make right now.'

Ben Stagg nodded. 'I guess I will have one of those cigars, if the offer's still open.' He leaned forward for his light and sagged against the wall, puffing gently.

The cook, for such short notice, did a good job. He had some roast beef and potatoes, with pan gravy reheated, and some peach pie. Gary didn't go into the mess building with General Caswell and McCabe. As soon as Stagg had eaten, he came out and walked across the compound to the barn where he spread out his bedding.

Gary remained in his office, while Captain Conrad along with Carl Beeman made sure that the Indians were being properly entertained. They were making a frightful racket. They always did when they were having a good time. As long as they whooped it up, Gary knew that they were happy.

He heard the shot, although it was muffled by the walls of the building, and he got up and went outside to the porch. The dancing and drum beating went on undiminished. Caswell poked his head out of the mess door and said: 'What was that? I thought I heard a shot.'

Jim Gary said: 'General, I'm afraid that was Jason Ivers resigning.'

Caswell threw his napkin down. 'What the hell's that? What are you talking about?'

'General, I wish you'd step inside and talk with me,' Gary said. He saw Conrad coming at a trot and made a motion with his hand, and Conrad veered, moving toward the quarters Jason Ivers occupied. General Caswell came down the walk and went inside Gary's quarters with him. Gary motioned him to a chair.

Before he could speak, Conrad came in, nodded once, and said: 'Right through the heart, Major. I guess it was the only way out he knew.'

Caswell's eyes darted from man to man. 'Suicide? That fine man? By God, somebody had better explain this and fast, too.' Then he looked at Jim Gary's expression, and he knew that he was going to get an explanation he wasn't going to like.

Lieutenant Carl Beeman was given the honor of calling on Commissioner Elwood Butler and Clive Maybank. All the way in to Fort Reno, Beeman had been turning over in his mind exactly how he intended to handle it.

When he decided, he measured the risks and found them substantial, but he was no longer afraid of risks, and he could hardly remember what it felt like not to have confidence.

He found the two deputy marshals, Hutchins and Speer, in their office, for the jail was still crowded, and after the shooting no one had ordered the prisoners released. The judge was waiting word from Major Gary concerning the pursuit and capture of Llano Vale. Carl Beeman took care not to tell the marshals that Vale was dead.

Butler and Maybank were still at the Drover's, and neither seemed glad to see Carl Beeman, which was understandable. They were even less pleased to see that Beeman had the two deputy marshals with him.

'I'm happy to have caught you two gentlemen in,' Beeman said, smiling in a most agreeable manner. 'I say that because it is more convenient to make an arrest here than to pursue you singly about the country. Wouldn't you agree, Marshal Speer?'

'It does beat chasin' 'em,' Speer said dryly.

'Arrest?' Maybank said. 'On what charge?'

'Of paying Llano Vale twenty dollars to kill Lovering,' Beeman said. 'Was that all he was worth?' He looked from one to the other, and shook his head. He made a clucking noise and polished his glasses.

'Wait until Senator Ivers hears of this,' Butler snapped. 'You won't be in the Army long.'

125

'I'm afraid there won't be any recourse there,' Beeman said. 'You see, Major Gary confronted the senator at Fort Reno. Before he killed himself, he made a clean breast of it and...' Mr Beeman paused.

Maybank was in a rage. He walked around the room, his temper in charge, swearing and accusing, and Butler was trying to shut him up. But the bung had been knocked out of the barrel; everything just spilled out until there wasn't any more. The marshals produced their handcuffs, and, only when they clicked around Maybank's wrists, did he stop talking. He tried to kick Mr Beeman, lost his balance, and fell. The marshals hauled him up and out of there. Butler was brought along, but he was quieter and gave up more easily.

After it was over, Beeman walked over to the saloon and sided Sergeant Geer, who had the detail lined up. They were cutting a great thirst. There was some time before the southbound was due, and Beeman toyed with the idea of getting drunk but decided it just wasn't the thing to do.

A man down along the bar sidled up, and at first Beeman didn't recognize him. Then he remembered him – Gunderson, one of the ranchers he'd helped out – it seemed like ten years ago.

'I want to buy you a drink, Lieutenant,' Gunderson said, and motioned for the bartender to move their way. With the glasses filled, Gunderson raised his. 'I like to do business with a tomcat. Here's to clean air and quick hangings.'

'Treat the Indians right so I won't have to come back,' Beeman suggested. 'I like it here, but...' He smiled and left the rest in the air, sure that Gunderson would understand.

By train time, the troopers were in a singing mood, but Geer had not allowed them to drink so much that they turned disorderly. They loaded their horses and their badly used gear, and Geer formed them into ranks. He got them into one of the passenger coaches, and the civilians stood around and watched, not quite sure how they felt about the Army, but certainly aware that they had caused a stir.

Mr Beeman had consumed enough whisky to brighten his eyes and bring colour to his cheeks, just enough to elevate his optimism to a high plateau. He rocked back and forth on his heels, a cigar jauntily clamped between his teeth, and surveyed his surroundings which he was sure were definitely beneath his station. He was thinking of Camp Verde and his wife and child, and of how much he had missed them, and within him was a determination to romp a bit with the child, and then...

A slight commotion disturbed his speculation. He looked down the platform where an Indian woman and a small child were being jostled by a civilian. The accumulated wrath of every down-trodden person since the beginning of time rose in Beeman, and he dashed there and grabbed the man by the collar. He bounced him heavily against the steel side of the coach and put a great lump on his head. The man lost his hat and his belligerence, and he sat down in the cinders and moaned and held his head. Beeman bowed to the Indian woman.

Then he saw the reddish-brown hair and the surprised blue eyes, and he knew that she as not an Indian. The child was part Indian, and everything became plain to Beeman.

He said: 'Madam, I'm sure you would be more comfortable in the other coach.' He offered his arm, and, after a brief hesitation, she took it. A pigeon-faced elderly woman with a prune mouth said – 'Well, I certainly never!' – and flounced onto the train, her sensitivity mortally wounded.

The crowd parted, and Beeman picked up the child to carry him. The woman would have walked behind him, Indian-style, but he would not permit that.

Sergeant Geer, wondering what had happened to Beeman, came to the vestibule step, looked out, and saw them. He grinned and said – 'Here, now, little bugger. – and took the boy, handling him gently.

They got in the coach, and the conductor

waved the train under way. Beeman and the woman took the seat Geer had been saving. Beeman introduced himself and the sergeant. The woman said: 'I've seen you on the reservation, and I waited.' She looked at Geer, grizzled, unshaven, with his kind brown eyes and tobacco-stained smile. 'My man was not good, but he was not bad, either. To go back ... well, I couldn't make a mistake.'

'What's your name?' Beeman asked.

'Elsie Breedon. I was ten then. That was nine years ago.' She put her arm around the boy; he was three, with large brown eyes and dark hair. 'There were two others, older. They died. He's all I have.'

'My dear,' Beeman said gently, 'life will be easier for you now.'

'There are others,' Elsie Breedon said. 'They're afraid to leave. You must help them.'

'We will,' Beeman said. 'Believe me, we will. We will never give up. Isn't that right, Sergeant?'

'It sure is, Mister Beeman.'

In the hour before dawn, General Tremain Caswell left his bed, dressed, and walked the short distance from his quarters to the headquarters building. A fire burned in the fireplace, casting an irregular, reddish light into the room, and through the front window he could see Gary sitting there, a cigar

129

between his fingers and a half-empty bottle by his elbow.

Caswell went in and said: 'I couldn't sleep worth a damn. You either?' He backed to the fire and let it warm him. 'Feels like snow in the air. An early winter, I suppose.'

Gary looked at him. He had been drinking some but he was not drunk. 'General, some years ago I had to tell her that her father was dead and that her fiancé had married another woman. Now I have got to tell her that her husband killed himself? Don't I ever bring her anything but grief?' He stared at the floor for a time.

'What the hell else can you tell her?' Caswell said gruffly. 'Who likes it, Jim? I sure don't.' He laughed without humor. 'Beeman sure slammed the door on Maybank and Butler, didn't he?' He fished through his pockets for a cigar, then bent to the fire, and used a glowing piece of wood for his light.

Gary got up and went over to the desk and brought back a piece of paper. 'This is my report, General. I'd like your endorsement so I can forward it.'

Taking it, Caswell turned so that the firelight fell upon it. He read a bit, then raised his eyes sharply to Gary who was watching with a neutral expression. 'Jim, you can't...'

He closed his mouth and read on. When he had finished, he stood there, saying nothing. Then he moved to the desk, scratched a match to light the lamp, dipped the pen into the ink pot, and scrawled his signature.

He left the report on the desk and turned back to the fire. 'Captain Conrad...?'

'Captain Conrad is in complete agreement with me as to how it happened,' Gary said quickly. 'An accidental discharge of his firearm while cleaning it.'

'And Beeman?'

'General, a bright young officer destined to make captain soon surely wouldn't question the report of his commanding officer.'

'I see,' Caswell said. 'Jim, I hope you get away with it.' He drew on his cigar. 'Are you going to take him back on the train?'

'No,' Gary said. 'We'll bury him here. Full military honors. If at a later date the government wants to move him...' He shrugged and let it remain a speculation. 'Or whatever they do with heroes.'

'There'll be stories.'

'They'll be lies.'

'Butler and Maybank will talk, Jim.'

'Their word against an official report endorsed by you, sir.'

Caswell gnawed his lower lip. 'Well, I suppose we can weather it out.' He shied his cigar into the fireplace. 'There are times when I've sat at my desk and looked out my office window and wondered if anything would ever really come out right. Do you ever get that feeling, Jim?'

'Often, General.'

Caswell drew a chair around and sat down in front of Gary, with the warmth of the fire between them. To the east the palest blush of dawn was turning the sky light along the edge, and it slowly marched up and over the far hills. Then a bugle broke the silence, clear and sharp in the cold air, and the Army began another day.

Caswell got up and said: 'I'll catch the train out of here, Jim. There's no need for me to go back.' He smiled warmly. 'There'll be paperwork six inches high on my desk, and you'll have problems of your own when you get back.'

'General,' Jim Gary said, 'I've got problems I've never even heard of.' He put away the whisky bottle and blew out the lamp. His depression was gone now. He flung open the door and let in the cold air and breathed deeply, filling himself with the biting freshness. He let it chase the staleness out of the room and out of his mind. Then he saw Captain Conrad approaching and went to meet him.

Yesterday was the past now. This was a new sun coming up, a new sun and yesterday's shadows died with the darkness. The world was born afresh each day.

PART TWO

1905

Chapter Eight

A child stick-balling a tin can down the street woke Martin Hinshaw, and, before he opened his eyes, he knew how the day was going to be – bad, just as every day had been for the last three months. Yesterday had been the worst of all for Martin Hinshaw. In the bucking horse contest, he had mounted a mean animal and got pitched badly. Later, in the bull-riding event, he had drawn one that had been sired by Satan and acted as though he had a belly full of hot chili peppers. When it came to the calf-roping even, his luck had deserted him completely for the little critter hooked his pony and gave him the worst fall of the day. An hour later a Louisiana sheriff had served papers on the rodeo owner and attached all the assets that weren't much to begin with. All of which left Martin Hinshaw sore in body, battered in spirit, and completely mangled in the pocketbook.

A fly began a droning dance on the dirty ceiling, and he gave up and opened his eyes. Carefully, so as not to excite strained muscles, he swung his bare feet to the floor. His room was small, one of the cheapest he could find on Bourbon Street, and he knew he'd spent his last night in it.

Hinshaw was twenty-five, a rather small man with a wiry, compact body. His face was broad and angular, and there was a bulldog bluntness to his features, a rough, unfinished look about him. He sat on the edge of his bed, clad only in the bottom half of his underwear. On the cracked marble top of the dresser he had laid out for easy counting a silver dollar, a quarter, two nickels, and six pennies. This was the end of the money, the end of the three-year-long thoughtless run that had led him to Canada and New York and all points in between. It represented to him the last hammered-home bit of bitter knowledge that he'd done his foolish things, hurt all the people a man had to hurt before he grew up, ignored all the advice, indulged his headstrong ways.

The street below began to grow noisy with peddlars, and he knew it was time to get out. He stood up, went to the washstand, and splashed water on his face, then got out his shaving gear. While he bladed his cheeks clean, he thought of his Texas again, and he could close his eyes and smell the eternal dust of the plains and then the sea breeze sweeping in the flavors of the Gulf, and the longing to quit this useless life was so strong that it knotted his stomach.

Finished with his shave, he dressed, picked up his small suitcase and silver-mounted saddle, and quit the hotel by tossing his key and a dollar on the clerk's counter as he passed through the lobby.

A pawnboker gave him thirty dollars for the saddle, although the silver alone was worth three hundred. Martin Hinshaw offered no argument at all. He pocketed the money and turned toward the nearest streetcar tracks and took one to the railroad station. He bought his ticket, declined to check his suitcase through, and went over to a vacant bench and sat down to wait for his train. He thought it strange that he should be going back in almost the same manner in which he had left – broke. Quite by accident he had passed through Laredo several years back, but he had remained aboard the train while it took on coal and water, and afterward he had cursed himself for being a coward. Yet his shame had been so acute that he couldn't leave his seat. And all the time he had kept telling himself that his father was dead, and it was done, and he could never change it. Yet he knew he had run out and left him alone to die, and it made a sickness in his stomach just thinking about it.

The dépôt was a busy place. People were rushing here and there and all talking until there wasn't much of a distinguishable sound, just a babble, a foreign tongue made up of words all run together. A child stopped before him and stared curiously at his high hat and spike-heeled Mexican boots, then the mother came along and scoldingly towed him away. Martin Hinshaw remembered that his mother had done that, and he'd always hoped the day would come when she'd stop it. Finally she did, but something else came along and towed him. He guessed a man would always be pulled by something.

Near the dépôt entrance, a crowd formed and moved along like bees around a hive. His attention was drawn there by the sudden run of Spanish, a language he had learned along with English. In the center of this throng he saw a high Texas hat with a high Texas man under it, an old man who limped along in spite of the crowd, making his way relentlessly toward the tiers of waiting-room benches.

Amid the noise and confusion, the tall Texan was a pinnacle of calm as he forced his way to one of the benches. It was then that Hinshaw saw that he had another man in tow, a young Mexican dressed in velvet and silver. An entourage of young girls swarmed about the Mexican, laughing and shoving one another to kiss him, and on the tall Texan's face there was no expression at all.

There was a year's bucking-horse prize money in silver on the Mexican's clothes, and it angered Hinshaw, raised again in him his Texas dislike for the race. Then he saw the handcuff on the Mexican's wrist, and, when the Texan brushed his coat aside, Hinshaw caught the glint of a familiar badge and the polished walnut butt of a pistol, and he felt better about it. The Mexican was the Texas Ranger's prisoner, something that seemed a natural relationship to Hinshaw.

The Texan was a tower of a man, gray at the temples and lined of face. He was crowding sixty, Hinshaw supposed, yet he was a solid man with a fierce, angular face. In his left hand he carried a heavy walking stick and used it to favor his left leg.

The two men, captor and prisoner, sat on the bench until train time, and the women made love to the Mexican while men brought food and wine and the women fed it to him. All the time the Mexican laughed and joked as though this captivity was merely a temporary thing.

Through it all the tall Texan sat like a stone image, a monument of patience, alive only in his eyes which darted about constantly as though he was determined not to be taken unaware. Occasionally he glanced at his watch to mark the passage of time. Then the caller announced the train, and the entourage set up a wail as the Texan forced his prisoner to his feet and made him walk slightly ahead through the wrought-iron boarding gates. Hinshaw left his place, for he was taking the same train, and he trailed the Texan through the crowd.

The conductor kept the Mexican's admirers from getting aboard the train, and they stood there on the platform, talking and calling their good byes, and some of the young girls cried. Hinshaw pushed his way through them and paused for a moment in the vestibule, making an eeny-meeny-miney-mo decision as to which coach to take. He took a left turn. People were jamming the aisle, finding seats, stowing luggage, and he pardoned his way through and sat down across from the Texan and his prisoner, and none too soon for he edged an irritated drummer out of it. The man said something unkind and went on down the aisle, which was just as well for Hinshaw had toyed with the idea of hitting him in the mouth.

The Texan's voice pulled Hinshaw's attention around.

'You'll have to move, sonny.' The Texan looked at him with eyes as unfriendly as two shotgun bores.

Hinshaw looked around and found the coach crowded. 'I paid for a seat, and I'm sittin' in it. If you don't think that's right, ask the conductor to look at my ticket.'

'That was an official request, not an argument. I'm Captain Guthrie McCabe, E Company, Texas Frontier Battalion.'

'Marty Hinshaw. My pleas...' He stopped and stared as McCabe pulled his long-barreled pistol and, with the muzzle, flicked aside Hinshaw's coat, looking for hidden firearms. 'Why, you nosy old...'

'Now don't get your collar too tight,' McCabe said gently. He put his pistol away. 'Just didn't want some armed stranger sittin' across from me. Just a precaution, you understand.'

The prisoner smiled, revealing straight, white teeth. 'He is a nervous man, *amigo*. A sick old man with a bad leg who will never get where he's going.' He raised his free hand and stroked his mustache. 'I am grateful for the company. We will talk and pass away the monotony of a dull trip.'

'About the only thing I ever say to Mexicans,' Hinshaw said, 'is get to work and get out of the way.'

The Mexican's face pulled into severe planes, and a dark anger came to his eyes. 'It is the kind of thing I expect from a Texan. Are you God, *señor*? Are you better than me? You are a fool. I have killed with my hand thirty just like you, proud Texans who only spit on the Mexicans.'

Guthrie McCabe smiled faintly. 'This ain't just any tamale-eater, son. This is Pedro Vargas, the bandit they call El Jefe.'

'Well what do you know,' Hinshaw said. 'Three years ago I saw Laredo a week after your bunch rode through. They were still burying the dead.'

'It was a glorious day for Mexico,' Vargas said.

'Your government's ashamed of you,' McCabe said flatly. 'Don't use the name of Mexico to excuse your hate and killings. There's a new rope waiting for you in Laredo, *amigo*.' Pedro Vargas smiled and shrugged his shoulders, dismissing the idea. This did not bother McCabe. 'It's kind of a game between Vargas and me, son. I'm bound and determined to see that he hangs, and he's determined not to. I've been chasing this rattlesnake since Nineteen One. Going on four years now. Twice I had him, and twice he slipped way. But this time it's going to be different, ain't it, Pedro?'

'You ask the wrong man, *señor*. I have much gold and many friends. Texas is a long way away, eh?' He reached out and poked McCabe in the chest with his finger, and paper in an inside coat pocket rustled slightly. 'The warrant, she is no good in Louisiana, eh? You break the law a little, so I break the law a little, too. Why you make such a big fuss? Because I shoot you in the leg? *Señor*, I am sorry. I meant to shoot you in the heart.' He moved his leg suddenly and jarred McCabe's thigh, and the old man grunted in quick pain.

Hinshaw then saw the growing stain of blood that had been hidden beneath the folds of McCabe's coat. 'That's a fresh wound!'

'Barely six hours old,' Vargas said, laugh-

142

ing softly. 'You will not take me back to hang, old man. By morning the fever will come and the sickness, and, when your eyes get heavy, I will be on you. I will sleep, but you will not. How long do you think you can last, eh?'

'I'll last,' Guthrie McCabe said. He looked at Martin Hinshaw. 'Son, you'd better ask the conductor for another seat. One's enough to watch. I can't handle two.'

'You don't have to watch me,' Hinshaw said. 'I wouldn't help this greaser if...'

'Don't tell me the story of your life,' McCabe said testily. 'I can see it for myself. You've got a suit about gone in the seat, and your boots are run over, and your luggage ain't much. Vargas buys men like you for a hundred dollars. He likes the down-and-outers because they've got a grudge against something, and, when he's through with you, he sends you down the road or leaves you layin' beside it.' He let his eyes roam past Hinshaw to all the passengers. There was no trust at all in this old man. 'I got the most wanted bandit in Mexico chained to my wrist. This train has to stop three times between here and Brownsville. Any of those places it could be boarded. If that happens, bullets are going to be zippin' around thick as flies around a honey house. So, if you're just a nice young fella down on your luck, you, of course, won't have any interest in stayin'. However, if one of Vargas's New Orleans' pals stuffed a hundred dollars in your pocket and told you to get him away from me, of course, you'll think this seat is just fine.'

'You have a nice way of putting that,' Hinshaw said. 'I paid for this seat, and I'll sit in it. If you don't like that then go to blazes. Think what you damned please. The way my luck's been running lately, I could buy a suit with two pair of pants and burn a hole in the coat.'

'Such pride,' Vargas said. 'Put two dollars in a Texan's pocket, and he thinks he is king.' He laughed. 'When I go to the *cantina* and hear a song that pleases me, I snap my fingers, and one of my men opens a bag of silver, and I throw a handful at the *señorita*'s feet.'

'Yeah, I know how you operate,' Hinshaw said. 'I saw you at the station kissin' and huggin' the girls. Take away the silver bangles and you'd just be another greaser with slick hair.'

The insult touched a raw spot in Vargas's mind, and he would have lunged out of his seat had not McCabe jerked him back. 'He don't like to be called a greaser, son. He likes to think of himself as Pedro Vargas, although he likely took the name off a headstone. He's El Jefe, friend of the poor and Texan-hater. But his ma was half Apache, and he never knew who his pa was. So you've got to watch that talk. When a man's got cur blood in him, a growl sets him off.'

'Before I die,' Vargas swore softly, 'I will cut out your heart, McCabe.'

'You might try,' McCabe said. 'Vargas, you just can't understand that Texans hate Mexicans, and Mexicans hate Texans. We didn't start it. It began a long time before either of us was born. But we ain't going to change it, either. Likely it'll never be changed. To a Texan you'll always be a greaser, and we'll always be *gringos* to you. Now you wouldn't like it none if us Texans came across the border in bands and raided your towns just because our grandpas died at the Alamo. You never learned to let a thing go, Vargas. Hell, we can get along without liking each other.'

The conductor came down the aisle with a distressed look on his face. He didn't like the law riding his prisoner in a day coach full of people. He stopped and punched Hinshaw's ticket. McCabe fished two fingers around in his vest pocket and handed the doctor two twenty-dollar gold pieces.

'You should have bought your ticket at the station,' the conductor said petulantly.

'I should have written to my mother once a month, too, but I didn't.' McCabe put his change away. 'At the first stop clear this coach, and before you give me some stupid argument, let me remind you that I'm a peace officer of the State of Texas, and I can

145

clear this whole damned train in the interest of public safety. In the meantime, bring me a telegraph blank. Better make it a whole pad. I've got a lot of friends I want to write to.'

The conductor, who was undisputed boss of the train, was irritated at being told what to do, yet he knew the authority McCabe had and went on down the aisle, punching tickets.

'We're still in Louisiana,' McCabe said, 'so he'll take his time, knowing I can't do anything about it. But he'll mind when we cross the border into Texas.'

'How long have you been shoving the law down people's throats?' Hinshaw asked.

'Since Eighteen Sixty-Seven,' McCabe said. 'I'm sixty and then some, but I don't look it.'

'I'd have sworn you were seventy,' Hinshaw said.

'Now if there's one thing I hate, it's some young squirt with a smart mouth,' McCabe snapped. 'Sonny, when I was thirty-one, I was the only peace officer in an eighty-square-mile piece of Texas. I battled varmints, Indians, the Army, and just about everything else that got in the way. For ten years I made up my own laws as I went along, and I didn't have any warrants, either, because there wasn't a judge who could write one out. My authority I wore on my hip, and people say that times have changed, and I guess they have because I traded that old single-action off and got me one of those self-cockers which speeds up my authority when I need it speeded up.' He patted his holstered revolver, then looked out the window at the scenery as the train moved along.

Hinshaw studied him. He was an old he-bear, all right, tough as Mexican beef and mean as a clawed cat. Hinshaw could well imagine the trail this man had left behind. He'd probably put a few in boothills scattered over the state and likely had more enemies than a man could count. But he would have friends, too, for he was the kind who drew to him staunch men, cut from the same tough cloth. Of course, there would be women here and there who would weep like blazes when he got it, and Marty Hinshaw was pretty sure that was the way McCabe would go, with a couple of spent shells in his gun, his enemy dead nearby, and no over-powering regrets about anything.

He looked at the Mexican and found him with his eyes closed, but Hinshaw knew he wasn't sleeping. The Mexican *bandido* was biding his time like a fox watching a hen on a roost, and, when the sap ran out of McCabe, he'd make his move, and it would be fatal to the Texas Ranger.

But none of this was really Hinshaw's business, and he kept telling himself that he had

147

learned long ago what to poke his nose into and what to keep out of. Yet he felt a surge of respect for this old man, a compulsion to invite himself into this game, as though he owed the old man a debt that had to be paid off now, before it was too late. Hinshaw did not really understand the source of this feeling, but it was there, too strong to ignore.

McCabe's leg was giving him a fit. Hinshaw detected the tightness around the mouth that pain built, yet the old man was a stoic.

It took the conductor more than an hour to bring the telegram blanks, but McCabe didn't voice any objection over the delay. He took the blanks, thanked the conductor, then fished a pencil out of his pocket. He handed the whole thing to Martin Hinshaw. 'You write for me.' He thought a moment. 'Sheriff Lyle Dunniger, Victoria, Texas. Have in custody, Pedro Vargas, alias El Jefe. Am on westbound out of New Orleans. Will arrive at your station.' He looked at his watch. 'One fifty-two a.m., day after tomorrow. Suspect attempt will be made to remove prisoner while train stopped. Request yourself and five deputies at my disposal until the train departs. Sign that ... McCabe, Texas Rangers.' Hinshaw finished it. McCabe read it then snapped his fingers to get the conductor's attention.

The man came up, annoyed at the peremptory summons, yet he took the wire and

148

three dollars, then went forward with it. McCabe sighed and seemed more at ease.

Pedro Vargas stopped looking out the window and said: 'In thirty-nine hours, I will be a free man. Don't you think a Mexican can read the telegraph code? There will be a hundred *bandidos* waiting in Victoria.' He laughed softly. 'Five deputies.'

'At my calculation,' McCabe said, 'one good Texan is worth thirty Mexicans in a fight. The odds are on our side, Vargas.'

Marty Hinshaw shook his head. 'McCabe, my old man had pride like that. He carried it right to the grave with him.'

'Then he didn't die whining,' McCabe said. 'Now shut up. I want to rest.'

It had stormed badly the night Hinshaw had left. Stormed outside the house and inside, too, Hinshaw remembered, for his father had always been a man of violent argument. He remembered that neither had thought to light the lamps, and the flashes of lightning now and then illuminated them as they shouted and swore and accused each other.

The remembering was no good, and the arguing had been no good, either. He had never convinced the old man that he had his own way of thinking, his own way of handling a trouble. A trouble that had started before he was born, started over nine hundred acres of Texas land, started really when Cortés

149

took Mexico, and the Texans came and took Texas away from the Mexicans.

He just couldn't explain why he had no killing hate against the Rameras family. The old man couldn't understand it, either; he believed that what he felt was good enough for his only son to feel. The old man wanted a fight with the Rameras clan. He had waited for it night after night with the lights out and weapons by his side. Martin Hinshaw didn't want it or think it would ever come, so he had left, and the Rameras clan had come, and his father was dead. Now he was sitting with another old man who was going to die, and all he had to do was change his seat, but he was held by the hand of his conscience. He wouldn't run from this.

The train stopped at Beaumont. McCabe took off his hat and laid it over his drawn revolver, the muzzle pressed against Vargas's side. They sat that way for twenty-eight minutes until the trail pulled out of the station.

Hinshaw could not understand how McCabe hung on. For thirteen hours he had sat motionless in his seat, one arm outstretched to brace himself against the rock and sway, a blossom of fever in his cheeks, and eyes that became increasingly bright. Hinshaw guessed that McCabe was afraid to move for fear that he'd just keel over if he did.

Pedro Vargas slept soundly, as though he possessed a soul of untroubled innocence. A

150

beard stubble was sprouting thickly on his cheeks, and his clothes were showing the soil of travel. All this pleased Marty Hinshaw who thought of all Mexicans as unbathed.

Guthrie McCabe sat the three and a half hours into Houston, then pulled a surprise. At gunpoint he ordered Vargas to leave the coach, and, in the same manner, he ordered Hinshaw to help him, for the leg was so bad now that he could not stand unaided. None of this made sense to Hinshaw, but he went along with it. Ten minutes later they were pulling out of the station, destination unknown.

Sagging back in his seat, McCabe seemed relieved. He motioned for Hinshaw to lean forward. 'Hope this doesn't inconvenience you,' he said, breathing heavily. 'We're on the Laredo train.' Vargas swore, and McCabe smiled. 'That telegram was a blind, greaser. Your men will run themselves ragged, but we'll be somewhere else. By the time they find out about it, you'll be in the guardhouse at Laredo.' Vargas's rage pleased McCabe to no end. 'Now don't get sore 'cause I pulled your fangs. With the best of luck I wouldn't have had a twenty-eight chance. And this bullet in my leg cuts that down to practically nothing.' He braced himself as the train picked up speed. 'I've got that rope danged near around your neck, El Jefe.'

He looked at Martin Hinshaw. There was a

plea there, a brilliance Hinshaw had never seen before, as though McCabe had reached some summit and knew it, and it was his best ever. Then he sagged like a wax candle suddenly exposed to heat, falling toward Hinshaw.

Hinshaw didn't reach out a hand to catch the old man. He went for Pedro Vargas who was making a stab for McCabe's holstered gun. He hit Vargas then, viciously, knocked him back completely senseless. It was a good feeling, the shock in his arm, the pain in his knuckles, and it evened up all those times when he was a kid and had been caught by the Rameras boys and taunted and hurt and humiliated.

The conductor, alarmed by the commotion, came hurrying down the aisle, pushing aside the curious. 'What's happened here? What's the matter with him?' He pointed to McCabe.

'Is there a doctor on the train?' Hinshaw asked.

'No, there isn't,' the conductor said. Then his expression brightened. 'Wait a minute. There's a nurse two coaches forward. She got on when we changed trains. I'll get her.' He turned to the crowd. 'Will you please take your seats? Clear the aisle, please. Step back.'

Hinshaw got McCabe back into the seat and braced him against the windowsill. Pedro Vargas lay on the floor motionless, and Hinshaw ignored him. He got his satchel down, opened it, and put McCabe's revolver in it, then brought out his own, an old single-action .38-40 Colt. He had a holster and shell belt for it and was buckling it around his waist when the conductor returned with the nurse.

She wore no uniform, just a dark skirt and a white shirtwaist with a flurry of ruffles at the bodice and cuff. 'This is Miss Sanders,' the conductor said. 'She's a nurse at the Mercy Hospital in Houston.'

'These gentlemen aren't interested in my credentials,' she said evenly. She looked at Hinshaw, who stepped a pace back, letting her get closer to the seat. The conductor stood there, a fretting expression on his face. He seemed annoyed that this was taking place on his train.

'I'm sorry, but I have no medicine or anything like that,' she said. 'We never carry anything...'

'There's a first-aid box in the caboose,' the conductor said.

'Then don't waste time getting it,' she said.

Hinshaw put her down as a serious-minded girl who knew how to keep a fresh fellow in his place.

She looked at Vargas, then said: 'Isn't he the Mexican bandit? I've seen reward posters on him.'

The question had been directed at Hinshaw. He said: 'Yes, ma'am. The other gentleman is a Texas Ranger.'

'I've seen Mr McCabe once or twice in Laredo,' she said. She turned to the conductor. 'Do you have a coach with a compartment?'

'Yes, but there's a colonel in it. You know how the Army is, lady.'

'I'm afraid I don't,' she said a bit tartly. 'What about the caboose?'

'That's for railroad folks,' he said.

'We'll use the caboose,' Hinshaw said. He stared at the conductor. 'Care to argue about it?'

'I guess not,' the conductor said.

Miss Sanders looked at McCabe's wound. 'How long has he had that?'

'Two days now.' Hinshaw bent forward and went through McCabe's pockets until he found the handcuff key. He unlocked the half around McCabe's wrist and snapped it closed on his own. 'The prisoner's got to come along. You might say that I'm minding him for a while.' He turned to the conductor. 'Bear a hand with the ranger and don't get rough with him.'

McCabe was not a small man, and the conductor had to ask two male passengers to help him. They took him to the rear of the train. Hinshaw got Vargas to his feet and propelled him groggily down the aisle and

154

into the rear coach. Vargas was just regaining enough of his senses to know where he was going, and he tried to turn on Hinshaw and got hit for it, a blow that drove him to his knees.

'I'm getting tired of belting you, Mexican. The next time I'm going to lay my gun barrel right across your hair oil.'

'A thousand dollars if you unlock the hand-cuffs,' Vargas said. 'You'd not be blamed.'

'Get up,' Hinshaw said, jerking on his arm. He shoved him on ahead and met the conductor at the door of the caboose. Vargas was forced inside, then Hinshaw unlocked the handcuff from around his own wrist, made Vargas get down on the floor, and locked him to some handrail pipes around the pot-bellied stove.

McCabe was placed on a bunk, and the conductor thanked the two passengers and shooed them out. He got the tin box containing the medical supplies, and Miss Sanders examined it.

'I think we can make do here,' she said. 'There's no need for you to remain if you have other duties.'

The conductor hesitated, then stepped out. She spoke to Hinshaw. 'Would you drop his trousers, please.'

There was a bottle of ether and some cotton, and she made a mask of this. When McCabe breathed easily, she took out the bullet with the sharp point of a small pair of scissors. Hinshaw was impressed with her efficiency and the way she made do with the few instruments she had.

'Will his leg be all right?' he asked.

'It's infected, but I think it will drain all right.' She went to the sink and washed her hands. 'Are you a peace officer, too?'

'No, I just happened along,' he said, looking at McCabe. 'There was a time before in my life when I had a chance to stand by a cranky old man, and I didn't. Afterward I wished I had, but I never thought I'd get another chance.'

'I don't understand,' she said.

'It's all right. My name's Marty. What's yours?'

'Ella. Marty what?'

'Hinshaw,' he said. He looked at Vargas. 'Guess we're stuck here a while. Hope you don't mind.'

'No, I don't mind,' she said, and smiled.

Major Carl Manners was in his adobe office, cleaning up some loose paperwork. A lot of his spare time was spent in this manner for the major was thirty, very young for so much responsibility. And he was driven by a desire to succeed, to prove to those older men who resented his position and youth that he was, indeed, more capable than any other man. He owed his job to a political appointment,

156

and he was new to the Texas Rangers, having served only six years.

He regarded them as impressive years and his contributions to the corps not without value. With some success he had introduced standardization, at least to the degree where rangers shaved regularly and didn't wear outlandish armament like a pearl-handled pistol on each hip and knife at the belt. His goal was uniforms, anything to make them stop looking like down-at-the-heels cowpunchers. He knew that would be some time coming.

A ranger came into his office with a telegram in his hand. 'Sorry to bother you, Major, but the telegrapher got this ten minutes ago. The ranger station over at Sweet Wells picked it up and passed it along.' He placed the message on Manners's desk, then stood there waiting. 'It's nearly twelve hours old, but I knew you'd want to see it.'

'Thank you,' Manners said, then glanced at it. Instantly his attention was caught, and he read it twice before he broke down and swore. 'Get Jennings in here! And Ackroyd!' The ranger ran out while Manners sat there mumbling about fools past the age of good sense.

The two rangers appeared a few minutes later, and Manners flung the telegram at them. 'Look what McCabe has done! I gave him three weeks' vacation to go fishing on the Nueces, and he goes to Louisiana and arrests

157

Pedro Vargas in some ... some prostitute's nest!' He rolled his eyes heavenward. 'God, I'll hear from the governor about this. He had no warrant except that old horse blanket issued three years ago.'

'Well, Major, he did arrest him. That's something,' Jennings said.

'Don't change the subject. I know what McCabe is thinking. He figures I'll be so glad to see Vargas under lock and key that I'll overlook this breech of law. Well, he's sadly mistaken. I'm going to have him dismissed from the service. Blast it all, times have changed. This is Nineteen Five! It's about time he found a porch to sit on.'

'McCabe and the governor are old cronies, Major, and...'

'Don't recite the man's lurid past to me,' Manners said. 'Well, he's got Vargas, and he's let everyone know it. That southbound will be blown up before it reaches Brownsville. Wire all the battalions near enough to reach the railroad. We've got to stop that train before it reaches Kingsville and take the prisoner off.' His expression turned bleak. 'That gallant old man alone...'

Ackroyd grinned. 'Thought you was mad at him, Major.'

'I can froth at the mouth and admire his guts at the same time, can't I? How do you deal with an institution? Go on, get those wires sent. We'll try to save McCabe's life.'

Chapter Nine

The caboose was old and drafty, and the night was cold now. McCabe lay on the bunk, asleep, drugged by the pain-killer the nurse had given him. The Mexican sat on the floor, his head wedged in the ell formed by the bunk and the coach wall. Ella Sanders sat on a small seat near the sink while Hinshaw hunkered down, his back to the door.

There was no talk, and he wanted it that way, for somehow all this brought up a bile of memory, and he had to taste the bitterness of it. He'd wintered out his first year in Wyoming, working for a transplanted Texas cattleman, and, in the spring, he'd joined a rodeo in Casper because he'd met a trick rider that had taken his fancy. Funny, but he couldn't remember her name, just that she had given him a merry, hellish year and left him broke and unable to decide whether he regretted any of it or not.

In Chicago, he had left the rodeo for a while. This girl's father was a big man in the stockyards, and Hinshaw had felt that here was a girl with whom he could be happy. As it turned out, she'd just been having fun and he wasn't, so he hopped a freight for Kansas

159

and joined up with another show.

He didn't like to think of all the prize money he'd won, or how much he'd thrown away on women and poor poker hands. Every time he'd get a stake something made him throw it away, as though he knew keep down that he did not deserve good fortune.

He raised his head and looked at Ella Sanders sitting there so pretty and composed. Hinshaw asked: 'Did you ever go for a canoe ride with a fella?'

She looked at him as people will when they think they have heard incorrectly. 'No, I haven't. Why?'

He shrugged. 'You've missed something.'

'Have I? What?'

He hesitated, thinking about it. 'I don't know. When you're young, people are always pulling at you, telling you to do this or that, and to be good. But when you push that canoe away from the shore, they can't reach you, and you can be what you want to be, bad or good, and, either way, it's an accomplishment.'

'I never thought of it that way,' she said softly. 'I suppose a nurse's cap is my canoe.'

He brightened. 'That's it exactly. You're on your own, and, no matter how it turns out, it's your doing.'

'Yes,' she said. 'What's your canoe?'

'I just stepped off of it a couple days back,' he said. Then he grinned to ease the seriousness of it all. 'Couldn't stand the rocking.'

'Stormy ride?'

'Blew a duster all the way,' he said, and rolled a cigarette.

Pedro Vargas smelled the burning tobacco and raised his head. Hinshaw hesitated and then tossed him the sack of tobacco.

After Vargas made his cigarette and pushed the tobacco back with his foot, he said: 'I heard you speak, *yanqui*. Why do you concern yourself with me?'

'Maybe it's because I hate Mexicans,' Hinshaw said. 'That wasn't something I was born with but something I was taught. And I ain't sure yet who did it, my pa or the Mexicans.'

'It is not so with me,' Vargas said. 'I was born in the dust of the street while a crowd of *yanquis* stood by and laughed at my mother's labor. The hate was a taste in my mouth from the moment I uttered my first cry, and the years have made it more bitter.' He turned his head and looked at McCabe. 'He does not hate me. To him I am just game testing the hunter's skill. He brings me back as a trophy of the chase, nothing more. One day I will kill him, but I will have respect for him when I do it.'

'Somehow,' Hinshaw said, 'it's hard to imagine you having much respect for anything since you've raided four or five towns, raped a hundred women, and left several hundred murdered men in your path.'

161

Vargas studied him at length. 'The name you are called by seems familiar to me, as though I had heard it before.' He smiled. 'It will come to me.'

'Your life will be richer for it,' Hinshaw said, and put out his cigarette in the sink. He ran some water to wash out the black spot, and Ella Sanders looked at him.

'You're cynical, aren't you? Did you lose faith in a woman or in yourself?'

He stopped and stared, then gave her an honest answer. 'With myself. Are you interested?'

'I guess not,' she said.

He went back to his hunker by the door. 'I've done some thinking along the line, and I've come to the conclusion that we're pretty cruel toward other people because we can't bring ourselves to be cruel toward ourselves, where likely it belongs.' He looked at her. 'We don't like being ashamed, and we all are ... of something.' He put his head on his crossed arms. 'If you want to sleep a while, I'll watch the ranger.'

'I'll stay awake,' she said. 'It's my job.' She smiled. 'And I'm not doing this one well because I fell down on another. I've learned not to spend my life making things up. You really can't, you know.'

'Is that what I'm doing?'

'I think you are,' she said. 'And I think it's right.'

Colonel James Gary waited thirty minutes with great patience, then he waited fifteen more with a mounting irritation. Finally he pushed his dispatch case full of papers aside and opened the door of his private coach. He was a tall, straight-bodied man in his mid fifties, still strong and handsome and commanding in manner.

He found the conductor approaching and buttonholed the man. 'Confound it, I asked you to have someone fetch me a headache powder nearly an hour ago.' He frowned. 'What kind of service do you offer on this line?' A bit of the drill field came into his voice, and the conductor looked at him with round, concerned eyes. He fingered his watch fob nervously and straightened his cap.

'I'm sorry, Colonel,' the conductor said. 'But there's a ranger on the train who's been shot. I've been pretty busy.'

Gary frowned. 'I heard no shot.'

'No, no. He was shot before he got on the train.' The conductor smiled. 'It's a little involved, sir, but the ranger has a prisoner, and the nurse took the bullet out of his leg. Never mind. I'll get your headache powder myself. It's in the caboose. I'll fetch it.'

'Wait a minute,' Gary said. 'I want to hear more about this. Who's the prisoner?' He frowned. 'You don't explain clearly, you know.'

'Some Mexican bandit. Pretty famous around Laredo. They call him El Jefe.'

'Pedro Vargas!' Gary said explosively. 'What a stroke of luck. Where is the prisoner now?'

'In the caboose, I tell you, two coaches back,' the conductor said. Gary ducked inside for his hat, and, when he reappeared, the conductor took his arm. 'Colonel, I don't think you can get in.'

'Nonsense,' Gary said. 'I represent the United States government.' He walked briskly down the length of the coach, now and then catching himself as the train swayed along.

Marty Hinshaw stood because Guthrie McCabe was resting peacefully on the couch, and Ella Sanders sat in the only remaining chair. He was beginning to feel weary, but he couldn't give in to it for he had taken McCabe's place, and he had McCabe's prisoner and McCabe's troubles.

'He'll sleep a long time,' Ella Sanders said, rousing Hinshaw from his own train of thought. 'He's a strong man who's run on nerve, and now he's run out of steam. By morning he'll have a fever and won't know where he is.'

'I'll know,' Hinshaw said. 'So it'll be all right.'

She looked at him. 'You stepped into his

troubles. You must have a reason.'

'We all have reasons,' he said. 'My pa was a bull-headed cuss. Never knew when to quit. Many times I cussed him for being a mule, but there never was a time when I didn't bust my buttons being proud of him. But when he needed me most, I ran off and left all my troubles behind. I never got a chance to make it up to him. He died before I ever saw him again. He was fifty when I was born. Three generations apart, he always said, and he never blamed me because I didn't understand him.'

'I see,' she said. 'So you're paying him back now, in your own way.'

'Put it that way, if you like,' Hinshaw said.

'I'd say that it was a good way to put it.'

He looked at her and wondered how long she'd been a nurse for the railroad, where she lived, and whether or not she had some slick-haired crackerjack waiting for her at the end of the line.

A firm step passed their door, came back, then a solid fist rattled the panel. Hinshaw drew his .38-40 and said: 'Who is it?'

'Colonel James Gary, United States Army.'

'You're in the right church but the wrong pew,' Hinshaw said. 'The smoking car is forward.'

'Confound it, I want to see the ranger,' Gary said impatiently. He rattled the knob of the door, and Hinshaw cocked his pistol.

165

'Do that again and I'll bust your hand.'

'Very well, I'll get the conductor.'

'Wait a minute,' Hinshaw said. He stepped back so that, when the door opened, he'd be shielded, then motioned for Ella Sanders to slip the bolt. Pedro Vargas watched all this in silence, and Hinshaw held a finger over his lips as a warning to stay that way.

Ella opened the door, and Gary stepped in. 'This is outrage...' He stopped when Hinshaw pressed the gun into his back and searched him for weapons. 'Who are you?' Gary demanded.

'Teddy Roosevelt in disguise,' Hinshaw said. 'All right, put your hands down. Lock the door again.' He looked at Gary, who was staring at McCabe. 'Something the matter with you?'

'McCabe!' Gary said. 'By all that holy, it's Guthrie McCabe.'

'Just keep back,' Hinshaw said. 'He needs the rest. Are you really a colonel?'

'Yes, and you can put that blasted pistol away before it goes off,' Gary said. He looked at Pedro Vargas. 'I can't say that this is a pleasant coincidence, seeing you chained to the radiator, but it makes me happy. President Roosevelt sent me here to look into this bandit situation. He's about ready to bring in federal troops and put this thing down once and forever.' He glanced at Martin Hinshaw. 'Will you put that weapon away?'

166

'It's not heavy,' Hinshaw said.

'You're an obstinate young man,' Gary said. 'All right, have it your way but let the hammer down easy before we have a nasty accident in confined quarters.' He studied McCabe with an expression tinged with affection and respect. 'We worked together many years ago. Kept in touch for a long time ... then I went East, and we just drifted apart. Quite a man then and now.'

Ella Sanders said: 'Colonel, wouldn't you like to sit down?'

'Thank you, no,' he said. 'But I'd like a headache powder.' He explained how the headache had led him to this compartment. She mixed the powder in a glass of water, and he drank it, then glanced at Hinshaw. 'The conductor only mentioned one ranger on the train.'

'I'm a friend of McCabe's,' Hinshaw said. 'Colonel, it's a little crowded in here, and since this ain't visiting hours...'

'Of course,' Gary said. He turned to the door, then paused. 'Say, I have a coach to myself. Why don't you remove the prisoner? We'll take turns guarding him.'

Martin Hinshaw shook his head. 'Mister McCabe wouldn't like that. When he wakes up, he'll want to see Vargas chained like a dog.'

'Your offer is kind,' Ella Sanders said, 'but Marty's right. I'm sure you understand.'

167

'Yes. I trust I can return in the morning?'

'Just don't rattle the knob,' Hinshaw said, and slid the bolt back. After he closed the door, he said: 'When the conductor comes by, I want to ask him about this colonel.' He holstered his pistol and looked at Pedro Vargas. 'If the Army ever marched on you they'd clean out your bunch like rats from a cellar.'

'We are not afraid of the Army,' Vargas said. 'I have an army of my own.'

'You can't fight the U.S. cavalry with Winchesters,' Hinshaw said. 'The trouble with you, Pedro, is that you don't know when you're licked.'

'*Si,* it is always the Mexican who is licked, who is stupid.' He laughed. 'I will match my army against the army of that colonel. We have machine guns, too.'

'You Mexicans couldn't pay for a belly full of beans, let alone machine guns,' Hinshaw said.

'I will see you stand before a wall and die,' Vargas said. 'I will kill you with a machine gun.' He looked at Hinshaw for a moment, then fell into a sulky silence.

'Kind of said a little more than you meant to, huh?' Hinshaw laughed. 'Now who'd sell machine guns to Mexican bandits, anyway? What do you figure on doing, attacking Texas?'

The conductor knocked on the door and

identified himself. Hinshaw opened up to him. 'How's the old man?'

'Resting,' Hinshaw said. 'About that colonel...?'

'Gary? Quite an important man. Served for years in Texas during the last of the Indian troubles. What I came to tell you about was a telegram that came for the ranger. The Mexicans showed up at Victoria. So did the rangers. A hell of a gun battle. Three rangers killed and seven wounded.'

'What about the Mexicans?'

'I guess they got away,' the conductor said, and went on down the aisle.

Major Carl Manners was an early riser every day, for in spite of his modern, college-bred methods he believed that a man was at his best when he went to bed shortly after sundown and got up at sunup. He was shaving when a ranger came to his room with a telegram. He read it and finished his shave. 'Well, it isn't the first wild-goose chase we've been sent on,' he said, and toweled his face dry. 'McCabe used his head. Vargas likely had men waiting to stop the train and take him off. Saved a lot of lives there, for when he stops a train, he pulls the spikes and spreads the rails or puts sticks of dynamite under the ties.'

The sergeant said: 'Major, now that McCabe's changed trains, do you want some of the other battalions alerted?'

'Hell, no,' Manners said. 'Let him go on into Laredo. We'll be there to meet him at the dépôt.' He thought a moment. 'I'd better not send a telegram to the sergeant at the Laredo station. The Mexicans might pick it up and wonder why we're suddenly increasing strength. Order two companies to march readiness. Have them ready to leave in an hour. Rations for three days and all their belongings.' He went to his desk and sat down, tapping his fingers lightly on the blotter. 'Vargas's capture is a good bit of politics, providing we can hold him.'

'There'll be a hell of a fight if they try to take him,' the sergeant said.

Manners smiled thinly. 'Grady, no matter what kind of a trial Vargas gets, it'll be in Texas, and the Mexicans will never believe it was fair. He'll be a hero. Even more so. I want you to go to Laredo. Pick two of the fastest horses in the stable and ride hard. Leave right away and keep your badge and gun out of sight.'

'I see,' Grady said. He was a man, forty-some, thin and listless in manner, as though he never in his life and gotten enough to eat or had enough sleep. 'What am I looking for, Major?'

'The condition of the town and the Laredo garrison,' Manners said. 'It would be pure hell if we locked Vargas in the stockade and

170

then lost him. Think of what the newspapers would do to that.'

'They're always doing something,' Grady said. He glanced at Manners and asked the question frankly: 'Do you think you can really cover up the mess Standers made?'

'I can try,' Manners said. 'One thing they didn't tell me about this job when I took it was that I not only had to enforce the law, but safeguard the ridiculous record of the Texas Rangers. It's difficult to polish something that has always been a bit tarnished.' He lit a cigar and offered one to Bill Grady. 'Our long history is filled with bad mistakes and periods of corruption that would sicken anyone. We've got our enemies, Grady, and they're always waiting for another mistake. It makes good newspaper copy.'

'Maybe it's because we're all human, Major. Except McCabe. He'll be here when we're all gone.' He laughed. 'And they'll probably put up a statue of him in the park at Austin. That's the way life is.'

'No doubt,' Manners said. 'And we'll both contribute five dollars.'

'Sure,' Grady said, rising. 'We're both fools.'

After Grady left, Carl Manners sat at his desk and wondered why he didn't get out and open a law office somewhere and try divorce cases. But, no, he had to fill himself full of high-flung notions about being a Texas Ranger, about carving his name in the monument of Texas history. What a rude awakening that had been, and he hadn't been the same since. There wasn't one administration that hadn't had some corruption in it, some stupidity in it, and some heroism that was undying. The records were filled with men who rode a hundred miles with a bullet in them to run down some criminal or another, but many times the truth proved less glorious than the deed. On one occasion a ranger had kept going when he suddenly realized that the chase had taken him into a Texas county where he was wanted for questioning concerning the ownership of a horse.

The rangers, Manners understood, had enlisted all kinds of men on their rolls, and there weren't really too many questions asked as long as he could ride fast, shoot straight, and be stupid enough to take the long hours and thirty-five dollars a month in pay. Or they commissioned men through politics, or kept on men like McCabe, *or men like myself*, he thought, and this turned him into a sour frame of mind.

Being a public servant was hell, Manners decided. Being a public hero was impossible. To keep his mind from dwelling further on the subject, he reached for a stack of recent correspondence, particularly the letter bearing the engraved seal.

Austin, Texas
April 11, 1905

Major Carl Manners
Texas Frontier Battalion
On the Border

My Dear Major:
   The governor wishes to advise you that because of the publicity in the Eastern papers concerning our minor brushes with the Mexican bandits, the true facts have so been distorted that the President of the United States has appointed a military man to come here and look the situation over. The governor does not wish to convey the impression that he is against government troops in Texas, but he is desirous of terminating these minor hostilities as quickly as possible so that the President's appointee can better exercise his time in some fine grouse shooting. There have been some rumors in Austin that El Jefe has armed his soldiers with automatic firearms. Please investigate this and send along your confidential report on where such weapons could be bought. Naturally the governor regards this as pure rumor, but he does not want the newspapers to get hold of it and distort it.

   Kindest regards,
   Paul Sterret
   Secretary to the Governor

Manners folded the letter and put it away. It was plain enough that the Army man needed the grand tour, and it was just as well for these minor brushes with the Mexicans had taken over a hundred lives in the last year, and the country from Langtry to Brownsville was an armed camp where no one trusted his neighbor, and the poor Mexicans living on the Texas side were neither friendly with their own people across the river nor trusted by the Texans.

The distorted facts, Manners decided, probably came a lot closer to the truth than the governor's reports. Well, it was part of the job he supposed, and wondered who'd be the best man to send along with the soldier, someone who liked to loaf and who would show him a lot of country and damned little else.

By the time the train drew near Laredo, Martin Hinshaw was as close to being worn to a frazzle as he had ever been. He had maintained a constant vigilance over the prisoner. Guthrie McCabe shook off the fever with surprising rapidity, although he still had a touch of it, evident in his cheeks and bright eyes.

When the train slowed just north of the switchyard, five men boarded and came to the caboose with the conductor. They were armed and wore their badges in plain sight

174

and put leg irons on Pedro Vargas and took him away.

Martin Hinshaw was relieved to be rid of the Mexican, and he could see that Ella Sanders was, too. The trip had been wearing on her with McCabe's being sick and getting no sleep at all. Hinshaw said: 'It's ten minutes into the dépôt. Let's go to the observation platform.'

'Why?'

He grinned. 'Because I've been alone with you longer than I ever have with a girl, and I haven't really been alone at all. Are we just going to say good bye and let it go at that?'

'Maybe we should,' she said. 'Marty, there'll be someone waiting for me in Laredo.'

'I might have guessed it.'

'No, we're not married. Just engaged. His name's Fred Early, and he owns the biggest store in town.'

'Figures that you'd get a successful man,' Hinshaw said. 'It's like I told McCabe, my luck's always been bad.'

His manner, his readiness to play the underdog rôle, touched her, and she said: 'Marty, why don't you come to supper tomorrow night?' She wrote the address on a slip of paper and put it in his shirt pocket. 'My father and I live alone. Please.'

'It won't put Fred Early's nose out of joint, will it?'

'He'll understand,' she said.

The conductor was going to see that Mc-Cabe was taken off the train. He explained that it was the railroad's responsibility, and Hinshaw didn't argue with him. He said good bye to Ella Sanders, took his satchel, and went to the nearest vestibule to wait. When the train pulled into the dépôt, he got off before it stopped completely and was walking toward the center of town before the rest of the passengers got down.

He found a hotel that was clean enough and cheap enough and took a room there, stowed his suitcase and revolver, then went in search of a shave and a bath. He had a bath first, then a shave, and all this felt so good that he spent an additional thirty-five cents on a haircut.

His intention afterward was to go back to the hotel and sleep for three days, but his curiosity got the better of him, and he walked along the main street until he saw the sign he looked for:

FRED J. EARLY
DRY GOODS – GENERAL MDSE.
LAREDO, TEXAS

Hinshaw stepped into the store and was immediately surrounded by the smells of leather and cloth and oil finely coating the racks of shovels and tools. A few customers

176

were being waited on, and Hinshaw walked about as though trying to make up his mind about something. He identified the clerk right away and Fred Early; one gave the orders, and the other took them.

Early was thirty, Hinshaw guessed, a very successful thirty. Tall and Texas straight. Early's hair was dark and wavy, and he wore a thin mustache and a white shirt with slick cuff protectors.

As Early waited on a customer, Hinshaw studied him while pretending to study a case of pocket knives. Early had a smooth, easy manner with people, and a way of smiling that convinced all that he was a friend, even while his hand rang up profit on the cash register. It wasn't difficult to see why Ella Sanders had picked him, for Early would amount to something. He had that serious turn of mind found in important people.

The customer left, and Early came over. 'May I help you?'

Hinshaw realized then that he would have to buy something. 'I like that little pearl-handled penknife,' Hinshaw said.

'A very fine knife,' Early said, taking a tray of them from the case. 'I sell a lot of these, here and all over. Import them from Germany, you know. Famous for their steel.' He demonstrated the keen edge on some paper he moistened. 'Only a dollar and a quarter.'

'I guess I'll take it,' Hinshaw said.

Earl took the money and made change. 'New in Laredo, aren't you?'

'Just got in on the train.'

Early's interest grew. 'Say, what's this rumor I hear about El Jefe being taken prisoner?'

'I guess it's so,' Hinshaw said, putting the knife in his pocket. 'Some ranger had him on the train.'

'Heard the ranger was flat on his back,' Early said. 'There was another fella...'

'I wouldn't know anything about that,' Hinshaw said. 'You hear all kinds of things these days. How's jobs around here?'

'Holding,' Early said. 'Which is about all that can be expected with the Mexican trouble and all. Out of work?'

'A man either has it or he hasn't,' Hinshaw said. 'I may look around.'

'Jobs are hard to find without a recommendation,' Early said. 'Any stranger in this part of the country is looked over pretty good.'

'I make friends quickly,' Hinshaw said. 'But thanks for the suggestion. If I need a commendation, I know of someone in town who might give me one.' He smiled pleasantly and went out.

His hotel bed was lumpy, and the afternoon was turning out hot, but it really didn't bother him for he was too tired to care. He slept until a cool breeze coming through his window woke him, and he found that it was dark outside. There was some traffic noise coming up from the street, but he paid no attention to it and went back to sleep.

Someone knocking at his door woke him. Hinshaw grumbled and lit the lamp, then opened the door. Two men stood there. One said: 'The name's Bill Grady. Martin Hinshaw?'

'Guilty,' Hinshaw said, and sat down on the bed.

Grady looked at his friend, then back to Hinshaw. 'What do you mean by that?'

'What? Oh, just a form of expression. What do you want?'

'We had a devil of a time locating you,' Grady said. 'This is Corporal Anderson. We're Texas Rangers. The major got in an hour ago. He'd like to talk to you.'

'Some other time,' Hinshaw said. 'I'm catching up on my sleep.'

Bill Grady frowned. 'I'm sorry, but the major don't like to be kept waiting. Now he's not asking much, just a little of your time.'

Hinshaw looked at him. 'Friend, I've got a few dollars to my name, the clothes on my back, and no job. But I have plenty of time and, since that's all I have, I'm inclined to be selfish about it. If he wants to see me, he can come here. Now leave me alone.'

'He's not very friendly,' Corporal Anderson said dryly.

'No, and I don't think he'll improve,' Grady said. 'All right, Hinshaw, we asked you nice.'

They moved together, and Hinshaw came off the bed. He hit Anderson an axing blow that spun him completely around and slammed him against the door, but it cost him dearly, for it gave Grady a chance to grab him, trip him, and pin him to the floor while Anderson recovered and snapped on the handcuffs. Hinshaw was hauled to his feet, and Anderson rubbed his jaw.

'Did you have to do that?' he asked. 'Gollee, I'm liable to get a toothache now.'

'What's the big idea, jumping me?' Hinshaw demanded.

'Now don't get your pin feathers all mussed up,' Grady suggested. 'We've got a buckboard downstairs, and we're going to see the major.' He glanced at Anderson. 'I owe McCabe three dollars. He said we wouldn't get him without a scuffle.'

'I get the toothache, and he gets three dollars,' Anderson said sourly. 'That's the whole of McCabe's life.' He picked up Hinshaw's hat, clapped it on his head, and laced his coat over his arm.

They went downstairs and through the lobby. Hinshaw got in the buckboard, and Grady drove out of town. As they neared the residential section, Grady pulled his team to

180

the side of the road. Anderson hopped down to hold them while an automobile approached, carbide lamps shedding a flushed glow ahead, clanking, puffing, smelling of oil. Hinshaw saw that Fred Early was driving, and Ella Sanders sat on the high seat, one hand keeping a firm grip on her hat.

He hunkered down so as not to be seen, then the car passed on. Anderson got back into the rig; he was in a sour frame of mind. 'God-damn' contraptions anyway! The only one in town, and Early has to own it. On Judgment Day he'll be selling ringside seats.'

'He just knows how to make a dollar,' Grady said. 'We all have our little talents.'

Ranger Headquarters was a half mile from town, a cluster of buildings with barracks and a stout stockade on the west side. As they pulled into the yard, Hinshaw knew that Vargas was in the stockade, for at least ten rangers formed a patrolling guard around it, constantly moving in a preset pattern.

Grady took him by the arm and steered him across the porch. Once inside he unlocked the handcuffs and said: 'Now behave yourself. He only wants to thank you.'

'He could have wrote me. I don't get much mail.'

'You wait here,' Grady said, and left him with Anderson to see that he did. He knocked, stepped into the major's office, then came right out. 'Go on in.'

Carl Manners got up and came around the desk, his hand outstretched. 'Mister Hinshaw, the Texas Rangers owe you a debt of gratitude. Please sit down. I hope I didn't inconvenience you, asking you to come here at this late hour, but tomorrow I'm going into the field for a few days, and I wanted to take the first opportunity I had of thanking you. Cigar?'

'No,' Hinshaw said. 'How's the old man?'

'Difficult to keep in bed,' Manners said. 'What are *your* plans?'

'Get a job. The old home place is fifty miles north of here. I'd like to buy it back someday.'

'I'd like to offer you work, if you'd accept it,' Manners said. 'We're always looking for good men. I won't insult you by asking if you can ride ... your boots show that. Can you handle a firearm?'

'Major, I could draw and put five shots into the palm of your hand from twenty feet in that many seconds.' He grinned. 'For a while I had a girl who was a rodeo trick shot. She taught me that and a few other things. But this isn't for me. I couldn't get used to calling you, "sir," and getting up when I was told, or doing what I was told. Besides, the pay's poor.'

'You've come highly recommended to me,' Manners said. 'Colonel Gary was impressed with your devotion to responsibility.

182

Will you think it over?'

'Don't have to,' Hinshaw said, rising. 'Give my best luck to the old man. He's going to need it if he keeps sticking his neck out so far. Good bye.' He offered his hand, and Manners took it, then Hinshaw stepped out. Grady was waiting, and Hinshaw said: 'Drive me back to my quarters, *boy*.' He grinned when he said it, and Grady's sour expression broke, and he smiled, too.

Chapter Ten

Fred Early parked his automobile near the bank of the river at a place where it bent sharply so they could see Laredo and the Mexican side and hear the soft whisper of water. The night was clear with only a part of a moon showing, but they could see the oldness of Mexico and the rawness that was still Texas.

Early smoked a cigar, while Ella Sanders chattered on gaily about her experience on the train. Finally Early said: 'My dear, in the past fifteen minutes you mentioned Martin Hinshaw's name eleven times. Have I a rival in this itinerant rodeo rider?'

She laughed. 'No, of course not. He's … well … interesting.'

'I am a fascinating man myself,' he said lightly. 'Ella, when are you going to give up that ridiculous job at the hospital?'

'Soon,' she said. 'When we're married. Fred, I've paid off the mortgage with that job. I'm proud of it.'

'I'd be more proud,' he said, 'if I had done it. How will I explain that I'm living in a house paid for by my wife?'

'Do you have to explain it?'

He shrugged. 'I think life should have reason to it, cause and effect. A successful man has to explain more than ... well ... your gallant friend Hinshaw. He has to account to no one, Ella. Drift here, then drift somewhere else. You pay no more attention to him than you do a tumbleweed.' He puffed on his cigar. 'Call me old-fashioned if you will, Ella, but I'm not in favour of a young girl pursuing a nurse's profession. One never knows who you'll meet.'

'Some good people and some bad people, Fred.'

He frowned. 'Selectivity of associates is man's right,' Early said. 'You were born to command servants, Ella, not to be commanded by some unwashed mother who has a fretful child and wants to be waited on because she's paid her bill.' He threw away his cigar and got out and cranked the car. As soon as the engine coughed, he came back to the seat and manipulated the controls to keep it running. As he drove toward town, he said: 'You must marry me soon, Ella.'

This pleased her for she gave him a quick smile. 'Why, Fred, you sound impatient.'

'About some things I am,' he said. 'I'm impatient to be more than I am so that, when I speak, men will accept that I am right and not debate with me. I'm impatient to have money, not to count or flaunt, but to be free from want. And I'm impatient to marry you so we can find happiness together.'

'Fred, I thought you were happy now. I know I am. I don't want to change what I am.'

'Then why did you go to school to become a nurse?'

'Because I was interested in it.'

'And the job with the hospital?'

She shrugged. 'I just wanted to see more of the world, that's all.'

He shook his head stubbornly. 'I don't think you're honest with yourself. We all want to change what we are. That's why we leave home, to get away from what we've been. I suppose we're all a little ashamed of our parents, that they weren't more. I know there was a time when I no longer looked at my father as a father, and looked at him as a man who had simply thrown away all his opportunities. That was the day I made up my mind to get away, and I've never gone back.'

'I wonder if that's what Marty thought. He

185

told me, you know...'

Early's laugh was brittle. 'I'm afraid, if you mention that huckleberry's name to me just once more, I'm going to form an intense dislike for him.'

'All right,' she said. 'Except that I've invited him to supper tomorrow night.'

'Oh, really,' Early said, but wisely said no more.

He dropped her off at the house, kissed her good night, then drove to the main street. He parked his car in front of the saloon, and he was pleased when some loungers gathered to admire it. Early went inside, bought a drink, then turned to some men playing cards under a hanging corner light. Their clothes marked them as ranch owners, and not exactly poverty-ridden, either. Early's position in the community was an invitation to join the game, and he did, betting with irritating caution.

The conversation was mostly about the rangers and the Mexican bandit being held in the stockade. In ten minutes Early had learned that a federal judge was coming in from El Paso to try the case, and the trial was set for next week.

Miles Cardeen, one of the biggest ranchers in the county, said: 'The clerk over at the hotel told me that that young Texas jack rabbit hauled off and whacked that ranger in the chops before they took him out of the hotel.' He bet. 'Give me two. So I figured you can't go wrong with a man who's tough and modest. When he hit me up for a job, I hired him.'

Fred Early glanced up. 'That's taking a chance, isn't it, Miles?'

'I don't see how.'

Early shrugged and studied his cards. 'What do you know about him, really? I'd let him go before he brings you trouble.' He threw in his hand. 'Especially now, with Vargas coming up to trial.'

The game stopped, and they looked at Fred Early. One of them said: 'I wouldn't hire any stranger. He might be a spy for Vargas's army. You never know, Miles.'

'The last time Laredo was hit,' Early said casually, 'Goheen hired a new swamper. I don't think any of us can doubt now that he studied the town and passed the information on to the Mexicans. Look at the way they hit the bank and the express office and every other cashbox in town.'

'Except yours,' Miles Cardeen said.

'That's right,' Early said. 'Remember that I was suspicious. The man spent too much time walking around, wandering in and out of places. I told you before the raid that I was taking my cash and hiding it, and I did. The ones who didn't listen lost plenty.' He put a match to his cigar. 'We know a little about Vargas. He's a smart man. We know damned

187

little about Hinshaw. So play it safe. Pat him in the hind end with a boot and send him down the road. This whole business on the train could be a put-up job with Hinshaw in it all the time. Vargas swore he'd come back to Laredo and burn it to the ground. I look for him to keep that promise.'

Miles Cardeen looked around at the others. 'I guess I don't really need another man. We ought to quietly pass the word around on Hinshaw. Nothing personal, you understand, but just to protect ourselves.'

'That's most sensible,' Early said, 'Vargas has always employed some renegade whites to do his advance work. This is the best way. After all, what's Hinshaw to us … just a drifter.'

Early played a few more hands, had another whisky, then left the saloon. He paused on the walk for a moment, looking up and down the street. A crowd still gathered around his automobile, and he put up with their jokes, cranked it, and drove home. He lived alone in the better section of town and a Mexican cleaning woman came in every afternoon and kept the house in order. Early put the automobile in the barn and locked it to keep the Mexican children from stealing all the brass off it. A man had to put up with those inconveniences when a large section of town was Mexican. One of Early's dreams was to clean it out once and for all, push them all back across the Río Grande where they belonged. He knew a lot of people who felt the same way. Important people, too.

The housekeeper had left the hall light burning, and he went in, turning on the parlor lights. The hall clock struck the hour, and he went out and wound it, then returned to the parlor, sat in his favorite chair, and read the latest papers. He took them from several large cities and even had two Eastern papers mailed to him.

Early read like a man killing time, a man waiting. When he heard a faint scratching on the wall, he got up, went through the kitchen to the dark back porch.

A Mexican waited there. He said: 'I have a message from Batiste.'

'What is it?' Early asked.

'He grows impatient for the rest of the shipment.'

'Tell him I'm expecting some freight to-morrow or the day after. Look for my motor-car. The usual place. Don't contact me until then. He'll have the money ready?'

'*Sí*,' the Mexican said. 'Batiste cannot wait long. A thousand men will march on the town, but we need more guns, more ammunition.'

'You'll get them. Watch for my motorcar.'

He turned and went inside and picked up his newspapers. This time he read like a man with his business behind him and now

189

ready to enjoy himself.

Martin Hinshaw spent the night in Miles
Cardeen's bunkhouse, and at dawn he rolled
out with the other hands and went to the
watering trough to wash before breakfast.
While he was combing his hair, the foreman
came up and said: 'Boss wants to see you.
Use the back door.'

Hinshaw frowned, then shrugged, and
walked toward the house. As he approached
the back porch, Cardeen came out. He came
to the point.

'I can't use another man, Hinshaw. Sorry.'

'Changed your mind suddenly, didn't
you?'

'That's the way I am,' Cardeen said. 'I'll
pay you for the full day, though.'

'Hell, never mind,' Hinshaw snapped, and
returned to the bunkhouse to get his
satchel. It was quite a distance to town, but
he walked it and never gave it a thought.
Anger could do that to him, block out the
uncomfortable aspects of his life.

He spent the day moving around, asking
in every store for work, but the answer was
always the same: there just wasn't anything
for him. In late afternoon he went into the
saloon and bought a beer and, after that, a
bowl of chili beans in a small restaurant,
and, when he paid for it, he held his fortune
in his hand, not enough for another night at

the hotel.

I'll be damned if I'll go on the bum, he thought and made up his mind before he reached the street. A man needed the dignity of work even if it was shoveling manure at the stable, and, when he got to the point where that was denied him, he was in trouble.

The afternoon was hot. When Martin Hinshaw reached the Ranger Company Headquarters, he washed at the watering trough before going in. An orderly took his name and told him to wait. Ten minutes later Major Carl Manners came across the porch. His clothes bore the dust of travel, and he beat it off with his hat. With Manners was Bill Grady who grinned and said: 'So soon?'

'Funny,' Hinshaw said. 'Major, is that offer still open?'

Manners gave it a moment's thought. 'You'll start as a private, Hinshaw. No favors, and you'll make it on your own.'

'I didn't ask for anything special.'

'Come into the office,' Manners said.

Hinshaw bathed and shaved before leaving for town with the clerk who went in every evening to pick up the mail. He didn't feel a nickel richer, yet he was conscious that again his life had a direction. At least for two years, which was the term of his enlistment. He got out of the buckboard on the main street, and, as he passed Fred Early's store, he noticed the two clerks checking crates of newly arrived merchandise. Hinshaw walked on and, after asking directions, found Ella Sanders's house, a neat two-story frame structure surrounded by shade trees.

A man sat in the swing with his pipe and evening paper and looked Hinshaw over carefully as he came up the walk. The man said: 'You must be Hinshaw. Ella spoke of you. I'm Joe Sanders. Pardon my not getting up, but I'm nearly crippled. Can't get around much.'

'Glad to meet you,' Hinshaw said. 'I guess I'm early, but I had a chance to catch a ride and…' He let it trail off. 'Nice place. Is Ella home?'

'Out riding with Fred Early in his newfangled motorcar,' Sanders said. 'Sit a spell. I don't see many people to talk to. They'll be back soon.'

Hinshaw sat on the porch railing and rolled a cigarette. 'Is the town all set to hang the Mexican?'

'They were all set to hang him the last time he was here,' Sanders said, 'only they couldn't catch him. They ought to take him some place else for trial. Feeling's too high around here to ever find a jury who haven't already judged him.'

'From what I hear, he's had it long overdue,' Hinshaw said. 'He was bragging on the train about how many he'd killed.'

192

'Somehow I can't blame Vargas for getting himself hung,' Sanders said. 'What else could the man do? He's a Mexican, can't read or write, so what's left for him but to steal? Son, we make a lot of this ourselves. Give a Mexican a job so he can hold his head up and you don't have any trouble with him.'

Early's car putted down the street. They could hear it before it turned the far corner. It came on and stopped in front of the house. Early hopped down and helped Ella out, then secured the brake, and turned off the gasoline valve while she came onto the porch.

When she saw Hinshaw, she smiled, then she saw the badge pinned to his shirt and clapped her hands in delight. 'Isn't that wonderful,' she said. Early was coming up the walk, and she turned to him. 'Fred, this is Marty Hinshaw. He's joined the Texas Rangers.'

Early presented his hand briefly and said: 'We'll all sleep safer in our beds because of this.'

Hinshaw frowned, thought of something to say, and held it back. Ella was taking off her hat and duster. 'Why don't you sit here and talk? I have supper ready to pop into the oven.' She hurried on into the house, and Early took the other chair on Sanders's right.

'Come into my store tomorrow,' Fred Early said. 'I'll sell you a pair of pearl handles for your pistol. All the rangers wear them, you know.'

'What's your beef against the world?' Hinshaw asked. 'Or don't you like Texas Rangers?'

Early shrugged. 'They leave me unimpressed,' he said. 'I would suggest that the flaw lies in their recruitment policies.'

'You never come out and say a thing,' Hinshaw said. 'Scared to, or don't know how?'

He was pleased to see the flat light of temper in Fred Early's eyes. Early said: 'My fiancée's goodness of heart is often greater than her judgment. Inviting you here for supper was a mistake. You can correct that by leaving.'

Hinshaw glanced at Joe Sanders. 'Is that what you think, too?'

Sanders shook his head. 'Son, something's started here that's not my business. You do what you want.'

'Mean that?' Hinshaw asked.

'I do,' Sanders said.

He came off the porch rail, had Early by the shirt front, and jerked him out of the chair before Early could set himself. Then Hinshaw's fist chopped through a short arc, and he lifted Early over the rail and into the lilac bushes. Early fell hard and stayed there, not out, but not ready to get up, either.

'You pick a good fight,' Hinshaw told him. 'But that's all.' He glanced at Sanders. 'Guess

194

he's right. I've got no business at your table.' He started off the porch, then hesitated. 'Try and tell her I'm sorry and at the same time that I ain't. Does that make sense?'

'Perfectly,' Sanders said and watched Hinshaw hurry down the walk. Then he looked at Early. 'Get out of there, Fred. You look silly.'

Ella came out as Fred Early climbed out of the lilac bush and brushed himself off. There was a spot of blood on his mouth and a swelling that would grow.

'What happened?' she asked. 'Well, someone say something!'

'Maybe a little too much was said already,' Joe Sanders replied.

Early shot him a glare, then said: 'It seems to me that no further proof is needed that my judgment of Hinshaw was substantially correct. I'm sorry, Ella, because I don't enjoy proving you wrong.'

'Just what have you proved, Fred?'

'That's fairly obvious, isn't it? The man struck me in the face. He's hardly the kind one invites to supper.'

'Fred, he doesn't strike people without a reason,' Ella said. 'I'm not trying to excuse it, but by the same token I don't want to see this warped out of shape.'

Early knew that he wasn't going to get anywhere. He said: 'Perhaps it would be better if I didn't stay for supper. Your judgement had been questioned, and your pride hurt and...'

'My pride has not been hurt,' she snapped. 'But you're right, Fred. Perhaps it would be better if...' She let it trail off. 'Damn it, my supper's ruined.'

'Good night,' Early said. 'I'll come around and see you tomorrow, Joe. There are quite a few papers for you to sign. Orders, receipts, and the like. Ella, this is the first day of your vacation, and you're tired from your trip. Perhaps if I called later in the week, when you're rested, you'll be more reasonable.'

He nodded and went on down the walk. After he cranked up his car and drove away, Ella and Joe Sanders watched him. Ella said: 'For a man I'm likely to marry, I understand him very badly. Pa, what are the things you sign? I don't understand this ... this partnership you have with Fred Early.'

'I've explained it a dozen times, honey,' Joe Sanders said.

'No, you've just told me that you loaned him a thousand dollars of your insurance money, and, as interest, he made you a one-fourth partner. That seems pretty generous, Pa.'

'In some ways, Fred's a generous man,' Sanders said. 'When you have a business like Fred's, there's a lot of paperwork connected with it. I must sign two hundred letters a week. He's a smart businessman, Ella. A mail-order business isn't limited to the income around town, and shipping stuff here and there is harder than it sounds. When Fred first talked about a partnership to me, I tried to explain that I'd gone to work at twelve and had never been much for reading and writing, but he said a clerk could do all that as long as someone else tended to the signing. I've been a help to Fred. Gives him more time to tend to other things.' He reached out and patted her arm. 'Sorry about the supper, honey.'

'I don't give up easily,' she said, and stepped off the porch.

'Where are you going?'

'To find Marty Hinshaw,' she said. 'I've a few things to say to him.'

'I wouldn't...,' Joe Sanders began, then let it go, for his daughter was at the front gate and turning toward the center of town.

Rather than immediately walk back to the ranger camp, Martin Hinshaw decided to wait on the main street and hope for a wagon or a buggy going out. He stood in front of the hotel, smoking a cigarette and cursing himself for letting his temper get the best of him when tapping heels along the walk drew his attention around.

Ella Sanders came into the light, and stopped. 'I want to talk to you, Martin Hinshaw.'

'I apologized to your fath...'

'I don't care about that,' she said firmly. 'You came to my house and created a fuss, and, if you think you can just turn your back on it and walk away, then you've got another think coming.'

'What do you want me to do?'

'I went to the trouble to fix a supper, and you're coming home with me and eat it,' she said. 'And if you're ashamed of yourself and sit there with your eyes on your plate, well … you'll just have to, I guess. Only you don't walk away from the things you do so easily.'

'Why don't we just skip all this?' he asked.

'Marty, I'll take you by the ear and pull you along if I have to.'

He looked at her. She stood tall and firm-minded, and he knew that she would do exactly that, and he laughed. 'All right, I couldn't whip you in a fair fight, and I know it.'

'You may take my arm and start acting like a gentleman,' she said.

They started along the walk.

'I suppose Fred Early's there,' he said.

'No, he left. But if he was, it would still be the same.'

'You're a real stubborn woman,' Hinshaw said. 'Early's going to have to change some if he expects to marry you.'

She gave him a quick glance. 'How do you mean that?'

'Well, he fancies himself the masterful type. One day he'll walk into the house and tell you he don't like where the couch is sitting, and he'll end up on the floor, seeing stars.'

'Why, I'm not like that, Marty!'

He stopped and took her arm and turned her so she faced him. 'You're like that, and I like your being like that, Ella. I like the way you handle yourself and the things you do and say. You're a better woman than Fred Early deserves.' They were halfway down a dark block, and there was no one to see him, so he put his arms around her and kissed her. When he released her, he said: 'That's my second mistake tonight, but don't expect me to apologize for it.'

'Don't do that again to me, Marty,' she said softly. 'You see, there are always enough doubts in our minds without building more.'

'Doubts about what? Fred Early?'

'Talking is no darned good. Besides the supper's getting cold.'

Colonel James Gary was in Carl Manners's office when Guthrie McCabe came in, his crutch thumping. Manners was pouring the drinks. He waited until McCabe lowered himself into a chair before passing them around.

'You ought to stay off that leg,' Manners said. 'Colonel Gary's been relating some experiences you and he had some years ago, Captain. I was most surprised to know that you had served together.'

'We've had some high old times,' McCabe admitted. 'And some low ones. Right, Jim?'

'Without the bad, a man wouldn't know what was good,' Gary said. He chuckled, and stroked his mustache. 'When I stepped into the nurse's compartment and saw you, you could have knocked me down with a gust of wind. It's been some nineteen years as I recall.'

'The fall of 'Eighty-Six,' McCabe said. 'How's the family, Jim?'

'Jane's fine. So are the two girls. We have a son entering West Point. You?'

'I never took a wife,' McCabe said, and he sounded as thought he regretted this oversight. Then he laughed. 'It'll be good to be working with you again, Jim. The major here tells me you're a military adviser to Teddy Roosevelt. Well, it comes as no great surprise to me. You always had the mark of a doing man about you.'

Gary laughed and waved aside this flattery. He finished his drink and stood up. 'I think I'll write a few letters before I turn in. If reveille comes as early in the rangers as it does in the Army, then a man my age needs all the sleep he can get.'

After he went out, McCabe said: 'He's a damned good soldier, Carl. He'll do his job.'

'The President couldn't have picked a worse time to send a man,' Manners said. He leaned back in his chair and looked at McCabe. 'When I first got wind that you'd arrested Vargas in Louisiana, I was ready to court-martial you and dismiss you from the service.'

'You've changed your mind?' McCabe asked.

'I've reconsidered,' Manners admitted.

'You talk like a man trying to trade horses,' McCabe said. 'All right, I've been a lawman long enough to know you have to make deals. Talk, and I'll listen.'

'The point is this bandit trouble is Texas business. We don't need the help of the federal government. Whether we do or not is going to be Colonel Gary's decision. I want to make certain it's favorable to Texas.'

'You won't lose your job if it ain't,' McCabe said.

'No, but the rangers will suffer a loss of prestige.'

McCabe shrugged. 'So? Right now that badge earns all the respect of any nickel-plated tin star. It's the man behind it who always builds respect for the law.'

'That's something neither here nor there,' Manners said. 'The point is that Vargas's attorneys have arrived in town. Grady says they came in late this afternoon. The fact that you arrested him in another state without a warrant may be enough to have the whole thing thrown out of court.'

Guthrie MacCabe shook his head. 'Carl, it'll never get to court.' He leaned forward, favoring his wounded leg. 'Vargas would never trust the legal court machinery to free him. No, his *bandidos* will be across the Río Grande before court convenes. If you want to make it legal to satisfy yourself, get a change of venue and have him moved to Austin and tried there. With the queen bee in the stockade, every Mexican across the river is waiting for the signal to charge and turn him loose. For that matter, seventy percent of the Mexicans here in Laredo will take up arms for Vargas the minute the attack begins.' He pointed his finger at Carl Manners. 'I know what's in your mind, and I'll tell you how I know. All my life I've dealt with men who had some kind of an axe to grind, men who were good men and bad, and I've made my share of deals, heard just about every proposition under the sun. No, Carl, I'm not going to use my old friendship with Gary to lead him on some snipe hunt while you sprinkle water to settle the dust. I'll tell you what I will do, though. I'll take that young recruit, Hinshaw, and Gary and escort the prisoner to Austin. And while I'm there, I'll stop in and see the governor ... we used to raise hell together some years back. So, if you want to make out those charges against me, you just go right ahead.'

Carl Manners's expression was smooth and tight, and it was a minute before he spoke. 'Guthrie, you sound like a man making threats.'

'I'm telling you which side your bread's buttered on because you're a young squirt who don't know his hind end from a warm bun. Laredo was hit once before, and it was bad, but this time's going to be a slaughter unless you do something about it.'

Manners sighed. 'Forgive me for saying this, but I'm hoping that Vargas will win acquittal. I've thought about it until my head aches, and it's the only way out of this. Oh, there'll be another time, and it will be different then, but he's got to be turned loose. Either that, or we risk every soul in town in a reprisal raid.'

'Do you think he won't raid, anyway?' McCabe shook his head. 'Major, I hate to tell you the facts of life this way, but Jim Gary is the best thing that ever happened to you. He'll make his report and bring in the Army and these spiks won't be dealing with the State of Texas any longer, but the United States government. The rangers will never wipe out the bandits because we can't cross that river into Mexico. But the government can put pressure on Mexico City and maybe cross the river. Now do we move Pedro Vargas to Austin or not?'

'Give me some time to think about it,' Manners said.

'You don't have much time,' McCabe pointed out. 'Every day Vargas's army gets stronger. We're outnumbered now nearly fifteen to one. Outgunned, too. We need more than we've got, Carl. We need an army to fight an army.'

Manners shook his head in weary agreement. 'How did it start, Guthrie? How did it all begin, this hate for one another?'

'I guess it began thousands of years ago when one man looked at his skin and saw it was a little whiter than the man next to him. So he hauled off and kicked the other in the ass to show his superiority. You … me … we all add to it. We call the Mexicans greasers and spiks and bead rattlers on account of their religion and, when they ask for a job, we put them on the manure pile.'

'Then why don't we do something about it?' Manners asked. 'If we know why, then why don't we fix it?'

'I guess we don't want to stand alone,' McCabe said. 'A long time ago I learned that a man can be brave in one respect and a coward in another. But it's important that Pedro Vargas hang, Carl. While he's alive, he's a symbol for every poor, uneducated Mexican who wanted to hit back and didn't dare. He's a cry on their lips… *¡Viva los bandidos!* It's a cry that has to be stilled,

204

Carl, or there's never going to be any peace between Texas and Mexico.'

Manners took his time lighting a cigar. After he shook out the match, he said: 'Maybe this is too big for us. I didn't want it to be. Glorious traditions of the corps and all that. I wanted it to be ended with Vargas swinging from the end of the rope, but it wouldn't be an ending at all but a new beginning of something more vicious than before.' He sighed heavily. 'All right, Guthrie. Tomorrow night, very quietly, you can leave for Austin with the prisoner. I'll call Colonel Gary in the morning and lay all the facts on the table. What's the use of hiding what can't be hidden?'

'You're going to work out all right, Carl,' McCabe said. 'But for some time there I had my doubts.' He smiled and slowly stood up. 'We need the Army, and the Army needs us. Vargas buys his firearms and ammunition from someone. We'll have to hunt out his source of supply and cut him off.'

'I don't think they're coming from this side of the border,' Manners said. 'It would be too easy for him to get them through Mexico.'

McCabe disagreed. 'Carl, the only reason I'm walking now is because Vargas shot me with one of those seven millimeter Mauser automatics. It had a jacketed bullet, and it didn't spread.' He reached into his pocket

205

and tossed it on the desk. 'The nurse on the train gave it to me.' He pointed to the bullet. 'I don't say that a weapon like that couldn't be bought in Mexico City, but I'm pointing out that to the Mexican government Vargas is an outlaw. He steals from his own people, too. It would be a lot harder to move guns through Mexico than it would through Texas and across the river.'

'Every time you open your mouth, you give me something more to worry about,' Manners said. 'I've heard talk, rumors, that Vargas had machine guns. If that's true...'

'Do you want to take a chance that it ain't?'

'No,' Manners said. 'We'll have to look into this.'

McCabe went to the door, opened it, and paused there. 'Carl, are you still going to have me court-martialed?'

'Oh, get the hell out of here,' Manners said, and smiled after McCabe closed the door.

Chapter Eleven

Sergeant Bill Grady and two other rangers maintained a guard post on the Texas side of the Laredo/Nuevo Laredo river crossing. To Grady it was dull, uninspiring duty, monotonous. A man soon grew lazy at it, smoked too many cigars, and counted the hours when he'd be relieved of it. There wasn't much traffic. What there was consisted mainly of Mexican people who had friends or relatives on the other side and passed back and forth. They were always stopped and asked their names and where they lived, and they always answered patiently and went on. Grady could see that anyone could cross any time they wished with no real barrier to stop them.

Four wagons approached the crossing, and Grady recognized them as belonging to Joe Sanders, who had been in the freighting business for more years than Grady had lived. The drivers stopped the teams, and the ranger approached.

Grady said: 'What've you got this time?'

'Two empties,' the foreman said, getting down. He handed Grady a sheaf of papers all signed by Joe Sanders. 'The two loads consist of trade goods, hand tools, knives, pots, and pans. The Mexicans go for the tinware. We're going to bring back leather, blankets. Texans go for them. Can you figure it out?'

'I'm not supposed to,' Grady said. 'You mind opening a crate?' He walked to a wagon and pointed at random. 'That one there.'

'Glad to oblige,' the man said and, with a crowbar, pried off the lid. Grady looked at the merchandise, then motioned for him to nail it up again. When the foreman tossed the hammer aside, he said: 'Would you mind yelling across to the Mexican police? I get tired of opening these damned things.'

'I'll take care of it,' Grady said, and signaled for the ferry to be warped into the bank. 'How's old man Sanders? I never see him any more since the accident.'

'Neither do I,' the foreman said, climbing aboard the wagon. 'He's crippled up and don't get around at all. Fred Early gives me my orders since he's one of the family, or darned near.' He picked up the reins. 'See you this afternoon.' He drove his wagon onto the ferry, and it was slowly pulled across. In a half an hour all the wagons were transported to the Mexican side, and Grady sat down in the shade, resigned to idling the day away.

In late morning a ranger rode up, spoke to Grady, then put up his horse and took

Grady's place as he mounted up and rode away to Ranger Headquarters. When he went into Major Manners's office, he found Guthrie McCabe there and Martin Hinshaw. Grady grinned at him and said: 'Hello, squirt.'

'Have a chair,' Manners said. 'Hinshaw, in the rangers we never pull duty with any man we don't trust completely.' He looked at Bill Grady. 'I've got a job for you, McCabe, and Hinshaw. Since you've never worked with this recruit...'

Grady smiled and scratched his chin. 'He'll do from what I've seen of him. What's the job?'

'Take Pedro Vargas to Austin for imprisonment and trial.'

Grady whistled softly. 'That's two hundred miles as the crow flies. When do we leave?'

'Tonight,' Manners said. 'You'll use horses and travel at night as much as possible. Stay clear of towns. I want him there before his bandit friends find out what's happened to him.'

'What we don't want is another raid on Laredo,' McCabe said. 'We've figured out a way to stop it, Bill. Tomorrow morning we'll pull all the guards away from the guardhouse, open the doors, and go on about our business. I figure there are enough Vargas spies in Laredo to let it be known that he's no longer here. There won't be any reason for a raid then.'

'It might do the job,' Grady said. 'You want me to stay in camp the rest of the day, Major?'

'Yes, you'll all remain here. After dark you can get the wagon ready and pick the horses and draw supplies. Take your saddle horses along. Tie them on back.' He glanced at Grady. 'Any activity at the crossing?'

'Four of Joe Sanders's wagons crossed over. They were on some of Fred Early's business.'

Manners sighed. 'That man would sell hot, roasted peanuts in the middle of a battle.' He grinned. 'I suppose the demand for peanuts would be great under those circumstances. Did you notice any massing of men across the river, Bill?'

'None that I could see, Major. Of course, his lieutenants would have them scattered all over the country. But not so far they couldn't be brought together in a hurry. If we could only cross that river...'

'We can't,' Manners said. 'You're going to have to forget that, so stop thinking about it.'

'I'd like to pick fifty men and raid his camp just once,' Grady said.

It was a thought Manners had entertained, too. He indicated that the meeting was over, and they went outside. They all moved to the shade, and Hinshaw rolled a cigarette. 'It seems to me,' he said, 'that we do a lot of running in circles. McCabe catches him, fights to bring him back, then we move him. Somehow I get the feeling that we're getting nowhere.'

'The mistake was mine, I guess,' McCabe said. 'Taking him into custody was a point of pride with me.' His lined face settled into an expression of regret. 'One man, one greasy-haired Mexican bean eater turning out to be more than the Texas Rangers can handle, makes me see red.' His manner softened. 'But it just ain't us. There's people in Laredo who look to us to protect 'em. The public safety has to come first. That's something I have to know and then remind myself not to forget.' He searched his pockets for a cigar, then accepted one of Bill Grady's. After he lit it, he stood there with his eyes squinted into slits, studying the river and Mexico beyond. 'If I was running this here shebang, I'd set a trap for Vargas's bunch that a snake couldn't wiggle out of. I'd hit 'em with every sneaky trick I could think of. Maybe I'd do me some moonlighting on the other side of the river, too.'

Grady laughed. 'McCabe, this ain't like the old days.'

'Too bad,' McCabe said, and walked away, bearing heavily on his crutch.

'I'd like to see him get his way for thirty days,' Hinshaw said.

'He'd get the job done,' Grady said, 'but he'd start a war between Texas and Mexico again. Let's go over to the mess hall and see if we can argue the cook out of some coffee and a piece of pie.'

Miles Cardeen ate at sundown, or shortly after, for he was a man who worked from daylight to dark, and his supper was the most pleasant hour of the day for him, an hour spent with his wife and two daughters. Afterward, he always went to his porch to sit and smoke. His foreman would come across the yard and get the next day's orders. They'd talk a while, settle what needed settling, then Cardeen would go in to read his paper a bit or listen to his older girl play the piano.

He was halfway through his cigar when a gun popped dully from somewhere away from the yard, then overhead there was another pop, and a star shell burst, spreading a bright light over the entire ranch yard and buildings. Cardeen was surprised, bewildered. He stood up and leaned over the railing to see what the devil was going on. He was standing that way when a machine gun rattled from some brush at the edge of the yard, and bullets slammed into him and tore splinters from the side of his house, and he fell dead.

Men poured from the bunkhouse, yelling and dashing across the yard, and the machine gun fired again and was joined by another placed at a broad angle. The men broke stride and dropped. A few made it to cover, but they had only their pistols and here and there a rifle.

A sudden commotion brought Colonel Gary from his room, and, when he stepped to the door, he saw most of the rangers standing in the yard, looking west at the bright light slowly falling from the sky.

'Star shell,' Gary said, and ran toward headquarters where Major Manners stood. 'What's out there, Major?'

'Cardeen's place. What is it?'

'A star shell,' Gary said. 'The Army uses them to light the field at night during an attack.'

'God damn!' Manners said, and began shouting his men to action. He split his command, for he had no other choice. In ten minutes he had twenty-five men mounted and was leading them at a fast pace toward the Cardeen ranch.

Martin Hinshaw had been left behind, whether by design or accident he never knew. He was none too happy about it. The corporal in charge saw that every man was armed with pistol and rifle and at his post around the stockade, then they settled down to wait. Hinshaw noticed Colonel Gary nearby and moved a bit closer.

213

The corporal came by, and Gary stopped him. 'Anderson, I'd advise you to have the men dig in. The likelihood of an attack...'

'The major didn't say anything about that, Colonel.'

'Damn it, I know what he said!' Gary snapped. 'That raid in all probability was a blind. They want Vargas. You've got to get the men under cover, in the buildings, in a dug-out hole, anything.'

'Colonel, I take orders just like you do,' Anderson said, and went on.

Gary pushed his rifle butt into the soft earth and furiously began to paw out a trench. Hinshaw watched him for a moment and thought that the idea had a lot of merit. He began digging, shoving the dirt away from him until he could stretch out flat or even roll over without exposing himself.

The night was very still, and beyond the lights of Laredo burned brightly. Gary snapped his fingers, drawing Hinshaw's attention.

'Have you seen McCabe?'

'He went out with the others,' Hinshaw said. 'There's only about twenty of us, Colonel.'

'Not enough,' Gary said. 'The smart thing to do would be to unlock the guardhouse door and turn the prisoner loose. It might save the lives of some good men.'

Cardeen's house still stood, but the outbuildings were burned to the ground by the time Major Carl Manners and the rangers arrived. Quickly Manners took a grizzly inventory and knew that no one had survived the raid. Cardeen was dead and so were his nine men. Grady found Cardeen's wife inside the house, dead, but he didn't find the two girls.

Manners said: 'Why do they always cut on them, McCabe?' He spoke softly with an angry tremor in his voice. 'All right, mount up! We're going back! Hurry it up there!' He swung to the saddle.

McCabe said: 'Think we'll get there in time to hit them from behind, Major?'

'That's precisely what I mean to do,' Manners said. He gathered his force with a circular motion of the arm, then stormed out of the yard.

Manners knew that the raid had been a decoy, suspected it before he ever left the ranger camp, yet he had to play the game and hope he could turn it to his favor. The men he had left behind would put up a strong fight, and they might hold the bandits at bay until he could charge from the rear.

Never before had he been given the opportunity to conduct a military maneuver against the Mexican raiders. The rangers were always outnumbered in a headlong fight. Most of the time the bandits had disappeared by the time the law arrived on the scene. This time, he believed, it would be another story. He skirted the town with his men, riding across country, cutting three fences and fording two creeks to do it, and, as he neared the ranger camp, he heard the rattle of gunfire and the sharp chatter of a machine gun.

His men spread out in a line, swung into a curve, and closed in, blocking the bandits from a retreat to the river. Manners was elated, when they suddenly saw this new danger and turned on him. The rangers fired as they came on, and the machine gun dropped four horses and sent the men tumbling. Three never moved, but the fourth one crawled along the ground dragging his wounded legs behind.

The firing lasted less than a minute, then it was finished, and Manners got off his jaded horse and shouted some order into the chaos. Lanterns were brought up, and men were detailed to duties. The guardhouse was checked, a useless gesture for the lock had been shot off the door, and Pedro Vargas was across the river. Five of the guards were dead and three others seriously wounded.

Piece by piece, Manners put it together, taking one report after another, as soon as he could summon the men. Colonel Jim Gary was more concise than the others. He came into Manners's office with Hinshaw.

They carried the machine gun and a metal case of ammunition.

'A German Spandau,' Gary said. His uniform was dirty, and he brushed at it. 'They hit us ten minutes before you arrived, Major. Four men died in the first burst, then the guards took cover. Hinshaw and I had dug trenches, and we were able to pin the machine-gunner down with the rifle fire. However, it didn't stop them from releasing the prisoner.'

'How many were in the raiding party?' Manners asked.

'Ten. Twelve at the most.' He patted the machine gun. 'With this, ten is enough.'

'There were two of those damned things at the Cardeen Ranch,' McCabe said. 'I saw Grady picking up some empty brass in a couple of places.'

'The surgeon ought to have a report in an hour,' Manners said wearily. He placed his hands flat on the desk. 'Colonel Gary, I am formally requesting that you return to Washington immediately and ask the President of the United Sates to send federal troops. The Texas Rangers are no longer able to cope with a war of this magnitude.' He looked at Gary. 'My clerk will put that in writing in the morning.'

'I'll send the telegram tonight,' Gary said. 'Major, you're doing the right thing. But the Texas Rangers still have a job to do. A job I think the Army is ill-equipped to do.' He glanced at all of them, then slapped the water jacket of the machine gun. 'Find the source of these weapons, and find the man who sells them, then leave him floating face down in the river. Waste no time on trials and free-talking lawyers. Find him and kill him.'

Guthrie McCabe laughed. 'Now you're talking like the old Jim Gary I used to ride with.'

'God help my soul,' Gary said. 'I thought I'd outgrown my wicked ways.'

Chapter Twelve

Colonel Gary dispatched his five-page telegram and the operator at Laredo picked it up and passed the somewhat stretched word over town so that, when the citizens' delegation called on Major Manners the next morning, their rage had subsided to a blind fury. Fred Early was the leader and spokesman, and the citizens of Laredo were proud of the bold way he stood up to Manners and even cussed him out a bit for being an incompetent political bloodsucker. The rangers were in general ripped thoroughly for a dereliction of duty in permitting the raid on

Cardeen's place, and they all wanted to know what was being done about rescuing the two abducted girls.

Manners endured this without losing his temper, for it was part of his job to deal with the angry and the injured, the do-gooders and the self-glory seekers. He placated them and got rid of them, then poured a glass of whisky and drank it straight, and afterward threw the glass against the adobe wall of his office. Wisely he was left undisturbed for an hour.

Piedras Negras was a sleepy village across the river a hundred-odd miles northwest of Laredo. Guthrie McCabe, Marty Hinshaw, and Bill Grady forded it at dusk and entered the town. They watered their horses in the square, looked the place over carefully, then went to the *cantina* for something to eat and drink.

They did not look like Texas Rangers. McCabe was dressed in a dirty corduroy coat with a rent in one sleeve, his hat was sweat-stained, and the dirt of three days' travel added to his ragged appearance. Whiskers on his face made him fierce in appearance, and, if he created the impression that here was a man who would kill another for five dollars, it was exactly what he wanted.

Travel and no razor and old clothes turned Hinshaw and Grady into convincing saddle-bums. Other than first glances, they attracted no attention in the *cantina*. They ate chili beans and drank tequila and left the place to wander around town. The lights in a store attracted them, and they went in. McCabe and Grady looked around, while Hinshaw ordered a side of bacon, some coffee, a box of cartridges, and a can of black saddle daub. They spent the night sleeping in the square, and they didn't talk much until the town grew quiet.

Hinshaw said: 'You see those knives and kettles and stuff? That's what Fred Early peddles.'

McCabe grunted some soft reply, and opened the can of boot daub. He put some on his hands and began to massage it into his hair until the gray was completely gone. He looked like an entirely different man. 'With all the years I've spent in this part of the country,' he said, 'it just wouldn't do for some chili bean to recognize me and pass the word along to Vargas. Tomorrow we'll get out and see if we can pick up Vargas's trail.'

'He won't be easy to find,' Grady said.

'Didn't say he would be,' McCabe said. 'But I want to find those Cardeen girls and fetch 'em back while they still want to go back.'

'What do you ... oh,' Hinshaw said, answering the question himself. 'I never thought of that.'

'Think about it, then,' McCabe advised. 'If Vargas don't want 'em, he'll give 'em to his lieutenants, and they'll pass 'em on to the sergeants, and then the soldiers can have 'em. If they ain't dead in two weeks, they won't want to come back. We'll work south in the morning.'

'What are we looking for exactly?' Grady asked.

'Some place where Mexican soldiers ain't,' McCabe said. 'There was a small garrison just outside of town, so I didn't expect nothing here. The Mexican army is after Vargas, too, that is, if they want to collect the reward. It's the *rurales* we'll have to watch for, the police. They're as bad as Vargas, only they wear uniforms.' He put his hat over his face. 'Go to sleep. We'll leave before sunup.'

They slept lightly. Before morning a squad of soldiers rode through town, waking them. It was the end of sleep. They got their horses, left Piedras Negras, and cut south. Before the day was out, they were in the mountains.

That night they had a fire, slept well, and were traveling before daylight. Two days more carried them near the village of Sabinas, a collection of adobes crowded against a small river. McCabe was in no hurry to enter the village, so they made camp high where they could study the land and the people down below. Hinshaw didn't think too much of the idea until McCabe pointed

221

out a few things: they hadn't seen a sign of a soldier for two days, and there were too many people in that village for the size of it.

After Hinshaw was told these things, he saw that they were true. From all the goings and comings, he felt that they had stumbled on Pedro Vargas's main camp. McCabe disagreed in that he felt that Vargas's camp was nearby but not in the town. The Mexican bandit only used the town.

At sundown they mounted up and left their place in the mountains and took to the ridges, moving in a circling way until they got a good look at the passes in and out. Before dawn they heard a horse snort somewhere below, and they stopped and waited for daylight.

Vargas had his camp in a cañon that at first glance seemed to have only one way in and out. A closer inspection revealed a narrow trail running from the floor to a far ridge. McCabe wanted to have a closer look at that.

This was no temporary quarters for the bandit, for crates were stacked about and several adobe buildings had been put up by a small creek that drained into the river. The rest was tents and lean-tos.

'Now ain't that some nest of rattlesnakes?' McCabe observed.

Hinshaw agreed that it was, and Bill Grady silently wondered what three men thought they could do to a camp of five hundred. But the way McCabe figured it, there really weren't five hundred. A hundred and fifty seemed to be in the village with another hundred drunk most of the time. He went to sleep, stretched out on a rock, as though he had already decided what to do and was just waiting for the right time to do it.

McCabe's interest in the trail to the ridge was not whether or not he could navigate it, but whether or not he could block it easily. After a careful look, he decided that he could. With that settled, he got them together and laid it out plain and simple.

'If we're going to get those girls, the best way is to go down and get 'em.'

'Just like that,' Hinshaw said.

'Move slow and you'll get killed,' McCabe said. 'Son, I've taken prisoners away from the Indians. I know how to do it.'

'Listen to the old man, squirt,' Grady said. 'How do we do it?'

'It's a safe bet the girls are locked up all the time,' McCabe said. 'They wouldn't have the run of the camp. How many buildings could be locked or guarded?'

'Four I counted,' Hinshaw said.

McCabe chuckled. 'That narrows it down some, don't it? Figure, too, that they don't expect anyone to drop in sudden-like, and we've got a bit of an edge. We'll go down tonight, about midnight.'

'Wouldn't early morning be better?' Grady asked.

McCabe shook his head. 'I want to give the ones a chance to get drunk who're going to get drunk, and the ones who went to town a chance to get back and get asleep. We'll move together, find the place the girls are locked in, then play it by ear. We'll make it afoot all the way.'

'With your bad leg?' Hinshaw asked. 'Hell, I'll be carrying you up the pass. You keeled over in my lap once. So you just pull up your rocking chair and let the young in heart do the heavy work.'

'I'm going to pin your ears back for that,' McCabe said. 'But this ain't the time or place to do it. We'll all go down. If you put a hand on me to help me, I'll bend my gun barrel over your head.'

'He ain't fooling, squirt,' Grady said.

'I'm getting a little tired of hearing you call me that,' Hinshaw said. He blew out a long breath. ''Scuse me for asking, Captain, but why is it so blamed important to get those Cardeen girls back? I can see some humanitarian reasons, but…'

'They marched with Vargas's army,' McCabe said. 'They've been in Vargas's camp. As far as we know, they've seen more of the inside of Vargas's army than anyone else. So anything they can tell us is to our good. That answer your question?'

'Sure enough,' Hinshaw said. 'Well, let's go down there and make the major proud of us.'

'In time,' McCabe said, 'but now we wait.' He settled back and put his hands behind his head. 'Come over here, son.' He waited until Hinshaw settled beside him. 'There was a time when I wasn't sure you had more nerve than good sense. But when we get into Vargas's camp, I'm relying on that good sense more than your nerve.'

'I don't quite understand,' Hinshaw.

'I'm talking about the way you feel about Mexicans,' McCabe said. 'I want to get in that camp and out without firin' a shot.' He turned his head and looked at Hinshaw. 'Where'd you get your hate for Mexicans? Over the kitchen table? Most of it spreads that way. A kid will laugh and play with Mexican kids and figure he's their best friend, then one day he'll hear the old man call them spiks because he's mad about something, and pretty soon the kid's doing it, too, and you've got a hate growing. And the poor Mexican kids have been thinking that he's a Texan that ain't like the rest, but they soon change their minds. If we hadn't taken Texas from the Mexicans, everything would be all right, but we've just got to hate what we defeat, or so it seems.'

'Did you ever know the Rameras family, McCabe?' Hinshaw asked.

'Tolerably well,' he said. 'Why?' Then he looked again at Martin Hinshaw. 'Say! Hinshaw! The name suddenly means something to me. Are you related to the Hinshaw who fought the whole damned Rameras family to a draw over some land?'

'That was my pa,' he said. 'McCabe, I learned my hate from the worst kind of Mexican, the Mexican with money, with land. Pa was squatting right in the middle of what Rameras claimed was all his land. Only it wasn't, and he knew it. When I was a kid, I used to take some damned good beatings from Batiste Rameras and his two brothers.' He looked at McCabe. 'I wasn't in that fight. No, I was smarter than that. I ran out on Pa and went to rodeo bumming. He fought 'em alone, much to my regret.'

'He done a good job, too,' McCabe said. 'Of course, if he'd lived, they'd probably have tried him and hung him. Texas has outgrown her feudin' days. One of the Rameras boys survived. The oldest one, Batiste. He hung between life and death for months, but he recovered. Now he runs a saddle shop and feed business in Laredo. It'll only be a matter of time before you two run into each other. When that happens, remember you're a Texas Ranger and not some rowdy looking for a fight.'

'I won't promise a thing,' Hinshaw said, 'but I wouldn't duck anything.'

'Wouldn't ask you to, son. Now go to sleep.'

Hinshaw figured this was impossible for the rocks were uncomfortable, and he was too keyed up for sleep, yet the next thing he knew was Bill Grady's hand gently waking him.

'Time to go, squirt.'

They picketed the horses in a sheltered spot, then slowly worked their way down the trail. The night was clear, but starless, which cut their vision sharply yet afforded them a black cover that was more important than being able to see. The trail was steep and narrow but not as difficult as Hinshaw had first thought. It would be difficult, if not impossible, to take a horse up it, which limited any pursuit in case they had to beat a hasty retreat.

Vargas's camp was typical, a welter of disorder, with many cook fires and many small, independent camps making up the bulk of the larger over-all encampment. The late hour and many empty wine bottles helped still the activity. The three rangers skirted it, moving toward the first of the adobes.

They crouched by a hide window and listened. They heard men sleeping, and McCabe motioned for them to move on. Hinshaw brought up the rear. They paused at two more of the adobes, and McCabe kept urging them on. At the fourth building McCabe nodded, and how he knew puzzled

Hinshaw. Then he heard a girl crying, two men laughing, and a wine bottle clinking against a glass, and he understood how Mc-Cabe had drawn his conclusions. The girls would be kept busy; there wouldn't be any snoring coming from that adobe.

McCabe made a cirling motion with his hand. Grady went one way, while Hinshaw and McCabe went the other. After circling close to the wall, they paused by the door. McCabe closed his fist and made striking motions. Both Hinshaw and Grady nodded, only Hinshaw looked around for something more solid than his fist. He didn't want to take a chance on being able to knock his man out with one punch. Some crates stood nearby, and Hinshaw gently took off a heavy board from the top and again went to the door. McCabe reached out and rattled the latchstring. From inside a man swore in annoyance. The door opened, and Hinshaw used the butt end of the board like a ram and caught the Mexican in the pit of the stomach. The man blew out all his air in a gush and went down, completely unconscious. Grady and McCabe bowled into the room.

A candle cast a faint light on the second Mexican and the two naked girls. Grady ducked a knife thrust, caught the Mexican's arm, and whirled him so that Hinshaw could swing the board. He used it like a ball bat, as though he were driving a hot one clean over the fence, and the edge of the board caught the Mexican across the base of the skull. He went down with no cry at all.

McCabe snatched up two blankets, threw them over the girls, and spoke softly. 'We're rangers. Make no sound.'

They nodded mutely, too frightened or surprised to speak. Hinshaw took a look outside and saw that they had attracted no attention. He went out, and the others followed, moving more rapidly now toward the trail leading to the ridge.

Before they cleared the camp, the younger girl started to whimper. Grady clapped a hand over her mouth and half carried her forward. McCabe, in spite of his bad leg, was keeping up. They worked to the top where the horses were hidden.

Grady put one of the girls on his horse, and motioned for Hinshaw to ride with the other one. Then Grady chuckled and said: 'Keeping that for a souvenir, squirt?' He pointed to the board in Hinshaw's hand, and only then did he realise that he still carried it.

He started to throw it away, changed his mind, and jammed it in his rifle boot. 'Yeah, I think I will.' He swung up behind the girl, and lifted the reins. 'Grady, did I do all right?'

'Don't you know?'

Hinshaw shook his head. 'I was too scared.'

'You did fine, son,' McCabe said. 'Now,

let's get the hell out of here. It's a long way
to the river, and that camp's going to be in
an uproar in an hour.'

Chapter Thirteen

At dawn McCabe's party was in the highest
mountain reaches. He stopped for a rest, got
a pair of field glasses from his saddlebag, and
studied the trail they had just traveled. For a
time he scanned it, then grunted softly. He
handed the glasses to Martin Hinshaw. Far
back, but following, was a group of *bandidos*,
forty or fifty strong, if the dust they raised
was any indication.

Hinshaw handed the glasses back. 'I didn't
think we'd get away with it.'

'We'll get away with it, but it'll be the last
time,' McCabe said. 'I was figurin' on the
Mexican way of doing things. They felt safe
in camp and had no guards. We did what
they thought could never be done ... walked
in and took what we wanted and walked
right out. But we'll never surprise 'em again,
son. Vargas will have guards posted from
now on.' He nodded toward the two girls
huddled together. 'Talk to 'em.'

'What'll I say?'

'It's a young man's job. You'll think of

something.' He gave Hinshaw a gentle shove.

Bill Grady was near the horses, watching Hinshaw, and Hinshaw wished that he'd stop that. He couldn't think of thing to say. A man just couldn't walk up and ask if they were all right when he knew that they weren't and probably would never be again. They were pretty girls, in a big-boned way. He went to his horse on impulse, opened his bedroll, and took out the extra shirt and pants and underwear that he carried.

He bundled them under his arm and went over to where they sat. 'It's the best I can do, ladies. I hope you understand.' The older one looked at him for a moment, then her lips moved soundlessly in a brief thank you. Hinshaw motioned for Grady. 'Bring my blankets here, Bill. You take one end, and I'll take the other. We'll hold this up and turn our backs, ladies. You tell us when you're dressed.'

They stood that way for a few minutes, then the older girl said: 'All right.' Bill Grady took Hinshaw's blanket back, rolled the pack, and lashed it behind the saddle.

'I wish we could offer you some coffee or somethin',' Hinshaw told them. 'My name's Marty.'

The older one said: 'I'm Rhea. My sister is Alice.' She looked at her hands and folded them in her lap. She remained sitting that way, her head tipped forward.

Guthrie McCabe said: 'We could risk a small fire for a pot of coffee. Tend to it, Bill.'

'The brush is too green to burn,' Grady said. 'Say, Marty, you want to contribute your souvenir for firewood?'

'It's in my rifle boot,' Hinshaw said. He reached out and touched Alice Cardeen's hand. 'You're going to be all right now.'

'Are we?' Rhea asked.

Hinshaw fell silent for a moment. 'Ladies, I hate to tell you, but they didn't leave any-one alive at your home place.'

'It doesn't matter,' Rhea said. 'We're not alive, either. Not really. Not now.'

Grady said: 'Hey, squirt, come here!'

Grady stood there, holding the board in his hands. McCabe came over as Hinshaw sided Grady. Then Hinshaw saw what had drawn Grady's interest. The board had been a part of the top of a crate and on it, in black paint, were some letters, smudged over but still legible.

**RLY
XAS**

Hinshaw said: 'Half of the R and half of the X. Fred J. Early, Laredo, Texas. Does any-one think differently?'

'Not likely,' McCabe said softly. 'Well, well, very interesting. Son, what kind of a crate did you jerk this off of? Or don't you remember?'

232

Hinshaw thought a moment. 'I guess it would have been about the size of a rifle case or a little bigger. You can see how long the board is.'

'Get your Winchester, Bill,' McCabe said.

Grady got it, and McCabe measured it and found the crate to be longer. He said: 'About the right length for a German Mauser rifle.'

'Or one of those machine guns,' Grady said. 'You still want the coffee, Captain?'

'Not if it means burning this piece of wood,' McCabe said. 'Express my regrets to the ladies, son.'

'How come I got to … oh, all right.'

'I think it best that we move on anyway,' McCabe said. 'Sorry, but we really have little choice in the matter.' He walked over and stood halfway between Hinshaw and Grady. 'I don't have to explain to a couple of Texas men the why of my next order. The Mexicans are not going to follow us for twenty miles and give up, so it becomes necessary to travel fast. Grady, I'll have to take the horses for the ladies.'

'No, that's not fair!' Rhea Cardeen said.

McCabe held up his hand. 'This is ranger business. Hinshaw, take the rifles and what supplies you two will need. And I'll see you in Laredo.'

After a glance at Grady, who acted as though this made no difference at all with him, Hinshaw hurriedly got what gear he wanted, then stood back while McCabe and the girls mounted up. He shook hands with each man, then rode off.

After they quickly passed from sight, Grady said: 'Let's backtrack. Take your knife and cut some brush. We'll wipe out a mile or so of tracks before the Mexicans catch up with us.'

Hinshaw said: 'My pa used to tell me that, when you traded with the Indians, you made your deal fast and got out before they figured out they'd been cheated. McCabe left in a big hurry, seems like.'

'McCabe used to be a trader with the Indians,' Grady said. 'Let's go, squirt.'

'I sure wish you wouldn't call me that,' Hinshaw said, and began chopping brush.

They worked along the back trail, dragging a clump of brush behind them, wiping out all sign of prior passage. After an hour of this Grady threw his piece of brush away and started to climb into the rocks. Hinshaw followed him, and, when they finally stopped, both men were out of breath. They hunkered down in a pocket that commanded a good view of the climbing trail. Far down it, a dust spiral rose in the still, dawn air. Grady said: 'Company.'

The Mexicans came into view, fifty mounted men led by Pedro Vargas. When Hinshaw saw him, he lifted his rifle and said: 'I can do what the State of Texas couldn't.'

'You want to get killed for it?' Grady asked. 'Simmer down, squirt. It's going to be a hot day.'

The Mexican bandits found the petered-out trail and stopped to talk it over. Vargas held a brief conference, then split his men into three sections, one to ride back and two to go on to see if they could pick up the trail ahead.

'Time to go,' Grady said, and they left the pocket, working on up the ridge and starting down the other side into a brush-choked ravine. They spent a miserable three hours beating their way through this and stopped at a small stream to fill their canteens.

'It's a good place to hole up,' Grady said. 'Tomorrow night we'll try to recross the ridge and make it to the river. I'd rather float along than walk.'

Traveling on the river had never occurred to Hinshaw. He said: 'How far does the river go?'

'It leads into a lake, that I know,' Grady said. He stretched out on the ground. 'We'll find it, when we get there.'

Hinshaw studied him at length. 'Don't this bother you, being afoot with the whole country swarming with bandits?'

'Squirt, if I let everything bother me that came across my path, I'd have worry lines on my face an inch deep.' He reached out and slapped Hinshaw on the arm. 'You just stick with your old Uncle Bill, and, by the time we get to Laredo, you'll be a grown-up Texas man.'

'You keep digging your spurs into me,' Hinshaw said, 'you'll have a fat lip by the time we get to Laredo.' He shook his head. 'For the life of me I can't understand why I didn't belt you instead of Anderson in the hotel room. You seemed such a nice guy at the time.'

'It just goes to show you that you never can tell,' Grady said. 'Hope the old man makes it back. He's got a job cut out for him, though. Those Mexicans have got a lot of Indian blood in them ... they're good trackers. It won't take them long to figure out that two of us are afoot, and they'll be trying to take up our trail. Late tonight will be time enough for us to break out. I don't think they'd expect us to move in their direction and break through, so that's where we'll go. I learned that fighting Indians.'

'Hell, there weren't any Indians to fight by the time you got old enough,' Hinshaw said.

Grady made a wry face. 'Now you've gone and ruined one of my favorite lies.'

They slept until dark. Grady seemed to be in no hurry to get going. Finally he moved out and started up the face of the mountain, but stopped as soon as the brush began to thin out. He and Hinshaw waited two hours, and they didn't talk. Finally Grady heard what he wanted to hear – horsemen moving around below them, pushing their way through the brush.

He led the way, climbing into the rocks, taking the hard, short way to the ridge far above them. The going was tough and Hinshaw's muscles began to ache and his breath grew short, but there was no stopping. When they reached the ridge, they found some mounted men moving along the trail. They waited until there was an opportunity, then slipped through them, and hunkered down two hundred yards beyond.

Grady thumped Hinshaw on the arm and made a silent clapping motion with his hands, then turned and slowly began to move down the other face of the slope. He came across a deer trail and took it, saying without stopping: 'The game will use this before morning. There won't be a trace of our tracks.'

'I suppose you learned that Indian fighting?'

'You're getting smarter all the time, squirt.'

Morning caught them in a valley. They took cover in some thick brush, ate cold beef and hard bread, then slept. The day was hot, and any sound woke them. In the afternoon a Mexican with a squeaky-wheeled cart came by. They watched him until he passed out of sight and didn't speak until the ox bell could no longer be heard ringing.

'How far to the river?' Hinshaw asked.

'Another day, I guess,' Grady said. 'We'll travel at sundown.'

'Couldn't we steal a couple of horses?'

'These peons don't have horses. Besides a missing horse would draw attention to us. Walking's good for the soul, squirt. If McCabe kept going, he ought to be near the border by now. The girls wouldn't slow him much, I don't guess. They're made out of tough stuff when it comes down to it.'

'That older one,' Hinshaw said, 'sounded like she'd about give up.'

Grady shook his head. 'She's been to hell and back, but one of these days a good man will come along and make her forget all that.'

'Yeah, but can that man forget?'

'I said, a *good* man, squirt.' He fell silent for a moment. 'She's kind of a pretty thing. I've seen her once or twice before … in town just last week.'

'I didn't know you knew about women,' Hinshaw said, smiling. 'I figured you for a curly wolf who liked his horse and that was all.' He stretched out. 'Ain't you a little old for her, Grady?'

'My pa was fifty the day he got married, and my ma was seventeen. He didn't worry about being too old for her, but her being too old for him.'

'I'll bet that's another of your lies,' Hinshaw said, and went back to sleep.

They walked out the night, moving north. It was tiring, for the miles were telling, and they just weren't walking men at heart. They had to be careful as they encountered roads and small farms and dogs, now and then, that would start barking. Every light they saw come on was a danger to them.

Twice they came close to meeting a posse of Mexican *rurales*, but they took cover, and this danger passed on. Hinshaw didn't have to be told what would happen if they were captured by *rurales*. This corrupt police force would sell them to one of Vargas's henchmen for a hundred *pesos*, and they'd die slowly and in a lot of pain.

A dark line of dense trees marked the riverbank. When they reached it, they sat down and listened to the water gurgle against the bank.

'I feel like a cigarette,' Grady said, and rolled one, then passed the makings to Hinshaw. They took their light off one match, then leaned back and enjoyed this brief pleasure. When the cigarettes were too short to hold, Grady got up. 'You go upstream and look for a dead log near the bank. I'll move down a ways. If you find something, whistle once.'

Hinshaw explored, but found nothing. Shortly he heard Grady's low whistle and went back. Grady stood near deadfall half over the riverbank.

'Just what I want,' he said. 'All those branches will keep it from rolling over all the time. Give me hand. We'll see if we can ease it in.'

They had to use the other branches as peaveys, and finally they managed to get the log afloat. Grady hooked a foot in one of the branches to keep the current from taking it on downstream. Then he took off his boot, switched feet, got the other off, and wrapped his boots in his coat. Hinshaw imitated him. They tied the sleeves of their coats around the bole of the log and thrust their rifles and gun belts between the bundle and the log.

'Always keep your gunpowder dry,' Grady said, and laughed softly.

'Boy, you sure know how to amuse yourself,' Hinshaw said. He lowered himself in the water and clung to the log. 'Shove off there, huh, admiral.'

Grady gave a push, grabbed the log, and the current started to move them gently downstream. He watched the bank move past, slowly, steadily, then he said: 'I can't even feel the blisters on my feet now. This is really livin', ain't it, squirt?'

'I don't know why it is,' Hinshaw said, 'but all the people I seem to associate with are real nuts. This damned water's cold.'

'So's a grave,' Bill Grady said. 'I'll take the water.'

Chapter Fourteen

Captain Guthrie McCabe and the two Cardeen girls made the journey from Lampazos de Naranjo to Laredo in complete comfort, riding in General Juan del Norte Vallejo Guadalupe Hildago's personal carriage and escorted by the general's aide-de-camp and fifty armed soldiers, picked personally for their bravery and devotion to duty and to Mexico. Under the existing treaty provisions, armed soldiers were not permitted on the American side, so the entire escort stacked arms on the Mexican side of the river and crossed in a body, delivering McCabe and his charges to Ranger Headquarters.

Major Carl Manners, alerted that his *ménage* was approaching, viewed the whole thing from his porch. Colonel James Gary stood by his side, and the colonel had a wry but sage comment to make about the whole proceedings.

'I never knew it to fail, Major. Send McCabe naked in the wilderness, and he will return on the shoulders of good fortune.' He smiled behind a wreath of cigar smoke. 'His explanation of this will be even more astounding.'

The carriage was approaching, and Manners could see McCabe, sitting between the two Cardeen girls. He was dressed in a fine dark suit, and he wore a spotless white shirt with ruffles running down the front. He carried a gold-headed cane. The Cardeen girls wore gay gowns and flaunted parasols.

When the carriage stopped, the Mexican captain immediately leaped off his horse and helped the girls and McCabe down from the carriage. McCabe carried a piece of wood under his arm. He spoke briefly with the captain. They embraced, then the captain got on his horse, wheeled his detail about, and recrossed the river.

Manners's curiosity was beyond control. He and Gary left the porch and met McCabe halfway across the yard. The old man said: 'May I present Rhea and Alice Cardeen. Major Manners, Texas Frontier Battalion, and Colonel James Gary, United States Army.'

'Captain,' Manners said, 'where are Grady and Hinshaw?'

'Being heroes,' McCabe said, 'but I suspect they'll wander in one of these days.'

'Perhaps you'd like to explain the grandeur of your arrival,' Manners said.

'I would,' McCabe admitted. 'But in the

shade.' He glanced at Gary, and smiled. 'Jim, would you see that the ladies are made comfortable?'

'You can use my quarters,' Manners said. 'The captain and I will have a drink in the meantime. I'm sure you'd like to hear this, Jim.'

'Having heard McCabe's explanations before,' Gary said, 'I wouldn't want to miss it.'

McCabe and Manners went inside. Manners took a bottle from his desk drawer and glasses, and brimmed three. He looked at the board under McCabe's arm. 'What's that?'

'A piece of wood Hinshaw picked up. A very interesting piece of wood.' He lifted his glass. 'To your continued health, Carl.'

'To hell with that. I never needed an excuse to drink a glass of whisky.'

Gary came in as though he had hurried a bit. He saw his glass and picked it up. 'I hope I haven't missed anything.'

'McCabe was about to explain,' Manners said, sitting down. 'Start from the beginning and leave out the lies.'

'My reports are always factual,' McCabe said. 'Long, perhaps, but factual.' He explained how they found Vargas's mountain camp and, in detail, covered the rescue of the two girls. He made certain that Manners understood his clever detective work. He knew this annoyed the major and dwelt on the subject until Manners began to drum his fingers. Gary was smiling faintly as though this were an old routine with him.

'This piece of wood, Carl, came from a weapons crate. Hinshaw snatched it in the heat of battle and brained a couple of Vargas's men with it. Due to some fluke of luck he carried it with him, and it was later discovered by Grady to have great importance.' He laid it on Manners's desk. Gary left his chair to have a look. 'As you can see, there's part of two words remaining on the wood. This was, I correctly assume, part of a shipping label. And you can figure out for yourself, the name spells Fred J. Early, Laredo, Texas.'

'It would appear to,' Manners said. 'All right, now where are Hinshaw and Grady?'

'In old Mexico,' McCabe said. 'In order to get the girls back safely it was necessary to take their horses. They volunteered, of course.' McCabe smiled. 'When a captain speaks, every ranger is eager to volunteer. In our own words, Carl, you've said that a ranger must be resourceful as well as brave and eager to do more than his fair share of...'

'All right, all right,' Manners said, waving his hand. He reached out and tipped up the board so he could again read the lettering on it. 'I trust you questioned the two girls?'

'Yes. They weren't able to see much, except that Vargas has a good-sized army and

244

plenty of weapons, including machine guns. They are without a doubt of German make, and my original notion, Carl, about them going south across the border…'

'Yes, yes, I won't argue with you there,' Manners said. He glanced at Jim Gary. 'I think this new evidence is enough to start a quiet investigation. I'm sure not going to approach Fred Early on the evidence of this board.'

'I'd like to accept this assignment, Carl,' McCabe said.

'All right. I was going to invite the colonel to give you a hand. Of course, this isn't Army business, Jim, but you might be…'

'I was holding my breath, afraid you wouldn't ask,' Gary said. He glanced at McCabe. 'You call the shots, Guthrie.'

'Just a minute,' Manners said. 'McCabe, damn you and your cloud of dust. You haven't told me how you got the carriage and the escort.'

'I thought you'd never get around to that,' McCabe said, smiling. He settled more comfortably in the chair. 'There I was, if you can picture it, deep in hostile territory with two women on my hands. What do I do about it? Grady and Hinshaw would pull the bandits off my back trail for a time, but they'd pick it up again. I figured I had a day and a half, or two at the most, so I asked myself just where the safest place for me

245

would be.' He clapped his hands. 'A guest of the Mexican army. Simple, huh? So I cut across the mountains to Lampazos de Jaranjo. I knew General Hildago had a large garrison there.'

'An old friend, I assume,' Manners said.

'As a matter of fact, no,' McCabe said. 'I figured the best thing to do would be to play this straight, for if the general caught me in a lie, I might end up in jail. Besides, there isn't an officer in the Mexican army who hasn't thought of collecting the reward for Pedro Vargas's capture, so the information I offered in the line of directions to his stronghold might buy me passage across the river. The general, it turned out, was a real gentleman of the old school. The Cardeen girls were cared for by his wife and three daughters. I got a bath, a shave, and one of his good suits.' He fingered the material. 'Not bad goods. Probably cost a man forty dollars in Austin.'

'Get on with it,' Manners said curtly.

'The general immediately dispatched three companies of infantry, one of cavalry, and a company of light artillery, then nicely supplied a carriage and an armed escort to the river.'

Carl Manners stared at him for a moment, then shook his head. 'Guthrie, if they ever hang you, I'm positive you'll talk them into using an old, weak rope.'

Jim Gary interjected: 'Guthrie, what kind

of an army does General Hildago have? By that I mean is it rag-tag or well drilled?'

'Spit and polish,' McCabe said. 'Enough to give Pedro Vargas a rough fight.'

'He won't do much with five companies after a four day march over rough terrain,' Gary responded. 'When I wired my report to the President, I asked for four regiments. Two of infantry, one of cavalry, and one artillery.' He sat for a moment in thought. 'Guthrie, I'd like to back out of our little investigation. If I can get the President's approval, I want to cross the river and talk with General Hildago. I'm not thinking of maneuvering Vargas between two armies ... he's too clever for that. However, we might try tricking him to this side of the river and have the Mexican army alerted to cut off his retreat back.' He got up. 'I think I'll compose a message and get it on the wire. Thanks for the drink, Major, and Guthrie, keep me posted on your investigation into the arms shipment.'

After he went out, Carl Manners said: 'He plays his cards close to his vest, doesn't he?'

'Is there any other way to play?' McCabe asked, and stood up. 'Well, I guess I'll get out of this suit. Wouldn't want to get it dirty wearing it around some office.' He wiped his finger across Manners's desk. 'Don't you ever dust?'

By travelling at night and hiding in the foliage along the river, Bill Grady and Martin Hinshaw made their way with the current. They let the river take them, after a week of slow motion, into the Río Grande. Then in daylight they reached the Texas shore, and Grady gave the log a push and sent it downstream. He declared: 'I never want to see so much as a tub of water for the rest of my life.' Then he looked at Hinshaw and laughed.

'What's so funny?'

'You ought to see yourself, clothes torn, knees out of your pants.'

'You're no collar advertisement yourself,' Hinshaw said. 'Where the hell are we?'

'About fifty miles southeast of Laredo,' Grady estimated. 'Lonesome country. Well let's start walkin'.' He shouldered his rifle. 'Come on, squirt. We've been gone too long now. You want the major to worry?'

'As Texas Rangers we ought to be able to get a couple of horses.'

Grady shook his head. 'You don't look like a Texas Ranger. Where's your badge and papers? The same place mine is ... in Manners's desk drawer. So let's start walking.'

They spent the whole day in a dreary march. That night they built a fire and cooked the last of their bacon and coffee. Before they bedded down, five men rode into their camp and pointed rifles at them.

It was Hinshaw who said: 'Now, wait a minute. Careful with those things.'

The firelight was not bright, and the mounted men were half shrouded in shadows. Bill Grady asked: 'Carlisle, is that you?' He peered at one tall, bearded man. 'It's me, Grady. I stopped at your place two years ago when you had the rustler trouble.'

The tall man dismounted, struck a match, and held it close to Grady's face. Then he whipped it out and said: 'Put up your repeaters. I know this man. We saw the fire from afar and thought a couple of Mexicans had crossed the river to rustle some beef. I've been running a few head in this area, and we were having a look-see.' He regarded Grady carefully. 'You look a little down in the heels.'

'We've been across the river,' Grady said. 'This is Hinshaw, a new recruit in my battalion.'

'Is that so?' Carlisle asked. He turned to one of his men. 'Let them have your horse, Harry. You can ride double with Smitty.' He rolled a cigarette, and passed the makings to Grady and Hinshaw. 'The next time I'm in Laredo I'll pick him up. Sorry I can't spare another.'

'Riding double suits me fine,' Hinshaw said.

Carlisle smiled, and looked from one to the other. 'I guess you've got your badge with you ain't you, Grady? I ask because I know a man don't enlist in the rangers for life, and I wouldn't want to lend a horse unless I was sure of getting him back.'

'I don't have my badge,' Grady said. 'But you'll get your horse back.'

'Well, now, it's just your word then, ain't it?' He drew on his smoke and shied it into the dying fire. 'It's kind of risky, being on a man's land with no real business. And having once been a ranger don't mean a thing to me. The worst sinner I ever knew had once been a fire-eatin' preacher.' He glanced at his men. 'We don't bother the law any more with our troubles, Grady. All you did was chase the Mexicans across the river. When I send one across, he don't come back.'

Bill Grady said: 'Carlisle, don't make a mistake now. Turn your men, and we'll go on about our business.'

'Now, I can't do that,' Carlisle said. 'All I know is that you're on my land and that I didn't invite you. I know you've been a law-man, Grady, but your friend I don't know from Adam's off ox. There's a stand of cottonwoods about two miles from here, near the river. They'll do.'

Martin Hinshaw said: 'Is this some joke? Mister, you're making…'

'This is the kind of a man you've got to do business with, squirt, the big Texas man who doesn't believe in taking the time to check facts before he shakes out a rope for a hanging.' He dropped his hand near his holstered revolver. 'Two to one, squirt. The odds scare you?'

Carlisle understood this and started to swing up the muzzle of his rifle. Bill Grady drew his .44, firing as it came level with his hip. Even then he shot a scant second behind Hinshaw who spilled a man from the saddle. As the man fell, he triggered his rifle into the air. The other two, moving slower than Carlisle, threw up their hands and quieted their horses with their knees, fearful that this animal skittishness would be misread.

Hinshaw walked over and rolled the dead man on his back. He said: 'I killed him, Bill.'

'Don't worry about it. Get their rifles.' He pointed his pistol at Carlisle, who sat on the ground with a smashed shoulder. 'I told you, you were making a mistake, and you're going to find it out when we get to Laredo.' He glanced at the two men still mounted. 'Get down. Help Carlisle on his horse and put the dead man across the saddle. Squirt, tie the two horses together.'

Grady covered the two men while they worked, then he had Hinshaw tie their hands behind them. 'Mount up, squirt, then cover them while I mount.' He doused the small fire with water from his canteen, then stepped into the saddle. 'All right, gentlemen, start walking. When you get to Laredo, your feet may have a few blisters, but that's nothing to what the judge will hand out.' He looked at Hinshaw and laughed. 'I've been a ranger for thirteen years, and that was the first time I ever pulled my gun quick. I didn't do bad, huh?'

'You were slower'n hell,' Hinshaw said. 'When we get to the barracks, I'll teach you how to do it right. I'm also going to teach you not to call me squirt.'

'That's going to be some education,' Grady said, and moved out with his prisoners.

Chapter Fifteen

Fred Early left his store and walked down the street a block to Batiste Rameras's saddle shop. Rameras was talking to a customer. When he finally finished, Early went over to the counter. Two men worked at their benches, and Rameras spoke to them in Spanish. They left the shop. He started to close the front door, and Early said: 'Don't do that. Sending your workers out before noon is suspicious enough. This afternoon I want you to come over and measure my motorcar for a new top. To anyone who's started thinking, that will stop them.'

'You're a cautious man,' Rameras said. He was short, very heavy through the chest and shoulders, and, although he was growing large in the stomach, there was still a great power in him. 'Recent events do not please me *Señor* Early. The two girls have been brought back, snatched from the very hands of El Jefe.'

'He ought to learn to take a better grip, then,' Early said. 'It's no concern of mine.'

'Men will talk of this and laugh. El Jefe does not like to be laughed at. The old one was gone and came back with an escort of Mexican soldiers. The other two have not returned.' He swore softly. 'Three men defying the army of El Jefe. It's not good.'

'One of those men was Martin Hinshaw,' Early said. 'You remember the father, Batiste?' He enjoyed the shock and rage on Rameras's face. 'What do you want from me now, Rameras? More machine guns?'

Rameras remained silent for a moment. 'So, the son comes back? Ah, it is a sweetness to me, a rare wine that I will drink. The old man, McCabe, must die. The other two may die with him, particularly Hinshaw. I want it arranged.'

'Arrange it yourself,' Early said. 'I'm a merchant, not a killer.'

Rameras shook his head. 'I will kill them myself, but first they must be brought to me under some pretense. Put your mind to it, *señor*. I'll send my man to you in two days.'

'I don't want any part of it,' Early said flatly.

Rameras smiled. '*Señor*, we both play a dangerous game. El Jefe will be the emperor of all Mexico, and you will be a very rich man. But to be either, no mistakes can be made. We would hate to lose you, *señor*, as a friend, but if you threaten us or refuse to co-operate, we would have to reveal the source of our arms and find another.'

'I see,' Early said. 'I either take orders or you cross me, is that it?'

'Plainly put, yes,' Rameras said.

Early shrugged. 'All right, I can't fight that. I'll see what I can do.'

He left the shop, returned to his own store, and went into his office, closing the door. This would take some figuring out, he decided, and spent an hour in deep thought, finally arriving at a conclusion. From his file he took a thick sheaf of folders, put them in a leather satchel, then went out in back of the shed for his motorcar. Early drove out of town and took the road to Ranger Head-quarters, stopping away from the main building because there were some horses tied there and he didn't want to booger them.

He went into the headquarters building, carrying the satchel, and spoke to the ranger on duty there. 'I would like to see Major Manners on urgent business, so if you'll tell him I'm here...'

'The major's got someone in his office now,' the ranger said.

'This is most vital,' Early said.

'There ain't anything that crossed the major's desk that ain't vital. If you'll just wait...'

'I can't!' Early shouted, and burst past the ranger, flinging open the door to Manners's office. The conversation stopped, and they all looked a round: McCabe, Grady, and Martin Hinshaw. The ranger recovered from his surprise and grabbed Fred Early by the arm, intending to pull him out.

'What the hell is this?' Manners demanded.

'Sorry, Major, but he busted past me.'

'If Mister Early's that determined,' Manners said, 'then let him come in. Resume your post, Hardin.'

'All right, Major. Sure sorry.' He looked at Early as though he blamed him for making him look bad, then closed the door.

'Take a chair, Mister Early. You look a bit agitated.' Manners offered him a cigar, which he declined.

'Major, I'd like to talk to you ... alone.'

'I don't think there's anyone here you can't trust,' Manners said. 'Besides, it'll save me from telling them later.'

Early appeared nervous, and he licked his

lips. 'I hardly know where to begin, really. The whole thing is so shocking, so monstrous.'

'You just tell me and let me decide,' Manners said.

Early looked at each of them, then said: 'I believe, much to my horror, that I can tell you who is getting firearms to the bandits.'

He waited for the shock of this to take effect. Manners merely puffed on his cigar, and McCabe went on paring his fingernails. Hinshaw and Grady said nothing at all.

Again Early looked at each of them. 'I'm not joking.'

'I'm sure you're not,' Manners said. 'But we hear so many accounts of treachery and violence that we're hardened to it. Go on.'

'You all know that I am a businessman. In addition to my local trade I operate a mail-order business. These last few years the paperwork began to mount up, and it was either neglect the local trade or take on a partner to handle the mail-order business.' He paused for several minutes, then spoke in a much softer voice. 'I took Joe Sanders into the company, much to my sorrow.' He closed his eyes and shook his head. 'This is difficult for me, Major ... he's soon to be my father-in-law.'

'We appreciate the difficulty,' Manners said. 'But let's have the whole of it.'

'Quite by accident,' Early said, 'I was

searching some back files for records four and five years old. I rarely go into them, and I came across these.' He patted the satchel. 'Immediately I saw that the merchandise ordered and delivered to my loading platform far exceeded the material sold over my counter or through legitimate mail-order channels. Indeed, the weight of many crates indicated that they bore firearms and ammunition rather than the line of cutlery and imported goods I generally handle.' Again he patted the suitcase. 'These bills of lading, invoices on shipments, were handled solely by Joe Sanders. Once my mind began working on the problem, it became horribly simple to see what was happening under my very nose. Sanders's wagons hauled all the merchandise from either the dépôt to my store, or from Corpus Christi to my store. His men handled it, unloaded it, uncrated it, and his men packed goods for shipment. Joe Sanders handled all the paperwork.' He struck his hand angrily against the satchel. 'To think that he's used me, all the while living on the fringe of poverty with that dear sweet girl working to support him while he hid his riches from this horrible business ... it makes me almost ill.'

'Don't throw up on the floor,' Grady said dryly.

Early stared at him.

Manners said: 'Mister Early, I trust you

intend to leave those papers here for our examination?'

'Yes. Naturally.'

'Then return to your business and leave this to us,' Manners said. 'In no way let Joe Sanders know that you suspect a thing. We'll lay a trap for him, catch him red-handed.' He got up from behind his desk and offered a hand. 'It's through civic, high-minded men like you, Mister Early, that we will bring peace and law to this troubled patch of Texas. We owe you our great debt of gratitude.'

'I was only doing my duty,' Early said. His expression grew impressively sad. 'That dear sweet girl. If only the truth could be withheld from her.'

'I'm sure,' Manners said, 'that she never need know the whole truth, if you know what I mean. I'm sure that you can, with patience, Mister Early, and great love, ease her over the shock.'

'Thank you, sir,' Early said humbly. 'Major, I'm very sorry for the things I said and my attitude when I called on behalf of the citizens.'

'I understood at the time,' Manners said, and escorted Early to the door. He went out to the porch, watched him get in his car, and then came back in and toed the door closed.

'Boy,' Grady said, 'if I could lie like that, I'd have a bottle in one hand, a woman on my lap, and not a worry in the world.'

'There's a strong chance that he's telling the whole truth,' McCabe said. He looked at Hinshaw. 'You're with Grady?'

'All the damned way,' Hinshaw said. 'Major, you didn't believe a word of it, did you?'

'I go by facts,' Manners aid. 'I don't make my judgment of a man because I like the girl he's engaged to.' He pointed to the satchel. 'Hand me that. I'll go through this stuff, and if I think there's enough to arrest him on, I'll have Sanders brought in.' He took out his watch and looked at it. 'I understand the judge is leaving on the five o'clock train. Grady, clean up and get into some decent clothes and ride to town. Ask him to stay over another week. We may need him badly.'

Grady and Hinshaw left the office together and walked to the barracks. Hinshaw said: 'Every time I get ready to teach you some manners, you up and say something that makes me like you. That's frustrating as hell.'

'You shouldn't let that stop you,' Grady said. 'You want to teach me something, squirt, then you just go ahead.'

'There you go again, destroying that nice feeling I had.'

They carried water for each other, took baths, shaved, and changed into clothes that were clean and unpatched. Since Grady was going to town and Hinshaw wanted to go along, he asked the major for permission. Since Manners was in a mellow frame of mine, he granted it.

They rode out together, stopped at the saloon for a drink, then went to the hotel to deliver Manners's request to the judge. Hinshaw's relationship with the bench had always been uncertain. He waited in the hall for Grady to conclude his business.

They found themselves on the street with time on their hands. Hinshaw said: 'I think I'll go see Batiste Rameras. It's been some years.'

Grady frowned. 'Better stay away. If there's trouble, the major won't like it.'

'Hell, there was trouble before the major ever came into my life,' Hinshaw said.

Rameras's place was easy to find, and Hinshaw went in, followed by Bill Grady. The Mexican was behind the counter, and he looked at Hinshaw a moment before a full recognition came to him. Then Rameras's heavy face pulled into solid planes.

Hinshaw said: 'It's been a long time, greaser. There's one Hinshaw and one Rameras left ... which is one too many.'

'I will not quarrel with the law,' Rameras said.

Hinshaw took off his badge and gun belt and handed them to Grady. 'You watch him, Bill. He likes a knife.'

'There won't be any of that,' Grady said.

'You're a fool, squirt. The old man will throw you in the stockade for this.'

'Who cares? Are you coming out from behind the counter, spik, or do I have to come back there and get you?'

Ramersas laughed. 'I will come to you gladly.'

He ran around the end of the counter, and Hinshaw found that he just couldn't wait. He rushed to meet Rameras, and they met with surprising impact. Rameras tried to grab Hinshaw around the neck, but the smaller man ducked away and smashed Rameras flush in the mouth. Rameras kited back, bounced against the counter with enough force to move it ten inches, then spat out a tooth and some blood.

When he came at Hinshaw, he came with a quirt snatched from a quill of them on the counter. He opened a cut on Hinshaw's shoulder with it. There was nothing to do but retreat and get cut, and Hinshaw did it, backing to the door, taking the blows on his arms as much as he could. The quirt opened angry cuts and tore his shirt to ribbons from shoulder to wrist, then he was outside, and a crowd was gathering.

At first the quirt hurt him terribly, then there was no more pain, and he just reached out with his hands and grabbed it and gripped hard so it wouldn't slip in the blood. He jerked Rameras clean off the porch, wheeling away as he pulled so that Rameras's weight came full on the hitch rack, splitting the long pole, and dropping him to the dirt. Without hesitation Hinshaw picked up a two-foot length of the wood. He never let Rameras get to his feet. He broke his shoulder and opened his scalp, and, as Rameras fell, he smashed him alongside the jaw, then threw the piece of wood away.

The crowd stood there, making no sound at all. No one offered to look at Rameras to see if he was dead or not. Hinshaw looked at the downed man, and he was sorry that it had ended so quickly, for he found no satisfaction in this at all.

Bill Grady said: 'Was it worth it, squirt?'

Hinshaw turned slowly to look at Brady. The buildings started to lean crazily, and, when he collapsed, Grady caught him and held him.

'Where's the doctor's office?' Grady asked.

A bystander said: 'Two blocks down and one to your right. But he ain't there.'

'Where the hell is he?' Grady wanted to know.

The man thought a minute. 'Over to Joe Sanders's place, I guess. He likes his checker games.'

'Thanks,' Grady said, and hoisted Hinshaw to his shoulder.

He hurried down the street, watching for loose boards in the walk so he wouldn't stumble and fall. *The damned young fool,* Grady thought. *All that hurt for nothing.* But there was no telling him anything. Had to learn it all himself. The squirt.

Sanders and the doctor were on the porch. Ella came out as Grady brought Hinshaw to the porch.

'Take him inside,' the doctor said, opening the door.

'What happened?' Ella asked.

'He had a fight,' Grady said. 'With Batiste Rameras.'

'What about?'

Grady put Hinshaw on the horsehair sofa, and the doctor brushed him aside so he could work. 'Get my bag,' he said. 'It's in the hallway.'

Ella got it, and gave it to him. 'I asked you what about?' she queried Grady again.

Bill Grady shook his head. 'I don't think he even knew. Maybe it was because he just had to lick Rameras once. Now he knows it wasn't any good. It never is. Why is it a man can't get smart without getting hurt?'

Chapter Sixteen

Dr Garrett left the Sanders house to go uptown and tend to Batiste Rameras. Ella Sanders was quite capable of getting Hinshaw on his feet. A shot of Joe Sanders's whisky helped. After Hinshaw was sitting up, she got one of her father's shirts to replace his ruined one.

'Some fight,' Bill Grady said, and Hinshaw looked around at him.

'I remember him falling before I did,' Hinshaw said.

'Yeah, you whipped him. Wait until the major hears about this.' He tossed Hinshaw's gun belt and badge on the sofa. 'I knew you wouldn't remember where you put 'em, so I brought 'em along. How do you feel?'

'Like my arms are afire.'

'You took a whipping before you got to him,' Grady said. He glanced at Ella Sanders. 'I guess I'll go out and finish a checker game on the porch. Whistle when you're ready to leave.'

After the front door slammed, Hinshaw said: 'It seems that every time we meet I've been fighting. I'm good for other things, you know.'

'No, I didn't know,' she said. She smiled. 'Yes, I really did know. Did it help your grudge any?'

He shook his head. 'Not a bit.' He got up, and stood unsteadily for a moment. 'Seen Mister Early?'

'Yes.'

'When's the wedding?'

'In the fall,' she said. 'Does it matter to you, Marty?'

'It might to you,' he said, and let the puzzled expression on her face remain there. 'Ella, I had no idea I'd end up here in your parlor, but since I am here, I'd like to talk to you.'

'All right, Marty.'

'Do you suppose we could go and sit on the back porch?'

She hesitated, then nodded, and went through the house. They sat on the steps where the shade was good and cool, and he rolled a cigarette before saying anything.

'Some of the things I'm going to ask are going to sound strange to you, but I'd like straight answers.'

'It's the only kind I give, Marty.'

'I hear that your dad's a partner with Fred Early. He must be doing pretty good with all Early's mail-order business.'

'It's constantly expanding,' she said. 'Dad pours the profit back into the business. I don't understand a lot about it because I'm

265

gone so much, and Fred doesn't discuss his business with me.' She smiled faintly. 'He has some old-fashioned notion that a woman's mind is incapable of understanding the ramifications of commerce. Why do you ask?'

'Curious mostly. It sounds like a real good thing … your dad being able to handle the paperwork right here at home. But knowing you, I can guess that he gets a lot of help.'

'Actually I've never helped him at all,' Ella said. 'Dad's the first to admit this, and I think he's even proud of it, but he never had a chance to finish the second grade in school. He can't read much at all, except figures. He always said that all a man had to know was how to multiply, add, and subtract. His writing is even worse. Watch him sign his name sometimes. He draws it like a picture.' She folded her hands around her raised knees. 'I've always thought that Fred took him on because of me. You know, his being almost one of the family. But it gives him something to do, and it makes him feel like he's worth something. It's not easy to be crippled, Marty. At first, I wanted to help him, but he wouldn't have it, and I was away most of the time on my job. Then I thought about it and just kept my nose out of it.'

'You're a sensible girl, Ella.' He got up. 'Well, I've raised my dust for today. Grady will want to be getting back.' He turned to the door and paused. 'You're going to marry

Fred Early. Do you love him?'

'Why, that's a silly question. Would I marry a man I didn't love?'

'I guess not. But what is it in him that you see, Ella?'

She thought about it. 'I really don't know. I suppose I'll have to find out, won't I?'

Grady had just lost his second game and was ready to leave before he lost another. They thanked Ella Sanders and her father and walked back toward the center of town to get their horses.

There was a sprinkle of loungers along both sides of the walk. They watched the two rangers while they untied their horses. Then Fred Early came out of his store and approached them. He took hold of the bridle of Hinshaw's horse.

'You are aware, I suppose, that you have without provocation assaulted one of our oldest citizens,' Early said.

'If you don't let go, I'm liable to assault another one,' Hinshaw said. 'How is the spik? Flat on his back?'

'You really hurt him,' Early said. 'Why?'

'Because the Rameras family taught me to hate them,' Hinshaw said. 'Ask around. Someone may remember my old man. He killed the whole damned family except Batiste. I may take care of that, if he gets in my way.' He pulled his horse around and rode out of town, Bill Grady trailing him by three yards.

As soon as they returned to the ranger camp, Hinshaw put up the horses, then went to headquarters to speak to Major Carl Manners. He had to wait fifteen minutes in the outer office before Manners invited him inside.

'Major, there's something important I'd like to discuss with you.'

'Anything discussed in this office had better be important, or I'll have you tossed out. Sit down, Hinshaw, and make it brief.'

'It's about what Fred Early said. I don't know if you had a chance to look at those papers yet, but I figure Fred Early for just about the smartest crook that ever squatted over a pair of boots. The whole set-up was perfect for Early, Major. He found a man who was still in the freighting business, an old salty cuss who couldn't read or write much. And the girl was out of town most of the time which gave Early all the leeway he wanted.'

'That's not very plain,' Manners said. 'Start again.'

'I'm not good at explaining,' Hinshaw said. 'But this is how it works. Early wants to keep himself clear in case there's trouble, so the easiest way to do it is to have a partner. A perfect partner, a man who's uneducated, a man who'd trust him. All right, Joe Sanders is near perfect in that respect. He trusts Early on account of his daughter being engaged to him. And Early always makes a point to bring papers over for Sanders's signature when the girl ain't there to check anything.'

'That last is a guess, Hinshaw.'

'But damn' close. Sanders is crippled. He can't get around hardly at all, so it's logical to figure that Early brings the stuff to him. Now ain't that so?'

Manners rubbed his chin. 'All right, I'll accept that. So Sanders signs for everything. But if Early has been using him, why did he come here and inform on Sanders?'

'Because in some way he no longer needs Sanders, or he wants out, and now it's time to get out with a clean shirt tail. That was the idea all along … to have Sanders as a partner for that time when the whole thing would be finished. That way Early could claim complete innocence while Sanders took the blame as the crooked partner.'

'It's a theory, and that's all,' Manners said. 'But it's a theory I'll keep in mind. What's the matter with your arms? They look fat.'

'I … ah … got in a fight, Major. He used a braided quirt, and I used a piece of wood. Those are bandages. That's what makes 'em fat.'

'Who did you fight with and what about?'

'Batiste Rameras, Major, and I guess it was just because he's a Rameras and I'm a Hinshaw.'

'Damn it, you can't do things like that! You're a peace officer with proud traditions to uphold.'

'Well, I took my badge and gun off,' Hinshaw said.

Manners closed his eyes for a moment, then said: 'Return to your barracks until I call for you. Was Sergeant Grady there?'

'He held my gun and badge.'

'Good Lord,' Manners said. 'Go to your barracks and tell Grady I want to see him right away. And you stay in your barracks where I can find you.'

Hinshaw left the building and walked across the dusty yard, whistling softly. He found Grady in his bed, smoking and reading an old newspaper.

'I told the major,' Hinshaw said, hanging up his gun belt. 'He wasn't mad at all.'

Grady lowered his paper. 'What did he say?'

'Oh, something about traditions of the something or other.'

'No, no. How did he say it?' He swung his feet to the floor. 'Did he shout?'

'No, I wouldn't say so,' Hinshaw said. 'Fact of the matter is, he was pretty nice about it.'

'Wait a minute now. Did he close his eyes?'

'Yeah, he did that. He wants to see you right away. Said I should tell you.'

'One more thing. Did he say … "Good Lord"?'

Hinshaw thought a minute. 'Yeah, he said that. How did you know?'

'I just lost my sergeant's rating,' Grady said. 'When your arms heal, I'm fairly going to take the difference in pay out of your hide.'

'Aw, he wouldn't do that,' Hinshaw said. 'I just did him a big favor.' He stretched out on his bed and reached for Grady's fallen newspaper. As soon as Grady left, he started to read it.

Colonel James Gary was writing a letter to his wife and children. The job depresed him for he could not help but compare the sheltered condition of his own with the Cardeen girls, homeless, without family, soiled by their horrible days of captivity. It was so sharp in his mind that he wrote of it in a separate letter meant only for his wife, and afterward he felt much better.

He had an appointment with Major Manners at four and lay down for a few hours' rest. The telegrapher interrupted him with a message that had just come in. Gary read it.

Colonel James Gary, U.S. Army
On the Border, Laredo, Texas
    Use your own judgment in negotiations. Have full confidence in you.

                                        T.R.

It was the key he needed. He got up and went to headquarters. Manners and McCabe were talking, and Gary hesitated to interrupt, but he was waved into a chair.

'Glad you showed up,' Manners said, 'for I was just about to send for you. We've had an odd bit of luck here, or perhaps it isn't that at all. When Grady and Hinshaw ran into Carlisle on the plains, they didn't realize that they were forgetting a vital link in the chain of circumstances surrounding the gun running. Carlisle and his men are being charged with murder. For some time we've known that he hangs every Mexican he finds on his property. One of his men broke, and he's offered us a deal.'

McCabe said: 'We still do make deals, Jim.'

'I'm not against it if the profit is high. What was the deal?'

'He'll reveal the hiding place of some goods that've been stored at Carlisle's place. Goods dropped off by Joe Sanders's teamsters and plainly designated for Fred Early's store.' Manners rubbed his hands together. 'In exchange he wants the murder charge dropped. We've agreed to aggravated assault on Hinshaw and Grady. That's sixty days at the most.' He looked at Grady. 'This doesn't sound good for Joe Sanders, Colonel. It's unlogical as hell that Early would store anything on Carlisle's place. A man in the gun-running business wouldn't trust another man that far. No, from all indications of it, I'd say that Sanders was doing the illegal business and holding out on Early.'

'Are you thinking about a warrant?' Gary asked.

'Yes,' Manners said. 'The judge will issue it. McCabe will serve it.'

Gary smiled. 'Major, I was going to ask for the loan of McCabe. I got permission to dicker with the Mexican army, and I thought we'd take a ride across the river.'

'You could send someone else with the warrant,' McCabe said. 'Grady's not on patrol or on duty.'

'Grady's been busted to private,' Manners said. He got up and went to the door to speak to the ranger on duty there. 'Get Hinshaw here on the double.' He came back and sat down. 'Somehow he's got the idea that duty's a lark. He might as well find out what it's like right now.'

McCabe frowned. 'Hinshaw's taken a fancy to the girl, Major. It's not really fair.'

'Since when have I been fair?' He looked steadily at McCabe. 'Are you afraid to see him put to the test to find out what kind of a man he is? He's run from the tough things in life before. Maybe he'll run now. If he does, it's better that we find it out before he runs when it can cost a man is life.'

Hinshaw was prompt, and Manners came

right to the point. 'In the morning I want you to go to town and have the judge swear out a warrant for Joe Sanders's arrest. Take a buggy with you so you can bring him back to the stockade.'

Hinshaw's mouth dropped open. 'Arrest him? Major, he's no more guilty than I am.'

'It's not my policy to debate my decisions with recruits,' Manners said. 'If you decline to accept your duty, say so, and I'll draw up your discharge papers.'

'Maybe you just ought to do that,' Hinshaw said flatly.

'That was easy for you to say,' Manners told him. 'Quitting gets easier every time you walk out, doesn't it?' He slapped his hand flat on the desk. 'Hinshaw, how many chances do you think life's going to hand you?' He waved his hand. 'I'll get someone else.'

'Never mind,' Hinshaw said. 'I'll serve the warrant. But I won't like it.'

'Nobody asked you to like it,' Manners said. 'I don't like it, either, because every time I have one served, I also run the risk of making a mistake.'

'You've sure made one this time,' Hinshaw said. 'I'll leave after breakfast, and I sure hope you'll excuse me if I drive slow.'

Chapter Seventeen

Pedro Vargas camped in barbaric splendor twenty-five miles from the river while his army licked their slight wounds sustained in the encounter with General Hildago's forces. Vargas's claim to having an army was valid only when judged by number. He had nearly twenty-four hundred men in his camp, and he kept them only when the looting was good. A handful of lieutenants carried out his orders or passed them on down the line, for this was an army of individuals, with a man free to come and go as he wished. After a good raid, Vargas always got new recruits, poor *peones* eager to share in the prize money, but that always turned out to be very small, and, if any of them could have manipulated simple mathematics, they would have soon realized that they fought and died for less than eighteen cents a day.

Vargas's share was somewhat larger. He took a straight fifty percent. The rest was largely divided up among his lieutenants. The soldiers were paid off in women and whisky. Like all revolutionary armies, Pedro Vargas was pressed hard by logistics. He had to carry his wealth wherever he went – for his was a pay-as-you-go army, and in dealing with Mexican police officials the pay was not cheap. Neither were the *yanquis*. He had been brooding about this.

Vargas spent much time in his tent, sleeping, thinking, hating, and loving the young Mexican girls who were about. He had two guitarists who played almost constantly for him and a dozen servants who tolerated his moods.

One of his lieutenants entered his tent, a risky thing since El Jefe's moods were unpredictable. 'A man from Batiste has come into the camp, *jefe*.'

'Bring him to me,' Vargas said, and held up his wine glass to be filled by one of the servants.

The lieutenant returned a few minutes later with a Mexican in tow. 'I am in the employ of Batiste Rameras,' the man said quickly.

'So?'

'He is unable to help you further, *jefe*.'

Vargas stood up. 'I will have his ears for watch fobs. What does Rameras think I am doing? Playing a game with the *yanquis*?'

'He is in bed with a split in the skull,' the Mexican said. 'There was a fight between him and the young ranger, Hinshaw. A most brutal affair, *jefe*. For hours my *patrón* did not regain his senses.'

Vargas cursed volubly again. 'That man

Hinshaw is a curse on my soul. First his interference on the trail, then his sneak attack on my camp to free the girls, now this.' He slammed his fist into his palm. 'I have had enough of this *gringo*. Luz, get me twenty men with souls of steel. We cross the border tonight.'

'Twenty, *jefe?*'

'Your ears are full of wax? Go!' As soon as the lieutenant dashed out, he turned to the Mexican. 'Sit. Eat and drink what you want.' He napped his fingers at the guitarists. 'Play him a bright air. *¡Andale!*'

'You are a savior, *jefe*. A true friend of the people.'

'Of all this I am aware,' Vargas said. 'But it is good to hear it from sincere lips.' He began to dress for war, buckling on a much-silvered cartridge belt and a pair of pearl-handled pistols. He said to the Mexican: 'You will become one of my *bandidos* tonight, my friend.'

The man was astonished and a little frightened by the prospect. '*Jefe*, my soul is not of steel, I am ashamed to say.'

'You will do even more dangerous work,' Vargas said. 'Go back across the river. Find Hinshaw, then come to the edge of town. I will be waiting along the river.' He clapped the man on the shoulder. 'I will make an example of him. You will be a hero in my camp. Now go!'

'But, *jefe*, I have yet to finish my meal. And

277

the song is not ended!'

'Would you deny me revenge because you are selfish and stupid?'

The roaring voice drove the Mexican from the tent, and Vargas stepped out a few minutes later. His lieutenant had formed a group of twenty men. They waited with their horses. 'We go,' Vargas said, and stepped into the saddle.

Martin Hinshaw's departure from the ranger camp was unauthorized, yet he went, understanding that, if he were caught, the major would likely dismiss him from the service. Taking a horse from the stable was just too risky, so he walked into town and kept to the back streets and alleys until he came to Ella Sanders's house. It was well after eleven o'clock, and he didn't expect to find any lights on. He went to the door and knocked until Ella came downstairs with a lamp in her hand. She parted the lace curtain over the door and held the lamp high so that it shone on his face. Then she slid the bolt.

'Marty, I should be angry with you, coming here at this hour. What do you want?'

'I've got to talk to you.'

She sighed. 'I have to leave on the six-fifteen train. Can't it wait?'

'No, it can't,' he said.

'All right, come on in.' She held the door open for him, then said: 'Who's that?'

He looked around and saw the man standing by the gate. He sprinted off the porch while the man wheeled and dashed down the street. Hinshaw chased him for a half a block, then gave it up as the man ran under a street light and disappeared into the darkness.

Hinshaw went back to Ella Sanders. 'Just some Mexican looking for something to steal,' he said, stepping into the house.

'Come on in the parlor but keep your voice down. Dad's sleeping.'

She put the lamp on a small table, and sat on the sofa. He said: 'I don't know how to start, Ella. The beginning, I guess. This afternoon I thought I could do my duty like the major said, but I guess I can't, because the major's wrong.'

'What's the major wrong about?'

'About your dad selling machine guns to the Mexican bandits.'

She was shocked and showed it. 'What a vicious lie! Is the major insane? He must be to think a thing like that. What proof could he have...?'

'Only what Fred Early gave him,' Hinshaw said.

Now she was hurt as well as shocked. 'Marty, you're lying to me.'

'Look at me,' he said. 'Do I look like I'm lying? Ella, I'm not much of anything, but I love you. I wouldn't hurt you if I could help it. When I came here tonight, it was to get your dad in a buggy and light out.'

'Is that all you know? To run?'

'I deserve that,' he said, 'only I know Fred Early's the one the major wants, not your dad. But I can't prove that. I've got nothing to base it on except my judgment of the man. He's no good.'

She studied him for a long moment, then said: 'You believe what you're saying, don't you?'

He nodded. 'Tomorrow, the major's handing me a warrant. I've got to take your father back to the stockade and lock him up. Early brought a whole satchel full of papers as proof that your dad was trading in guns. And a few other things have come up that look bad. I know Early's no good. Someday I'll prove it, and I hope it's before you're married to him.'

His manner added credence to his words, gave them force and truth. Ella knew him for a simple, direct man, and, as shocked as she was, she knew she had to hear the rest of it. 'What do you intend to do, Marty?'

'I wanted to spare you,' he said. 'I still do.'

She shook her head. 'We've got to do more than that. It's the truth we want, no matter how it hurts. Dad would want it that way. So do I. Tomorrow when you come with the warrant, Dad will be ready to go with you.'

'And Fred Early?'

She thought about it. 'I think it's easy for us to blame him. I love my father and assume him innocent. You love me, and because of that you assume he's...' She stopped, and lightly brushed a hand across her forehead. 'Did you say you loved me?'

'I said it. Shouldn't have, but I'm always saying things I shouldn't.'

A cane thumped on the ceiling. 'Dad's awake. You'd better go up. He'll want to know what you're doing here.'

Martin Hinshaw said: 'What'll I tell him?'

Ella smiled. 'You might say that you were courting me.'

'He'd never understand that.'

'He'll understand it better than the other. I'll tell him after you've gone.' She put her hand on Hinshaw's arm. 'I've got to prepare myself to lose either way, don't I? I mean, if Fred is right then I've got something to live with.'

'He's not right.'

'Then I've loved a man who's worse than a thief,' she said.

'You never loved him,' Hinshaw said. 'Just think of the things he's said that you really didn't like but overlooked, and you'll know that you never loved him.'

'How can you know he'd say anything...?'

'Because he's no good, and a no-good man has a lot of funny notions.'

Joe Sanders thumped again with his cane,

and Hinshaw turned to the stairs and started up. Ella went into the parlor to get the lamp.

Hinshaw reached the top landing before the front door crashed open. He whirled and saw the Mexicans crowding in, and he acted without thought, drawing his gun and firing as it came level with his hip. Two men fell, and the ones crowded behind fired back, the bullets puckering the steps around him, gouging strips of plaster and paper from the wall. Instead of retreating, he vaulted the banister and dropped level with the hall and crouched there, working the hammer, driving them back with their wounded. For a moment he thought he saw Pedro Vargas, but he was sure that he was mistaken.

Hinshaw realized that he couldn't defend the house from the bottom floor, so he grabbed Ella by the arm, jerked her into the hall, and shoved her up the stairs. The front windows lost their glass as two Mexicans forced themselves into the house, and glass came down in the rear of the building as they broke into the kitchen.

When he and Ella reached the top of the landing, Hinshaw stopped. 'Get a mattress!' he yelled.

The door to Joe Sanders's room opened, and he dragged himself out. He had his pistol and a box of cartridges. Ella came back with the mattress. Hinshaw rolled it and used it for a shield while he went belly down on the landing. The Mexicans were crowding into the house. He could hear them talking as he punched spent shells from his gun and reloaded.

Hinshaw's view of the front door was uncluttered, and the Mexicans did not try to enter that way. Instead, they congregated in the parlor and the kitchen, out of sight. Then he heard Vargas curse them. *He was here!* And surely the bandit knew that the gunfire would attract attention, and that time would be running out for him, or maybe he didn't care. A man could want something so badly that he lost all care. It never occurred to Hinshaw that Pedro Vargas wanted him. He had automatically assumed that it was Joe Sanders whom Vargas sought.

Vargas's men had to get up the stairs, so they rushed it, ten strong, and Hinshaw fired point-blank into the mass while bullets thudded into the mattress and nipped the collar of his shirt. The men retreated, and Hinshaw turned his attention to his empty gun.

Joe Sanders made no sound. Hinshaw looked at him and found him leaning on the mattress, blood dripping down his face from the hole in his temple. Quickly he looked around and saw that Ella had barricaded herself in the bedroom. He was glad of that at least.

He reached over and took Joe Sanders's gun from his still hand and broke it open. It was unfired. *Well*, Hinshaw thought, *they got what they came after*. Three dead Mexicans lay in the open front door and two more on the stairs. One had rolled to the bottom.

Outside the house there was a stir, a rumble, the sound of men approaching on the run, and Vargas got out the back way. They had horses nearby, and Hinshaw heard them ride away. He got up and took a deep breath because he had the hard part to do. He went to Ella's bedroom and opened the door and found her standing by the dresser, her complexion like chalk.

'They've gone,' he said. 'You'd better sit down.' When she hesitated, he put his hands on her shoulders and forced her to sit on the edge of the bed. 'Ella, I don't know how to tell you, but your dad was unlucky.'

She looked at him, and her expression melted into grief. She began to cry silently. He turned away from her as, downstairs, men ran into he house. He met a crowd on the stairs. They stopped and looked at Hinshaw, and he realized that he was still holding his revolver. He holstered it and looked at Fred Early, who seemed to be leading them.

'Where is she?'

Hinshaw jerked his thumb toward the bedroom. 'In there, crying.'

Early started to push past so he could go

284

in to Ella's room, but Hinshaw blocked him with a stiff arm. 'Don't bother her.'

'We're engaged. I *never* bother her.'

'You bother me,' Hinshaw said, and shoved him into the arms of his friends.

'Poor Joe,' one man said sadly.

'Yes,' Early said, looking at Sanders. 'But maybe it was a blessing in disguise.'

'That's a hell of a thing to say,' a merchant remarked. 'A couple of you fellows give me a hand. We'll carry these Mexicans out and stack 'em in the yard.'

They left Early and Hinshaw standing on the stairs. Neither exhibited any intention of moving. Early said: 'You're a damned hero now, aren't you?' He laughed. 'Samson slaying the Philistines with the jawbone of an ass. Or rather an ass slaying…'

'You want to take a fast ride down the stairs?' Hinshaw asked. He grabbed Earl by the coat. 'Old Joe's dead, ain't he? Old Joe who couldn't read or write, he's dead and can't say a word in his defense. What did you do, tip Vargas off and have him come here and kill him?'

'You're out of your mind,' Early said, and knocked Hinshaw's grip loose. Ella opened the bedroom door and peered out. Early rushed to her and folded his arms around her. 'My dear, my dear.'

'Fred, I'm so confused, so lost.'

'I know. I know.'

Martin Hinshaw's expression turned bitter, and he walked slowly down the stairs and went out to stand on the front porch. He saw a Texas Ranger in the yard with a lantern. When the ranger saw Hinshaw, he showed a moment's surprise, then came to the porch. 'I guess the major'll want to talk to you.'

'Undoubtedly,' Hinshaw said.

Chapter Eighteen

The ranger rattled his keys until he found the right one. He unlocked the cell door and said: 'All right, Hinshaw, they want you to testify.' He stood aside as Hinshaw stepped out, then walked with him across the yard to the major's office.

The porch was crowded, and the inside waiting room was jammed. The two passed on through and went into Manners's office that now served as an inquest room.

Hinshaw was sworn in and took his seat. The judge asked the questions.

'State your name, please.'

'Martin Hinshaw.'

'Are you under arrest, Mister Hinshaw?'

Manners stood up. 'He's under disciplinary arrest, your honor. Purely a formality until the conclusion of the hearing.' He smiled

286

briefly. 'Mister Hinshaw is sometimes difficult to keep track of, and I wanted to assure your honor that he would be present when called.'

'Thank you, Major.' Judge Everett Calender stifled a smile. He was a gaunt, gray man well past the meridian of his life, solemn of manner, yet not without a deep stream of humor. 'Mister Hinshaw, will you relate the happenings of the night before last for the court?'

Hinshaw glanced at the people seated, especially at Ella Sanders, then gave a complete account of the gunfight at the Sanders house. When he finished, he thought he would be excused, but Judge Calendar had other notions.

'Mister Hinshaw, since you were confined to quarters at the time you broke house arrest and went to the Sanders home, you must have had a compelling reason, considering the consequences should you be found out. Will you state those reasons?'

'I went to warn Joe Sanders and give him a head start on the warrant I was ordered to serve. The deck was stacked against him.'

'I see,' Calendar said. 'Well, that's a matter for Major Manners to settle. Mister Hinshaw, when the battle started and you exchanged fire with the Mexican bandits, did you understand the purpose of the attack?'

'No,' Hinshaw said.

'But the attack broke off as soon as Joe Sanders had been killed?'

'Yes, sir,' Hinshaw said. 'But a lot of people were coming toward the house. The Mexicans had to get out or fight them.'

'That will be all,' Calender said.

Hinshaw stepped down, then asked: 'Can I remain?'

The judge glanced at Carl Manners, who nodded imperceptibly. Hinshaw took the chair next to him, and everyone in the room grew quiet. McCabe and Colonel Gary sat near the far wall, directly in back of Ella Sanders. Fred Early sat on the opposite side of the room, a sad expression on his face.

Calendar said: 'I want it clearly understood that this is not a trial but a preliminary hearing into the manner and cause of death of Joseph Sanders. In view of the written and spoken evidence, I have reached a conclusion. It seems evident that Joseph Sanders was engaged in the illegal sale and transportation of automatic weapons to the Mexican bandits. It also seems reasonable to conclude that due to some misunderstanding, some argument with the bandit leader, Pedro Vargas, he was killed. An indictment would have been in order had Joseph Sanders survived the attack. Since he is dead, and the arms traffic stopped, I direct that the matter be closed. Major Manners, you will so note it in your official report.'

288

'That's not true!' Ella shouted, and Fred Early immediately came forward to silence her.

'You and your god-damned law!' Hinshaw snapped, turning on Carl Manners. He doubled his fist and knocked Manners backward into the lap of the man sitting behind him.

One of the nearby rangers grabbed Hinshaw from behind and pinned him while Manners scrambled to his feet. His face was white with anger, and he ripped the badge from Hinshaw's vest.

'You're through as a ranger! Now you've got thirty minutes to clear out! Do you understand? Thirty minutes to gather your gear and git!'

'That suits me just fine,' Hinshaw said. 'The whole thing stinks.' He turned and rammed his way clear of the room, walking rapidly back to the barracks. It took him less than thirty minutes to pack what little he owned, check out with the paymaster, pocket his money and head for town.

The rest of the day he spent in the saloon, drinking beer, or walking around with his hands in his pockets, looking in the store windows. In the late afternoon he went to Ella Sanders's house. A stern-faced woman answered the door and told him Miss Sanders didn't want to see anyone.

Hinshaw had supper in a small restaurant

289

and played cards in the saloon until after ten. Then he walked down to the river and looked for a good spot under the trees where he could make night camp. For a time he seemed unable to make up his mind, then he selected a grove and found McCabe, Bill Grady, and Carl Manners waiting there.

They shook hands, and Manners said: 'You didn't have to hit me that hard, damn it.'

'Didn't you want it to look good?' Hinshaw asked. 'Bill, you got any heifer dust? I've run plumb out of smokings.'

'You're always out of something,' Grady said, handing over his sack of tobacco. 'What's Early been doing today?'

'Minding his store,' Hinshaw said. 'Do you think he was convinced that I've been given the boot?'

'Yes,' Manners said. 'Your being under arrest and all … then that outburst. Yes, I believe he's sold. Now you've got to sell him, Marty. He's lost his man, and he'll need another one, a desperate one. From now on you'll only be in contact with Grady. Here or across the river.'

'We'll work it out,' Grady said.

McCabe said: 'If I've got Early pegged right, he'll let the money greed drive him back in business. This time we want to make sure he doesn't weasel out of it and put the blame on a dead man.'

'Nailing his hide to the fence is a personal ambition of mine,' Martin Hinshaw said.

'Good luck,' Manners said. 'We'll be watching every move you make.'

'Don't get so close you shy off the game,' Hinshaw advised.

They left him then. He spread his blankets, stretched out, watched the stars, and finally, when he thought the time was right, he left his camp and went back into town. An easy cruise along the street found Fred Early. He was playing cards in the saloon.

Hinshaw used the alleys. With a rock, he broke the padlock off Fred Early's store. He went inside and fumbled around until he found a hammer and chisel. Methodically he pounded away at the dial on Early's safe. After he'd left a few deep chisel marks, he put the tools down and went to the front window where he hunkered down to watch the saloon across the street. He had quite a wait before he saw Early step out and pause on the porch. Hinshaw struck a match, holding it below the level of the window, but high enough so that Early was attracted by the light. Quickly he whipped out the match and went back to the safe, tapping and chiseling away at the lock. He felt a movement of air as Early eased open the rear door. He managed to be convincingly surprised when Early said: 'Don't move or I'll blow a hole in your back.'

Early moved to the lamp and lit it, then stood there, pointing a small .32 at Hinshaw. Early smiled and said: 'I never keep more than two hundred dollars in there. Hardly worth the trouble it's going to cause you.'

'To a man who's broke, that's a lot of money,' Hinshaw replied. He nodded toward the gun. 'Going to shoot me?'

'I guess not,' Early said. 'You can get from five to ten years for safe-cracking.' He looked at the badly battered dial. 'You don't even know what you're doing, Hinshaw. Come on in the office and close the door. And I don't have to remind you not to put your hand near your gun.'

'I'm not stupid,' Hinshaw said, and moved ahead of Early. As soon as he was in the office, Early closed the door and locked it. He put a match to the lamp, then went behind his desk and sat down. 'I had you pegged as a no-good from the day I first saw you.'

Hinshaw laughed. 'That's funny, because I had you pegged the same way. Now what?'

'You didn't last long in the rangers.'

'I don't last long anywhere where the pay is poor and boneheads are always telling me what to do.' He grinned. 'Now, you're no bonehead, Early. You packaged Joe Sanders up nicely and came off smelling like a flower. I kind of thought it would be nice to bust open your safe just to show you that someone could take something away from such a smart man.'

'But it didn't work out,' Early pointed out. 'You're still broke, and I'm holding a gun on you.'

Hinshaw shrugged. 'It's my luck, I guess.'

'You always work for the wrong people,' Early said. 'I could have told you that the rangers wouldn't do for you. Hinshaw, there's a wild streak in you. Law enforcement isn't your kind of business.'

'What kind is?'

Early thought for a moment. 'You ought to be a trader.'

'A man's got to have something to trade before he...'

'Oh, you have,' Early interrupted. 'You've got a five-year stretch in the Texas pen to trade.' He laid the .32 aside. 'I'll give you your choice. You can take the five years for breaking into my place and bunging up my safe, or you can take a job that will pay you a lot more than is in my safe.'

'Do you think you can trust me?' Hinshaw asked.

'Why not? You like freedom well enough to do as you're told.' He leaned back in the chair. 'No, I wouldn't trust you, Hinshaw. I don't trust anyone, but I can handle you.'

'Like you handled Sanders?'

'I didn't have anything to do with him

getting killed,' Early said.

'Then why set him up for the major?'

'Because Batiste Rameras wanted me to get you and McCabe up for a killing. Murder I want no part of. It was time to get out.'

Hinshaw frowned. 'You've told me a lot, Early.'

'Nothing that I couldn't take care of. You see, I could pick up this gun and kill you before you could make it through the door. And if you did make it, who would believe you? Especially after that blow-up in the hearing room.' He shook his head. 'You'll have to do this my way, Hinshaw.'

'All right,' Hinshaw said. 'What do I do?'

'You'll first straighten up the mess you made when you shot Carlisle. Hinshaw, you've caused me no little inconvenience. First Carlisle, then crippling Rameras. He won't be on his feet for another two weeks.'

'So soon? I thought I hit him harder than that.'

Early laughed. 'When he's up and around, I'm going to let you kill him.'

'I'll do it free,' Hinshaw said. 'What's at Carlisle's besides some stuff stored there? Maybe you didn't know it, but one of Carlisle's men shot off his mouth to the major.'

'There's nothing there but imported hardware,' Early said, smiling. 'The other merchandise was moved weeks ago. Carlisle's place is just right for certain purposes. It's

294

barren land, and most travelers steer clear of it. There are times when I wish to meet people and not to be seen, so I use Carlisle's place. I also conduct business there and, now and then, see a demonstration of a certain item offered for sale. It is also used as a stop-over and repair station for Sanders's wagons that I will now take over. You can run this place for me. I'll pay you a hundred and twenty a month, with more when you've shown me you're worth it.'

'I'd have asked for half of that,' Hinshaw said.

Early laughed. 'I don't believe in hiring cheap help.' He took out paper and pen. He wrote for a few minutes, then turned the paper around for Hinshaw's signature. 'That states that I caught you in a felonious act and have agreed to employ you as a means of rehabilitation. In the event that fails, I am releasing you to the custody of a peace officer and pressing charges. Now put your name to that or we don't do business.'

'You sure know how to cover your bets,' Hinshaw said.

'That's the only way to do it. Now sign it.'

Hinshaw scrawled his name, and Early put the paper away. 'There's one more thing,' he said. 'I know you've formed an unwarranted attachment to Ella Sanders. At no time do I want you to press yourself on her, or attempt to communicate with her. If she responds to my urging, we'll be married in two weeks. I wouldn't want there to be any doubt in her mind that she's getting the right man.'

'If it's part of the job, all right,' Hinshaw said.

'It is part of the job. If you go to the stable, I'll see that you get a horse. You can leave for Carlisle's tonight. And don't leave there without my permission.'

'Wouldn't think of it.' He started to get up, then stopped as Early put his hand on his revolver. 'What's the mater, Mister Early? Are you nervous?'

'Hiring a new man always entails some risks. Now don't disappoint me, Hinshaw.'

'I won't.' He turned, unlocked the door, and left the store by way of the alley. He went to the river and the grove of trees to get his blankets, and, as he was rolling them, Bill Grady appeared, stopping well back in the shadow of the trees. Grady spoke softly. 'Don't turn your head, squirt. If you can hear me, whistle softly.'

Hinshaw did, then stopped. 'I've got a job. Good pay but lousy business.'

'I'll tell the major.'

'I'm on my way to Carlisle's,' Hinshaw said.

'I'll see you there.'

'Be careful,' Hinshaw warned. 'He'll be watching me or having it done.' He put his bedroll over his shoulder and walked back to town. It was a comfort to him to know that Bill Grady would always be close by.

When he reached the stable, he found Early there and a saddled horse. 'Now and then you'll have guests at Carlisle's,' Early said. 'Be polite. Take care of them. And keep your damned nose out of their business.'

'That won't be hard,' Hinshaw said, mounting up. Before he turned out he asked: 'When does my pay start?'

'It's started,' Early said, and gave the horse a slap.

Chapter Nineteen

Bill Grady volunteered to take a buggy and drive Rhea and Alice Cardeen into town to meet the eastbound train. Colonel Gary and Guthrie McCabe were halfway to General Hildago's headquarters, so Grady did the job as a favor to Gary, and because he wanted to.

Their tickets were already bought so there was nothing to do but wait on the hard benches and grope for things to say. Grady smoked a cigar and kept watching the clock. Finally he said: 'It's best, I suppose. The colonel must have a nice home. You'll like it.'

'Yes,' Rhea said. 'But I've never been

underfoot in someone else's house.' She turned her head and looked at Grady. 'Why did he do it? Because he and his wife felt sorry for us?'

He thought a minute, then shook his head. 'I don't think Colonel Gary wanted you to be alone. He and his wife ain't offering you a place to stay, Rhea. He's offering you a home. That's more than I could offer, I guess.'

'What do you mean, Bill?'

He shrugged. 'I'm older than you. Maybe too old.' He laughed softly. 'Not much to look at, either. But I'd be good to you, Rhea. And Alice … she could live with us. I guess you think I'm a hard drinker, but I really ain't. I wouldn't drink at all except that it gets so blamed lonely at times. I've got eight hundred dollars in the bank at Corpus Christi, and half interest in a fishing boat. This job don't mean so much to me that I wouldn't give it up and go back to Corpus Christi.'

This was the longest speech Bill Grady had ever made to a woman, and Rhea knew it. 'Do you love me, Bill?'

'I guess I do,' he said. 'Maybe you don't believe I do on such short acquaintance, but it's a fact. I don't want to see you go away, Rhea.'

She studied her folded hands a while. 'It would be better if I did for a while. In the fall, maybe I'll come back.' She didn't look at him when she spoke. 'If I have a baby, you won't know it, Bill, because I'll come back alone. It's got to be that way.'

'It don't have to be,' he said. 'Hell, it ain't as though you'd...' He let it drop. 'Write to me, and I'll write to you. I don't write good, but I'll write anyhow.'

The station agent came over. 'Train's due in, folks. Sorry about your family, girls.' He went back to his duties. Grady gathered their grips and took them to the cinder platform.

At the edge of town, three blasts indicated the approach to the grade crossing. Rhea said: 'A shack is better than a mansion, Bill, when a woman ain't underfoot.'

'You'll have a house,' he said. 'As soon as this is over, I'm getting out and going to Corpus Christi. Everything will be dandy when you come back.'

The train rumbled into the station and stopped. The conductor got down with his step, and they had to get aboard. Alice went first and paused in the vestibule as Rhea said: 'Do you want to kiss me, Bill?'

'I guess I do,' he said, and clumsily put his arms around her. His embrace was brief, but he was smiling when he let her go. 'That was good, Rhea. I can wait.'

'Yes,' she said. 'The waiting isn't really long.'

She turned and went into her coach. Grady stood there until the train pulled out. Afterward he drove back to Ranger Headquarters and put up the rig.

Major Manners was in his office, and Grady sat down. Manners said: 'What's the smile for?'

'I sort of got myself engaged, I guess,' Grady said.

'To the older one?'

'Yep,' Grady said. 'When she comes back, I'm leaving the rangers.'

'A married man's no good to me,' Manners said gruffly, but there was a warm light in his eyes. 'I always knew you were a special kind of man, Bill.'

'That's what I've been trying to tell you,' Grady said. 'I'll be leaving in about an hour for Carlisle's place. I figure I'll camp on the prairie in one of the old buffalo wallows and keep an eye on the squirt. If he makes one mistake, he'll never live to make another.'

'Keep him alive,' Manners said. 'Keep yourself alive. Every day, along about sundown, there'll be a pair of rangers patrolling away from sight of the house. Contact them and pass any information back to me. I want to catch Fred Early red-handed.'

'Vargas has been pretty quiet on the other side of the river. Ain't it about time for him to pull off another raid?'

'His pattern of activity is changing,' Manners said. 'Gary and I were discussing this. He compared it to some of the revolutionary armies in Europe. In the beginning Vargas raided for money and guns. Gary tells me that this is the pattern until there is enough stolen money to buy arms and a source of supply established. Since Fred Early is running guns and ammunition, Vargas doesn't have to rely on raids for that purpose. He's building up for something big. And I'm beginning to agree with Gary's theory.'

'What's that, Major?'

'That Vargas is going to launch a full-scale attack against Texas.'

Bill Grady laughed. 'Hell, he'll never make it.'

'No, but how many will be killed before he's stopped? Two thousand? Three? How many towns will be ashes? There'll be scorched earth from Del Río to Brownsville. How many ranches will go? Eighty? A hundred? And cattle? Thirty-five or forty thousand head. God knows how much in money. Probably a million dollars in the banks alone.'

Grady's humor vanished. 'The Army had better get here in a hurry.'

'It'll take six weeks to establish strength,' Manners said, 'and Gary assures me that this is moving very rapidly, indeed. So we're going to have to break Vargas before he breaks us. To do that we've got to cut off his supply of guns, assuming, of course, that he still needs more before he can move into the field. I want him to start raiding again, scrounging for what he needs to support himself. An army can't grow on scrounging, Bill.'

'Seeing as how we can't kill it, we keep it from growing, huh?'

'That's it exactly. Laredo was hit hard once and survived. We can take those raids and come back for more. And that's what we'll do, hold him off, take the punishment until the Army gets here. Then between the Mexican army and ours, we ought to be able to fight him on his terms.'

'I never clearly understood what his terms were,' Grady said, rising. 'Well, I'll see you when I see you, Major. Don't wait up for me.'

Martin Hinshaw approached the Carlisle place just after dawn, and it built a tightness in his stomach, riding in cold this way. Two men came out as he dismounted by the porch; they carried rifles in the crooks of their arms.

One said: 'I know you. Beat it. There've been enough rangers around here.'

'I got kicked out,' Hinshaw said, and tied his horse. 'Got a new job. Your boss.'

'Like hell,' the man said, and Hinshaw kicked him in the groin. The man dropped his rifle and rolled on the ground, his knees pulled up tight.

Hinshaw pointed to the other. 'If I get any argument from you, I won't kick you. Now show me Carlisle's room, then get all the men together who live here.' He brushed past the man and went into the house. Like most men who live alone, Carlisle's place was a litter ground. Hinshaw turned and found the hand standing in the doorway. 'Get this place dunged out from top to bottom. Don't waste time about it, either.'

He spent the rest of the day getting settled. One man left the ranch to go to Laredo to talk to Early, to see if this was really so, that Hinshaw was the boss. Hinshaw let him go because he understood how Early meant this to be. If Hinshaw was tough enough to force his authority on them without letter or prior notice of change, then he would be able to handle anything that came up.

The ranch ran little stock, but the wagon yard was large, and two wagon makers were employed as well as a blacksmith and a harness maker. Three other men made up the work force, plus a cook and a servant in the house. The three men seemed to have no function other than to act as guards, and Hinshaw, with one kick, had already reduced that to two. The injured man was unable to get out of his bunk without help, and he would be doing no riding for a week or so.

Hinshaw spent the night in a state of suspended judgment, and he realized that Early really had him on the hook, for all he would have to do to get rid of him would be to deny ever hiring him, and Hinshaw would have a gunfight on his hands.

The hand returned from Laredo around breakfast time the next morning. He sat down to eat while everyone watched him. Finally he said: 'We're expecting company tomorrow or the next day. The boss wants him treated nice.' He looked at Hinshaw when he said it.

'I treat everyone nice,' Hinshaw said. 'Who's the guest?'

'You'll know when he gets here,' the man said.

That day he got to know some of the men at the ranch or at least their names. The two wagon makers were named Carl and Luke. When Hinshaw went to the shop in the barn to watch them work, Carl stopped him at the door.

'We know our jobs. We don't need any help or advice or anything.'

'I was only going to look around,' Hinshaw said.

'There's nothing to see,' Carl said. He was a strapping man with heavy arms and a hammer in his hand, so Hinshaw shrugged and went back to the porch to sit.

The next day, Pete, one of the guards,

hitched up a buggy and drove to town to meet the train. He didn't go to Laredo, but to a small spur junction fourteen miles northeast of the Carlisle Ranch. He returned late at night, and the visitor went immediately to his room and locked the door, and at breakfast time the cook fixed a tray.

As he started to take it in, Hinshaw said: 'Put that back in the kitchen. If he wants to eat, let him come to the table like the rest of us.'

Pete said: 'That's not friendly.' He looked at Hinshaw and saw that he wasn't going to change his mind, so he shrugged and went on eating.

The cook took the tray back, and Hinshaw went to the visitor's room and knocked. 'Breakfast is on the table, if you want to eat.' He went back and sat down. Ten minutes later the man came out. He was rather small and round-bodied, and he wore glasses and a flowing mustache. He said nothing at all, just sat down and ate, and afterward returned to his room and locked the door.

Pete left again with the buggy and returned with Fred Early. The men were eating supper, but Early didn't seem hungry. He went into the parlor, sent Pete for the visitor, and closed the door. An hour later he came out and sat down at the table.

To Hinshaw he said: 'Tomorrow morning we're going out a few miles north of the

305

place for a demonstration.'

'All right. Need anything special?'

'Tell Carl to bring an old wagon. We'll need the buggy and saddle horse for myself.' He sliced his steak. 'Getting along all right?'

'I'm getting paid a lot for sitting,' Hinshaw said. 'Never knew a man could make so much money without knowing what he was doing.'

'It's not what you know, but who you know,' Early said. When he finished eating, he picked his teeth and lit a cigar. 'If this works out right, I'll have apiece of merchandise to sell at a good price. Carlisle used to be in charge of all the wagon freight. In a week or so you may have to take some wagons across the border to Nuevo Laredo for me. Just trade goods. Nothing to worry about.'

'I don't worry about it,' Hinshaw said frankly. 'You give the orders, and I'll take them.'

Early laughed softly. 'I wondered how you'd get along out here. They tell me that Charlie's swollen up like a pair of apples. You play rough.'

'That's only because I was unfamiliar with the rules.'

'The only rules you have to remember are the ones I give you. Treat me right and you've got a soft place. Treat me bad and you won't last.' He leaned back in his chair. 'I saw Rameras before I left Laredo. He'll be up and around in a week or so.'

'So?'

'I need Rameras,' Early said frankly. 'He's the only man who can come and go in Vargas's camp. It doesn't do a man any good to have merchandise if he can't reach his market. That makes sense, doesn't it?'

'Everything you do and say makes sense,' Hinshaw said.

'Rameras will take my proposition to Vargas. If he deals, we're both going to come out ahead. There's a five-hundred-dollar bonus in it for you.' He shrugged. 'Of course, if you make a mistake, it'll be a nickel bullet.'

'I don't like lead in the gut,' Hinshaw said. 'This must be big.'

'Very big,' Early said, his eyes bright. 'I'm not a fighter, Hinshaw. My kind are never in the front of a battle, but without us there wouldn't be any battles. Let the fools have the glory and the heroics. For me I like the manipulations, the logistics of war, big or little. God, how I envy the Rothschilds ... they financed empires, you know. Broke them, too, when it suited them. Vargas would be a petty bandit if it wasn't for me, and he knows it. I am the real builder of his army, and he won't move a horse or a man unless I want him to.'

'That's a lot of power for one man to have.'

Fred Early smiled. 'Hinshaw, you speak like

307

a baby ... so innocent. Do you know how much money I have? A million dollars, give or take a few hundred thousand. I made it by buying items for twenty-one cents and selling them for two dollars and ten cents.' He brushed ash off his coat. 'Or rifles for twenty-one dollars and selling them for two hundred and ten dollars. These small merchants with their fifty percent are fools. It's not for me.'

'No,' Hinshaw said solemnly, 'you sure ain't a fool. I guess, if you go on, you'll own railroads and steel mills and whole towns and all the people in them.'

'Exactly. What can stop me?'

'Not much, I guess. It gives a man something to think about, doesn't it?'

Chapter Twenty

Alice Cardeen looked out the window of the day coach for a long time, then she said: 'Are we out of Texas yet?'

'No, dear,' Rhea said. 'Why don't you sleep, Alice?'

'I'm not tired.'

Rhea Cardeen frowned and watched her sister who seemed only to have a dull interest in the passing land. A young man in a brown suit sat across the aisle. He kept glancing their way and smiling politely. Rhea kept freezing him out until finally he gave up and read a newspaper.

She thought of Bill Grady, big, ungainly Bill Grady with his soft words and gentle hands. He was her hope for a new happiness, and the promise in his eyes was the courage for her to go on. Had she been alone, she knew, she would never have left him, but Alice never smiled now and her mind always seemed far away on another plane, and it wouldn't be good to leave her alone. Perhaps, she reasoned, the change would bring her back to her old self. When that happened, she'd come back to Texas and Bill Grady.

By her estimation they were only forty or fifty miles east of Laredo and the roadbed followed the natural floor of the shallow valleys formed by undulating land. The coach swayed and rocked along, trucks clacking over the rail joints. It was a lulling thing, and she hoped it would make Alice drowsy.

The sudden clamping on of air brakes threw her against the forward seat, then the engine and forward cars ground through the ties. She heard the thundering crash as the locomotive went over on its side, and the baggage coach plowed into it. The coach in which she rode teetered dangerously, but did not go over, and the din was unbelievable – women and children screaming and men shouting for order.

Above this came the rattle of machine gun fire, and she grabbed Alice and threw her to the floor as bullets shattered the glass all along the coach and puckered the sides. Some were hit and fell, thrashing, in the aisles. Then the firing stopped, and a silence, broken only by moans, spread along the length of the derailed train. Next the sound of horsemen thundered down over the brow of a hill, and the Mexican bandits boarded the train from both ends.

Alice began to whimper, and Rhea said: 'Oh, God, not twice!'

They came into the coach with their laugher and brutality and drawn pistols and stripped purses and jewelry from the women and relieved the men of their wallets and pistols. Then one of the bandits stopped and looked at Rhea Cardeen and laughed.

He spoke to another man who raced away and came back a moment later with Pedro Vargas. He holstered his pistols grabbed Rhea Cardeen by the hair, and pulled her to her feet.

'My little bird, you flew away,' Vargas said, smiling. 'We must build a stronger cage.' He jerked her into the aisle and threw her to her knees. The young man in the brown suit was thinking of something gallant, and he got to his feet to do it but sat down again when a Mexican pressed the muzzle of his pistol

310

against his stomach.

'Bring the other one, too,' Vargas said, and went forward.

They were taken off the coach and surrounded by shouting Mexicans. Alice stopped her crying and said: 'Bill will come for us, won't he, Rhea?'

'Yes, dear. Be quiet now.'

She nodded. 'Will it be like before, Rhea? Will it?'

'No,' she said, and knew that it wasn't really a lie. It would be worse, and she closed her eyes and tried not to think about it. *She'll die this time*, she thought. *Die slowly and hard.* It was almost too much for her to think about.

A grinning Mexican stood near her elbow, and she turned to him and smiled and slipped her arms around him as though she thought him beyond resistance and tried not to think of what she was doing. Her hand reached for his holstered pistol.

Inside the coach, the young man in the brown suit watched this, and it made him sick to see her loving the bandit. He watched her whirl away suddenly and heard the gun go off. He spoke softly to the man standing next to him. 'God, she shot the other girl. God, she just up and killed her!'

Martin Hinshaw first thought that Fred Early wasn't going to take him along. The wagon and the men had already left, and Early dawdled with his breakfast. Finally he came out on the porch and said: 'Get your horse.'

They rode to a place a mile or so from the ranch buildings, and Early's guest was already set up to demonstrate his weapon. He had a machine gun on a tripod, and it was unlike anything Hinshaw had ever seen, slimmer, lighter, more mobile than the heavy Gatling guns the Army used. The ammunition was contained on a belt of metal links and small caliber, not much larger than .30-30 rifle cartridges. Slung on his shoulder was another gun in a leather case.

'Dis a new weapon,' the German, whose name was Schilling, explained to Early in an accent thick enough to saw. 'Ve are developing many new arms. As you can see, dis machine gun iss small enough for one man to carry. Herr Spandau, the inventor of the veapon, claims it will fire nearly five hundred rounds a minute.'

Fred Early whistled. 'The old gun wouldn't do better than two hundred, and it was heavy as hell.'

'The German army iss being equipped with many of these new guns,' Schilling explained. 'I am sure you can see the mechanical advantage one vould have vith such a veapon.'

'And you have some to sell? If they're so good, why?'

Schilling smiled. 'Ve vish to test the veapon.'

Early looked at him sternly. 'I know you Germans. You've tested the hell out of this thing. What's wrong with it?'

'You are a suspicious man.' He shrugged. 'Actually the veapons I have for sale are not quite acceptable by the German army.'

'They work, don't they?' Early asked. 'I can't sell Vargas something that doesn't work.'

'The veapon will function,' Schilling said. 'Ve are making rapid advances in many veapon fields. The machine guns I have for sale have been improved upon. Yet ve vould like to place them into the field for ... testing. It iss the theory of certain German officers that one of these guns vill equal a company of riflemen. Naturally dis vill remain a theory unless tested. Ve have here a situation dat iss ideal. The forces on one side are armed with rifles and pistols vhile on the others ve arm them vith these new veapons. If the Mexicans defeat the other force, ve vill have some assurance that the veapon iss effective.'

'What are you going to do ... read about it in the newspapers?' Early asked.

Schilling smiled. 'Ve have men in Corpus Christi who vill send us information. Now I vill demonstrate the veapon, firing at the oak sides of the vagon parked six hundred yards away. You vill see how powerful the

313

machine gun iss.'

He threaded ammunition through the mechanism, pulled on the crank handle, then squatted behind the gun and began firing. As the empty shells ejected out the side, the metal links fell apart. Without attracting any attention, Hinshaw picked up an empty shell and a link and put them in his pocket.

Schilling fired several hundred rounds, and then they went to examine the wagon. The wooden sides were splintered and shot through. Early said: 'It's powerful, all right. What I'd like to...' He stopped when Schilling pulled on his arm and pointed.

On a small rise, three hundred yards distance, a horseman wheeled and started to gallop away. Carl grabbed up his Winchester, but Early said: 'Save your shells. He's out of range.'

'Not for me,' the German said and uncased a bolt-action rifle with a long telescope on it. With maddening calm he squatted, put on the sling, and dumped the rider from the saddle with one shot.

Early spoke to Hinshaw. 'Get the horses and we'll take a look.'

Hinshaw ran back, got the horses, and returned. They mounted and rode out, and Early swung down to turn Bill Grady over with his foot. Hinshaw felt his stomach knot, and it was with a great effort that he held himself from running to Grady.

The ranger was shot clear through, stomach and back, yet he was alive. He looked at Early, then at Hinshaw, and with an effort that cost him his remaining strength he tried to draw his gun and shoot Martin Hinshaw. But he dropped the gun and strangled on his blood and died there.

Fred Early said: 'Send a couple men out to bury him.' He looked at Hinshaw's colorless complexion. 'You sick?'

'I don't like to see any man cut in two,' Hinshaw said, and turned to his horse and swung up. He rode slightly ahead of Early on the way back so Early couldn't see the bleakness of his expression or the tears he constantly fought back. In his last living moments Bill Grady had thought to play out the game so that Fred Early would have further proof that Hinshaw was an enemy of the Texas Rangers.

Hinshaw had control of himself by the time he rejoined the group. He nodded toward that spot of prairie where Grady lay dead and said: 'Pete, take a shovel and put some sod over him. Someone might come along and find him.'

'We don't get many travelers through…' He looked at Hinshaw's expression and broke off his argument. 'All right.' He took the German's shovel and got his horse.

Early walked over to where the German was casing his piece of portable sudden death. 'I'm impressed. How many can I have?'

'I haf forty pieces and five thousand rounds.'

'How much?'

'A thousand dollars each,' the German said.

Early made some mental calculations for his profit. 'When can you deliver?'

'The boat...' He stopped when Early raised his hand in caution.

'We'll talk about it later,' Early said. 'Hinshaw, see that all this is brought back to the ranch. You can ride back with me in the buggy, Herr Schilling.'

Hinshaw waited until Early and the German drove away, then he mounted his horse and rode out to where the wagon had been parked over the rise. Carl and the signalman were hitching a team to it. Hinshaw examined the splintered holes in the bed where the many bullets had gone clear through.

'That was some shooting,' Hinshaw said.

Carl glanced at him. 'I wouldn't know.'

Hinshaw had a rage to work off, and he came off his horse before Carl knew what was happening. He axed Carl flat, then said: 'I'm going to teach you how to say sir to me.'

'Maybe it'll be the other way around,' Carl said, rising. 'I had the job coming, and Early gave it to you.' He had the size and weight and a grudge of his own, but it was nothing to the fire inside Hinshaw. He caught the wagon maker as he bore in, and, when he hit him, he saw Grady sprawled out there, dead, and it was a joy to feel pain in his fists and to see blood spring to Carl's lips.

Hinshaw's advantage was his rage over Grady's murder, and it made him immune from pain, yet it left him clear-headed, coolly calculating, and he went after Carl like a butcher reducing a side of beef to steaks and chops. He closed an eye and pulped the man's nose and got hurt a little himself, but he was slowing the wagon maker down, making him sluggish and unsteady on his feet, and he was sapping the man's strength with his punches.

Hinshaw worked him around with his back to the wagon and hit him with all he had and felt the fight go out of the man. Then he stepped back and let him fall. A moment later he walked over, took his canteen from the saddle, and poured it in Carl's face. That brought him around, slowly, and he sat, leaning against the wheel for support.

'The next time I walk to the barn, you open the door and step aside. You understand?'

'Next time,' Carl said in a mumble, 'I'll have something in my hand.'

'And I'll have my gun. You want to play this right out to the end?'

'I guess not,' Carl said.

Hinshaw got on his horse and rode back to the ranch and found Early waiting on the porch. He had his satchel by his side and picked it up when Hinshaw rode into the yard.

'Drive me to the dépôt,' he said, and got into the buggy. Hinshaw got in, picked up the reins, and turned out of the yard. Early lit a cigar and said: 'As far as anyone in Laredo is concerned, I took the eastbound on business. Drop me off, and I'll catch the train back, then you drive to Laredo and meet me in town.'

'At the hotel?'

'Yes. Stay away from my store. I don't want anyone to know that you work for me.'

'Ashamed of it?'

Early laughed. 'Friend, very few people really know much about my business, and those that do can't prove a thing. There isn't one scrap of paper that ties me to anything illegal. As for what goes on at Carlisle's, it can stand inspection anytime. I use the place for a wagon repair dépôt, and I store merchandise there because I don't have the room in town. If I entertain a guest now and then, that's also in the line of business.' He looked at Hinshaw, and smiled. 'As for the little demonstration you saw, there's no connection between that and arms traffic to Pedro Vargas. If I want a man to show me

318

something, I tell him to come right ahead and show me.'

'It pays to be careful,' Hinshaw said.

'Too bad that ranger wasn't more careful,' Early said. He looked at Hinshaw. 'You knew him, didn't you?'

'Yes, he always called me squirt.'

Early laughed. 'That must have set just dandy with you.'

'I always meant to teach him different,' Hinshaw said softly. 'It doesn't matter now.' He flipped a glance at Early. 'Do you have to talk all the time? It gets on a man's nerves.'

A stain of temper came to Early's cheeks, but he laughed and passed it off. 'You're like a cocked gun. Well, I guess it's an asset to you.'

He fell silent then, and Hinshaw drove until well after dark. They finally came to a junction with a railroad shack, some loading pens, and a siding full of freight cars. He let Early off. He went in and checked the train time, then came back.

'Thirty-five minutes. Might as well get started. I'll see you tomorrow afternoon.'

'Give me some time to sleep,' Hinshaw said.

Early laughed. 'All right. Day after then.' He stepped back, and Hinshaw drove away. As soon as he was clear of the dépôt, he veered south and drove steadily through the night, arriving just before dawn at Bill

Grady's unmarked grave.

He parked the buggy in the old buffalo wallow and gathered up all the pieces of splintered wood he could find and built a small fire. Then he ripped out the wooden luggage bin beneath the buggy seat and made a cross, tying it together with a piece of wire he found. Then using a clevis pin, he heated it and burned Bill Grady's name on the head marker and planted it by the grave.

Dawn was rinsing away the night when he kicked out the fire and drove away, heading for Laredo. He looked back and could make out the grave marker. He said: 'If there's any patrols around here, I hope they got eyes and can read.'

He tried not to think of the way Grady died, but he couldn't keep it out of his mind. He remembered how close he had come to breaking down and giving the whole thing away. He guessed that Grady had sensed that for he had drawn his pistol, reminding him that his duty to the State of Texas was bigger than a man's duty to his friend.

And that's what he was, Hinshaw thought. *My friend. The best damn friend a man could ever have.* There wasn't any need now to hold it all back, so he dropped the reins and let tears mar his vision. He didn't think Bill Grady would think less of him for crying.

Chapter Twenty-One

Martin Hinshaw stopped at the barbershop for a haircut, shave, and a bath, took a room at the hotel, then ate in the dining room before going on to the store for some smoking tobacco. With a cigarette between his lips, he stepped out to the walk, feeling like a different man. This feeling had a short life for Ella Sanders was walking toward him.

She stopped and looked at him. Hinshaw took the cigarette from his mouth. 'I can step across the street until you pass,' he said.

The sincerity, the simplicity touched her, and she came up to him. 'Marty, I think we'd better talk.'

'Why don't I take you down to the Shattuck House and buy you a cup of coffee?'

She shook her head. 'I've got a little shopping to do. Come to the house in a half hour.'

'Fred Early may not like...'

'Fred Early didn't ask you,' she said, and went on into the store.

He loitered along the street until he figured a half hour had passed, then he walked over to Ella Sanders's house. She met him as he came onto the porch. She held the screen door open for him, and he stepped inside, placing his hat on a bench by the hall tree.

'I'll make some lemonade,' she said, going to the kitchen. Fresh plaster covered the bullet holes in the walls, but the gouges in the woodwork had not been repaired. 'The weather's turning out warm, isn't it?'

He laughed, and she turned and looked at him. 'You could have said that on the street, Ella.'

'Yes. I ought to know better than to make small talk.' She sliced lemons and squeezed them. 'When Dad was killed, I'd been hurt, and I wanted to make others hurt, too. I haven't been fair to you, Marty. You risked your life the night Dad was killed, and I never even thanked you for it.'

'That doesn't matter,' he said. 'I wanted to help you, and you turned to Early. I knew that I was licked, but I didn't understand it. I still don't. He brought those papers to the major, and somehow you just forgave him for it.' He shook his head. 'Pa used to say that love was blind, but I never believed it.'

She looked squarely at him. 'Not love, Marty. I don't really think there ever was love.' She added sugar and water in the pitcher and got two glasses. 'The things you said got through to me in spite of everything. Fred came back this morning on the train. I saw him.'

'How was the trip?' Hinshaw asked innocently.

'He didn't go on a trip,' she said. 'At least not where he said he went. He got off somewhere between here and the sixty-mile watering tanks.'

'Did he say that?'

'He didn't have to,' she said, sitting down across from him. 'You know how Fred is, talking a lot of the time. Right away he told me about the good time he had. Only it was a lie, all of it. He never got to the sixty-mile tanks because the east-bound train, the one I would have been on if it hadn't been for the funeral, was hit by Varga's bandits, de-railed and looted. Fred Early knew nothing about that, Marty. Nothing at all.'

Hinshaw whistled softly. 'You didn't call him on that, did you?'

'No,' she said. 'Because I really didn't know what it meant, his lying like that.'

'Well, he's going to hear about it before the day's out and wonder why you didn't catch him up. Your answer had better be better than his was.'

'That's worried me some,' she said. 'I don't know what I'll say. I've thought about it since I saw him, and nothing comes to me.'

Hinshaw sipped his lemonade and thought about it, then said: 'Did he come here?' She nodded. 'Good. Then tell him you haven't left the house since the funeral and didn't know about it yourself. And after the delivery boy told you, you thought he was sparing your feelings by withholding the grim truth.'

Her expression brightened. 'He might believe that. Fred likes to think of himself as always being most considerate and kind. But I'm afraid of him now. I know too much, and yet I really don't know anything.'

'He's in this right up to his eyeballs,' Hinshaw said. 'I know because I'm working for him.' She actually recoiled from him, and he took her arm for fear she would turn and run. 'Ella, you've got to understand. That was all a put-up deal at the hearing, me socking the major, and him booting me out of the rangers. You see, it was the only way they could convince everyone that I was in disgrace. I managed to convince Fred Early that I was desperate for money, and he gave me Carlisle's job out at the ranch. That's where I've been the last few days.' He felt her relax and let go of her arm. 'Grady was my contact, but he's dead, and I've got no way of passing on information to the major.' He shook his head. 'I know Early. He'll use me, then put a bullet in me just like Grady. When he hired me, I knew it was a short-term deal.' He shrugged. 'I don't mind the chances, but I've got to contact the major and let him know what's up. Early's too careful and too smart to be trapped unless he could be caught with guns and ammunition on him. But he never goes with the wagons when they cross the river.'

'There's nothing to stop me from going to the major,' Ella said.

He looked at her, then shook his head. 'Early would have you killed if he suspected...'

'Marty, I'm not afraid. Let me ... for Pop's sake.'

'All right. Early contacted a German at Carlisle's place. He's buying a new machine gun, lighter, faster firing. One man could pick this up and run with it. If Vargas ever gets his hands on a dozen of those, he could terrorize the whole border. In the mountains he could hold off an army. In a couple of weeks, Early will have those guns. Right now they're on a boat somewhere offshore. Tell the major that.'

'I will. Anything else? How will he get them into Mexico?'

'With the wagons some way,' Hinshaw said. 'I never got into the barn, but he keeps two wagon makers on at Carlisle's. You'll just have to tell the major to sharpen the guards at the crossing and hope they figure out how he's doing it.'

'Are you going back with him?' Ella asked.

'I've got to. No telling how much longer he's going to need me around, and I might pick up some additional information about the boat or how he gets the guns across. There are other questions I'd like answered

… like how he arranges the pay-off. I figure Batiste Rameras is taking care of that.'

'Marty, if you learn anything more, how will you contact me?'

He shook his head. 'I won't. Once is enough.'

'You're shutting me out, and that's not your decision to make. Marty, the Cardeens were on that train. They were taken off.'

He stared at her for a moment, then said: 'Good God!'

'Do you see why I have to help? They machine-gunned the train to cow the passengers. Some were hit. Those guns were bought from Fred Early. Next it will be something more terrible.' She took the empty glasses to the sink. 'I've made up my mind, Marty. Don't argue with me.'

'How would you do it? You can't go out on the prairie, and I won't get a chance to come to town.' He shook his head. 'Let the major put a man on it.'

'What could a man do that I couldn't? Get shot like your friend?' She came back to the table and sat down. 'Marty, I think Fred trusts me because I'm a woman, and, to him, all women are a little stupid. We're all human, Marty, and we all make mistakes. I might be able to find the ones Fred Early has made.'

'All right, but you stay in town. If I have to get word to you, then I'll figure some way to do it. Is that understood?'

'Yes, Marty.'

He looked at her and smiled. 'I think you're kind of pretty, you know that? If I ever get two dollars in my pocket, I'm going to buy a marriage license.'

'Well, now! I haven't said I'd...'

'I know. So wait until I ask.' He got up, and went into the hall for his hat and returned to the back door. She stood there as though she was waiting for something, so he put his arms around her and kissed her.

After he left the house, he carefully threaded his way through two alleys before going back to the main street. He went to his room at the hotel and stretched out on the bed to wait for Fred Early.

Since the train's derailing, Major Carl Manners hadn't had a decent sit-down for a meal. Now he returned to his office and ordered his meal brought there. He was just starting to carve the roast beef when the guard knocked.

''Scuse me, Major, but the Sanders girl is her. Wants to see you.'

'Show her in,' Manners said and sighed, resigned to having the roast grow cold. He stood up and plucked the napkin from the collar of his shirt as Fred Early opened the door and ushered Ella Sanders into the office.

'Nice of you to receive us,' Early said, offering his hand. 'Miss Sanders suggested that since you were so considerate during her trying time, that she come out here and thank you personally. Naturally I was glad to escort her.'

'Glad you came,' Manners said, sitting down. He glanced at his roast and started to push it away, then Ella got up and took off her gloves.

'Let me carve that for you, Major. Fred, why don't you get two glasses and pour a drink for yourself and the major?'

'I believe I will,' Early said, and got up, turning toward a wall cupboard.

Quickly Ella Sanders took a folded piece of paper from her purse and slipped it under Manners's plate. He saw this but did not let on by word or expression when Early turned back with bottle and glasses. Ella sliced the beef and insisted that the major eat while they visited.

'The crying is over,' Ella said. 'Fred and I have talked about it, and I think people will let me live my life in peace.'

'Yes,' Manners said. 'If you were a man, it would be different. It's a tragedy, but we all must live through them.' He glanced at Fred Early. 'A miserable business, that train's derailing. I hope you weren't harmed.'

'Only my purse,' Early said. 'Fortunately I was carrying only ninety dollars in cash.

Had I been carrying more, they might have thought I was rich and held me for ransom.'

Ella reached out and patted his hand. 'And the dear never said a word to me about it in consideration of what I'd been through.'

'You've got breeding, Mister Early,' Manners said. 'I knew that the first moment I saw you.' He motioned toward the roast. 'Are you sure you won't join me?'

'Thank you, no,' Early said. 'We've really intruded long enough. Don't bother to get up, Major. We'll show ourselves out.' He shook hands again. 'When you come to town, drop in at the store. I'm going on another buying trip tomorrow, but I'll be back before the week is out.'

'I may do that,' Manners said. 'By the way, have you seen that saddlebum, Hinshaw? When he left here, he was riding a company horse. I'd hate to slap a horse-stealing charge on him. So, if you run into him, tell him I said to bring the animal back, and we'll forget it. He's half wild and will get in enough trouble before he's dead without adding this to it.'

'It seems that I recall someone saying he had a job on a ranch,' Early said. 'However, if I see him I'll tell him to bring the horse back.'

They left, and Manners waited until they drove away, then motioned for the guard to come inn. 'Send for Corporal Anderson.'

He then took the paper from beneath his plate, and read it. When he was finished, he sat there with his fists clenched.

Anderson came in, and Manners waved him into a chair. 'The Sanders girl slipped me this. She saw Hinshaw, and I guess we know why Grady's horse came back alone. He's dead. Murdered by one of Early's men.' He tossed the note to Anderson who read it slowly. 'That part about the new machine guns may just be the thing we've been waiting for. Damn it, I wish Gary were here. He'd know about those things.'

'You want me to take Bill's place near the Carlisle Ranch?'

'No,' Manners said. 'It's too risky. Early will be on the look-out even more now that Grady was caught.' He slapped the desk. 'I told Early that the horse Hinshaw was riding was taken without permission. Knowing how cautious Early is, it might bring Hinshaw here for a talk.'

'How do you figure that?' Anderson asked.

'Early may tell him to bring it back. He wouldn't want a warrant sworn out. So we'll sit tight until we see Hinshaw. Maybe by then he can give us a lead on that boat. If we knew the location, we could board it when it docks, or board her at sea.' He lit a cigar and paced up and down the office. 'It seems to me that, if Early ever takes those wagons across the river, the weapons will get into

Pedro Vargas's hands, and there won't be one solitary thing we can do to stop it. So we've got to do Early a favor and keep the guns on this side and make Vargas come and get them.' He looked out the window. 'He's camped over there somewhere, probably near enough so that he can see with a telescope. I say that because there must be some signal arrangement between him and Early, some sign used that's big enough to be seen across the river.'

'Yeah, and so ordinary that we've never noticed it.'

Manners turned and looked at Anderson for a long moment. 'You've hit on something real smart there, and I don't see how I ever overlooked you for sergeant.' He slapped his hands together. 'That's what we've got to find out, that signal. I want every corporal in my office in a half hour. Somehow, if enough questions are asked, enough thought put to it, we may pretty well put down on paper just what Mister Early's obvious habits are, and, out of those, something very commonplace is going to come up again and again, and we'll find it. Now get out of here and pass the word.'

Chapter Twenty-Two

Hinshaw grew tired of waiting, but he'd been told to wait, and he was getting paid to wait. So he smoked and sat on some grain bags in the rear of Fred Early's store. Finally Early arrived. He went into his office and motioned for Hinshaw to follow him.

'Close the door.' He lit a cigar and sat down. 'Miss Sanders and I have been out to Ranger Headquarters. A little politicking.' He looked at his watch. 'It's later than I thought.' He took a twenty-dollar gold piece from his pocket and tossed it to Hinshaw. 'Get yourself a railroad ticket to Corpus Christi. I'll meet you at the dépôt just before train time. Get aboard after I do. Sit in the same coach but several seats behind me. I'll be carrying considerable money in my valise, and I don't want to lose it.'

'All right,' Hinshaw said. 'Is that all?'

'You do the job right and that's enough,' Early said.

Hinshaw got up and went to the door. 'In Corpus Christi what do I do?'

'I'll tell you what to do when the time comes,' Early said.

Hinshaw left the store and went to the

dépôt and bought his ticket. He put it in his coat pocket and walked back to the saloon where he nursed a beer and played solitaire to whittle away time. He kept watching the wall clock and the degree of the sunset and hoped that it would be fully dark before train time. After waiting as long as he dared, he left the saloon and, by the back alleys, worked his way to Ella Sanders's house. She was in the kitchen, doing the supper dishes, when he scratched lightly on the screen door. He heard her step, then she unhooked the door, but, to keep her from opening it, he put his foot against it. He didn't want to step in the light.

'I'm leaving on the eight o'clock east-bound for Corpus Christi. Early's carrying the money for the pay-off and...' He heard a chair scrape as someone got up from the table.

'Run!' Ella screamed. 'Run, Marty!'

He knew it was Early, and he cursed himself for being such a damned fool, for being so careless, yet he wasn't stupid enough to stay. He wheeled and dashed for the back fence and vaulted over it, ripping the leg of his pants as Early opened up with his .32 pocket pistol. The bullets came close, but not enough so as to touch Hinshaw. He sprinted on down the alley, all the time hoping that Ella would have sense enough to get out of the house before Early turned his attention to her.

At the end of the alley he paused and heard Early coming up fast from behind. Hinshaw sprinted for the street, grabbed the first horse he came to, and went into the saddle. His rodeoing paid off, and he did an Indian sling, grabbing the mane and falling low along the horse's side as he fogged out of town. He didn't think that Early would follow him to Ranger Headquarters, and, as soon as he cleared the street, he straightened in the saddle and let the horse run.

A surprised ranger waved him on into Manners's office. McCabe and Jim Gary were there, both unshaved and bearing the marks of hard miles traveled. They looked in surprise as Hinshaw burst into the room.

'Major, I blew it!' Hinshaw said. 'It was a fool thing to do, and I don't have any excuse except that I got careless.'

'Well,' McCabe said, 'somewhere along the line you've learned how to be honest even when it hurts.'

'Calm down,' Manners said. 'What happened?'

Hinshaw sat down. He explained that Early was going to Corpus Christi with the money to pay for the weapons. He told how he'd gone to Ella's house to tell her so she could pass the information on and foolishly revealed both himself and her to Fred Early who had been out of sight, sitting at the kitchen table.

Manners nodded, and scratched his chin. 'Well, maybe we can save some of it. I have no doubt that you'd never have come back from Corpus Christi alive, Marty. Early surely would have had you killed and dumped into the sea. So you may have saved yourself a close one. Also we can assume that Early won't be aboard the train since he knows I can telegraph ahead and have him arrested. It may mean that he won't get to Corpus Christi on time, as he planned, but we might be able to.' He glanced at Jim Gary. 'Colonel, do you want to bring Hinshaw up to date on developments across the border?'

'We didn't do well at all with the Mexican army,' Gary said. 'They might be interested in a combined campaign later, but it will have to be cleared through diplomatic channels in Mexico City and Washington. Lord knows how long that will take. Three months. Maybe six. By that time Vargas will have sacked half of Texas.' He brushed some dust from his shirt sleeves. 'We'll have to get Vargas to come on this side of the river, Major. Your plan has a great deal of merit.'

'Yes, and I've just had another idea,' Manners said. 'Marty, do you suppose Early was going to meet that German in Corpus Christi?'

'He might. Why?'

'Suppose we detain Early as long as we

335

can while you go on ahead and meet the German. He's met you at Carlisle's place, and he knows you're an Early man. You just might be able to buy those damned guns in Early's name. If we had them, it might be enough to draw Vargas across the river into a trap. Colonel Gary is familiar with that type of armament, and he agrees that such a weapon would be of great value to a fast, mobile army.'

'Well, I'm game to try it, Major. But how'll I catch the eastbound? It's likely out of the station by now.'

'A telegram will hold it at the tanks for two hours, and, by taking a spare horse along, you could make it.' He frowned. 'Hate to send you alone, but...'

'You don't have to,' McCabe said. 'I'll go with him.'

Manners shook his head. 'Too many people know you, Guthrie.'

'They don't know me,' Jim Gary said, smiling. 'Besides I'm an old cavalry soldier who can ride anything with hair on it.' He looked at Hinshaw. 'Pick four good mounts, boy. We'll be moving fast.'

'In the meantime,' Manners said, 'I'll do everything I can to detain him in town, but I won't promise too much. Better figure on him arriving in Corpus Christi a day after you do.'

'You could arrest him,' Hinshaw said.

'On what charge? Your word against his? A smart lawyer would have him free in twenty-four hours.'

'He threw a cylinder of lead at me.'

'Because he caught you snooping around his fiancée?' Manners shook his head again. 'Who could ask for a better story than that? No, we'll do the best we can. Give me fifteen minutes, then come back here for the money. How much was Early going to take?'

'About thirty thousand,' Hinshaw said.

Manners whistled. 'I wonder if I have that much in the safe? It's division payroll and expenses for a year. Well, let me worry about it.'

Hinshaw picked horses with the legs for speed and the deep chests for show, and, to save the horses, he suggested that they ride bareback, for the weight of a Mexican saddle would tell over the distance of miles. Gary agreed to this, and they returned to headquarters. Manners came out with a leather dispatch case that Hinshaw put inside his shirt.

'There's twenty-six thousand there in bills. I've wired ahead, and the eastbound will be sided at the tanks until you arrive. Good luck, both of you, and bring me back those guns.' He extended his hand up. 'Or at least get them on Texas soil. A full company of rangers will be on patrol near the waterfront. If you get to shore, we'll surround you like bees around a hive.'

'What's going to keep Vargas from finding out we're holding the guns?' Hinshaw asked.

'Nothing,' Manners said. 'In fact, we'll do everything in our power to make sure he finds out. It might be an irresistible plum for a vain bastard like him … to take the guns away from the Texas Rangers.'

Hinshaw laughed and wheeled his horse and rode out with Jim Gary a pace behind. They cut across country, riding fast, and the only time they stopped at all was to open fence gates. In two hours they reached the road and followed it for nearly ten miles, then they pulled to a walk to spare the horses.

Gary checked his nose and suggested: 'We ought to swap mounts now.' He looked back at the two horses they been leading.

'Too early,' Hinshaw said. He sniffed the air. 'Do you smell dust?'

'I don't smell anything,' Gary said. 'This pounding's made my nose bleed. Guess I'm not as young as I thought.'

They stopped for several minutes. 'I still smell dust,' Hinshaw said. 'Someone's ahead of us and traveling fast.' He sniffed again. 'Something else, too. Like hot oil.' He swore. 'Damn it! Early's automobile! He's ahead of us in that damned automobile of his!'

He drummed his heels against the horse, and they rode on at a trot, letting the miles fall back. Hinshaw kept smelling the dust and the hot motor oil. At midnight they swapped horses and turned the jaded mounts loose on the prairie. Hinshaw said: 'That dust smell is getting stronger.'

'How far to the tanks?'

'Two hours. Maybe a little less. How do you suppose Early found out the train was sided there?'

'Likely the telegrapher in town picked it up and passed it on,' Gary said. 'Let's go.'

They rode for nearly three miles, then Hinshaw pulled up sharply, and sniffed the air. 'No dust,' he said.

'He couldn't have left the road,' Gary said. Then he peered ahead. 'What's that? Looks like a light.'

Hinshaw saw what had attracted Gary's attention, a small glow of light, as though someone were standing in the road with a lantern.

'He's broke down,' Hinshaw said gleefully. 'Come one!'

They rode forward without regard for caution, and, as they drew near, they could see Early's automobile in the middle of the road. Early heard them approach and dropped the lantern and ran across the road, hopped over a fence, and disappeared in a pasture. Hinshaw looked at the car. The engine cover was up, and it was not running. He drew his pistol and fired repeatedly into the mechanism as though it were the brain of some monster and he wanted to make sure that he killed it. Then he reloaded and shot out three of the wooden wheel spokes so that the hub collapsed on the rim. He went on, leaving the car sitting askew in the road.

Gary sided him and said: 'We ought to get Early, son.'

'To hell with him. He's got a long walk ahead of him.'

The train sat at the siding, engine idly huffing, and they got aboard, and it pulled onto the main line. They went into the caboose and had some coffee and sat down. The conductor ventured back, and Hinshaw asked: 'When's the next eastbound due through Laredo?'

'Day after tomorrow,' the man said. He looked at them, at their dusty clothes, and at Gary's beard and bloody shirt front. 'You don't look important enough to hold up a train for.'

'He's the Grand Duke of Russia,' Hinshaw said, nodding to Gary. 'You wouldn't want an incident that would lead to war, would you?'

'You can't stay here in the caboose,' the conductor said, getting fussy. 'It's for railroad people.'

'We don't want to go up and sit with the peasants, either,' Hinshaw said. 'Ain't that right, your Highness?'

340

'If you say so,' Gary said, smiling. 'After all, your father owns the railroad.'

The conductor wasn't going to get anywhere and he knew it, so he went forward to take his irritation out on the passengers. Gary poured some coffee and stretched out in the seat. 'This sit-down feels mighty good. It's hell what years will do to a man.' He saw Hinshaw rolling a cigarette and took the makings from him. 'When I was a second lieutenant many years ago, I didn't smoke. But I got promoted and graduated to cigars. Actually, that was more important than the promotion, for you couldn't keep a good sergeant unless you smoked good cigars that he could bum off you. When I made captain, I had to have cigars and whisky.' He smiled and sighed and closed his eyes. 'Those were hard days, but good. They must have been, for I remember them so fondly.'

'I hope I live through this so I can remember it,' Hinshaw said. 'Colonel, if we carry this off and make Vargas swim the river, I'd kind of like to make a present of him to McCabe.'

Gary opened his eyes and looked at Hinshaw. 'What do you mean by that?'

Hinshaw shrugged. 'Well, McCabe's chased Vargas quite a spell, and I get the feeling that, if it was over, he'd retire to some front porch with a good dog at his feet and a newspaper in his lap. I guess an old he-bear

341

like McCabe never quits on the down swing, so I'd like to run Vargas right into his arms.'

'Son, you're talking my language,' Gary said. 'We'll have to work something out. That's for sure.' He studied Hinshaw most carefully. 'I guess you figure on getting Fred Early personally?'

'No,' Hinshaw said. 'I don't care who gets him. If it's me, I'll be sorry for it, because there's a woman I'll have to face afterward. Sure she doesn't love him, but she thought she did, and it wouldn't be right, me having to kill him.'

'So that's why you didn't go after him across the pasture?'

'I guess it is,' Hinshaw agreed.

'That could have been a mistake,' Gary said. 'He may get lucky and catch a horse or make some connections and throw a kink in your rope.'

'It's a chance I'm taking,' Hinshaw said. 'But if you thought it was a mistake, Colonel, you could have done something about it.'

'That's right,' Gary said. 'But I'll tell you something, son. I've got you pretty well pegged, and I'll take you along any time, anywhere. Back to back with you I'll never worry about any yellow rubbing off on me, and, if we're unlucky and catch a bullet, I'll know that it'll go in the front. Bill Grady knew that. So does McCabe and the major. You've finally made the grade as a ranger, squirt.'

Hinshaw grinned and colour came to his face. 'Thanks, Colonel.'

'You've earned it.'

'Naw, I don't mean that bull. I mean calling me squirt.'

Chapter Twenty-Three

Batiste Rameras was in the saddle shop when he heard the back door open and close, and, since few people ever came in that way, he went to the rear of the store to investigate. Fred Early sat on a bale of leather. He had his shoes off and was rubbing his feet.

'You cannot stay here,' Rameras said, his manner unfriendly. 'The rangers are looking for you.'

'I know that,' Early said, showing his weariness. 'I've been ducking and hiding and running all the way back here. Batiste, you've got to help me.'

'Why?'

'Because I helped you,' Early said. 'What kind of a question is that?'

'You have been paid well for anything you did,' he said. 'Leave my store.'

'Wait,' Early said, holding up his hand. 'Let me stay here until tonight. I'll cross the river and work my way to the coast.' He took paper and pencil from his pocket. 'Here's the combination to my safe. Not the one in my office. Slide my desk away from the wall. You'll find a trap door in the floor. There's a safe there with over a hundred and thirty thousand in it. As soon as it gets dark, get the money and come back here. Then take me to Pedro Vargas's camp. You'll be rewarded.'

Batiste thought of this then said: 'Why don't I tell the rangers where you are and keep the money?'

'They'd take it away from you,' Early said. 'Batiste, the only safe place for us is in Mexico. Don't be a fool now. I told you I'd reward you, and I will, generously. I'll give you five hundred dollars.'

'That's a lot of money,' Batiste said, and nodded.

He left the back room and closed the door, then he moved to the front of the store and motioned for one of his workers to come over. Quickly, in Spanish, he told the man what he wanted done, then pressed a ten-dollar gold piece into his hand.

'Go like the wind. Tell the soldiers at the river crossing that your mother is sick and that you would visit her. El Jefe will admit you. Tell him I will be there late tonight ... with the *yanqui*. A big *fiesta* should be held in his honor. Now, go.'

Rameras did not go into the back of the store until late afternoon. He found Fred

Early pacing up and down. Immediately he grabbed Rameras by the arm. 'Where have you been? I've been worried sick wondering.'

'There is nothing to worry about,' Rameras said. 'I have dispatched a man to El Jefe's camp. There will be much dancing, and the *señoritas* will laugh and sing for you tonight. El Jefe will be pleased that you are his guest.' The gaiety left his voice. 'But El Jefe will not be pleased about the weapons you promised.' Then he shrugged his shoulders, and smiled. 'Ah, why speak of it? El Jefe is a man with a big heart, and he will remember the good things you have done.'

'I want to make arrangements to go to the coast,' Early said. 'Naturally I'll pay for any help I get.'

'Naturally. The people of Mexico are poor, and the dollars are of great value. You will want a boat to take you to New Orleans. It can be arranged.'

'Once I get out of Texas, I'll be safe enough,' Early said. He laughed briefly. 'They really have nothing to charge me with. I'll hire some attorneys and start litigation to protect my property here. Those damned rangers can't do a thing to me. Not a thing.'

'Then why are you afraid of them?' Rameras asked.

'Because Hinshaw's alive,' Early snapped. 'He's a reckless, headstrong fool, and he's

345

liable to shoot me on sight as not. Who wants to die at the hands of some idealistic fool?' He looked at Rameras. 'Why did Vargas have to bungle the job when he had the chance? Couldn't fifteen men kill one wild Texan?'

Batiste Rameras smiled. 'To kill a Hinshaw is no small thing, *señor*. I know that well. My family learned it and took the knowledge to the grave.' A brightness came to his eyes. 'His death to me is a thing long desired, but he is a man unafraid. To my face he comes to me, like the thunder. He does not run and hide, and someday I will meet him, and one will die, but it will be a proud thing, with honor.' He looked at Early again. 'I can see why you are afraid of him. Myself, I know fear of him, but to me it is an excitement, like a fiery woman's love. You do not know what I mean?'

'I never understand half of the things you people say or think,' Early said. 'See if you can get me something to eat. And a tub of water and a change of clean clothes. I'm crawling with dirt.'

Rameras shrugged. 'We cannot have everything, *señor*. The money I will bring, but no more.' He went out and closed the door, and he heard Early shoot the bolt home. It pleased Rameras to have the man gripped by fear, and he went down the street for a leisurely supper at a restaurant.

As soon as it was dark, he let himself into

Early's store by the back door and, without using more than match light, worked the combination of the hidden safe. He packed the money, mostly bills, in a saddlebag and left the store the way he came in.

In his own shop, Rameras put the saddlebag beneath the counter, then went in back, and tapped on the door. 'I have the money. When I tap on the back door, come out. I'll have horses waiting.'

'All right,' Early said. 'But for God's sake hurry. I don't like being cooped up in here.'

'I will make haste,' Rameras said. He left the shop, went to the alley, and saddled two horses he kept in the barn. Then he went back for the saddlebag and finally tapped on the rear door. Early immediately came out.

'No one saw you?'

'Who pays attention to a Mexican?' He stepped into the saddle.

'Where's the money?' Early asked, mounting.

'I have it here. It is safe.'

'I'll carry it myself,' Early said, and Rameras handed it over without argument. When they reached the end of the alley, they stopped, for a party of six rangers were entering town, towing Early's damaged automobile. Three rangers had their ropes dallied tight and were dragging the car along, the wheelless axle scuffing the ground. One of the rangers sat in the driver's seat, loudly blowing the bulb horn.

A crowd began to collect.

'The swine,' Early said. 'No respect for anything!'

'We go now,' Rameras said. 'No one will notice us with the machine taking their attention.' He rode out, and Early followed, still swearing softly over the treatment of his automobile.

Rameras knew all the spots where the river could be crossed unobserved, and they went in the water, swimming the horses. They emerged on the other side and paused in a grove of trees. Twenty minutes went by, then Rameras's helper appeared on a burro.

'Everything is in readiness,' he said. 'The camp is not two hours' ride from here.'

'Then let's get going,' Early said.

It seemed to Early that they wandered over a circuitous route. There were times when he felt they were near the river, and far from it, and lost, for he was a man with little sense of direction and no ability to get from one place to another unless he followed the road or took the train. They were in wooded, hilly country when they came to Pedro Vargas's camp. Early was stunned by the enormity of it. They rode for fifteen minutes just getting from the fringe to Vargas's headquarters.

It was, he believed, the noise that bothered him the most, for everyone seemed to be talking or singing or yelling or getting drunk.

He felt a momentary regret in coming here, and he hoped that he would be leaving before morning. Surely Vargas would understand his desire to hurry.

Vargas's headquarters was a huge tent surrounded by his retainers, and he welcomed Early with a laugh and an embrace. 'Ah, my friend, you do me the honor to come to my humble house.' He snapped his fingers. 'Music, dancing, *andale!* Sit down, sit down. Bring food and wine here.' He smiled and led Early to a chair. 'Misfortune falls upon you, eh? It is life. Tomorrow the sun will shine.'

'I must get to the coast and to New Orleans,' Early said.

'Of course. It will be arranged. But now you will rest and eat and be entertained.' He glanced at Batiste Rameras, then at the saddlebag Early held. 'What have you there, *amigo?*' He indicated the saddlebag.

'A bag of *yanqui* dollars, *jefe*,' Rameras answered for him. 'The property of *Señor* Early.'

'So! Sanchez, Luz! Stand over the property of our guest with your rifles. Kill the first man who dares place his hand on it.'

'*Si, jefe*.' They stood on each side of the saddlebag with cocked rifles as Early set it down. He said: 'That really isn't necessary, Vargas.'

'It is a courtesy,' Vargas said. He smiled. 'In my camp, you may call me *jefe*.' He threw his leg over the arm of his chair. 'A pity there will be no more guns. You promised me new machine guns, and I have not seen them.'

'They're aboard a boat right now,' Early said. 'As soon as I get to New Orleans, I'll take legal steps to take possession of that cargo.'

'Splendid,' El Jefe said. 'Ah, here are the servants with food and wine.'

Early sat there, paying no attention, while he was being served. Then the feeling grew strong in him that he was being watched, and he realized that no one in the vicinity was talking. He looked up and found a young, dirty-faced girl staring at him, and, in the lamplight, he could hardly make her out, then a full recognition came to him.

'Why, it's Rhea Cardeen, isn't it? You've been in my store.'

'What are you doing here, Mister Early?'

One of Vargas's lieutenants raised his hand to strike her, but Vargas snapped: 'Let her speak. *Señor* Early is my guest. We are ... business partners.'

'We needn't discuss it,' Early said. 'My dear, are you a prisoner here?'

'She is my property,' El Jefe said. 'She was taken from me once by that tall *yanqui*.' He laughed. 'This time I am watching for him.'

'Grady?' Early said.

'He is the one,' Vargas said.

'You will wait long, *jefe*,' Rameras said

softly. 'Grady is dead. Is that not the truth, *Señor* Early?'

Early glanced at Rhea Gardeen and found her eyes steady and hard on his. Suddenly he felt the need to be moving on and stood up. 'I thank you for your hospitality, Vargas, but if I can have a horse and a guide to the coast, I'll be moving on.' He reached for his saddlebag, and the muzzles of two rifles pushed into his stomach. A hard, frightening suspicion came to him, and he looked at Vargas and found the man smiling.

'Sit down, *señor*. That's better. You are in haste, and you haven't eaten yet.' He glanced at Rhea Cardeen. 'And you have not told her how *Señor* Grady died. Was he shot in the breast, *señor?* Man to man ... did you fight him and kill him?'

'I didn't kill him,' Early said. 'I don't go around killing people.'

'No, that is probably true,' Vargas said. 'You would have it done.' He leaned forward slightly. 'In the back, then?' He let Early sweat for a moment, then laughed. 'Carve the bird, my little flower. Give our guest the choice piece.'

Rhea Cardeen picked up the long carving knife and never took her eyes off Fred Early. Suddenly she thrust the point against his stomach and he reared back in the chair. He held himself that way, his eyes round and frightened.

'I loved him,' Rhea said. 'We were going to be married, Mister Early.'

'God, I'm sorry!' he gasped.

'Are you?'

She threw her weight against the knife, and he screamed and fell backward and thrashed on the ground, both hands clutched around the wooden handle. Vargas sat there with a smile on his lips. He said: 'How much money is in the bags, Rameras?'

'*Mucho dinero, jefe.*'

'Help ... me!' Early gave this cry, then began to gag, and finally he stopped kicking and lay, staring at the stars with vacant eyes.

Rhea Cardeen said: 'Kill me now if you want. I don't care.'

'Who speaks of killing?' Vargas asked. 'Rameras, get a horse. Take her to the river. You are free, my little flower. With the stroke of your hand you have earned your freedom. Go with El Jefe's blessing.'

She stared at him, stunned. 'Why?'

'Because El Jefe is kind,' Vargas said. He motioned toward Fred Early. 'Put a rope on his feet and drag him to the edge of camp. In tomorrow's heat he will draw the flies.'

Rameras brought up a horse and almost picked Rhea Cardeen up and placed her astride him. 'We go,' he said. 'El Jefe may change his mind.'

'I wouldn't care,' she said.

Rameras went with her, and another man,

and it was only a short ride to the river taking a direct route. On the way Rameras and the other man talked in Spanish and laughed. Occasionally they mentioned Fred Early's name. At the river's edge they stopped and got down.

Rameras asked: 'Can you swim, *señorita?*'

'Yes, very well,' Rhea said.

'The current is not swift here,' Rameras said. 'And the only deep part is in the middle.' He pointed upstream. 'Laredo is not far. You will make it before dawn if you do not stop and sleep.' He dug into his purse and handed her two gold pieces. 'It will buy you a new dress and a flower for your hair. I am sorry about the *yanqui*.'

'I believe you are,' Rhea said. She turned and went into the water to her knees, then looked back for a moment before going on.

Rameras and the other man mounted. They sat and watched her swimming strongly. There was a sliver of moon, and they could see her head and the wake she made. She made midstream without difficulty then Rameras swore softly. 'She has stopped swimming. Swim, *señorita!* Swim!' He thought she turned and looked back, then her head disappeared from sight. They waited many minutes, but she did not reappear. 'She stopped swimming,' Rameras said again.

'*Si,*' said the other man matter-of-factly

and turned his horse and rode back toward Pedro Vargas's camp. A moment later Rameras followed him but made no attempt to catch up.

Chapter Twenty-Four

Two small Mexican boys, spearing frogs along the river, found Rhea Cardeen. They told their father who hastily hitched his burro to a cart and drove seventeen miles to Laredo for the Texas Rangers. Guthrie McCabe and Major Manners answered the call personally. The two Mexican boys were each given a silver dollar for their prompt honesty, and they ran whooping toward the adobe a mile away to show their mother this great fortune. The Mexican farmer helped pull Rhea Cardeen to the bank, and McCabe made a close examination of her.

'She hasn't been in the water too long, Carl. Fifteen hours, maybe. No marks on her, either. Drowned, I guess.'

'The question in my mind is how did she get away from Vargas's camp?' Manners asked.

McCabe pointed to her feet. 'They're not cut up. No blisters. Either she was brought to the river, or the camp isn't far from it.' He

354

looked up stream. 'How far would something float in that length of time.'

'All the way from Laredo,' Manner said. 'Does that suggest that his camp is somewhere across from town?'

'It could,' McCabe said. He turned to the Mexican and, in Spanish, hired him to take the girl to Laredo in the cart. Then he and Manners mounted their horses and rode back.

As they rode along, Manners said: 'Would she leave her sister? The young one wasn't quite right in the head, you know. Leastways not since Grady and you and the kid brought 'em back.'

'She wouldn't leave her unless she was dead,' McCabe said. 'When we get back, I'd like to check the investigation reports on that train's derailing. It seems to me that some fella testified that a woman shot another. Do you remember?'

'Yes, Collins. A salesman for a windmill firm.'

'The pieces sort of come together,' McCabe said. 'Rhea killed her sister before they ever left the vicinity of the train. And somehow she got loose, or was turned loose, and drowned trying to swim the river.'

'The Mexicans could have held her under.'

McCabe shook his head. 'It ain't their way of killing.' He fell into a thoughtful silence. 'She didn't have anything on but her chemise. To me that suggest that she could swim. A person who couldn't wouldn't shed a dress before getting in the water, or take it off after she went in.' He shook his head again. 'The river ain't so wide that even a passable swimmer couldn't make it. It's my guess that she just gave up and let herself sink. What was there to come back to? She'd killed her sister and that preyed on her mind. And Grady's dead.'

'She didn't know that,' Manners said.

'How can you be sure of that?'

'I guess I can't,' Manners said. 'The older I get, the less I'm sure of.'

Colonel Gary and Martin Hinshaw swung off the train as soon as it reached the station. They immediately lost themselves in the crowd and worked their way clear. On a street corner two blocks away they found a saloon and went in, bought two glasses of beer, and took them to a table in one corner.

'I hate to confess this,' Gary said, 'but I haven't the slightest notion as to how to go about contacting the German.'

'I don't know, either,' Hinshaw said. 'Early must have had some kind of an arrangement, but I don't know it.'

'Do you suppose Schilling is put up at one of the hotels?'

Hinshaw shrugged. 'Your guess is as good as mine. One thing for sure, we don't have time to play around with this. Early is liable to show up tomorrow, or the next day for sure.'

Four rough men staggered into the saloon and made a lot of noise ordering their drinks. Then unexpectedly they veered toward the corner table, and, before Hinshaw or Gary could rise, they were surrounded.

One man made a rude joke and gave Hinshaw a push in the face with the flat of his hand that upset him. Gary made a move for his pistol, but one man grabbed his arm and shook his head. Before Hinshaw could rise, they piled him, three of them while the fourth held Gary neutral. Under a smother of bodies, a soft, sober voice said: 'Play along, Hinshaw.'

They started to brawl, wrestling against the table until they broke it. Then the bartender came over with his shotgun and said: 'All right! Now take it outside! Go on, get out of here!'

Gary exchanged glances with Hinshaw, and, in that brief instant, he saw that there was more to this than he understood. They went out to the street, making a lot of noise. After they walked down a piece, they ducked into an alley, and the four men grinned.

'You two cleared the station awful fast, or we'd have contacted you there.' They presented their badges, and Gary blew out a relieved breath.

'There ought to be a simpler way of doing business,' he said.

'Well, we've been trying. I'm Dick Aiken.' He introduced the others. 'We've got the German spotted in a waterfront hotel. The same with the trawler. We'll point the place out to you. Room seventeen at the far end of the hall and to your right. But from there on out, we'll just be looking on and standing by.'

'Thanks,' Hinshaw said. 'We'll get busy. But keep a watch on the dépôt and roads. Early's apt to show up.'

'There's men stationed there,' Aiken said. 'From the latest report from Laredo they ain't caught up with Early yet.'

'I don't like the sound of that,' Gary said.

Hinshaw and Gary left the alley and walked toward the waterfront. Dick Aiken was half a block ahead of them, sauntering along. When he passed the hotel, a cheap dockside dive, he looked up but gave no other indication.

A clerk in a dirty shirt glanced at them as they passed through the lobby and went up the stairs, but paid them no other notice. At the right door both men stopped, then Hinshaw knocked. There was a soft, scraping sound, then Schilling asked: 'Who iss it?'

'Early,' Hinshaw said.

'That iss not Early's voice.'

'I'm Early's man. You know me. Open up

358

a crack and look.'

The key turned, and Schilling opened the door enough to peer out. He recognized Hinshaw and opened the door wider. Then he saw Gary and tried to close it, but Hinshaw butted his shoulder against it.

'He's with me. He works in town.' He and Gary stepped into the room, and Gary closed the door.

'Why iss Early not here himself?'

'Something came up.' Hinshaw patted his pocket. 'He gave me the money. We'll go through with it as planned.' He took out his tobacco and rolled a smoke. 'Have you got the merchandise ready to come ashore?'

'I can signal the boat,' Schilling said. He looked from one to the other. 'The boxes are all marked mining machinery and made in the usual vay. Have you the men here to handle them?'

'The boss sent a good dozen along,' Gary said. 'Anyway, that's our problem, not yours.'

Schilling shrugged. 'Den ve go to the boat.'

Gary frowned but said nothing, and Schilling got his hat and coat. Farther down the dock and at the end of a long quay, he had a small catketch, and they got in while he cast off and hoisted sail. They sailed for better than an hour, then put into a deep cove, and he dropped anchor. He broke out his pipe and sat in the stern sheets and smoked; he wasn't a man for talk. After an hour of this, Hinshaw said: 'How long are we going to sit here?'

'Dere iss no hurry,' Schilling said in his thick accent.

Gary and Hinshaw exchanged glances and stretched out to rest. The boat rocked gently, and finally the tide swung it so the anchor rode, and the night began to fall. The faint huff of a stream trawler brought them erect, and, when they glanced at Schilling, they found him still sitting there, only he had a large black automatic pistol in his hand instead of his pipe.

'Remain quiet, please,' he said. 'It matters not to me vether I shoot you now or later.'

'What is this?' Hinshaw asked. 'Early ain't going to like this.'

Schilling smiled. 'He vill thank me. You didn't follow the plan. I knew it vhen you came to the hotel.'

The steam trawler came into the cover and dropped anchor. She was seventy foot on the waterline, a seagoing vessel flying some flag of a South American country. Schilling tapped his pistol against the gunwale to get their attention. 'Take in the anchor. There are oars under the seat. Row to her.'

Neither Hinshaw nor Gary thought it would be smart to argue with a copper-jacketed bullet, so they fitted the oars to the locks and clumsily pulled toward the anchored trawler. A ladder was put over the side amidships, and three seamen with rifles stood there while they came aboard. Schilling spoke to them in German, and they were taken forward to the captain's cabin, a well-appointed cuddy forward of the galley. The captain was a short, stern-faced man with a squared-off beard.

'So,' he said. 'You wish to intrude in business that is not yours?' He looked at Schilling. 'What went wrong?'

'I'm not sure, Herr Hauptmann. But it vas not as arranged. They came to the hotel and said that Early sent them.'

'He did,' Hinshaw maintained. 'You people got to act like spies or something? Hell, he got held up in Laredo, and all he had time to do was send Jim here to me with the money. There wasn't time to explain all this password and countersign business.'

The captain considered this. 'It may be as he says. How much did he give you?'

Hinshaw raked his memory for the figure Early had casually quoted and ended guessing. 'Feels like close to thirty thousand. He didn't tell me to count it, and I don't get paid to snoop.'

'No, sir,' Gary said. 'Mister Early don't like a man who can't do as he's told and mind his own business.'

The captain laughed. 'Put the pistol away, Schilling. Can't you see they're too stupid to have invented this?' He turned to his locker

361

and brought out a bottle of schnapps and four glasses. 'Tonight we'll put the merchandise ashore. But in the future, tell Herr Early to explain more fully. Schilling might have killed you.'

'We sure did think he was going to,' Gary said. 'And, golly, we was only followin' orders.'

'I like a man who follows orders,' the captain said. 'You may rest on deck. Tell the cook to give you food.'

They went to the galley and got a tin plate of seafaring slop that was a cross between a thin stew and thick soup. They sat on the fantail to eat, and, since no one was near them, they talked softly.

'Maybe I'm wrong, but the captain bought that a little too quick to suit me,' Gary said.

'I was thinking the same thing,' Hinshaw said. 'I'll bet you Schillings get to shoot that damned pistol before this is over. He killed Grady just as casually as a man would slaughter a hog.'

'If I was the captain, I'd take the money, kill the two fellas, and wait for the next buyer,' Gary said. 'I figure the next step will be to take our guns away, then the money. When that happens, you can figure us for dead.'

'Yeah,' Hinshaw said, and thought about it. Darkness was coming on fast and, in the channel, another fishing boat puffed its way toward the open sea. Hinshaw said: 'Let me try something.' He found a heavy clevis fastened to a hawser and freed it, then, with Gary's body blocking him, he slipped his pistol out of the holster and thrust it in his belt in the center of his back. He took his plate and bent over the fantail and dropped the clevis with a splash.

'Hey!' he yelled, and two seamen and the captain came aft on the run. Hinshaw stood there and swore for a minute. The captain interrupted him.

'What's going on here?'

'I dropped my gun overboard,' Hinshaw said angrily. 'I bent over to wash this damned plate, and my gun slipped out of the holster and fell in the water and...'

'Silence!' the captain roared. 'You are stupid. We have men who wash the dishes. It serves you right to lose your gun. A man as stupid as you should not be allowed to carry one.' He snapped his fingers. 'Hans, get the other man's gun. He is also stupid and is liable to hurt someone with it.'

The seaman picked Gary's revolver from the holster and handed it to the captain. He inspected it briefly, then threw it over the side. 'Inferior workmanship. Can't you Americans do anything right?'

'We try,' Hinshaw said.

'Silence. Finish your food, then come to my cabin. I will take the money now, before you

363

lose it.' He held out his hand, and, when Hinshaw did not respond quickly, he snapped his fingers. 'Come, come! You're on my ship, and I'm the captain, the law on this vessel. Hand it over.'

'Well,' Hinshaw said reluctantly, reaching to his inside pocket. 'All right, but hadn't I ought to get a receipt or something?'

'You have my word as a gentleman,' the captain said. 'I'll expect you in my cabin. Herr Schilling wishes to speak to you.'

He turned and went forward, and the two seamen went with him. Gary said: 'That wasn't such a dumb move. There's always an advantage when dealing with an arrogant man ... they always consider you more stupid than you really are. The captain and Schilling are going to count the money, then *bang*, twice.'

'I'm not going to wait for it,' Hinshaw said. 'Come on.'

He moved forward with Gary right behind him. A seaman stood anchor watch on the forepeak, and Hinshaw sledged him unconscious before he knew what had hit him. Gary caught him and eased him to the deck, while Hinshaw inspected the anchor. It was a mudhook riding to a manila rope leading between two rail bits. He quickly cast the rope off the towing bit and let it slip over the side. The trawler began to drift gently with no unusual motion. The catketch remained

364

to her anchor and marked the trawler's progress.

There were no lights aboard, and the night was dark. Somewhere in the channel a steamboat chugged slowly along. Together they eased the seaman over the side, then started toward the galley. But the cold water brought the seaman around, and he yelled and dog-paddled. This brought Schilling and the captain out on the run.

The open door threw light on the deck. Schilling had his automatic. Hinshaw drew his .38-40 and opened fire and watched Schilling sprawl and the captain stagger, a bullet having shattered his arm.

'The ball's opened,' Hinshaw said. 'Care to dance?'

Chapter Twenty-Five

The shaft of flung light from the open cabin door and the two rose blossoms of gunfire against the blackness of the cove were beacons to Dick Aiken. 'Hard a starboard!' he yelled. 'Close! Close! Floodlights! Fire a rocket!'

A huge light on the wheelhouse went on, bathing the trawler in brightness. Then a rocket went up, and the whole cove was illuminated. They were only a hundred yards from the trawler now. Aiken could see the seamen moving about on deck, all armed with rifles.

'Open fire!'

A two-pounder on the bow spoke. A geyser of water shot up astern of the trawler. Someone on deck answered with rifle fire, a burst replied, and a German seaman sagged against the midships rail.

'Stop engines!' the American captain yelled, blowing through the tube to the boiler room. The thumping throb of the steam engine died.

They eased alongside the trawler, crunched against her, then Aiken and a dozen rangers boarded the vessel, hastily disarming the crew.

The captain was made prisoner and herded into his cabin. Gary and Hinshaw left their forward place and came aft. Dick Aiken grinned, and said: 'We were about ready to go when the shooting started. Did you do that?'

'They were getting ready to shoot us,' Gary said. He looked at the captain, whose face was gray and filled with pain. 'Better take good care of him. I think he'll testify. Have some men break open the cargo hatch. They've got some mining machinery aboard that I want to look at.'

Aiken went to the door and detailed two

men to this job, then came back. The captain was staring at Hinshaw. 'I thought you lost your revolver overboard.'

'You never want to believe all you hear,' Hindshaw said. He stepped out. Gary followed him to where two men were breaking free a hatch. With a lantern they went below and looked at the stacked crates, shored heavily so they wouldn't shift with the boat's motion.

'Get a fire axe and let's break these out,' Gary said.

Aiken got the tools off a bulkhead, and Hinshaw took one. They broke the shoring and freed the crates. He knocked the top off one. Gary raised the lantern.

'Hydraulic cylinders,' Gary said. 'I suggest we get this ship to a dock and unload her. Those machine guns are buried in the cargo somewhere.'

'I'll remain aboard with you,' Aiken said, and went on deck to order a towing hawser made fast. The German sailors and junior officers were taken aboard the other boat, then they got underway.

Hinshaw remained in the wheelhouse for a time, but progress was slow, and it would be hours before they reached the dock. He took a lantern and went into the cargo hold and broke open a few more crates. He found more cylinders and some other parts. This bothered him for he couldn't shake the notion that he was seeing something and not seeing it at all. He didn't possess much mechanical knowledge, but he had a curiosity not easily pushed aside. Finally he tried to take one of the cylinders apart. He found the piston and rod end to be a dummy that unscrewed easily. He tipped up the cylinder and spilled the packing sawdust and a rapid-fire Spandau machine gun on the deck. He whistled, and Gary came aft.

'Don't tell me that people ain't clever,' Hinshaw said, showing him the machine gun. 'There wouldn't be a customs man in Texas who'd think hydraulic cylinders were stuffed with machine guns packed in saw-dust.'

'Where's the ammunition?' Gary asked.

Hinshaw shrugged. 'Probably in boxes marked peppermint candy.' He put his hands on his hips and blew out a breath. 'Early had the whole thing well-organized. He told me he'd made a million dollars, and I thought it was hot air. I guess it wasn't.'

'A weapon like this would bring five thousand dollars on the illegal market,' Gary said. 'It's a modern improvement, and the Army would like to test a few of these in their arsenals.' He picked up the lantern and led the way on deck. They stood by the rail and looked at the dark sea. 'We can ask ourselves just how this all could have happened right under our noses, and it's easy to see. Take a man like Early, highly respected in the community, who could come and go as he pleased without question. Add to that his mail-order and importing business to cover his receiving odd and varied shipments. On top of that add his use of Carlisle's place and poor Joe Sanders, and you've got a pretty sound set-up for making money.'

When the vessels were docked side by side, the rangers and local police took complete charge. The trawler's crew was hustled off to jail and the cargo unloaded and taken to the dépôt where boxcars and more armed rangers were waiting.

Gary saw no need to hang around, and Hinshaw expressed an impatience to get back. He put it: 'I never did get that look in Carlisle's barn.'

They caught an early passenger train west and got off at a small whistle stop shortly after dawn. They ate breakfast in the hotel before renting horses. Late in the afternoon they approached Carlisle's ranch and found it deserted except for the cook.

He grumbled as he put on the coffee pot. 'I ain't leavin' till I get my pay. Got nothin' to hide. Broke no laws, either. I was hired to cook and I cooked. Never left the house 'cept to fetch wood and water and unload the wagons.'

'Where's Carl and the others?' Hinshaw asked.

'Skipped out. Day before last. Ain't you heard? Early's dead.'

Gary and Hinshaw exchanged glances but said nothing.

The cook prattled on. 'Rameras was here. Early went to Vargas, but that greaser took his money. It was that Cardeen woman who done it. Put a butcher knife right through his gizzard. Vargas turned her loose. Heard they fished her out of the river, though.'

'Where's Rameras now?' Hinshaw asked.

'In town, I guess,' the cook said.

They took their coffee and went to the barn. Hinshaw knocked the lock off the door with a piece of scrap iron he found nearby. Carl had a nice shop with all the tools he needed, and a partially finished wagon was sitting there where he had left it. Hinshaw and Gary looked it over carefully but could find nothing wrong. Then Gary placed his coffee cup in the bed before kneeling. The sound of the cup against the floor planks was hollow.

'That's odd,' he said, and had a closer look. At first glance it seemed that there was a hair split in each plank, so he got a wrench and unbolted one. He saw the extent of Carl's cleverness. Each plank had been split and planed for careful mating, but hundreds of holes had been drilled in the inner edges, a perfect place to carry several thousand rounds of rifle ammunition.

Hinshaw said: 'So that's why no amount of crate opening at the crossing ever turned up anything. Hell, even when the wagons crossed empty, they were carrying cartridges.'

'I've seen enough,' Gary said. 'Let's get going.'

They caught up fresh horses and rode out. Other than one brief rest on the prairie, they made no stops until they reached Ranger Headquarters. Major Manners had been wired from Corpus Christi about their success, and he took them to his office. He also ordered hot water and towels and a razor so that Hinshaw and Gary could shave as they talked. They brought Manners up to date in a few sentences. He asked a few questions and got his answers.

He got out a train schedule and consulted it. 'The machine guns ought to arrive tomorrow afternoon. Colonel, how long would it take to assemble them and place them operationally about the camp?'

'Five hours at the most,' Gary said.

'Good, because I want Pedro Vargas to get a personal invitation to come and get them.' He took a piece of paper and drew the plan of the camp. 'Here's the river. I would like some of these pieces zeroed in on the river so that I can cut off Vargas's retreat. There isn't a man in this camp who isn't looking forward to this fight. We're dug in and we're

371

well-armed with Mauser rifles. As soon as you get freshened up, Gary, I'd like you to go over the whole thing with me and add what you feel necessary.'

'I'd be glad to do that,' Gary said.

Manners glanced at Hinshaw who was toweling his face dry. 'You get to town. Someone's been asking for you, and I promised her you'd come in as soon as you got back.'

'Does she know that Early's dead?' Hinshaw asked.

'Yes,' Manner said. 'I guess the whole town knows it. Two of his men from Carlisle's came through and said he was dead.' He shook his head. 'It's hell to think of, but, you know, half the people in town don't believe Early did any of these things. Somehow the truth is hard to believe.'

'When do you want me back, Major?'

'When I send for you,' Manners said. 'There's one crackerjack still on the loose... Batiste Rameras. He was Early's contact and Vargas's right-hand man. If you should happen to find him, do your duty as a Texas Ranger. I won't burden you with a warrant.'

Hinshaw grinned. 'Major, I heard that you didn't approve of McCabe's shoot-from-the-hip methods. Ain't this kind of against the grain?'

'Never you mind that,' Manners said, waving his hand. 'Now get your bath and clothes changed and hie into town.' He turned to Jim Gary. 'If you wanted to draw Vargas here, how would you word the invitation?'

'I think I'd play on his sense of vanity,' Gary said.

'I agree,' Manners said, sweeping a paper off his desk. 'Listen to this … Pedro Vargas, bastard son of an Apache squaw. You call yourself El Jefe, The Chief, a title better suited to your horse. You have boasted of killing Texans, but the truth is that you have grown fat like an old woman. Why don't you go back to sleeping in the sun? We have the machine guns you want, and, although you have thirty men to our one, we know you are afraid to cross…' He looked at Hinshaw. 'I thought I told you to get going?'

'I was just listening, Major.'

'The devil with that. Get out of here.' He turned again to his message and Jim Gary. 'Don't you think I'm putting this nicely?'

When Hinshaw closed the door, Manners was reading Gary the rest of it.

The bath and change of clothes were as good as a night's sleep to Martin Hinshaw. After cleaning and oiling his gun he changed horses again and went to town. The aroma of beer caught him as he passed the saloon. He wheeled around, tied up, and went in to have one. The bartender shoved a full schooner his way, then came up for conversation.

'Hard to believe about Fred Early,' he said. 'Always seemed such a nice fella.'

'What's hard to believe about it?' Hinshaw asked. 'What did Early ever do to make you think he was a nice fella? Spend a little money in here?' He drank some of his beer, then pushed the stein away from him, and rang a dime on the bar.

The bartender picked it up, then said: 'Got a message for you from Rameras.'

'What kind of a message?'

The bartender reached down and came up with a Mauser rifle and five rounds of ammunition. 'He left this here. Said he had one just like it. Said you'd know where to find him so the Hinshaws and the Rameras family could finally settle their old differences once and for all.'

'When was this?'

'Yesterday, I think. Yeah, yesterday. He rode north.'

'I know that,' Hinshaw said, and unbuckled his gun belt and laid it on the bar. 'Keep this for me until I come back.'

'Suppose you don't?'

'Then sell it and take the money and get drunk,' Hinshaw said.

He picked up the rifle and the ammunition and went out. Pausing on the walk, he opened the bolt and shoved the cartridges against the magazine spring, then closed the bolt, and slipped on the safety. He mounted his horse, turned out of town, and cut north.

Each mile he traveled became more familiar to him. It was the land of his childhood. He knew where the rabbit warrens were and where the wild game fed. Going back now was really a relief to him, yet all the time he had felt a dread. He supposed it was because he had run away once, and it had been the secret shame that had held him back. But he was going now. It wasn't the old fire of family animosity that pulled him, but a clean, legal duty and a pride in the Texas Rangers. Rameras wouldn't understand that because he only wanted to kill the last remaining Hinshaw. He couldn't be blamed for that.

At nightfall, Hinshaw camped cold and slept on the ground with a blanket around him. At dawn he was mounted and moving again. He came to the old home place just before noon. Little remained except half an adobe wall and a crumbling stone fireplace. His father was buried somewhere nearby, but he didn't know exactly where. No one had thought to erect a marker. An open grave had been freshly dug.

Three miles to go, he thought, and rode on. The Rameras mansion loomed ahead finally, a gaunt, low, rambling building, decaying after years of desertion and neglect. There was no sign of life, and Hinshaw stopped well out of rifle range and dismounted. A movement in a grove of trees attracted his attention. He eased closer. Batiste Rameras was digging in the family plot, and he had no weapon on him or near him.

When he waved Hinshaw on in, Hinshaw hesitated, then mounted and rode over. Rameras wiped the sweat from his face and said: 'I have already dug your grave, *señor.* Not ten feet from your father's. I will bury you beside him, where you belong.' He threw his shovel aside. 'But I am a realist. Perhaps you will have to bury me, so I have saved you the trouble of digging. Place me by my father.'

'You're a funny cuss, Rameras.'

'We have our ways, all of us,' Rameras said. 'Tonight, you would please me by eating with me and sharing some wine and my tobacco. Afterward, I must ask you to camp away from the house. When it is dawn, I'll be waiting for you. I have five rounds, too.'

'I'm a Texas Ranger with orders to bring you in,' Hinshaw said, raising his Mauser. 'Why don't I just do it now and save this foolishness?'

'A Hinshaw cannot act in shame,' Rameras said. 'Neither can I. It is a curse we both bear. Had it not been so, I would have ambushed you, or you would shoot me now. Come ... I have a bottle of wine in the cistern cooling.' He smiled and walked to the deserted house.

Chapter Twenty-Six

Colonel Jim Gary rode into Laredo early in the morning. He had some important dispatches that he wanted to get out on the afternoon eastbound. There was also a letter to his wife that he wanted to get off. He dropped these off at the dépôt where they were placed in the mail sack, then he rode on to the center of town. A question to a swamper sweeping out the saloon gave him directions to Ella Sanders's house. He tied up at the hitching post outside and went down the walk. She was on the porch, washing windows, and she smiled when she saw him.

'Why, Colonel Gary. This is a surprise. Come in. I'll put on some coffee.'

'Thank you.' He looked at the pail and soap and drying cloth. 'It seems that you'd have Marty doing that.'

She laughed and went into the kitchen, Gary following. 'My mother taught me not to wait until a man did household chores. How is Marty?'

Gary frowned. 'Don't you know? I thought he was here.'

She looked at him. 'I haven't seen him.'

'He left the ranger camp yesterday to see you.' His manner mirrored some alarm. 'Thank you for the offer of coffee, but I've got to look into this.'

He turned and went through the house and down the front walk. Riding back to the main street, he dismounted in front of the hotel and went in. The clerk didn't know anything, but suggested the saloon, and Gary crossed the street. The bartender was a man who took pride in knowing everyone's business and repeating it. He told Gary about Batiste Rameras's challenge, and Gary stormed out of the place. His first impulse was to ride to the north, but he thought better of it and went to Ella Sanders's house. She met him at the gate, and he quickly filled her in on the details.

'Please go to Major Manners and inform him of this,' Gary said. 'I'll ride north and see if I can get Hinshaw out of this before his hot head gets him killed. Any particulars I should know about finding the place?'

'Follow the wagon road north,' she said. 'You can't miss the old Rameras place.'

'Thank you. Don't waste any time informing the major.' He turned his horse and galloped out of town.

Batiste Rameras had gone to considerable trouble to be a good host to his enemy. On a pack horse he had brought along dishes and cooking ware and food. He cooked as though he were eating his last meal. Hinshaw, suspicious yet of Rameras's motives, brought his rifle along, but when he saw that Rameras had put his away, he leaned the Mauser against the outer wall and forgot about it.

When they sat down to eat, Hinshaw said: 'How could you be sure I'd share this with you?'

'I did not think you would be so uncivilized as to refuse,' he said. 'In truth, I was as sure that you would accept as I was sure you would come here to kill me. It is a thing enemies should do, break bread and share a bottle of wine before settling their differences.'

'I sure don't understand you, Rameras.'

The Mexican shrugged. 'Why should you? Tonight I will pray and move the beads on my rosary, and it will not matter to you that I pray not for me but for my wife and children. Miguel and Sanchos, they must grow strong and be men of honor. And Lita with her small, soft hands and big eyes, she must see a world of beauty.' He looked at Hinshaw. 'You didn't know I had a family? It's no matter.'

'I'm not leaving a son to pass my hate onto,' Hinshaw said.

'Nor I,' Rameras said. 'It was the hate of our fathers, handed to us, forced on us, molding us to a path that had to lead here.

379

But it will end here, Hinshaw. It must come to pass.'

Hinshaw thought about this and said: 'My old man used to see you and your brothers in town or on the range, and he'd tell me that I ought to waylay those spiks. I guess he kept after me all right, from the time I knew what talk was to the time I left home.'

'The words of our fathers were never taken lightly,' Rameras said. 'But it has never been so in my house. I have taught my sons not to hate the *yanquis*. I do not hate you, Hinshaw, but my father did, and I must honor the wishes of my father. It is the same with you, I think.'

'If you're so all fired full of this good feeling, why did you work with Vargas and Fred Early?'

'For Early I had no use,' Rameras said. 'He was to me, as you were to him, a man to be used and then killed when he was through with you.'

'And Vargas?'

Rameras shrugged. 'He is Mexican. We have much in common. The hate we feel toward Texans binds us. Neither of us can forget. He never wanted to, and I cannot. But I differ from Vargas. The things I feel are bad, and yet I'm helpless against them. They are my own to bear. I do not want to pass them on. Vargas preaches hate. I wish to suppress it.'

Hinshaw stared at him, then said: 'You're a liar.' He threw his plate aside and stood up. 'All of this ... this last supper business and talk about your kids ... it's all a put-on, Rameras. You're a no-good, hating Mexican trying to make out differently, but it's all a damned lie. You don't preach hate? What do you think you're doing every time Vargas hands a rifle to some Mexican sodbuster and takes him into his army? What do you think you're doing when a Texan dies or a child is taken by the Mexicans?' He shook his head. 'You almost lulled me into making a mistake, Rameras. You almost had me thinking that I wasn't a cop, and you wasn't a criminal. Get on your feet, Rameras. I'm arresting you in the name of the State of Texas.'

'I was afraid you would take that attitude,' Rameras said, and stepped back. He reached down into the top of his boot and brought out a knife.

'So you weren't armed, huh?' Hinshaw laughed. 'How many rounds do you really have for the Mauser?'

Rameras grinned. 'A bandoleer.' He flipped the knife over in his hand so he could throw it.

There was no hesitation in Hinshaw. He whipped out with his foot, caught a folding chair, and sailed it at Rameras, who threw the knife and ducked at the same time and wasted his one chance. The knife fell far

381

behind Hinshaw, out of Rameras's reach. Hinshaw went into the Mexican, chopping with his fists, opening cuts on his face.

Rameras had the strength, and he wanted to wrestle. He grabbed Hinshaw over the arms and crushed him, lifting him off the ground. The strength of the man was enormous, and Hinshaw felt his ribs contract. He felt a moment of panic that he immediately beat down. With his thumbs, he jabbed into Rameras's groin, and it was enough to free the grip momentarily and allow Hinshaw to slip clear. Then he laced a punch into the Mexican's kidneys and hurt him.

He hit him again, and Rameras cried out. Then Hinshaw put him down with a blow behind the ear. Rameras fell heavily and rolled over on his back, and Hinshaw went to the Mexican's horse and got the rope off the saddle. He cut a short length of it to bind the man's wrists behind him. He slipped the noose around Rameras's neck and went to fetch his own horse and rifle.

When Rameras regained consciousness, he was hauled to his feet, and Hinshaw mounted his horse. He tied the end of the rope to the saddle horn and said: 'We've got a long walk back, so don't drag you feet.'

'You are without honor,' Rameras said. 'I always knew it.'

'A touching speech,' Hinshaw said, and rode out, Raneras following on the lead rope.

A horse's walk is different from a man's, and Rameras was soon breathing hard for he had to half trot to keep up. Hinshaw stopped now and then but not out of pity for the prisoner. He had no intention of camping out the night with Rameras. He used the rests so that he could travel on without wasting hours.

'If a man was meant to walk, he would have a hoof like a horse,' Rameras said. 'It would only be merciful if you let me ride with you.'

'I'm not merciful,' Hinshaw said. 'I'm just a dumb fella trying to do my duty, and I damned near let my feelings get in the way of it.' He shook his head. 'It sure takes a man a long time to smarten up. Come on, let's trot.'

'You are without soul,' Rameras said. 'I should have killed you when you approached the grave, but it pleased me to toy with you.'

'You want to be more careful with your toys,' Hinshaw said.

As he rode on, he divided his time between the trail ahead and looking back to see how his prisoner was coming along. He didn't figure there was much chance of Rameras's slipping off the noose, not with his hands tied behind him, but he did not reckon with the man's cleverness nor his dangerous nature.

Rameras was already fifty yards away and

running by the time Hinshaw discovered he was dragging just rope. He stopped, dismounted, and shouldered the Mauser. He took his time aiming, and then he touched it off and watched Rameras go into a tumbler's roll. Rameras started to get up, then fell. Hinshaw mounted and rode over to him. Rameras was bleeding at the shoulder, and he glared at Hinshaw, who dismounted and fastened the rope around the man's neck. This time he looped it, put a knot in it, and snugged it up so that Rameras couldn't work it off.

'I'm bleeding badly,' Rameras said.

'I know what kind of a shot I am,' Hinshaw said. 'I just took a little meat off your shoulder.' Still he stripped off his bandanna and bound the wound before getting on his horse again. 'We've still got a long walk. There's no use tiring yourself out by running.'

They wore out the night by marching slowly south. In the morning they stopped at a stream to drink and wash. When Rameras complained that he couldn't function with his hands tied, Hinshaw pushed him in, saying: 'Now no one'll know if you wet your pants or not.'

In mid-afternoon, Hinshaw saw a spiral of dust in the south and the dark speck of horse and rider that caused it. He stopped and freed the Mauser. Finally he could recognize Colonel Jim Gary, and he put the rifle away.

Gary stopped and got down to rest his lathered horse. He saw Rameras on the lead rope and sighed with relief. 'I rather expected to find you dead, Marty. Rameras is not exactly the most sneaky cuss on earth, but he'll take a close second.'

Hinshaw grinned. 'Well, to tell the truth, he almost got to me with the sad story of his wife and kids.'

'What wife and kids? He baches it in a room behind his shop.'

Hinshaw turned and looked at Batiste Rameras. 'You're the most convincing liar I ever met. You really had me believing that stuff.'

Rameras shrugged. 'I tried to once before ... on another Hinshaw, and it worked.'

'On my father?'

'*Si*,' Rameras said. 'My brothers were dead and my father. Alone I was left with the *yanqui*. So I went to him with a white cloth and tears in my eyes and asked him to spare me. He lowered the muzzle, and then I drew from the folds of my clothing a *pistola*, and I shot him. But even on the ground he summoned the strength to shoot me before he died.'

Hinshaw said: 'You've confessed before a witness. That makes you as good as hung, Rameras.'

'I will be hung anyway,' he said. 'Let us go ... my shoulder gives me pain.'

'Let me ask you something,' Gary said. 'Who rode on whom? Did the Rameras clan start the fight, or did Hinshaw?'

Rameras nodded toward Martin Hinshaw. 'We waited until he went away. The old man was alone, the lion without his cub. We rode on him, my father and brothers, but he was waiting for us, his claws sharpened. My father died first, a bullet in his breast.'

'I'm glad I didn't kill you, Rameras,' Hinshaw said. 'Shall we go, Colonel?'

A sleepless night and the long ride called for a glass of whisky when Hinshaw reached town. With this small fire burning in his stomach, he did what he had started out to do – went to see Ella Sanders.

She answered his knock and said: 'A little tardy, aren't you?'

'Some,' he admitted. 'Should I throw my hat in first?'

'No, I'll allow you this mistake.' She turned into the house, and he followed her. Then he took her arm and pulled her around to face him.

'Don't I get a kiss?'

'Do you think you have one coming?'

He smiled. 'Well, I've had a trying few days with mighty slim pleasures. I was sort of looking forward to it.' He put his arms around her and held her loosely. 'I thought I'd kiss you a couple of times and talk marriage. I don't believe in long engagements.'

'Are you going to stay in the rangers, Marty?'

He sobered in expression. 'Yes. Do you mind? The money isn't much, but we could live off it if we didn't get too high on the hog.'

'Is it what you want to do?'

'It's a good thing to do,' he said. 'Funny, but I never cared one way or another about the law. I don't figure I ever broke many laws because I was never in any real trouble. But it was just something I never thought much about. Now it's different. I like the responsibility, Ella. It makes me a part of something, and I need that. A man just can't live for himself.' He grinned. 'I guess I've turned out more serious than you expected. But I guess it's an improvement.'

'You're a good man, Marty. I always thought so.' She put her arms around him and kissed him, and she gave him more than he had bargained for, exposing to him the banked fires of passion he had never realized existed. When she pulled away, she laughed and patted his cheek. 'I baked a pie for you. Hope it isn't stale.'

'That wouldn't matter to me.'

She studied him seriously. 'It's like you to say that. You take life as it comes, Marty. You never prod it and turn it and try to perfect it to suit yourself. I'm going to like being married to you because I'll never have to pretend or be anything but what I am. If I've had a bad day and the meat's cooked too long and the potatoes half raw and the biscuits burned, you'd eat them and smile and never make me feel that I'd failed in any way.' She kissed him again briefly. 'Now I'll get you the pie. The major sent in word. He wants you back on the post right away. They expect Vargas to attack at any time. Most of the people have left town already.'

'Then what are you doing here?'

She smiled. 'I stayed to cut the pie.'

Chapter Twenty-Seven

Laredo was a ghost town when Martin Hinshaw and Ella Sanders rode through. The people had all packed blankets and food and moved away, camping out on the open range, or staying with friends who lived some distance away. Marty drove Ella's buggy on to the ranger camp and put up the team while she went to the headquarters building. Colonel Gary and Carl Manners were there and both expressed some annoyance that she hadn't gone with the others, yet they openly admired her courage for staying.

Gary said: 'The doctor has kindly consented to stay. He may need a capable assistant. The stockade is the strongest building on the post. We'll put you up there.'

'I hope it's no trouble,' she said.

Manners smiled. 'Compared to the trouble we're expecting, it is nothing.' He took a pair of field glasses from his desk and motioned for her to step to the door. He handed her the glasses to study the Mexican side of the river. For a full minute she moved them back and forth before handing them back, her expression grave.

'He must have a thousand men camped there,' she said.

'Yes. And he wouldn't have them in the open that way unless he was getting ready to move.' He took her arm. 'Colonel Gary will show you to your quarters.' He saw Hinshaw walking toward the porch and beckoned him inside. 'Good job on Rameras, Corporal.'

'I almost didn't… Corporal?'

Manners half hid his smile. 'Well, with off-post rations and an increase in pay, it ought to amount to about seventy-five a month. A married man needs that to live properly.' Then he swung the subject around, moving to a wall map of the camp. 'Here's where we've placed the machine guns. Gary has trained teams in their use, and they've already been zeroed in on the river. Our entire defense depends on those guns, Marty. We're going to let the Mexicans get to our side before opening up, then we'll lay down a barrage and make them ride through it.'

'They will,' Hinshaw said.

Manners nodded. 'Yes, they'll try to take the weapon positions, but you can see that they're well back from the entrenchments. It will be up to you riflemen to protect the weapon positions and drive the remainder back. Even in retreat they'll have to go through our fire again.' His manner grew severe. 'We may not whip them, Marty. The best we can do is to so reduce them in numbers that their backs will be broken. Weakened, the Mexican army that is marching north may finish them off. Yes, it was the deal Gary made. We'd weaken them, push them back, and the Mexican army would have the glory and honor of finishing the job. It was the only way he could work it. They wanted the biggest piece of cake, or they wouldn't play.'

'Well, I guess if I got to die, I'd rather do it for the State of Texas than anyone else,' Hinshaw said. 'See you around, Major.' He went out and off the porch and found a place in a trench. There he noticed that all the rangers were armed with Mauser rifles and plenty of ammunition.

'Where'd these come from?' he asked.

'McCabe and Gary found 'em at Carlisle's place,' the ranger said. 'In the wagon shed. In between all the two by four uprights, rifle racks had been built. They ripped off some of the wall sheeting and found over a hundred of 'em.' He slapped the walnut stock. 'They sure beat a .30-30 for power and accuracy.'

'You're liable to get plenty of practice,' Hinshaw said.

The day turned out long and warm. Hinshaw grew tired of waiting. Finally he left the trench and went to see the major who sat on the headquarters porch, binoculars in hand and rifle by his side.

'Yes, what is it, Hinshaw?'

'Major, I'd like to have permission to cross the river and talk to Vargas.'

'You're out of your mind!' He waved his hand. 'Go back to your trench and keep your hat on. The sun's getting to you.'

'Major, it's a lot better for one man to run the risks than to get half or more killed.' He took hold of Manners's sleeve. 'Let me hold a parley with Vargas.'

Manners studied him. 'What would you say?'

'I'd put the cards face up on the table, tell him what he was up against if he crosses the river. I'll try to show him how much better it is to walk away from this one. We've cut off his guns and ammunition source. Six months from now he'll be on the die-up, his men deserting to go back to the farms. I can't believe the man's enough of a fool to risk four or five hundred men just to...' He looked at Manners who was holding the field glasses to his eyes. He handed them to Hinshaw, and he could see the movement across the river, the movement toward the river.

'Too late for talk now,' Manners said, taking the glasses back. He began shouting orders while Hinshaw went back to his trench and picked up his rifle.

It was too bad, he thought, that the crossing would be just out of rifle range, for the rangers could do a lot of damage with the Mausers while the Mexicans advanced.

Guthrie McCabe sprinted across the yard, surprisingly spry for his age. He jumped into the trench with Hinshaw, and said: 'Feeling brave, squirt?'

'Nope.'

'When the shootin' starts, a man could move around considerable without being noticed,' McCabe said.

'What's on your evil old mind?'

'Catchin' Vargas before he gets away. If we had him prisoner, we could force the others to withdraw.'

'You're crazy.'

'Sure, and I'm looking for someone as crazy as I am to help me. Game?'

Hinshaw grinned. 'I'll probably have to carry you back, but let's go.'

They made their way toward the crossing and took cover in the brush. McCabe had no rifle, just his long-barrelled .45. He advised Hinshaw to put the Mauser aside and use his pistol. 'You won't have time to use that,' he said. 'Besides Vargas has got to be taken alive.'

'What about them flyin' bullets?' Hinshaw asked. 'Seems to me we're hunkered down in the middle of the target.'

'Naw,' McCabe said. 'We're too close to the river. The machine guns are all zeroed in fifty yards behind. They didn't want to catch the Mexicans in the water.' He pointed to the first file of mounted bandits approaching the crossing. 'Seven or eight abreast. There's Vargas on that white horse.' He squinted. 'Maybe a hundred-yard dash to him as soon as the shelling starts. Get your runnin' shoes on, squirt.' He wiped the sweat from his palm and took a new grip on his revolver.

'Scared, ain't you?'

'Plumb scared,' McCabe said. 'I ain't a fool, you know. I like livin'. Hate dyin'.'

The Mexicans were in the water when they broke into a trot and, above the sound of mounted men, came the sparkling tones of a brassy bugle and an answering call, and suddenly a scattered rattle of small-arms fire. Already Vargas was to the Texas side of the river. He paused, sitting his splendid horse, while he turned and looked back.

His column was halted. From the rear firing broke out in a furious rattle, and Mc-

Cabe swore gleefully. 'That damned Mexican general's attackin' 'em!'

Vargas was shouting orders, trying to wheel his column about to meet this new challenge. Several of the weapon positions opened up, and the rain of bullets thinned their ranks, frightening the horses.

'Now,' McCabe said, and left his cover one jump ahead of Hinshaw.

As they covered the ground separating them, Hinshaw was again amazed at how spry the old man was. They were within thirty yards of Vargas before he ever realized he was in danger. He pulled one of his pearl-handled pistols and started banging away, but the machine gun fire behind him was setting up a din, an impassable wall. Vargas fought his horse, and the beast was almost unmanageable, which made his aim poor.

The bulk of Vargas's command was already returning to the Mexican side where the Army had them pinned down. Vargas, realizing that he was alone and virtually cut off, jabbed spurs to his horse. McCabe stopped, sighted, and coolly killed the animal.

Vargas fell in a roll and lost his pistol, and they closed with him. The firing was thick and bullets dimpled the earth near them, but Hinshaw was too frightened to care. McCabe was on Vargas, clubbing with his pistol. Hinshaw felt something nip the calf of his left leg, and he spun around and fell heavily. When he looked down, he saw blood soaking the leg of his pants, and he knew he'd been hit.

'Go on!' he yelled to McCabe. 'Go on, get out of here!'

The machine gun fire suddenly ceased. McCabe began to drag Vargas away from the river. Then he dropped him and came back for Hinshaw, who cursed him for being an old fool.

'Always pay my debts,' McCabe said, and pulled Hinshaw two dozen yards. He put him near Vargas, who was groaning and trying to sit up.

Hinshaw laughed and said: 'It seems we're always hitting him on the head.'

'Ain't that a fact,' McCabe said. He went over and ripped open Vargas's sleeve and took a small automatic pistol from the spring clip. 'Got nipped with this once,' McCabe said. 'And once is enough.'

A dozen rangers came toward them at a run, Major Manners leading them. When he got close enough, he yelled: 'I'm going to court-martial both of you!' He had Hinshaw helped to his feet and Vargas made prisoner, and they hurried back away from the river.

But the danger had passed, for the Mexican army, bolstered by three companies of cavalry, were already surrounding the bandits. Little by little, the shooting died away as isolated pockets of resistance fell.

Hinshaw was placed on the porch, and the doctor summoned. Ella Sanders ran to him and would have thrown herself in his arms if the doctor hadn't peered at her over his glasses and said: 'Act like a nurse, now.'

A ring of rangers surrounded Pedro Vargas. McCabe was one of them. Manners said: 'I see you accepted my offer, bandit.'

'How could I refuse?' Vargas asked. 'Permit me to have a cigarette?'

'Give him a smoke,' Manners said. A retinue of Mexican army officers were crossing the river. The battle was won, and Manners supposed they couldn't resist bragging about it. 'Lock him in the stockade. Put him in a cell next to Rameras. They might as well enjoy the conversation because they'll hang together.' He looked at Hinshaw. 'I don't think you're going to die. Miss Sanders, have someone hitch up a buggy and take this squirt home. Keep him in bed, so I'll know where to find him.' He blew out a long breath, for he was a man with many problems and an uncertain control over his men. 'And I want to talk to you, McCabe.'

'Suits me because I want to talk to you,' McCabe said. 'About retiring.'

'Can you really mean that?' Manners said.

'Now you know you're going to miss me,' McCabe said. 'I'll go along with the squirt, but, when I come back tomorrow, I'll expect my papers to be ready. I'm going to California and sit under an orange tree. Never saw one, you know.'

'Oh, my,' Manners said, and went off the porch to meet the approaching army officers.

McCabe said: 'He won't last. Ought to get him another job. Gets rattled too easy.' He looked at Hinshaw and grinned. 'Who'd you say was going to carry who, squirt?' He hauled Hinshaw to his feet and held him. 'Miss Sanders, I hope you can take this. He ain't going to change, you know. He'll never have good sense. He'll always be doing one fool thing or another.'

'Why you old billy goat!' Hinshaw said. 'You talked me into this!'

McCabe laughed. 'See what I mean? If he'd had good sense, he wouldn't have listened to me. Take his other arm, and we'll get him to the buggy before he falls and hurts himself.'

Oldham
Council

FIT

FITTON HILL

Please return this book before the last date stamped.
Items can be renewed by telephone, in person at any library or online at
www.oldham.gov.uk/libraries

In   e
Co   o
his   e
wo   n
ca   .
Su   s
pr   s
sp   o
La   n
re   s
Ga   t
pr   s
wi   n
history.

UNTIL DARKNESS DISAPPEARS